Happy Never After

Kathy Hogan Trocheck

HEADLINE

922126

First published in Great Britain in 1995
by HEADLINE BOOK PUBLISHING

First published in paperback in 1995
by HEADLINE BOOK PUBLISHING

10 9 8 7 6 5 4 3 2 1

ISBN 0 7472 5019 7

Printed and bound in Great Britain by
Cox & Wyman Ltd, Reading, Berks

HEADLINE BOOK PUBLISHING
A division of Hodder Headline PLC
338 Euston Road
London NW1 3BH

DEDICATION

For my own girl group, Las Malas Chicas; Linda Maring Case, Debbie DeWitt Cox, Sue Boore Foster, Nancy Bushman Graff, Debra Justus and Margaret Crist Wood. Old friends are the best.

ACKNOWLEDGEMENTS

The author wishes to thank family, friends and neighbors for their support and encouragement, and to express special gratitude to the following for the generous gift of their time and advice in research. Any errors in fact or judgement are my own, not theirs.

Kathy Kincer and Sally Devlin of DDI Investigations, John Rogers and the staff at Dallas Austin Recording Projects, William T. Hankins III, Robert Waller, Tim Shoemaker, Katherine Adams CPA, Matt and Doug Monroe, Russ DeVault, Sonia Murray, and Eileen Drennan, Susan Percy, Gary McKee, Susan Hogan, RN, Dr Loren Garrettson of the Georgia Poison Control Center. As always, Sallie Gouverneur and Eamon Dolan were the good shepherds who led me out of the darkness and into the light. Tricia Davies kept the carpool going, and Tom Trocheck was there when I needed him most.

1

'Is this Callahan Garrity?'

I'd probably heard that voice thousands of times over the years. Heard that high, gutsy contralto pining for lost love in the sixties girl group hits that made her a star. And later, after the songs ran out in the early seventies, on those sappy BurgerTown radio jingles. But now, on the phone, she sounded like just another pain in the butt.

Of course, the two-pack-a-day Kools habit had laid the sandpaper to the vocal cords, and the hot-and-cold-running Dewar's had done the rest. So when she identified herself as Rita Fontaine, the name meant nothing. 'Yes,' I said impatiently. 'What's this in reference to?'

What pays the bills around here is House Mouse, the cleaning business my mother and I run. We get a lot of women calling looking for work, but I already had all the mice I could handle. I just assumed Rita Fontaine was looking for a cleaning job.

'I'm Vonette Hunsecker's cousin,' she said, as though that made everything okay. She obviously didn't know that Vonette was not on my hit parade. Vonette is the

1

ex-wife of an old friend and the wife-in-law of the old friend's second wife, Linda Nickells, who is a good pal of mine.

'Vonette said you could help,' Rita said. Her voice said she doubted it. 'You're the private detective, right?'

'That's right,' I said warily. 'Just exactly what kind of help do you need?'

She let out a long wheezy sigh. 'You never heard of me, of Rita Fontaine, have you?'

'Afraid not,' I said. 'Should I have?'

'That depends. Ever hear of the VelvetTeens?'

Who hadn't? I'd been a little kid the year when the VelvetTeens hit it big with 'Happy Never After,' but I can still remember watching their first early appearances on *Platter Party*, a locally produced teen dance show that ran on WSB-TV, and then later, of course, on *The Ed Sullivan Show* and *American Bandstand*. Since they were from Atlanta, like me, the VelvetTeens were hotter than the Chiffons, the Shirelles, or any of those other mix-'n'-match Motown inventions as far as I was concerned.

Now it came back to me. She was the lead singer. Of course, that voice. Then I had a brief vision: long skinny legs, mile-high beehive, odd almond-shaped eyes fringed by inch-long fake eyelashes.

I said it before I could stop myself. 'I thought you were dead.'

'Me too,' she said.

What do you say to something like that? 'I didn't know Vonette had a famous cousin,' was all I could think of.

'Vonette was famous too,' she said. 'You didn't know she was a VelvetTeen?'

All I knew about Vonette was that she was hell on wheels if you crossed her. Before she and C.W. split up, she'd cut out the crotch of every pair of pants the man owned. If Rita Fontaine was Vonette's cousin, famous or not, she probably meant trouble.

'Uh, no,' I said. 'Listen, what kind of help is it that you need? See, I don't know if Vonette mentioned it, but my real job is running a cleaning business. I just do the private investigation thing once in a while. And right now, I've got...'

'Forget it,' she said. 'I'll find someone else.' And she hung up .

2

When Neva Jean came bursting through the back door a few seconds later, bawling her eyes out, I did what Rita Fontaine had suggested. I forgot about her.

'Hey Callahan,' Neva Jean sobbed. Her face was red, and twin tracks of melted mascara ran down her cheeks. She staggered over to one of the oak kitchen chairs and heaved herself down with another loud sob.

I looked at the kitchen clock. The kitchen is as close as we come to an office for the House Mouse. It was only four o'clock.

'Aren't you through for the day a little early?' I asked. Mondays are usually booked solid for all our girls, and Neva Jean was no exception.

'Oh,' she said, sniffing. 'That Mrs Clifford is so sweet. She saw how torn up I was about Kevin, and she told me to go on home. I'll dust the Levolors next week.'

'Kevin,' I said quickly, my pulse quickening. 'What's wrong with Kevin?' My older brother and I are not exactly close. He lives right here in Atlanta, but we see each other only on the major family occasions that demand it.

'Oh my Lord,' Neva Jean said, her upper lip trembling

5

like a bad Elvis impersonator. 'You didn't hear? Kevin got run over by a drunk driver today. He's in an irreversible coma. The doctors say he'll never walk or talk or nothing. When I heard I nearly died.'

I felt a chill run down my spine. I reached for the phone. 'What hospital? And where's Edna? Does she know?'

I was dialing my sister Maureen's number at work. She works in Grady Memorial Hospital's emergency room. She'd know what my brother's chances were.

Neva Jean was flat-out blubbering now. 'I ain't seen Edna since this morning,' she cried. 'After all Kevin's been through, this had to happen. First that sorry Roberta trying to convince him the baby was his when she knew all along it was really Sean's, and then being kidnapped by those awful Estonian extremists, and now this.'

I put the phone back on the hook. 'What the hell are you talking about?' I demanded. 'Who the hell is Roberta? What Estonian extremists? Which Kevin are you talking about?'

She wiped her tears on the hem of her pink House Mouse smock. 'You know. Doctor Kevin Saint Germaine. He's the black-haired fella with the eye patch. His first wife, Monique, now she was a real cute girl. But she got amnesia and forgot she was married and run off to a convent. Shaved off all those beautiful blond curls...'

'Wait,' I bellowed. Neva Jean looked hurt.

It had finally dawned on me. 'Is the Kevin you're talking about a character on one of those cheesy soap operas of yours? Is that what you're in hysterics about?

6

A soap opera character? Jesus Christ! I thought you meant our Kevin. That Kevin Garrity was hit by a car and in an irreversible coma somewhere...'

'What?'

We both whipped around to see Edna, my mother, ashen-faced, holding an armful of grocery sacks, and standing in the kitchen doorway.

'Kevin's been hurt?' Edna whispered. 'How bad? What hospital?'

She let the grocery bags slide out of her arms and onto the floor. A bag of Granny Smith apples burst open and the fruit went rolling all over the floor.

'No,' I said quickly. 'No, Ma. Not our Kevin. Not Kevin Garrity. It's some soap opera guy on TV.'

'What?' she repeated, bending over to pick up the bags. She seemed even more alarmed now. 'Not Kevin from *The Young and The Breathless*. Have they told Roberta yet?'

She took the sacks and set them on the red Formica countertop.

I kicked at an apple that had rolled under my foot. It had been a long, strange day. I wasn't in any mood for a *Soap Opera Digest* update.

But Edna was. She's my mother and my roommate and my business partner in the House Mouse, but we couldn't be less alike. I like cop shows. She likes the soaps. I like the flea market. She likes Home Depot. I like Jack Daniel's. She likes white zinfandel.

Right now she and Neva Jean were yakking a mile a minute about Monique and Sean and the rest of the *Breathless* cast of dozens.

7

Edna had brought in the mail along with the groceries, so I started leafing through the stack. There were a couple of handwritten envelopes that looked like checks. Good. A Rich's department store bill. A fat envelope full of grocery coupons, and a wedding shower invitation.

I held it up and showed it to Edna. The shower was for my cousin RaeAnn. 'Didn't we just go to a baby shower for her last year?'

'That was Roxanne,' Edna said, opening a cupboard to start stowing the groceries away.

'I can never keep those twins straight,' I said, looking at the invitation. 'Do we have to go to this thing? I could spend the rest of my life without tasting another cup of that Hi-C and lime sherbet punch Aunt Olive always makes.'

She pursed her lips and considered. 'Well now, I believe this is wedding number four for RaeAnn. We've given her a blender, an electric blanket, and a SaladShooter in the past. I'm about out of ideas.'

'Who's she marrying?'

'You remember Alton? The guy with the droopy earlobes?'

'Her first husband? The one who took out a bank loan to try and corner the market on Billy Beer? Even RaeAnn can't be that dumb.'

'She is though,' Edna said. 'According to Aunt Olive, she ran into him at an Amway meeting, and they fell in love all over again. She went home and packed her Barbie doll collection and left a note for poor old Wayne telling him it was over.'

I was just about to get the rest of the gory details when the phone rang.

'Hey!' It was Mac.

'Hey yourself. What's up? Are you home from work this early?'

'I've been home all day,' he said. 'Took a personal leave day.'

Andrew McAuliffe may be a bureaucrat (he works for the Atlanta Regional Commission as a compliance officer), but he's not exactly your typical government freeloader. He never takes sick days and the only personal leave days he's taken in the four years we've been together have been to help me out of a jam.

'What's up?' I repeated.

'I've been on the phone with Birmingham all day,' he said glumly.

'Is Stephanie okay?'

Mac's nineteen-year-old daughter and evil ex-wife Barbara have lived in Birmingham ever since their divorce years ago. He always refers to the ex as Birmingham, claiming he still can't utter Barbara's name without flashing back to the bad old days.

'Oh yeah,' he said. 'Stephanie's great. Except that she came home from school last night and announced to her mother that since she was flunking all her classes anyway she had decided not to bother with finals.'

'Uh-oh.'

'She and Barbara had a knock-down drag-out of course.'

'The kid was really flunking everything?'

9

'Chemistry, English lit, and sociology. Oh yeah, and badminton.'

'Can you flunk badminton?'

'My daughter is a model of consistency,' Mac said. 'She could, and she did.'

'She went all the way through the quarter and decided to quit just before finals?'

'Fourteen hundred dollars down the toilet,' he said quietly.

'What did you say to her?'

'I yelled. She cried.'

'So what now? Does she have any plans?'

He laughed. 'She did have. I think the plan was to go running to Atlanta, complain to Daddy, have Daddy take sides against Mama, spend the summer with Dad, work on a tan, party hearty.'

'I like it,' I said. 'Can I play too?'

'I've already nixed plan A,' Mac said. 'You know I've only got the one bedroom and bathroom out here. Do you have any idea how long it takes a nineteen-year-old to do her hair and makeup these days?'

'I have some idea, yes,' I said. 'So what's plan B?'

'I don't know,' he sighed. 'We didn't get anything worked out on the phone. The upshot of all of this is that it looks like I'm going to run over there and try to get the two of them speaking to one another again. Stephanie was hysterical when I told her she couldn't come live with me. And Barb was pissed off too. She thinks Steph should spend the summer away; give each other some space before they kill each other.'

I could hear it coming. 'When are you going?'

'I've got Rufus packed in the car already. I'll leave as soon as I get off the phone,' he said.

'Goddamn,' I said. 'Do you know what I had to go through to get these Jimmy Buffett tickets? Bucky had two extra tickets, and to get him to sell me two we're going to have to clean not only his place but the new girlfriend's playpen too. Can't you go tomorrow or Sunday?'

'I'm sorry,' he said. 'Hell, I wanted to go as bad as you did. But it can't be helped. Stephanie was threatening all kinds of wild stuff on the phone today. I've gotta go calm her down. Can you switch the tickets for tomorrow night?'

'I doubt it,' I said. 'Just tell the little brat to get her butt back in school. Can't you do that on the phone?'

'I would if I could,' he said. 'You think I want to go? I'd rather have a root canal than get in between those two. Look, I gotta go before traffic gets too bad. I'll call you when I get back, okay?'

'Fine,' I said rather nastily and slammed the phone down. I eyed the picnic basket on the kitchen counter. I'd splurged and gotten a couple of catered dinners to take to the Buffett concert at Chastain Park. Cold lobster salad, crusty French bread, some pâté, and key lime tarts. The chardonnay was chilling in the frig. Now I'd have to call Bucky and ask about a ticket switch, which I knew was hopeless. Jimmy Buffett plays two concerts in Atlanta every spring. They sell out immediately. I'd probably end up eating the lobster salad by myself in front of the television tonight. A fine way to spend a glorious spring Friday night.

Edna and Neva Jean looked at me expectantly. They'd been eavesdropping, of course.

'Well?' Edna said expectantly.

'There's bad news and good news,' I said. 'Mac's daughter Stephanie flunked out of college, and he has to go over to Birmingham tonight and referee a fight between her and her bitchy mother. So much for the concert.'

I took the shower invitation and ripped it to little bits, and let them drift into the trash. 'The good news is that the Waring blender we gave RaeAnn the first time she married has a five-year warranty. And it's only been four years by my count.'

3

I was sitting on the front porch, stomping red ants with the toe of my sneaker when the shiny late-model Cadillac pulled up to the curb. I was supposed to be cutting the grass, but it was hot for May, and I was still in a lousy mood over my broken date with Mac. He usually cuts the grass for us; the man actually enjoys doing yard work, but I hadn't heard from him that morning, so I assumed he was still in Birmingham.

The Caddie was white, not brand new, but it was somebody's cherished baby, with gleaming chrome and those gold-plated wire wheel covers. Two black women sat in the front seat, deep in discussion, even after the driver had cut the engine. While I waited to see who our company was, I rid the world of at least another dozen red ants. I hate those suckers.

When I looked up, the driver was getting out of the car. The other woman stayed where she was. I used my hands to shade my eyes. The woman walked up the sidewalk toward me, striding quickly in high-heel yellow sandals. Without the shoes, she was petite, maybe five foot three, and slim, dressed in a stylish bright yellow pants suit with a yellow-and-orange print blouse. Her hair was frosted shades of blond and brown and big dark sunglasses obscured half her face. As she got closer I could see she was in her late forties, but she had that well-preserved look you see in successful women her age.

When she came within hollering range the woman flipped off her glasses and looked me over. 'Callahan?'

'Shit,' I muttered to myself. It was Vonette Hunsecker. I glanced down at myself. I was wearing a faded stretched-out T-shirt, baggy black gym shorts, and my most holey pair of sneakers. Not exactly how I like to look when receiving company.

'Vonette?' I asked in the same tone she'd used on me. 'Is that you?'

I hadn't seen her since the divorce, it must have been three years. I hate to say it, but the woman looked fabulous.

She turned around and looked back at the woman sitting in the car, gestured to her to join us, but I could see the woman shaking her head no. Vonette put her hands on her hips and jerked her head toward me, but the woman stayed put.

'Callahan,' Vonette said, moving onto the porch to where I was now standing. 'It's been a long time.'

I shook her hand reluctantly. Hers was tiny and fine-boned, with long nails done in one of those fancy French manicures that leave you with weird-looking white half-moons on each finger. Mine were clean, and that's the best I could say.

'Can we talk a minute?' Vonette asked. 'I know you're busy, but this is really important to us, and C.W. says

14

you're the best at what you do. It was his idea for us to call you.'

I didn't know whether to be more surprised that C.W. had praised me or that he had managed to have a civil conversation with his ex-wife.

'All right,' I said. I gestured to a pair of white wicker rockers on the porch. 'Have a seat and tell me what's on your mind. But I can't guarantee I'll be able to help.'

'We're sure you can help,' Vonette said firmly, her peach-painted lips forming a big confident smile.

'We?'

She sighed. 'That's Rita, my cousin, in the car. She's, uh, a little shy about talking to you after you hung up on her yesterday.'

'What?' I said. 'Now wait a minute. She's the one who did the hanging up. I was just trying to tell her that I'm not really taking any new cases right now, because with the House Mouse and all . . .'

'Money is not a problem,' Vonette said, deliberately interrupting. 'I invested most of my money from the VelvetTeens, and I'm selling real estate now. I can afford the best, and I want you.'

'What is it you want me to do?' Curiosity will get me killed some day.

Vonette looked back toward the car again, still annoyed at her cousin.

'We need you to find someone.'

'Who?'

'Rita's sister, Delores. The third member of the VelvetTeens.'

15

'Find her where?' I asked. 'When was the last time you saw her?'

'Just a minute,' Vonette said. She got up and walked quickly to the car, opened the door and said a few heated words to her passenger.

Rita Fontaine followed Vonette reluctantly back to the porch, staying four or five steps behind her, her eyes intent on the pattern of bricks in our front walk. Rita was taller than her cousin by four or five inches. She was skinny all over, except for a small potbelly that protruded from the tight white slacks and Braves T-shirt she wore. While Vonette looked sleek, chic, and petite, Rita just looked used up.

Her beehive was gone of course. Architecture like that was never meant for the ages. Now her hair was cut close to the scalp. Her skin was two shades lighter than her cousin's, sort of a chocolate milk shake shade as opposed to Vonette's coffee-colored complexion. But there were deep creases at the corners of her eyes and her face looked puffy. She had amazing if somewhat bloodshot eyes, huge and liquid brown, with long curling lashes. An unlit cigarette dangled from the corner of her mouth.

'Callahan,' Vonette said, 'This is Rita, lead singer of the fabulous VelvetTeens.'

'Nice to meet you,' I said, offering her a chair. 'Vonette was saying your sister Delores is missing?'

'Thought you said you were too busy,' Rita said. The voice was just as raspy in person.

'She didn't understand how important this is to us,'

Vonette said soothingly. 'Callahan wants to know all about Delores.'

Rita took a pack of matches out of her pants pocket, struck the match and went to light the cigarette. When she saw Vonette glowering at her, she dropped the match onto the porch floor. 'She's trying to quit,' Vonette explained.

'What you want to know?' Rita asked, ignoring her cousin.

'Well, everything,' I said. 'When you saw her last, what she was doing, where she might be now.'

'Ain't seen Delores since sixty-seven,' Rita said, wriggling in her chair. 'She married that Jewboy, and we ain't seen her since.'

'David Eisner,' Vonette put in. 'He was our accompanist. Keyboard man. He and Delores eloped in May of 1966.'

'Sixty-six?' I said, not bothering to hide my surprise. 'You haven't seen your sister, your cousin, a member of your group in twenty-eight years? Was there a fight or something?'

'We got a postcard from her in seventy-four,' Rita said. 'She was in Vegas. Card said Delores was singing backup for Ike and Tina. Old Delores fancy-britches was an Ikette.'

'And that's the last word you had?' I couldn't help being incredulous. My own family is big and strange. We fight all the time and have little in common, but we at least connect occasionally for the sake of my mother.

'I been busy,' Rita said. 'Delores, she was her own

thing. She'd call Mama every year on Mother's Day, but Mama died in seventy-six.'

'Wait just a minute,' I said. I opened the front door, went to my bedroom and got one of the yellow legal pads I use to take notes. When I got back, Rita had closed her eyes tightly and appeared to be asleep.

'Let's just start with the basics,' I said loudly.

Rita opened her eyes and stared at the ceiling.

'Did your sister use her maiden or married name? And I'll need her age and social security number and last known address.'

Rita shrugged helplessly.

'Look,' I said, impatient. 'It would help if I knew whether I was looking for Delores Fontaine or Delores Eisner, or even if she calls herself Delores.'

Vonette blushed. 'Uh, Callahan. Delores's last name was never Fontaine. Rita's mama had Delores by a different man. Her name was Delores Carter. That's the name she used professionally the last time we heard from her.'

'In seventy-four,' I added.

'Well actually,' Vonette said. 'I saw an item in *Cashbox* in seventy-seven. It was a picture of Captain and Tennille. And there was a backup singer who looked exactly like Delores used to. This girl had those same unusual almond-shaped eyes and that long straight black hair.'

'Delores had good hair,' Rita said, apropos of nothing. 'I believe Mr Carter's mama might have been Cherokee Indian. I heard that one time. Delores, she liked to tell people she was an Indian princess.'

I wrote it down. It was a start. I looked up expectantly.

Vonette shrugged. 'That's all we've got. It's not much. But you've got to find her for us.'

'I'm not cheap,' I said. 'A hundred an hour, plus expenses. I'll want a ten-hour minimum, and you pay half up front. I'll have to have some old photos of Delores, and I'll need you to answer a lot more questions.'

'Then you'll do it?' Vonette looked relieved. She reached for her purse and got out her checkbook. 'Can you start right away?'

'Tell me something,' I said. 'You haven't seen or heard of Delores in all these years. Why the big hurry now? Is there a family reunion coming up?'

The two women exchanged glances. 'Go ahead and tell her,' Rita said.

'They're making a movie,' Vonette said. 'Oldies are big right now, real big. Ever since *The Big Chill* everybody in Hollywood is on a nostalgia kick. You heard of Davis Zimmerman?'

I nodded. Zimmerman made pleasant comedies, most of which seemed to draw heavily on his own teen years in the Midwest. His last two movies, *Summer Love* and *Top-Down* had been big box office, if not critical hits. Edna and I had been trying to rent *Top-Down* at Blockbuster for weeks, but it was always gone by the time we got to the store on Friday afternoons.

Vonette lowered her voice. 'He wants to call his next movie *Happy Never After*. Julia Roberts and Tom Cruise are already signed up. And the movie's theme song would be ours! 'Happy Never After!' God. We haven't

19

talked money yet, but I just know this could be the beginning of something big. For all of us. They're saying they might even give us small parts in the movie. As the original fabulous VelvetTeens.'

'If we can find Delores,' Rita reminded her cousin. She was rubbing her hands together, turning the unlit cigarette in her fingertips, like some rare jewel.

Vonette finished writing the check and handed it over to me. She stood and looked thoughtfully at her cousin. 'Rita, why don't you go on and get in the car,' she suggested. 'Callahan, would it be all right if I used your phone for a minute? I'm supposed to show a house at noon and I want to make sure the owners left the key in the lock box.'

Rita nodded at me and walked slowly toward the car. When she was out of range, I opened the front door for Vonette. 'You want to tell me what's with her?' I asked.

Vonette shook her head yes, rolled her eyes. 'I thought we might have a little private conference,' she said. 'So you know what you're dealing with here.'

'Which is what?'

She looked around the living room and gave it an approving nod. 'Nice light in here. I like the way you've left the moldings and the original windows. Buyers like this old stuff. Have you ever considered selling?'

I showed her to a flowered chintz armchair I'd rescued from my neighbor's curb a few weeks before on trash pickup day. 'No, we like it right where we are. Now, what were you going to tell me about Rita?'

She clasped her hands around her crossed legs. 'Look. Rita's had it hard. Her mother, my aunt Louise, had

seven kids by three different men Rita was oldest, which
meant she took care of everybody. When the VelvetTeens
started cutting records and it looked like we'd make it
big, everybody in the family started lining up to get
theirs. And Rita never turned anybody away. Houses,
cars, lawyers when somebody got thrown in jail, good
old Rita forked over the money for all of it.'

'And then what?'

'And then it was over,' Vonette said. 'First it was the
British Invasion, then all that psychedelic crap. Girl
groups were a big joke. We hung on as long as we could.
But in sixty-six, when Delores left, we knew we
couldn't go on. Rita may have been the lead singer, and I
was the oldest, but Delores was the heart of the group.
She was the one who came up with our look, our sound,
all of it. People said it was Stuart Hightower, but that's
a lot of bullshit. We were the VelvetTeens way before he
found us.'

'Hightower,' I said. 'Where have I heard that name?'

Vonette snorted. 'You are a lot younger than you look,
girl. Stuart Hightower started SkyHi Records in fifty-
nine. Him and Phil Spector and Berry Gordy, they made
rock 'n' roll.'

'And he discovered you guys?'

She nodded. 'We'd hang around outside this confec-
tionery across the street from Brown High, practice
singing, hoping the guys would notice how high we
teased our hair and how short we wore our skirts.
Delores made us dress alike. We even wore the same
color lipstick and eye shadow. The fabulous VelvetTeens,
child, that was us. We were messing around outside

21

that candy store one day when this white guy came walking down the sidewalk. He stopped and leaned against the wall and watched us. Never said a word. Next day, we were there again, and there he was again. This went on for a whole week, till one day Delores stepped right up to him and asked him what he thought he was doing. That was the way Delores was. She'd say anything to anybody.'

'I'm watching my next big act,' Stu said. 'You girls ever been to New York City?'

'And the next thing you know, there you were on *American Bandstand*.' I said.

Vonette tilted her chin. '*Bandstand, Hullabaloo, Where the Action Is*. We were on *Soul Train* at the very beginning. We went to England and went on this show there called *Ready Steady, Go*. We even did a television special with Andy Williams, in sixty-six, I guess it was. Had mink coats and diamonds. Chauffeured limos. When our second album went gold, Stu bought us each a white Mustang convertible.'

All this talk about the glory days wasn't telling me much about why Rita Fontaine was such a hard case. 'And then you weren't a big deal anymore,' I said, not unkindly. 'You've obviously done well for yourself. What happened to Rita?'

Her mouth tilted down at the corners. 'Men is what happened to Rita. Men and booze. Three bad marriages to three major losers. And in between, she learned to drink with the best of 'em. What her brothers and sisters and the rest of 'em didn't chisel her out of, Rita managed to piss away all by her own self.'

'How bad off is she?' I asked.

Vonette gestured toward the open window through which we could see the Caddie, with Rita asleep in the front seat. 'Bad as you can get,' she said, sighing. 'She's been working as an aide at a nursing home, when she can stay sober. She had a beautiful big home she bought after 'Happy Never After' went gold, but that's long gone. She was living in her car for a few months last winter, till she got pneumonia and spent a month in the hospital at Grady. Now she stays with Andre over near the stadium.'

'Who's Andre?'

'The only good thing ever happened to Rita since we cut that record,' Vonette said. 'Andre's her son. Twenty-eight years old and the best-looking boy walking around Atlanta on two legs. He sings too, you know, works a day job in a warehouse, and tries to keep his mama straight.'

'Oh,' I said.

She gave me a level look. 'Rita got kinda upset after she talked to you last night. She found some money Andre had hidden, bought herself a bottle of Cold Duck and had a little party. But she's been on the wagon, and I'm trying to get her to stop smoking, too. We start rehearsing tomorrow, I got a piano player hired, and I found some of our old sheet music. Now we need you to do the rest. I've got some old scrapbooks at the house, now that I think about it. Might be something in there that would help. Maybe you could come by around two o'clock tomorrow? By then, maybe Rita will feel more like talking.'

'She hasn't been real helpful so far,' I pointed out.

'It's Rita's last chance,' Vonette said. She stood up and smiled wryly. 'Mine too,' she said. 'I'm forty-nine years old. My husband is married to a second wife almost as young as my daughter. I woke up the other morning, looked in the mirror. You know what? My boobs had moved two inches south. The rest of it too. I know we're not ever going to be eighteen again. I know that. I just want a little of it back. You know? Just a little. Think you can understand that?'

'Yeah,' I said, getting up to walk her to the front door. 'I guess I can relate.'

4

Edna pulled into the driveway just as Vonette and Rita were leaving. She has a standing beauty parlor appointment on Saturday mornings.

'Who was that?' she asked, sitting down next to me on the porch steps.

I looked closely at her hair. In the sunlight it had a definite blue tint.

'Frank using something new on you?'

She put her hand to her head and regarded me suspiciously. 'Some new rinse-in conditioner. Why?'

'No reason,' I said. 'Is it supposed to make your hair look like blueberry cotton candy?'

She got up and ran inside the house. A minute later she was back, grim-faced. 'It's really blue, isn't it? In the lights at the salon it looked fine, just white. Dammit, now I'm gonna have to walk around for a whole week looking like your aunt Alma. She always had blue hair.'

'It'll be fine,' I said, patting her hand reassuringly. 'Just stay out of natural sunlight.'

She swatted my hand away. 'Thanks a lot. Now who were those women?'

'Oh them,' I said. 'That was Vonette Hunsecker. C.W.'s ex-wife. And her cousin. They want to hire me.'

'To clean their houses?'

I shook my head. 'Nope. They want me to find somebody. Back in the sixties, Vonette and Rita Fontaine, that's the cousin, were part of a group called the VelvetTeens. Remember them?'

'Vaguely,' she said. 'All that jiggedy-jig music you kids used to play all sort of sounded the same, you ask me.'

'It was supposed to,' I pointed out. 'Anyway, some Hollywood type wants to make a movie using their song, so they want me to find the third member of the group, Rita's half-sister, a woman named Delores Carter.'

'Well that shouldn't take long,' she said. 'When's the last time they heard from her?'

'Sometime during the Nixon administration,' I said. 'Not what you call a close family.'

'The VelvetTeens' Edna repeated. 'What was their big song?'

'"Happy Never After,"' I said, 'and there were four or five other big ones too.'

'You know, I think Kevin used to have a bunch of their records,' Edna said. 'There's a whole box of his old forty-fives up in the attic. I keep meaning to call him and tell him to get that crap out of there. It's a fire hazard. He and Wanda need to put that stuff up in their own attic.'

I stood up and offered her a hand to help her up. She took it, then dusted off the seat of her slacks.

Back in the house, I called directory information in Las Vegas and asked if they had a listing for a Delores Eisner or a Delores Carter. No go, but then I really didn't expect that she'd have stayed in Vegas all these years.

'I think I'll go look for those records,' I told Edna. 'Get me in the mood for the job.'

'What about the grass?' she said. 'I thought you were gonna cut it this morning.'

'The day's still young,' I assured her. 'Besides, Mac may show up yet. And he owes me big-time after last night.'

I found the box of records in a corner of the attic. I had to dig through piles of crumbling paperback books, stacks of *National Geographics*, and sweaters my brother hadn't worn since his junior-high graduation, but in the end, I found them. I also found an old box-type record player I remembered using for games of Musical Chairs.

Edna was standing at the bottom of the pull-down attic stairs when I climbed down with the dust-covered cartons. 'Take that filthy stuff right on out of this house,' she said, hands on her hips. I took them out onto the porch, then went back in the house for an extension cord and some cleaning rags.

Clouds of dust mushroomed out of the carton when I started lifting the records out. Kevin had obviously been a connoisseur of girl groups. Mixed in with the Beach Boys and the Beatles and Sonny and Cher and the Righteous Brothers and stacks of Motown singles, he had the Shirelles, the Chiffons, the VelvetTeens,

Martha and the Vandellas, the Marvellettes, the Ronettes, Patti LaBelle and the Bluebelles, the Crystals, and the Supremes. He even had 'Leader of the Pack' by the Shangri-Las. I blew the dust off that one and held it up to show Edna, who was now sitting nearby sipping a glass of iced tea.

'Hey, Ma, remember this one?' I asked. 'Maureen and I lip-synched the parody of it, "Leader of the Laundromat" at the Girl Scout talent show.'

'Lord, yes,' she said, grinning. 'Your father thought it was the funniest thing he'd ever seen in his life, you two little-bitty things with teased hair and lipstick and black leather jackets. We've got a home movie of it somewhere around here.'

I plugged in the record player, switched it on and was gratified to see the turntable start spinning. I dusted off the VelvetTeens' 'Happy Never After.' The B side of the forty-five was a song I'd never heard of: 'Dreams of Us.' Both sides were written by Stuart Hightower.

As the record started to spin I sat down in the rocker next to Edna.

The song started with a string section, joined by pianos and drums and an entire symphony. Then came that high contralto. 'Happy Never After,' Rita Fontaine wailed. 'If you ever leave me I'll be happy never after.' In the background Delores and Vonette sweetly chanted 'Never, no never, never, ever ever.'

'Now I remember them,' Edna said. 'Kevin nearly wore the grooves out on that song. And he'd turn the volume up so loud the neighbor's dogs would howl two blocks away.'

We played all of 'Happy Never After,' twice. Played the B side too, which wasn't bad, but wasn't nearly as good as the A side. Then, because it was hot and I was feeling lazy, I listened to all the rest of the Kevin Garrity sixties collection. I felt newfound admiration for my big brother's taste. In music anyway.

If he was such a big fan, I thought, maybe he could remember something useful about my new clients.

'The VelvetTeens?' he said, after Wanda woke him up from his afternoon nap. 'Hell yeah, I remember 'em. They were the best. I bought all their records, of course. And I saw them at least twice. The first time I was still in high school, but a buddy of mine invited me to a frat party over at Tech. It must have been around sixty-five, so I guess they were sort of on the skids by then. But man, were they sexy. Especially that lead singer.'

'Rita Fontaine? Sexy?' It was hard to jibe the idea with the image of the puffy-faced woman who'd just left my house.

'Oh yeah,' Kevin said softly. 'She had big old bedroom eyes, kind of Oriental-looking, almost, and when she sang, all the guys got a hard-on, just listening.'

'Thanks for sharing that,' I said.

'Hey, why are you asking me about the VelvetTeens?' he asked. 'Mac's a lot older than me. He probably remembers them a lot better than me. You ought to ask him about them.'

'I will,' I said. 'I've got a client who wants me to find Delores Carter, she was the youngest in the group, Rita Fontaine's half-sister. The VelvetTeens are trying to make a comeback.'

'Cool,' Kevin said. 'Can you get me free tickets?'

'You'll never change,' I said. 'Mom says for you to come get your junk out of our attic.'

'Yeah, I'll be over,' he said vaguely. 'See ya.'

When I got off the phone and went back to the porch, Mac was sitting in the armchair, sifting through the box of records. He stood up and kissed me briefly. 'I'm sorry about the concert,' he said. 'I'm just now getting back to town. I came straight here, didn't even go home.'

'How nice,' I said evenly. I had no intention of letting him off the hook so easily. Those concert tickets had been twenty-five dollars a piece, and the fancy supper I'd scarfed at midnight had given me a forty-dollar bellyache.

'How are Stephanie and Barbara?' I asked, sitting down beside him.

'We've worked out a cease-fire,' Mac said. He kicked the carton of records with his foot. 'What are these doing out here?'

'Research for a new case I've taken,' I said. 'You're just getting back, huh? Where'd you stay last night?'

'At Barb's,' he said. 'I took Stephanie out to dinner and we got back late and I finally got the two of them talking to each other. By that time it was after two, so Barb let me sleep there.'

My raised eyebrows weren't easy to miss.

'On the sofa in the den,' he said quickly. 'Don't be an ass. What kind of a case?'

'Missing person,' I said. 'I'm supposed to find one Delores Carter, whose loving family hasn't heard from her in twenty years.'

'You're kidding!' he said. 'Delores Carter of the VelvetTeens? Is that why you've got all these records out here? Who hired you?'

'You won't believe it,' I said. 'Vonette Hunsecker. She was a VelvetTeen. The other two members were her cousins. They need me to find Delores so they can make a big comeback.'

He grinned broadly. Mac's smile is one of the sexiest things about him. His hair and beard are gray, and there are laugh lines at the corners of his eyes, crow's-feet, Edna calls them, uncharitably, but Andrew McAuliffe ain't no senior citizen. His belly's flat, he's got a great set of buns, and the rest is nobody else's business but mine.

'You mean Vonette Hunsecker was Vonette Brown?'

'I guess,' I said, shrugging. 'Don't tell me you even know all their names?'

'Vonette Brown, Delores Carter, Rita Fontaine,' he said promptly. The VelvetTeens were the best. I can't believe you're working for 'em. Did you meet Rita Fontaine? What's she like?'

'Down and out in Atlanta, Georgia,' I said. 'Vonette looks great, but the years have not been kind to Rita. She's not the heartbreaker I hear she used to be.'

'That's too bad,' he said, shaking his head. 'God, Callahan, I can still see them up on the stage of the old Civic Auditorium. The first time they came to Atlanta was with some rock 'n' roll revue. They had the Drifters and the Platters and Leslie Gore, she had just hit it big with "It's My Party," and the VelvetTeens were the warmup act. All the other girl groups then, they always

31

looked like they were going to a mother-daughter social. But the VelvetTeens were tough, you know? Real tight dresses, and when they sang, they had these moves. They were real teases, I'll tell ya. Definitely not the kind of girls you'd take home to the folks, especially Rita Fontaine.'

'So my brother, Kevin, says,' I said.

'A VelvetTeen comeback would be great,' Mac said wistfully. 'Think you can find Delores?'

'I'm going to try,' I said. 'They haven't given me a whole lot to go on. Last they heard, she was in Vegas with Ike and Tina Turner, back in seventy-four.'

'Hey,' he said suddenly, snapping his fingers. 'You know who you ought to talk to? Jacky Rabbit.'

I picked up the records and started putting them one by one back into the box. 'While I'm at it, why don't I interrogate BooBoo Bear and Fuzzy Squirrel too?'

'No, idiot,' he said. 'You grew up here. Don't you remember Jacky Rabbit? He was the hippest guy in Atlanta radio. He had that show on WPLO, all the kids listened to it. Every rock and roll act that came through town turned up on his show, and he hosted *Platter Party* too.'

'I remember *Platter Party*,' I admitted. 'But I didn't remember who the host was.'

'Jacky Rabbit,' Mac said. 'Me and my buddies used to go down and sit in the audience at WSB when they did those shows. The cutest girls in town were always there. I saw Sam and Dave, and the Coasters, and Little Eva. I can still do the Loco-Motion.'

'I'll remember that when we double-date to the

Private Investigator's Prom,' I said. 'Now how would you suggest I go about finding Mr Rabbit? Aren't radio people notoriously transient types?'

'Probably,' Mac said, 'but I happen to know that Jack's still in town. He's using his real name now, Jack Rabin. Only reason I know is that the *Constitution* ran one of those "where are they now" pieces about him a couple years ago. At the time, he was selling airtime at WPCH.

The Peach, as it's known around Atlanta, plays mellow-fellow doctor's office Barry Manilow stuff.

'I'll look him up,' I said. 'Monday I'm gonna call Jane Cooper. We went through police academy together. She was in the GBI until a couple years ago, now she's opened her own office and she subscribes to one of those computer databases. I'll see if she'll rent me some time on the network to do a trace. I'm supposed to go over to Vonette's house tomorrow to pick up some scrapbooks and stuff, I'll ask her then about what kind of union they might have belonged to. Chances are, if Delores is still in the business, she has an agent representing her. Hey. I wonder if Jack Rabin is still in the phone book?'

Jack Rabin had a telephone and an address in Dunwoody and an answering machine.

'Hi! This is Jacky Rabbit's Golden Oldies Platter Party,' a cheery voice said. 'Leave a message, and remember Jacky's motto: Be Young, Be Foolish, and Be Happy!'

I did as I was told, and fifteen minutes later, as I was carting the records back into the house, the phone rang.

It was Jacky Rabbit's wife, a tired sounding woman named Bonnie.

'Jack's working today,' she said. 'He's setting up for a party over at the Days Inn on La Vista. Some class reunion, I think. You can probably find him there.'

I changed out of my shorts and into a cotton skirt and a blouse. Mac was outside, putting gas and oil into the lawn mower. I'd guilt-tripped him into taking over my yard work.

'I found your friend Jacky,' I told him. 'He apparently does DJ work on the side these days. Wanna come with me?' I was actually hoping he'd refuse, but since it was his lead, I thought I'd offer.

He wiped his hands on a rag and stood up. 'That's okay,' he said. 'Middle-aged hipsters I can pass up. I'll finish up here, then run home and get a shower. What do you want to do tonight?'

I shrugged. 'I dunno. Let's talk about it later.'

On the way to the Days Inn, I picked apart the little Mac had told me about his trip to Birmingham. So he'd stayed all night. At his ex-wife's house. So what? His daughter was there. It was late. It would have been stupid to go to a motel. And Mac has a cheap streak. Forget it, I told myself. Just forget it.

I found Jacky Rabbit where his wife said I would, at the Days Inn near Northlake Mall. Or rather, between his car and the motel. The parking lot was half-empty, but an overweight, bald guy dressed in black knee-length shorts and a black Bruce Springsteen T-shirt was unloading plastic milk crates full of records from a battered Buick station wagon.

I held the heavy glass door to the lobby open for him. 'Jack Rabin?' I asked.

He glanced at me. 'Are you Marcia? The program chair for tonight?'

I shook my head. 'Sorry. I'm Callahan Garrity. I'm a private detective. I was hoping you could help me with something I'm looking into.'

His eyes narrowed a little. 'Whose ex-wife are you working for?'

I laughed. 'Nobody's at the moment. I don't usually do domestic work. How about I give you a hand with your equipment, and then we'll talk?'

He nodded his head toward a set of opened double doors. The brass plaque on the wall said it was the Dogwood Ballroom. 'This was the last load. Let me just hook everything up and see if we got juice. Then I'll let you buy me a beer in the lounge.'

I followed him inside the ballroom. There was a small raised dais at the front of the room. A table held a complicated-looking turntable and control panel, and a couple of five-foot-tall amplifiers flanked the table on each side. There were blue and white streamers criss-crossing the room, blue and white balloons, and a blue-and-white banner strung from the ceiling. 'Welcome Avondale High Class of '75,' it said.

Rabin was on his hands and knees under the table, connecting a set of snaking black cables to the back of his turntable. He struggled uneasily to his feet and flipped a switch. He moved a mike stand to the center of the table. 'Test, test,' he said. The sound bounced across the room. 'Good,' he said.

In a minute he was by my side. 'The lounge is back this way,' he said, pointing down the carpeted hallway. 'I don't want to go far. That's five thousand dollars worth of equipment you're looking at there. Not counting the records. Some of those forty-fives were demos I got as a DJ in the late fifties and sixties. They're irreplaceable.'

Rabin was shorter than me, about five five, but he walked briskly, and his forearms were muscular rather than fat. I followed him into the darkened lounge. A bartender was slicing lemons behind the counter. We sat down at the bar. 'Hiya Jack,' he said. 'Moosehead?'

Rabin nodded. 'How about you?'

I usually like bourbon, but I'm a closet traditionalist. After Easter I wear beige shoes and switch over to gin and tonic or cold beer. Moosehead sounded good today. 'The same.'

After he set the two foaming glasses in front of us, Rabin turned to me. 'So what's a private investigator want with a washed up jock?'

His face was tanned, and he had light blue eyes under pale blond lashes. For the first time I noticed he wasn't really bald, but that what little hair he did have was shaved close to the scalp.

'I've been hired to find Delores Carter,' I said, sipping my beer. 'I'm sort of at a loss as to where to start. A friend thought of you.'

'Delores Carter,' he said, chuckling. 'Now there was a piece of work. You mind telling me who's looking for her?'

I thought about it. Secrecy didn't seem to be an issue

for Rita and Vonette. Besides, maybe Rabin could help them resurrect their career.

'Her sister and her cousin,' I said. 'They're planning a comeback.'

'The VelvetTeens,' he said, rolling the word around on his tongue and making it come out sounding classy. 'Yeah, why not? All these other oldies groups coming out of the woodwork. Why not them? At least those girls had some real talent. Cute girls, too. They had a real unique sound. Good stage presence. The kids loved 'em. They'd be great on the oldies revival tour.'

'They haven't heard from Delores since seventy-four,' I said. 'She was touring with Ike and Tina Turner.'

'That sounds like Delores, just dropping out of sight like that,' Rabin said. 'She was the little one, right? She was a pistol, that one. In the beginning, when they did a lot of live shows, one-nights, that kind of thing, the girls would send her around after the show for their money. And she wanted it in cash, baby. They'd been ripped off once too often out on the chitlin circuit.'

'Chitlin circuit?' I said. 'What's that?'

'How old are you?' Rabin said, sweeping his eyes over me. 'What, thirty-three, something like that?'

'I'm thirty-eight,' I said. 'Thanks for the compliment.'

'You'd be too young to remember,' he said. 'The chitlin' circuit was all these little clubs all over the South. Back in the early sixties, before desegregation, these joints were the only places a black group could perform live. Race music, they called it up until then. You know, Jackie Wilson, Sam Cooke, Little Richard, Otis Redding. Mamas did not like for their little white kids to listen to it, either. Of course, the kids ate it up. The VelvetTeens came in on the tail end of the chitlin circuit, but they did their time. Yeah, Delores, she was a pistol.'

'Her sister and cousin really want me to find her,' I said. 'Vonette said she thinks Delores might have been touring with Captain and Tennille in the late seventies. After that, nobody's seen or heard from her.'

'Well hell,' Rabin said, 'I seen her since then. I did a stint as promotions director at an oldies station in Columbia, South Carolina, in the late eighties. Must have been eighty-eight or so, she came to town, singing backup with Diana Ross. Kid looked good, too. What is she now, forty-eight, something like that?'

I shook my head. 'You tell me. I know she was the youngest in the group. Vonette is forty-nine. So you saw her. Did you talk to her, by any chance? What can you tell me about her? Did she go by Delores Carter?'

'Whoa,' he said, putting out his hand. 'The station did a ticket giveaway, I just came out on stage, announced the winners' names, and went backstage. I passed Delores as she was going onstage. That's it. We didn't talk, nothin' like that. It wasn't until a few minutes later that it hit me, hey, that was Delores Carter of the VelvetTeens. I got no idea what name she was going by.'

I sighed. 'How about her husband? A white guy, played the keyboards. She married him when she left the group. David Eisner's the name. Did you know him?'

He shook his head. 'I maybe knew him thirty years ago, but I wouldn't know him from Adam's housecat now. One thing I can tell you, Diana Ross wasn't travelling with no musicians, except her accompanist. And he's the same guy she's worked with for a dozen years. I don't know the name, but it ain't Eisner. A tour like that, they pick up musicians locally.'

'Figures,' I said. 'If you were me, where would you start looking for her?'

'LA,' he said promptly. 'Delores was never the lead singer type. She was always strictly backup. If she's still working in the business, she could be anywhere. But LA is where most of the session work is being done these days, unless she's gone country, in which case she'd maybe be in Nashville.'

'Thanks,' I said, taking a final sip of my beer. I got a five dollar bill out of my purse and laid it on the bar beside my glass. 'I guess that's where I'll start. I appreciate all your help, Jack. You want me to let you know if she turns up?'

'Yeah,' Rabin said. 'Gimme a jingle. I'd like to see those kids get back together again. They had a nice sound.'

I was walking out of the bar when he called out to me again.

'Hey, Callahan,' Rabin said. 'What's Stuart Hightower gonna have to say about the VelvetTeens making a comeback?'

The question puzzled me. 'What do you mean?' I said. 'Why should he care?'

'Oh baby,' Rabin said, shaking his head. 'You don't

know Stu Hightower. He'll have something to say about it, believe me.'

'Where is Hightower now?' I wanted to know. 'Is he still in the business?'

Rabin looked at me as though I were retarded or something.

'You're kiddin', right? Ol' Stu-Baby is right here in the Big Peach. Moved back from LA four or five years ago. He's got a new label, BackTalk. They got a big state-of-the-art studio in town, and I hear he lives out in Alpharetta, at Riverbend, where all the professional athletes and rich guys live. BackTalk's one of the biggest independent labels in the country. Now don't tell me you never heard of Junebug either?'

I admitted I hadn't.

'You must be living under a rock or something,' Rabin said. 'The guy just won a Grammy for Best New Male Artist of the Year. His first album, *Diss Dis*, went platinum in like five minutes. Stu Hightower has struck gold again. And it couldn't have happened to a bigger jerk. He should have a heart attack and die.'

'So you know Hightower?'

He shrugged. 'Everybody in the business knows him, and everybody knows what a crook he is. Did your clients mention how he stole from them?'

'They're pretty bitter about him,' I admitted.

'Watch out for the guy,' Rabin said. 'He's a sicko. Enjoys screwing up other people's lives. Always has.'

5

The waiter had just cleared the salad plates and was pouring us all another glass of chardonnay when Linda Nickells made me spit water through my nose.

'None for me,' she told the waiter, covering her goblet with her open hand and exchanging a meaningful look with C.W. 'I'm pregnant.'

'What?' I sputtered. Most of the water went on my one good silk blouse, but a few droplets landed on Mac. I mopped them up with my napkin. 'Is this a joke?'

C.W. was hurt. A moment before he'd been grinning like an idiot. Now he looked like somebody'd swiped his favorite toy. 'What's that supposed to mean?' he demanded. 'You think I'm too old to be a father again? Is that what you think? Because let me tell you something, Garrity – I'm only fifty-two years old. I got more energy than guys half my age. I run five miles a day and bench press two hundred and eighty—'

'Whoa,' I said. 'No, no, C.W., that's not what I meant at all. I'm just surprised. That's all. You're younger than springtime. I think you'll be a great dad again.'

I gave Linda a long searching stare. 'So you guys changed your mind?'

She shrugged. 'C.W. changed my mind. I know I told you no way did I want a kid. But we kept my little niece for a night a few months ago, and she was so sweet, so cuddly, and beautiful, I just fell in love with the idea of having a baby. And Mr Carver Washington here was only too happy to oblige me.' She fluttered her eyelashes and beamed dopily at C.W. who beamed right back. These two were impossible.

'Well, I think it's great,' Mac said. He reached across the table and pumped C.W.'s hand in one of those old-boy bonding rituals. 'Congratulations, buddy. When's the big day?'

'Thanks,' C.W. said. 'November. And the doctor says it's a boy. Now how about that?'

'That's great,' Mac repeated. He raised his wineglass in a salute. 'To babies,' he said. 'And to faster cars, older whisky, and younger women.'

'And more money,' C.W. added.

We all laughed and clinked our glasses together. But I'll admit, I felt a pang of something. Envy? Regret? Linda and I were running buddies. I'd come to count on her when I needed somebody along for the ride in an investigation or just a quick trip to the mall. But with a baby on board she wouldn't be doing a lot of hanging out in the future.

The men had started right in on a deep discussion of how C.W. was going to teach little C.W. III how to hit the fastball, shoot from the outside, and dig for night crawlers. I turned to Linda, who was by now digging into mountain of penne al forno. The girl always could eat like a farmhand and never gain an ounce. Now she was packing the groceries away again. Three months pregnant and she was still rail thin. I reminded myself to hate her.

'All I can say is, better you than me,' I told her. My hand was reaching for the butter dish, but my brain was telling me no. Instead I took a big bite of butterless bread. Then I reached again for the butter. Some things in life are too important to skip.

Linda raised an eyebrow. 'Take it from me, Callahan, never say never. Haven't you and Mac ever talked about having a baby together?'

I speared a piece of asparagus from my own plate of pasta primavera and nibbled at it primly.

'Are you kidding? We can't even figure out the logistics of living together, let alone how to get married and have a kid. Besides, Mac's been there and done that. I don't know that he's all that anxious to take another stab at fatherhood after all these years. Hell, he was just over in Birmingham yesterday trying to straighten out his nineteen-year-old daughter. I don't know that he's ready to cope with an infant.'

'What about you?' Linda said. She wasn't going to give up. Pregnant women are like reformed smokers. They all insist everybody should do what they've done. 'Isn't your clock ticking?'

'Honestly?' I wound a piece of fettuccine around and around the tines of my fork while I thought about it. 'Not really. Growing up, I always assumed I'd have kids. But I also assumed I'd marry Paul McCartney. Now, I don't know. I like what I do. I work for myself, answer to nobody but Edna, who I mostly ignore. Marriage and a kid would change all that.'

She nodded her head vigorously. 'I know that's right. C.W.'s already making noises about me taking a desk job somewhere like the traffic bureau. I told him, no way. I like the strike force. And besides, it's not like I'm really on the streets or in any physical danger. Most of the bad guys I deal with are computer geeks. You ever hear of assault with a deadly modem?'

Linda had met C.W. when he was her captain on the homicide squad. Once they started a relationship, she transferred out of his unit; first to the vice squad and later to the Atlanta Police Department's newly formed white-collar crime strike force. She said she loved the challenge of out-smarting con artists and rich college-educated jerks who couldn't keep their hands out of the till.

'I haven't told McKee I'm pregnant yet,' she said. 'I figure, why mess up a good thing? When I start showing, then I'll break the news. He'll probably put me on phone duty until my due date. These old dudes are scared to death of a pregnant woman.'

The rest of the dinner we spent discussing C.W.'s plans to buy a house in the suburbs, and Linda's insistence that they would stay right where they were, in her cozy midtown condo, until the kid was old enough to figure out that the ladies who strolled their street at night weren't ladies at all, and mostly weren't even women.

At one point Linda got up to go to the bathroom. C.W. leaned across the table. 'Did uh, Vonette call you?'

'Yeah,' I said. 'How come you never told me you were married to a rock star?'

He was annoyed with me. 'It was a long time ago. By the time me and Vonette got married, she was ready to quit the business. I hadn't thought about the VelvetTeens in years. Neither had Vonette, probably, until this movie thing came along. So, what do you think? Think you can find Delores?'

'I'm gonna give it a shot,' I told him. 'I'm supposed to go over there tomorrow and get with her and Rita.'

He turned around in his chair to get a better look at the ladies room door, just in time to see Linda emerging. 'Do me a favor,' he said urgently. 'Okay, Callahan? Don't mention the uh, baby to Vonette.'

Men amaze me. 'I'm not telling Vonette anything that might piss her off,' I said. 'But don't you think she'll find out sooner or later? Like from Kenyatta? Or didn't you plan to tell your daughter she's fixin' to be a big sister?'

'I'll tell them both when I'm ready.'

Linda was back at the table then, so he busied himself with finishing his chocolate mousse.

On the way home from the restaurant, Mac turned the radio to the oldies station he listens to. The Beachboys' 'Help Me, Rhonda' was playing. He snorted his disapproval. 'Can you believe that's considered an oldie?'

I smiled sweetly and patted his hand lightly. 'It is to me, Pops.'

'Thanks for reminding me of how ancient I am,' he said. 'I'm younger than C.W., you know.'

'I know,' I said. I decided to change the subject before

it veered over into the baby-marriage-living together area, which I try to avoid.

'So how was Barb?' I asked. 'Was she civil to you?'

He glanced at me, then turned his eyes back to the road. 'She's fine,' he said. 'Surprisingly cordial. She's got a new job at a travel agency. She's taken up running. She did her first marathon this spring. She's really changed.'

'For the better?'

'Yeah,' he said slowly. 'Better.'

He pulled up into the driveway and put the car in park, but I noticed he didn't cut the motor.

'You're not coming in?' Saturday nights Mac usually sleeps over at my house. We make a ritual of Sunday mornings. Coffee. Bagels and fresh-squeezed juice from the farmer's market. We take turns reading the newspaper and usually go back to bed midmorning for a long leisurely session of lovemaking.

'You mind?' he asked, reaching over and kissing me. 'I'm beat. That sofa-bed at Barb's was murder. And Rufus needs to go for a long run in the morning. Barb's got a cat now, so he had to stay in the Jeep. He's kinda pissed at me, I think.'

'What about me?' I said, pulling away from his arms. 'I got stood up for an expensive concert. Doesn't it count that I'm pissed?'

'Hey,' he said, obviously surprised. 'You're still mad about that? I thought you understood. Stephanie really needed me.'

'I needed you,' I said coldly. 'You could have run over there this morning, instead of just dropping everything last night because a spoiled kid wants to drop out of school. I need you tonight, too, but I guess that doesn't count.'

'Wait,' he said, putting his hand on my bare arm. 'I'll stay, if it's that big a deal. We can ride out to my place in the morning and get Rufus and take him out to the mountains. Okay?'

'No,' I said, grabbing my purse and opening the car door. I got out and leaned in the open window. 'Go home and play with your dog, you big jerk. Maybe he'll keep you company tonight when your feet need warming up.'

I slammed the car door and flounced off into the house.

6

I heard piano playing and singing as I walked up the sidewalk to Vonette's front door. She lived in a neat brick ranch house in a middle-class subdivision on the city's southside. The Caddie was parked under a carport.

The piano playing must have drowned out the doorbell and my repeated knocks at the front door. Finally, I opened the door myself and stepped inside.

The scene in Vonette's living room reminded me of one of those funny 1950s home movies you see sometimes about the roots of rock and roll. All the furniture in the living room had been pushed to one side. Vonette, her daughter Kenyatta, and Rita were standing close together beside an old upright piano. The pianist, an elderly black woman, was thumping the keys and pumping pedals with Pentecostal fervor, her flower-bedecked straw turban bobbing in time to the music, her eyes closed and her lips singing along loudly with the music.

Which was 'What a Friend We Have in Jesus.'

Vonette nodded at me but kept singing, so I seated myself on a gold antique satin armchair and commenced

49

to listening. When they finished, I applauded. 'Y'all sound great,' I said, meaning it. 'Kenyatta, I didn't know you could sing.'

She was C.W.'s daughter, but except for those gray-green eyes all the Hunseckers have, she looked like her mother: petite and slender with high cheekbones, fine dark hair pulled into a knot at the nape of her neck and a chin that jutted enough to let you know she was no pushover.

'Oh yes,' Vonette said, squeezing her daughter's shoulders. 'Kenyatta started singing when she was only four with the junior children's choir at Big Bethel AME. She's a voice major at Spelman, you know.'

'Thanks to mama,' Kenyatta said slyly. 'I wanted to major in elementary education, but she talked me out of it.'

'Well, now, I'll be going along back to church,' the elderly pianist said in a quavery voice. Vonette introduced her as her aunt Lillian, and walked her to the door. 'She stays at church,' Kenyatta said, giggling.

When Vonette came back, we chatted back and forth a little, about the VelvetTeens career and Vonette's hopes for Kenyatta, but Rita was quiet, leafing through a copy of *Jet* magazine, contributing nothing to the conversation.

Vonette went into the dining room and brought back a stack of thick red leatherette scrapbooks. 'Aunt Lillian kept these up,' she said. 'She never had any children of her own.'

She flipped open one of the books and showed me a

page with a black-and-white snapshot showing three skinny preteens dressed in frilly church dresses standing on the steps of a white clapboard house.

'That's us,' Vonette said. 'What were we in this one, Rita, thirteen, fourteen, and fifteen?'

'Yeah, probably,' Rita said. She'd seated herself on a chair nearby, and was sipping from a can of Old Milwaukee.

Vonette shook her head slightly in exasperation. She put her finger on the girl in the middle, whose hair was worn in two beribboned pigtails. 'That's Delores. Twelve or thirteen then, I guess.'

She flipped some more pages until she came to one that held what was obviously a publicity still supplied by the record company.

The girls were women in this picture, with upswept hairdos, exotic makeup, tight cocktail dresses, mink stoles, and elbow-length gloves. In this photo, Rita stood in the center, slightly apart from the two girls on either side. A long lock of hair curled seductively over a bare shoulder and her lips were slightly parted. Oh yeah. Now I could see what Kevin and Mac were talking about. Definitely come hither.

'Aunt Rita,' Kenyatta said, acting shocked. 'You were a stone fox.'

'Uh huh,' Rita said, glancing over at the photo briefly before turning her attention back to the beer she was nursing.

'Well, you can look at the rest,' Vonette said, abruptly setting the scrapbooks in my lap.

'There's some postcards and things in there, stuff we

found in Aunt Louise's things after she died. Maybe there'll be a lead for you there.'

When she put the books in my lap a photo fell out and slid to the floor. Kenyatta picked it up and examined it. It was another black-and-white snapshot of the VelvetTeens. A man stood in the middle of the group, with his arms around their shoulders. He was tall and thin, with a prominent hawklike nose, black-rimmed Buddy Holly glasses, and an exaggerated pompadour hairstyle.

'Who's the white dude?' Kenyatta wanted to know.

Rita glanced over. 'Shit,' she said softly. 'Stu-Baby.'

Vonette snatched the photo from her daughter and ripped it in half. 'That's Stuart Hightower. That's who that was.'

Kenyatta's eyes widened. '*The* Stu Hightower? Like the Stu Hightower who owns BackTalk records? Did you guys know him? How come you tore up his picture, Mama?'

'Cause that's what he did to us,' Vonette snapped. 'Tore us up. Oh yeah. We know Mr Stuart Hightower all right.'

'How?'

Rita slammed her beer can down on the glass-topped coffee table, spilling a little. 'I gotta pee,' she announced, then stalked out of the room.

'Mama?' Kenyatta said.

Vonette sighed loudly. 'Stuart Hightower discovered us. Or so he liked to say. The VelvetTeens, that is. He was our producer, our manager. He owned the record company we sang for, SkyHi. And when he got tired of us, well, he just threw us away like we were an old used-up candy wrapper.'

'Stu Hightower has some of the hottest acts in the business,' Kenyatta said. 'How come y'all never mentioned him before?'

We heard the toilet flush in the other room, then the sound of water running. 'It's old news,' Vonette said. 'Besides, he did us dirt. It's not something we like to dwell on.'

'Hey,' Kenyatta said, snapping her fingers. 'You know what? BackTalk is having a big listening party this afternoon at Cafe Caribe for Junebug. I bet we could get in if they knew you were the VelvetTeens. Let's go, okay? It'll be fun.'

'No way,' Vonette said, sounding genuinely alarmed. 'I don't ever want to see that man again.'

'No way what?' Rita said, popping the top of a new can of beer.

'There's a big party at this really cool nightclub in midtown, Club Caribe, for Junebug. I think we should go down there and check it out. But you know Mama, the biggest party pooper in the world.'

'She's a sorry old party pooper,' Rita agreed, her speech slightly slurred. 'Never was any fun. Come on honey, you and I'll go down there. We'll show them people what's what. Even I heard of Junebug. He's fine.'

Rita walked unsteadily to the door, where she picked up her pocketbook from a table. 'Come on, Kenyatta,' she said. 'Let's blow this pop stand.'

Vonette was at her cousin's side in a moment, tugging urgently at her purse strap. 'Now Rita, you can't be driving. You've had a little too much to drink. If the police stop you again, this time they'll take your license away for good.'

'It's okay, Mama,' Kenyatta said, digging in her own pocketbook. 'I'll drive us down there. We won't be gone long, I promise.'

Vonette was not happy about this turn of events. 'We got rehearsing to do,' she said, grasping for a reason her daughter shouldn't go. 'We need to run through "These Two Arms" and "Love's Too Late" and...'

'We'll do it in the car,' Rita said, opening the front door. She saw my van in the driveway, parked behind Vonette's Cadillac. 'She can drive,' Rita said, jerking her head in my direction, 'while we rehearse.'

Which is how I came to load the new fabulous VelvetTeens into the back of my pink House Mouse van, headed for midtown Atlanta.

'Smells like Pine Sol back here,' Rita said, wrinkling her nose.

'Never mind that,' Vonette snapped. 'This was your idea. Now let's get busy. We got work to do. Are you too drunk to remember the whole reason we're here today?'

They managed to stop bickering long enough to run through three songs on the way to Club Caribe, despite the fact that Rita, who was still singing lead, kept forgetting the lyrics.

'Been a long time,' she said, taking a sip from the beer can she'd produced from her purse. 'Don't worry. I'll get it right.'

'You better get it right,' Vonette muttered from her seat beside me. 'Better get straight too, or we'll be making the VelvetTeens a duet.'

Sunday afternoon in midtown should have been quiet, the streets deserted, except for an occasional dog-walker or in-line skater. But the Club Caribe was the city's newest, trendiest club, located in one of Atlanta's oldest buildings, a long-abandoned five-and-dime store at the corner of Peachtree and Tenth. Empty streets suddenly became clotted with traffic as soon as we got within three blocks of Juniper.

With traffic at a dead standstill, and Rita asking 'What the hell's goin' on?' I finally put the van in park, got out and walked three cars in front of me. From there, I could see a traffic cop directing cars into what had been an empty lot, apparently commandeered for the occasion for a parking lot.

It took us ten minutes to get into the lot and for me to maneuver the van into a too-small parking slot.

Car doors slammed all around us. The party-goers streaming past us seemed to have received instructions to dress in black. There was black leather, black satin, black denim, and acres of black spandex. The average age of the invitees seemed to hover around eighteen. 'I got shoes older than these people,' Vonette mumbled. 'And what's that they're all holding?'

Everybody except us seemed to be grasping a square of black-and-silver cardboard in their hands.

'All right Miss Thing,' Vonette said to Kenyatta. 'These people all got invitations. And those people,' she pointed to two large uniformed men at the door to the club, 'are obviously checking for invitations. Which we don't have one of. Let's just go on back home.'

'Just a minute,' Kenyatta said. 'I can fix this.' She quickly stepped behind the van, which I'd parked next to another van. She reached her hands up, unsnapped the rubber band holding her hair and shook her head, letting a cloud of soft dark curls tumble around her shoulders. She set her pocketbook down on the pavement and while the three of us watched, with our mouths hanging open, she untucked her blue work shirt and unbuttoned all but three buttons, tying the shirttails in a loose knot and leaving her midriff bare. The blue jeans skirt that had looked so schoolgirlish seconds ago got partially unzipped, the waistband rolled and worn slung down around her hips, exposing still more skin and her navel and yards of thigh.

Grinning mischievously, Kenyatta cocked her hips and shook her head, letting the hair go even wilder. She looked like a junior Tina Turner.

'You look fine!' Rita said approvingly. 'Like I used to look back in the good old days.'

'No ma'am,' Vonette said firmly. 'You ain't goin' nowhere dressed like that.' She hurried over to her daughter's side. 'You just get your little butt zipped up and buttoned up and get your behind in this van. We're going home.'

But Kenyatta danced away. 'Be right back,' she called over her shoulder.

'Come back here,' Vonette shouted. But Kenyatta just laughed and swished her hips in reply.

We watched while she skipped to the head of the long

line of people waiting to get inside. At the door, she pulled one of the two guards aside and engaged him in a long sincere discussion, pausing once to gesture in our direction. A moment later she was back, tugging at Rita and Vonette's arms. 'Come on,' she said. 'I told him y'all are the original VelvetTeens. He's into retro, and he thinks y'all are really cool.'

'I'll retro your butt,' Vonette said halfheartedly, but the three of us followed Kenyatta's lead, pushing our way to the head of line.

The guard favored Vonette, Kenyatta, and Rita with a gushing tribute to their talent. He was tall, about six four, with wavy blond hair that fell to his shoulders. He stopped me, extending his forearm to block the way, as I started to follow the others through the door. 'Who's this?' he said suspiciously. I guess he'd never seen a white VelvetTeen.

'Our manager,' Kenyatta said quickly. He frowned, but let me past.

The interior of the club was dark as a tomb. I was momentarily blinded because of the contrast between daylight and dimness.

After I blinked three or four times, I could see better. Hard to imagine this had once been the kind of place I'd shopped in as a kid. False ceilings had been ripped out to expose old beams and a welter of old pipes and wires, all painted dead black. Yellow, green, pink, and orange neon pulsed from the walls; neon pineapples, bananas, palm trees, and parrots. The fronds of twenty-foot-tall potted palms soared toward the ceilings. Two neon-banded bars lined the long walls of the room, and at the back was a raised stage. There were big-screen televisions mounted on all the walls, all of them showing a rap-dancing artist who was apparently the much-celebrated Junebug.

I suddenly felt ancient. From the looks of him, Junebug was about fifteen, with hair in dreadlocks, and a baseball cap worn with the bill in the back. In the video, he wore a sleeveless neon green fishing vest and huge baggy pants that looked like they were made of an old parachute. He was singing 'Diss Dis' and twirling a semi-automatic assault rifle like a majorette's baton.

Vonette, who was close beside me, sniffed in disdain. 'Now, tell me how they can call this music. Huh? Can you tell me that? Can you say he's a Sam Cooke or an Otis Redding? Or a Roy Orbison? And look at those moves. James Brown could move better than that in a wheelchair.'

'I know,' I said, agreeing with her. We get cable at our house, mostly so we can watch the Braves games and old movies, but every time I flip past MTV or VH-1, I'm always stunned. Just this week I'd seen Guns n' Roses doing their version of 'Since I Don't Have You.' Of course, the Skyliners' version hadn't featured a video with frontal nudity or a vignette with the lead singer bound and gagged, so if it hadn't been for the slightly familiar refrain, I never would have recognized the song.

As unimpressed as we were, Kenyatta was obviously enthralled. She was bobbing and swaying and rapping right along with our friend Junebug.

When the music stopped momentarily, she got busy scanning the crowd. 'Do you actually know some of these people?' I asked.

'Not really,' she admitted. 'I was hoping Serena might be here. I heard she and Stuart Hightower have split up, but she's still one of BackTalk's biggest acts.'

'Serena,' I said. 'Can't any of these people afford a last name?'

Kenyatta indulged me by laughing briefly. 'Seriously, Callahan, you never heard of Serena? She's BackTalk's answer to Whitney Houston. But she hasn't had a hit since "Something on the Side."'

The room was jammed shoulder to shoulder. A thick cloud of cigarette smoke – at least I hoped it was cigarette smoke – drifted toward the ceiling. Waiters were trying to move through the room with trays of filled wineglasses, but the crowd was too thick. I took a glass off a tray as the waiter nearest me stood motionless.

Vonette was craning her neck, looking around the room. 'Where'd Rita get to?' she said, shouting to make herself heard.

'I don't know,' I shouted back. We both tried to edge forward.

Suddenly, the music stopped, and lights were focused on the stage. Black curtains parted and a tall distinguished-looking man with a hawk nose, dark glasses, and silver hair slicked back into a chic little ponytail, stepped forward to a microphone. The silver hair contrasted nicely with his Acapulco tan.

Beside me, I heard Vonette suck in her breath. 'My

God,' she whispered. 'I'll be damned if he didn't go and get better looking.'

She was right. Stu Hightower reminded me of one of those foreign-born Sylvester Stallone action movie clones, Jean Claude something or other.

As the crowd hushed, Hightower said he was pleased to introduce his newest, hottest protégé: 'The most exciting act it's ever been my pleasure to work with.'

'Most exciting act,' Vonette said. 'Hah. That's what he always said about us.'

'Shush,' Kenyatta said, staring raptly at Hightower, who was now reciting the numbers of hit records Junebug had sold, the awards won, the accolades received. I wasn't really listening, searching the room instead, for the missing Rita Fontaine.

'Uh oh,' I said. I'd spotted Rita standing at the edge of the bar, three feet away from the stage. She was drinking straight out of what looked like a vodka bottle.

'Where?' Vonette said, knowing what I meant. I pointed my finger toward the bar.

'Uh oh's right,' she said. 'That's the hard stuff she's drinking now. Vodka. She gets crazy when she drinks that stuff. 'Come on,' she said. 'We gotta get her out of here. You gotta help me before she starts something.'

By now though, Junebug himself had appeared on stage. He was rapping to a prerecorded track, and the crowd had gone nuts. People were rapping along with him, holding their hands above their heads and clapping their hands, jumping up and down and milling closer to the stage to try to get close to the young star. We couldn't see the bar or the stage now.

'Look, that must be Junebug's mother,' Kenyatta said, hollering to be heard above the music. The woman she pointed at was standing in the wings, arms folded over her chest, a rapt expression on her face as she watched her million-dollar baby capering around the stage.

I glanced at her, then back at the bar. 'Let's go,' I said. 'We've got to get Rita.'

Kenyatta trailed behind us. The three of us pushed our way through the moving, pulsating crowd. The sound blanketed the room, with the steady bass beat pounding our eardrums in rhythmic waves.

We finally reached the bar, four-deep with people now. None of them was Rita Fontaine.

Vonette squirmed her way to where the bartender stood. 'The older woman who was here a minute ago,' she hollered, trying to be heard above the music. 'Did you see where she went?'

A look of disgust crossed his face. 'She grabbed a bottle of Stoli. Handed me a ten dollar bill, like that's all Stoli costs. You catch up with her, tell her she owes me twenty bucks more.'

Vonette slapped a twenty down on the bar. 'Where'd she go?' she repeated, frantic now.

He pointed to a small door near the edge of the bar. 'Don't ask me how, but I saw her going backstage, right after Mr Hightower went off.'

'Oh shit,' Vonette said, looking panicky. Another large security guard stood beside the door, arms crossed menacingly. 'Stay here,' I told her. 'But be ready to move when I come out.'

I dug in my purse until I found my generic brass-plated police badge. It's actually just a four-dollar, ninety-eight-cent mail-order special from a law enforcement equipment mail-order catalog, but it's roughly the same size and shape as the Atlanta PD shield, and pinned to a black leather case, it's gotten me in and out of some tight spots.

I stepped right up to the guard and shoved the badge under his nose. 'Fire marshal's office,' I barked. 'You assholes got any idea how far over legal capacity you are in this place?'

He glowered at me, but he knew I had a point, and he thought I had some authority.

'I'm going back here to talk to the management,' I said, my hand on the doorknob. 'Unless you want me to have my people clear out the place right in the middle of this kid's act.'

He opened the door and stepped aside.

I bolted up a short flight of stairs to the backstage area. More crowds milled about in the narrow hallway, and up ahead, through the buzz of glad-handing, I could hear a commotion that had a familiar sound.

I held the badge out like a weapon. 'Fire marshal,' I yelled. 'Everybody outta here, right now. Fire marshal.'

Heads turned. People began to move. I enjoyed the heady sensation of power for maybe thirty seconds.

The crowd had parted enough to give me a clear sight of Rita Fontaine and Stuart Hightower. The woman Kenyatta had identified as Junebug's mother was there too. She had kinked-out reddish brown hair that looked like it had been zapped by lightning, and she was dressed in a form-fitting silver jumpsuit, the zipper undone to show a set of overripe breast. She was clearly terrified by the scene unfolding in front of her.

Hightower didn't look scared. He looked mad. He'd ditched the dark glasses now. Rita's face was twisted in fury. She was six inches shorter than her old friend, but she'd managed to get her face right up into his, her long fingers gripping his wrist like claws.

'Listen to me, you lying motherfucker,' she was shouting. 'I'm gonna tell all these pretty people about Stu-Baby. Oh yes, me and Stu-Baby go a long way back. Don't we baby?'

'Go home, Rita,' he said, trying to sound good-natured, acting like he was shaking off a minor annoyance. 'We'll catch up on old times some other day. I've got business to attend to.'

That set her off again. 'Business,' she shrieked. 'Yeah, I know what dirty business you're into. Who you gonna screw today, Stu? You gonna steal some money from that little kid out there? You gonna fuck with him like you fucked with us?'

'Rita,' I called out. The people in the hallway stood frozen, fascinated with the ongoing drama. She turned and looked at me, but didn't loosen her grip on Hightower.

'Hey Callahan,' she called. 'That's our new manager,' she told Hightower, smiling triumphantly. 'the Velvet-Teens are making a comeback. Callahan, tell Stu here about how we're gonna be in a movie. Tell him how we're gonna cut a new album and go on the road and be bigger stars than ever.'

Hightower shot me a look of pity mixed with contempt. 'You'd better get her out of here,' he said. 'She always was a sloppy drunk.'

Rita reached up and slapped his face so hard he stumbled and nearly fell. 'Bastard,' she screamed. 'Filthy scumbag.'

Junebug's mother inched away toward the door. Hightower's eyes narrowed with hate. 'Call security,' he said to a nervous young black man who fluttered ineffectively at his side. 'Get them out of here.'

I grabbed Rita's arm and jerked her away from him. She stumbled, but regained her balance. 'Don't bother,' I told him. 'We're outta here.'

But Rita wasn't done. 'Rat bastard,' she yelled, struggling to free herself from my grip. 'I'm gonna tell all these people how you cheated me. You dirty, thieving lowlife.'

Somehow I got her down the steps and out the door to the backstage area, just as three more burly guards raced through it. 'They're back there,' I said. 'Go get 'em, boys.'

7

The first mistake I made on Monday was in assuming I had things under control. Nothing in my life is under control. Ever. Sure, I'd managed to get Neva Jean to her 9:00 a.m. job at the Highams' on time; with a full supply cart. I'd gotten Ruby dropped off at the Schwartzes' on time too, and we'd picked up her new blood pressure prescription on the way. Jackie picked up the key for some new clients who live in Morningside and called in later to say they'd even remembered to leave the check. We were so busy I'd even gotten David Gennaro, our only male House Mouse, to clean an efficiency apartment being rented by a client whose wife had kicked him out of the house. Sometimes divorce works out nicely for us.

I was having a second cup of coffee and making a list of places to look for Delores Carter when Edna, who was working on our bank statement, looked up from her calculator. 'That car door slamming outside sounds familiar. Did you ask the Easterbrookses to come in this morning?'

I hadn't. Baby and Sister Easterbrooks don't work full-time. Neither one will tell her age, but a good guess is that they're in their late seventies or early eighties. If you overlook the fact that Baby is deaf as a post and Sister very nearly blind, they're both in remarkably good health.

'Orneriness,' Edna said. 'That's what keeps them two going. Each one is bound and determined to outlive the other. I never have seen two old ladies so full of piss and vinegar.'

They knocked once at the back door as a formality, then came in, arguing as usual.

'You know that was my bingo winnings you used to buy that ticket,' Sister said loudly as Baby guided her into the kitchen. 'I'm not so blind that I can't see money missing from my pocketbook. So now, half that ticket is rightfully mine. Ain't that right, Miss Edna?'

Baby pulled out one of the oak kitchen chairs and more or less shoved her older sister into it. Then she took a seat herself.

'Tell that old fool *she* spent all her bingo winnings buyin' them no-good scratch-off tickets and a big can of Brown Mule snuff, and we both know it,' Baby said. She pulled a wrinkled and creased cardboard rectangle from her bosom and smoothed it with long, timeworn fingertips.

'This here is worth a hundred and forty-two dollars and fifty-seven cents and Miss Priss over there ain't a-gettin' a durn dime of it,' she said, chortling to herself.

Edna put on her dimestore bifocals and peered at the ticket. 'So that's what a winning lottery ticket looks like,' she said. 'What are you fixin' to do with all your loot?'

Baby smiled happily. 'Yes ma'am. I'd love some fruit, thank you for asking. A banana would be real nice. I been kind of stove up lately.'

Sister guffawed loudly, but Edna got up and got Baby a banana and a paper napkin.

'No, fool,' Sister hollered. 'Miz Edna wants to know how you fixin' to spend the money you won on the lottery by stealin' from me.'

Turning to Edna, Sister's cataract-clouded eyes gleamed maliciously from behind the thick-lensed glasses.

'She probably gon' spend it on her new boyfriend,' Sister said. 'Ask Miss Snip there if she's gonna give that money to old Pop Wilbanks.'

Baby fixed her sister with a suspicious stare. 'What's she tellin' y'all now? Is she tellin' that lie about me having a boyfriend again? Cause if she is, I might need to give her a smack on the chops like I used to when she got that mouth a-running.'

Edna sipped her coffee and tried to smother a laugh.

'Well, what about it, Miss Baby?' I said. 'What are you going to do with all that money? Miss Sister says you're sweet on Pop Wilbanks. Are you gonna take him to dinner at a nice French restaurant?'

'That old fart?' Baby said. 'I wouldn't take that old goat to the Varsity, let alone someplace nice. Besides, he ain't got a tooth in his head. Miss Priss over there is mad 'cause he served me double helpings of Mexican casserole last night at the covered dish supper at the senior center. No, Callahan, I am fixin' to take me a trip to Myrtle Beach, South Carolina. That's what I'm aiming to do. And Miss Priss,' she said, glaring at her sister. 'Ain't invited.'

'Hee, hee,' Sister laughed. 'Myrtle Beach, my behind. Can't nobody go clear to South Carolina with not but a hundred and forty-seven dollars.'

'That's what you think,' Baby said quickly. 'I'm going on a package trip with the Swinging Seniors. We got us a chartered air-cooled Greyhound motor coach and deluxe double-occupancy rooms at the Sea Star Motel with tile baths, steam heat, complimentary continental breakfast, and free Putt-Putt Golf passes.'

Sister crossed her arms over her chest and sulked. 'If I wanted to go, I reckon I could,' she said. 'But somebody got at my bingo winnings, and I'm a little bit short.' She looked at me expectantly.

I looked down at our appointment book. I'd already marshaled all my forces for today's bookings.

Edna reached over and pulled the book away from me. She turned the page to Tuesday and ran her finger down the entries, wrinkling her brow in concentration. We try to take it easy with the Easterbrookses. They can mop, dust, vacuum, and tidy, but they're not really up to a lot of stairs and heavy lifting.

'Here's one,' Edna said, tapping her pencil on the listing. 'Maggie Brown. Got a ranch house over on Superior Avenue. No dogs, no stairs, no burglar alarms.'

I'd forgotten about the burglar alarm debacle. A couple months earlier we'd sent the sisters to a new client who'd neglected to mention her silent alarm system. Ten minutes after Baby and Sister unlocked the back door they were surrounded by private armed security guards who were ready to haul the two of them off to the jail, until they checked with the owners and found that they'd just busted a couple of septuagenarian cleaning ladies.

'It's only a seventy-five-dollar job,' I said. 'And that's for the two of you to split. Will it help any?'

Baby started to mumble something about her missionary circle meeting, but Sister clapped her hands happily. 'Yes ma'am,' she said. 'I got a little piece of money put away that Miss So-and-So don't know about, so that'll just be so nice. What time you wanting us there?'

Edna wrote down the address and the directions in half-inch capital letters and handed the house key to Baby, who immediately tucked it into her bosom, along with her prized lottery ticket.

'Reckon we'll be going along now,' Baby said, standing up and reaching for her pocketbook. Sister stood up too, and gave us both a quick peck on the cheek. 'I'm gonna bring you back a nice box of saltwater taffy from my trip,' she promised. Lowering her voice so Baby couldn't hear, she whispered 'And I'm gonna watch out for Pop Wilbanks too. Eula Wilbanks ain't been dead three years yet. It's a scandal, the way he's chasing my sister.'

After they'd gone, Edna cleared away the coffee cups and got back to her bank statements. 'I'm going to get this thing balanced or die trying,' she vowed, clenching her teeth.

I went into the bedroom and looked at the list of phone calls I'd made. Vonette had told me that she thought the

VelvetTeens paid dues to AFTRA, the American Federation of Television and Radio Artists. There was an Atlanta listing for the union, but when I called I got an answering machine telling me nobody was available to take my call. I left my name and number and hung up.

On a whim, I called directory information for Los Angeles and Nashville. Neither had a listing for Delores Eisner or Delores Carter. I even asked for a Delores Fontaine, just in case she'd adopted her sister's last name. There were plenty of listings for Delores Carter. I called some, and the few people who actually answered their phones said they'd never heard of the VelvetTeens. Fame is fleeting for sure. To cover all the bases I tried Detroit, New York, and Chicago, too. I found a Delores Carter in Detroit who said she'd been a dancer on *American Bandstand*, but that's as close as I got.

Jane Cooper, my friend with the private investigation firm, had suggested I come to her office around 10:30. It was 10:00 now.

I called Vonette from my car phone. 'How's the patient?'

'Gone,' Vonette said. 'I think she was too embarrassed to face me. Drunk as she was, she knew she'd messed up. I called Andre last night, told him she was staying here. I didn't tell him she was drunk. He probably knew it anyhow. I think he's used to phone calls like that.'

To say that Rita had messed up was a bit of an understatement. She'd ranted and raved, kicked and screamed and cursed a blue streak about that no-good sonofabitch Stu Hightower the whole way home. It had taken all three of us to carry her into the house and get her undressed and into bed, where she immediately passed out. Looking down at her, her hair wild and uncombed, lipstick smeared around her mouth, clothes wrinkled and ill-fitting, it was hard to see the rock goddess Rita Fontaine had once been. I could still see the shocked look on Kenyatta's face. If Vonette believed Rita was on the wagon before, she obviously knew better now.

'She didn't used to be like that,' Vonette said, reading my thoughts now. 'Everything had to be just so with Rita. She'd put on makeup and fix her hair just to rehearse at home with the two of us. The handbags always matched the shoes, and the shoes matched her belts. You know, she used to iron her nylon stockings. She got to drinking right after the VelvetTeens broke up. I didn't realize it then. I just thought she was tired a lot.'

'How'd she manage to raise a son?' I wanted to know.

'That boy just raised himself,' Vonette said. 'It's a miracle he turned out as well as he did. Never knew his daddy, and had a mama who didn't know who she was half the time. He finished high school, went in the army, came home, and of course, he had to start looking after Rita. Andre is a worker.'

'Who was his daddy?'

'A man named Cleveland Strong,' Vonette said. 'He'd been the bus driver for one of our tours. We came off the road and next thing I know, Rita says she's married him. He stayed around until Andre was nearly two, and one day he just wasn't there any more.'

'You really think she's going to be up to performing again?' I asked.

'You never knew her when she was singing,' Vonette said. 'The rest of us, we liked the money, the traveling, the fame. Rita loved to sing. She lived for that audience. If we could get the VelvetTeens back again, I think it might save her life.'

The tenderness in Vonette's voice surprised me. 'Well, I'm going to see a private detective friend this morning, to run a computer trace on Delores,' I told Vonette. 'I'll call if I find anything.'

Cooper-Kelleher Investigations had office space in an upscale new development of office condominiums up north of the city near Roswell. The two-story brick townhouse looked more like somebody's house than the offices for a PI.

After I told the receptionist who I was, she buzzed Jane and told her she had a visitor. Soon I could hear the clicking of high heels on the polished parquet flooring. Jane Cooper had gone corporate. Big time. She'd tamed her wild black tangle of frizzy curls into some kind of upswept grown-up hairdo. She was dressed in an expensive-looking teal blue business suit and wore what the women's magazines like to call 'important jewelry' on her earlobes, around her neck, and on her wrist.

I felt instantly tacky in my cotton peasant skirt, blouse, and sandals.

'Callahan,' she said warmly. 'Come on back.'

We chatted on the way to her office, a large, high-ceilinged room with a big picture window that looked out on the newly paved parking lot. 'Great view, huh?' she said, gesturing toward the window. 'My partner got the office overlooking the woods. One of the perks of seniority, he claims.'

She sat down at a computer, pushed a few buttons, then looked up at me expectantly. 'Name, DOB, social security number,' she commanded.

As I dictated, she typed. A moment later, she looked up. 'Found her.'

I wheeled my chair over to look at the screen. Jane had gotten a hit on the name Delores Eisner. In 1978, she'd listed a post office box in Vegas as her address. There was a phone number too. The next listing, 1982, had her at 885 Los Bravos Avenue in Los Angeles. By 1987 she'd moved, to Thousand Oaks. There was a phone number. Jane picked up the phone and handed it to me. 'It's a long shot, but maybe she settled down and stayed.'

I dialed the number and got a recording saying the number had been disconnected. I shook my head and hung up.

'Pretty fancy stuff,' I said, getting out my pad and pencil to copy the addresses.

'I'll print it out for you,' Jane said. 'Yeah, this software isn't cheap, but it's our bread and butter with all the corporate work we do.'

A moment later the white box on her desktop spat out a sheet of paper, which she handed to me.

'Most of this info comes from rental deposits, utility hook-ups, things like that,' Jane said. 'It's odd that she seems to have just dropped out of sight. Could she have moved in with somebody else? A boyfriend or relative maybe?'

I shrugged. 'Eisner is her married name. So at least I know that's the name she was using in eighty-eight. As for a boyfriend or relative, I just don't know. My client says she's called all the relatives and nobody's seen or heard from Delores. Got any other ideas?'

Jane played with the heavy gold chain at her neck. 'I assume you'll get a Criss-Cross directory, talk to the neighbors and landlord at the last address, stuff like that?'

'Yeah,' I said. 'There's plenty I can do on the phone, but I don't know that my client is going to want to foot the bill for a plane ticket to California. I guess I'll try to reach her union again. I left a message this morning.'

'The union's a good lead,' Jane said. 'I haven't dealt with AFTRA, but I know trade unions usually keep up with members.'

I was looking around the office now. Jane's digs were definitely upscale. The desk and credenza were carved cherry, the walls held nicely framed original art and a love seat and sofa took up one corner of the room.

'You're doing pretty good, huh? How many investigators have you got working for you?'

'Right now?' She turned in her chair to study a map mounted on the wall over the desk. The map was of the Southeast. There were little colored pins stuck all over it, mostly clustered around Atlanta. Each pin had a little paper flag attached to it, with someone's name.

'Twelve,' she said. 'Of course, not everybody's full-time.' She looked at me closely, those bright blue eyes taking in the faded cotton skirt and scuffed sandals. 'Why don't you think about coming to work for me?' she said. 'You could keep the cleaning business. Let your mother run it. We'd have a lot of fun. And I could use somebody with your instincts.'

I laughed. Somehow I couldn't picture myself working in this kind of a setup. The kitchen table and a beat-up van suited me fine for now.

'I don't think so,' I said. 'Sounds like you've got a great business going for you, but that's the problem. You're a little too corporate for my taste.'

Just then the phone on her desk-top buzzed discreetly. Jane leaned over and pushed the intercom button.

'Sorry to disturb you Jane, but Leon's on line two. He says you're waiting to hear from him. Can you take it?'

'Tell him I'll be right with him,' she said.

I got up to leave.

'Think about that job offer,' she said. 'You want to hang around and go to lunch? I just need to talk to Leon first. He's been following a gal out in Douglasville who tells our client that she was bit by a brown recluse spider while trying on a bathing suit in the dressing room of his department store. Now her lawyer's trying to shake our client down to the tune of six hundred thousand dollars for loss of consortium, because she says she's lost all sensation in her pelvic area. I've seen this woman, and let me tell you, she's doing her husband a favor not screwing him. She must weigh two hundred and fifty pounds. Leon's been tailing her since last week. He called in right before you came to say she'd checked into the Alamo Motor Court out on Highway

Five with the guy who was at her house earlier in the week to read her gas meter. I just hope Leon remembered to put film in the camera this time.'

'I can't stay,' I said. 'Call me and we'll get together. You've got my address to bill me for the computer time, right?'

She waved a freshly manicured hand. 'Forget it. It's on the house. And don't forget about that offer. Okay?'

8

When I finally did get someone at Delores' union on the phone, the news wasn't promising. The last time they'd had a recorded payment for her had been in 1988, and it had been sent to a post office box in LA. I struck out with the husband, too. He hadn't had an AFTRA payment since 1979.

Vonette knew little or nothing about her cousin's husband. 'He was from up north somewhere, I remember,' she said. 'New Jersey maybe. I know his mama was alive, because Delores told me she didn't like it much having a black girl for a daughter-in-law. Don't ask me what he did before Stu hired him, because I don't know. I had a boyfriend of my own at the time and I was certainly not interested in some skinny little white piano player.'

I told her I'd found an old address for Delores, in a suburb of LA. 'Well keep making phone calls,' she said. 'I know I told you the money wasn't important, but I don't like throwing it away, either.'

Not an hour after I'd called her, Vonette was back on the phone again, this time so angry she was beside herself.

'Do you know what that lowlife cheatin' snake has done?' she demanded.

'Who?' I said warily, afraid she had been informed about her ex-husband's impending fatherhood.

'Stu Hightower, of course,' she said. 'That bastard has gone and got himself a uh, yeah, an injunction. Yes ma'am. I was served with an injunction five minutes ago that tells me that Stuart Hightower and SkyHi Records are the sole owners of the identity of an entertainment unit known as the VelvetTeens.'

'Uh-oh,' I said.

'This piece of paper says we can't perform as the VelvetTeens, we can't use the name and we can't sing any of our hit songs,' Vonette screeched. 'He's saying we can't sing "Happy Never After."'

'Can he do that?'

'That's what I intend to find out,' Vonette said. 'I've called my lawyer, and he's looking at this injunction. But the problem is, I have no idea what kind of contract we signed back then. Stu's lawyers have attached something to the injunction that they say is our contract, but I don't know. We were just kids at the time. We didn't know what we were signing. Hell, we didn't even have our own lawyers. My mama looked at the contract, and Stu's lawyers said it was a great deal, so we signed.'

'What will this do to your movie deal?'

'I don't know,' Vonette said. 'My lawyer's supposed to call their lawyer tomorrow.'

'In the meantime,' I said, 'Have you heard from Rita? Does she know about any of this?'

'This paper lists her as a defendant,' Vonette said, 'but I haven't heard from her all day. If she went in to work, she won't be home till after four. Now I got to worry about what she might do when she sees this thing. I can't take another of her toots, I swear I can't.'

My call waiting line beeped then, and then again, so I hung up and got back to attending to House Mouse affairs.

I was just penciling in two new clients for Thursday, one apiece for Jackie and Neva Jean, when Mac came in the back door. He kissed me, then held out two tickets in his hand.

'Box seats for tonight's Braves game. They're playing the Dodgers,' he said. 'And I'm sorry about the concert. Really.'

'What makes you think I don't have plans for tonight?' I didn't, and he knew it, but I was still sore about being stood up.

'I know it's last minute, but a buddy of mine who works at Coca-Cola came by this afternoon and dumped these on my desk. All the big wheels are out of town at a marketing meeting, so the peons can invite friends. Larry says it's a great view of the game. What do you say?'

He had me, and he knew it. I'd never sat in one of those Club level boxes at the stadium, and Coke's was supposed to be the best. Besides, I hate the Dodgers. I even quit drinking Slim-Fast this year to get back at Tommy LaSorda for past sins.

We decided to take my van because of the car phone.

Mac drove. We shared a cold bottle of Heineken, and left the windows down. I slipped out of my sandals and propped my bare feet up on the dashboard. The oldies station I keep on the radio was having a Beach Boys extravaganza, and I thumped my toes in time to 'Good Vibrations.' I felt like a sixteen-year-old.

'You think I'm getting too upset about Stephanie's dropping out of school?' Mac asked, giving me a sidelong glance.

'You've got a right,' I said. 'Sounds to me like she could use some lessons in responsibility. Maybe you should let her come live with you. Keep her on a tighter rein.' I couldn't believe I was saying it, but there was nobody else in the car, and the voice uttering the words was definitely mine.

'Huh?' He was as stunned as I was. 'Are you serious? I love Steph. But where would I put her? She sleeps on the sofa when she comes for weekends, but have you ever seen the amount of clothes these kids haul around with them?'

'You could move.' There was that voice again.

'You're serious, aren't you?'

Oh boy. Now I was hip deep in it. No way but up. 'Well, you're always complaining about how bad traffic's gotten on Georgia Four Hundred. Your office is downtown. Why couldn't you move closer in?'

The above was true. Mac's a civil engineer. He works for the Atlanta Regional Commission, which has planning responsibility for all the counties in the metro area. But I also knew about Rufus, his black lab. And the fact that Mac, the original outdoor guy, loved living someplace with the woods and a creek in his backyard. He hikes, fishes, camps. The only place he could fish in a neighborhood like mine would be in old Mr Byerly's weed-choked lily pond.

'I could move, I guess,' he said unhappily. 'You really think it's that important that Stephanie be with me? She's lived with Barb all this time. And spent weekends and summers off and on with me. Why suddenly does she need more?'

He had me there. And what business of mine was it anyway? I should never have opened my mouth.

'How about this?' I offered. 'Why don't you have her come to Atlanta next week? You guys could go camping up in the mountains. You told me you used to do that a lot when she was younger.'

He gave it some thought. 'Okay. Camping's a good idea. Don't know why I didn't think of it. Want to go with us?'

I did and I didn't. The north Georgia mountains are cool and green this time of year, and every town has a strip of cute little junk shops. But my idea of exploring the mountains consists of a bed and breakfast with warm croissants and fresh-squeezed orange juice in the morning. Mac, on the other hand, likes to get up at 5:00 a.m, hit the trout stream, and eat his catch for breakfast. We Garritys have never been high on eating trout before 1:00 p.m.

'You go,' I said quickly. 'I'd just be a third wheel.'

'Sure?'

'I'm sure,' I said. Traffic had slowed as we neared the

stadium. I pointed up ahead. 'Look. There's a guy waving us into that gypsy lot.'

We parked the van and got out. At the corner of the lot, which was actually the Mt Moriah AME churchyard, a couple of men were barbecuing a kettle-drum full of ribs. We walked closer to take a look.

One of the men had a white bath towel wrapped around his head. He was slapping a dark red sauce over the meat with a long-handled paintbrush. When the sauce hit the coals fresh waves of vinegar and tomato-scented smoke rose in clouds around the grill.

'How much?' I managed to ask, at the same time inhaling the fumes.

'Sandwich is four, slab is seven,' he said with admirable economy. A skinny pre-teen boy, barefoot with faded baggy shorts, held out his hand for the money while the older man layered the meat between two slices of Wonder Bread and then wrapped the sandwich in waxed paper.

As soon as we'd paid for two sandwiches, another man appeared by our side. He gestured toward a battered red cooler in the trunk of his car. 'Cold beer? Two dollars. They want four inside.'

Mac picked two cans of Miller Lite out of the ice. We took our dinner back to the van and perched on the bumper to eat. 'We must dine here more often,' I told Mac, between bites.

As it turned out, our al fresco dinner was the best part of the game. The Braves tried four different pitchers, who gave up a total of seven runs, including a two-run homer in the first inning. The Club level box was nice, but Mac's friend Larry had decided to watch the game at home, and you can only drink so much free diet Coke in one night.

We left at the bottom of the seventh, feeling guilty about deserting our team in their hour of need.

'McGriff will probably hit a grand slam as soon as we get out of the parking lot,' Mac grumbled, trying to edge the van out of the lot.

We turned the radio on, but Skip Caray's voice sounded gloomy. I switched it off and the car phone beeped.

'Callahan?' It was Vonette. Her voice sounded panicky. 'Andre just called from his night job. When he got home from his day job he found an empty Scotch bottle in the trash. And nobody's seen Rita.'

'I'm sorry, Vonette,' I said. 'But you hired me to find Delores, not baby-sit a drunk. If I were you, I'd check Rita into some kind of alcohol rehab. Get her dried out.'

'We will,' Vonette said. 'But right now I'm worried sick that she's in real trouble. Andre says she called him at work when she got home. She got served with the court papers too. He says she was cursing and carrying on about getting even with Stu. Talking about going out to his house and having it out with him.'

'She's drunk,' I said, trying to calm Vonette. 'Besides, does she even know where Hightower lives? I'll bet she's leaning on a bar somewhere, or passed out cold in her car.'

'No she's not,' Vonette insisted. 'We've called all the places she likes to drink. Nobody's seen her. And Andre said she said she was going out to Riverbend. Kenyatta says that is where Stu lives. She saw a big piece about his house in some magazine.'

'All right,' I said, glancing over at Mac. 'I guess we'd better go after her.' Normally I would have preferred to go by myself. But I'd seen Rita drunk once, and it would take all three of us to get her away from Stu Hightower.

We arranged to meet in a shopping center about a mile away from the country club, and I dropped Mac off at my house so he could get his car. 'They've got security out the wazoo up at Riverbend,' he pointed out. 'Half the pro ballplayers in town live up there, not to mention all those rockers and rappers and corporate CEOs. Big stone wall and gates and guards. How do you think Rita got in there?'

'I don't know how she got in and I don't know yet how we'll get in to get her,' I admitted. 'I'll let you know how it works out.' Mac made a halfhearted offer to accompany me, but he knows I can handle myself.

I got to the shopping center a few minutes before Vonette and Kenyatta, which gave me time to go into a Mister Donut and get a cup of coffee. While I waited, I worked on my plan.

When Vonette pulled up next to the van, I got out and hopped in the back seat of the Cadillac. 'Let's go over there to that Pizza Hut,' I said, pointing to a storefront at the far end of the shopping center.

'We've eaten,' Vonette said, but she did as I asked.

'Pull over there,' I said, directing her to a spot beside a row of parked economy cars, all of them bearing the lit-up 'Pizza Hut to Go' signs clamped to the car roofs.

I dug in my pocket and pulled out a ten dollar bill. 'Listen, Kenyatta. Go in and get a large pizza. Any kind will do. And stand in front of the doorway, so you block their view outside.'

'Okay,' Kenyatta said. But she looked dubious. I stopped her before she got out of the car. 'Do that thing with your hair and your clothes again,' I said. 'You gotta stop hiding your light under a bushel basket, girl.'

She stepped out of the car, shook her hair loose and adjusted her shorts so they rode on her hips, with her blouse tied under her midriff.

Then she went inside and stood in front of the door. She glanced out once, nodding her head.

'Okay,' I said to Vonette. 'Let's get us a sign.'

We chose the car farthest from the parking lot street-light. I'd been afraid the delivery signs might be permanently attached to the car tops, but luck was with us. The signs were attached with nothing more complicated than a super-heavy magnet.

By the time Kenyatta came sashaying out of the res-taurant with the pizza, we had the Cadillac looking like the delivery car to the stars.

'You're going to get us arrested,' Vonette fretted as she followed my directions to Riverbend. 'How's that going to look in the newspapers?'

'Mama,' Kenyatta said, 'How's it going to look in the newspapers if we don't catch up to Rita and stop her from whatever she's planning on doing?'

'My point exactly.'

I pointed to a turnoff in the road just ahead. 'Pull over right in there,' I told Vonette.

'Now what?' she muttered, but she pulled the Cadillac into a single lane road that turned off Old Alabama Road, and she cut the headlights without being told.

'You're getting the hang of this,' I said. 'Shame about that silk pants suit though. But it can be dry-cleaned? Right?'

'This outfit cost me three hundred dollars,' Vonette said, her voice rising an octave. 'I hope you don't expect me to go tromping through the woods or anything. Because that's where I draw the line. Rita or no Rita. I'm not studying no woods. You hear?'

'No woods,' I said, trying to calm her down. 'But you and I are going to ride the rest of the way in the trunk, while Kenyatta sweet-talks her way past the security guards at Riverbend.'

'What?' Mother and daughter said in unison.

'You ever seen Diana Ross delivering pizza in a three-hundred-dollar outfit?' I asked, playing to Vonette's vanity. 'It's only for a couple of blocks. Once we're inside and out of the guard's sight, Kenyatta's going to stop and let us out.'

Kenyatta looked as alarmed now as Vonette.

'How am I supposed to get them to let me in?' she screeched. 'I bet those guards are big old rednecks. Probably got guns too.'

'You're the cutest, sexiest little pizza delivery chick they've ever seen,' I promised. 'Tell them anything you like. The problem is not going to be getting past them, the problem is going to be keeping them from getting into the car and going with you.'

'This will not work,' she said, shaking her head. But

she got out of the car and watched while Vonette and I climbed into the Cadillac's spacious trunk.

It looked spacious until we were both curled up on opposite sides of the trunk, and Kenyatta closed the hood. Then it was pitch black, and hot. Vonette had put some kind of cherry-scented air freshener in the trunk, and the sweet smell closed up around me in the dark.

'You all right in there? Got enough air?' Kenyatta's voice was muffled but audible from the car's front seat.

I sneezed twice. 'We're okay,' I said loudly. 'Just get going.'

We felt the car start, back up, and then pull out onto the main road again. Smooth ride.

'She better not put a single scratch on this thing,' Vonette whispered. Five minutes later we felt the car slowing again, and then stopping. We heard a deep man's voice on the driver's side of the car, but I couldn't tell what he was saying. I did hear Vonette whispering something about sweet Jesus.

Kenyatta's voice was surprisingly clear. 'Pizza delivery for Clete Andrews,' she said, referring to the Braves All-Star outfielder.

'I didn't know he lived out here,' I whispered.

'Shhh,' Vonette hissed.

We heard the man's voice again, and then Kenyatta, giggling in a most conspiratorial way. 'Oh no. Mr Andrews said he'd be out by the pool with a friend. He was going to put the money in the mailbox, and said for me to just leave the pizza on the doorstep. I don't think he wants to be disturbed, if you know what I mean.'

The guard said something else we couldn't hear.

'Call if you want,' Kenyatta said breezily. 'I wouldn't want you to get in trouble or anything. It's just that Mr Andrews said he'd be out in the pool, so I don't know if he'll answer the phone.'

She giggled again, laying it on really thick. 'I bet you work out, don't you?' And then. 'I knew it. I knew those legs had spent some time on the StairMaster. I'll bet you lift weights, too, huh?' After another spasm of giggles, we heard her give him a phone number, and the car start up again and slowly roll forward.

'Thank you, Jesus,' Vonette whispered. And then, louder. 'All right now, get us out of here. We're almost out of air.'

'He's standing in the road staring at the car,' Kenyatta said. 'Let me just go down this street a ways, till he can't see the taillights. Then I'll turn off and let you out.'

The air in the trunk was hot and stale and I was starting to feel like a baked potato. I was getting stabbing pains in my lower back, and there was something hard and metallic digging into my shin.

'I'm turning the corner now, it's a street where they're just building the houses,' Kenyatta called out. The car stopped, and a moment later, she pushed a button and the motorized hood started to rise open.

We sat up stiffly, then climbed quickly out of the trunk. Kenyatta stood there grinning in the half-light of a street lamp.

'Hey y'all, I'm starting to like this private investigation gig,' she said, preening a little. 'You were right, Callahan, that fool believed every word I said.'

'Don't quit your day job yet, Miss,' I warned. 'That

guard was either totally besotted or not a baseball fan. The Braves just finished playing thirty minutes ago. Forty miles south of here. He must have been cute though. We heard you give him your phone number.'

She snorted. 'That old dude? Not! He was at least thirty. That was the Pizza Hut delivery number you heard me give him. I read it right off the pizza box.'

I took the Pizza Hut sign off the roof and put it in the trunk. Vonette stretched her hands over her head, bent and touched her toes, then straightened and moved toward the driver's seat. 'Let's get to that house,' she said briskly. 'I want to get Rita and get the hell out of here.'

9

We cruised the quiet dark streets looking for a pink hacienda that resembled the one Kenyatta had seen in *People* magazine.

'That house right there sold for four point two million in February,' Vonette said, pointing to a sprawling white contemporary that resembled a lunar landing module. 'And that one there,' she said, pointing to a house under construction next door, a three-story wooden skeleton, 'Helen somebody, I forget the name, she owns that mail-order catalog with the furniture and all. I heard the lot by itself was eight hundred thousand. I'd like to have the commission on that.'

Finally, on a cul-de-sac at the back of the subdivision, we spotted a house that fit Kenyatta's description. 'Oh Lord,' Vonette said. 'That white Nova looks like Rita's. I still can't figure out how she knew Stu lived all the way out here or how she got in.'

'They probably get *People* at the nursing home,' Kenyatta said. 'Rita is always bringing home magazines from there.'

'Maybe so,' Vonette said. She pulled the Cadillac into the driveway and parked behind the Nova. Then she turned to me with a grim expression. 'You got another plan for getting her out of here in one piece?'

I looked at the house. There were lights on in every room, it looked like. Rita's car was parked in front of a double garage, but both doors were closed.

'At least the cops aren't here,' I said. 'I guess the only way to handle this is to just ring the doorbell and hope Rita will be willing to leave without throwing too big a fuss.'

'Right,' said a disbelieving Vonette.

Music, loud music, was coming from somewhere. We rang the doorbell and knocked for what seemed like five minutes. Then we walked around the front of the house trying to look into the windows, all the while glancing over our shoulders to see if anyone was watching. But the windows were all covered by wide louvered plantation shutters, obscuring all but a sense of light and color inside.

'Hey,' Kenyatta said, stepping gingerly out of a bed of azaleas in front of a window near the corner of the house. 'That music is coming from around back. Maybe they're not fighting at all.'

'We'll just see about that,' Vonette declared, brushing away a leaf that had fallen into her hair. 'I'm tired of skulking around in the bushes looking for that girl. Come on.'

Vonette marched off with Kenyatta and me trailing behind. The music got louder as we rounded the back of the house.

'Wow,' Kenyatta said in a breath.

Countless spotlights hid in the treetops revealed a

series of terraces, formally planted with flowers and shrubs and small perfect ovals of lawn that fell away from the rear of the low-slung Spanish-style house. The first level held a small formal fountain with a statue of a dolphin spitting water. The second was apparently a three-hole putting green.

At the bottom of the garden lay a long narrow swimming pool, glowing turquoise in the dark. Facing it was a pool house that was an exact miniature of the main house.

'Six million easy,' Vonette said. 'I hope that fool Rita didn't break anything.'

The pool house was lit up too, and the music seemed to be coming from it. We moved quickly down the stone steps toward the pool. 'There's somebody on one of those chaise longues,' Kenyatta whispered. 'Maybe Rita just fell asleep.'

It was Rita, all right, sprawled out on a chair under an umbrella. Vonette leaned over. 'Rita,' she said loudly into her ear. 'Wake up. Now. It's time to go home.' But Rita didn't move, and her arms hung limply at her side. Vonette shook her violently. 'Rita,' she cried. But the only sound was of something heavy and metallic falling and striking the tile pool deck with a clatter.

Vonette sucked her breath in sharply. It was a small nickel-plated .22.

I moved quickly to the inert woman's side. She was breathing shallowly, and when I checked her pupils, they looked dilated. She reeked of Scotch, and there was an empty Dewar's bottle tucked in the crook of her arm.

'Girl, what have you done?' Vonette said softly, looking down at her unconscious cousin.

I sent Kenyatta up to the house, to see if she could find anyone, like Stu Hightower. We heard her open one of the French doors that lead into the house from a small brick patio. 'Hello,' she called. 'Anyone home?'

'Don't go in,' I told her.

Vonette was sitting on the chaise beside Rita, gently patting her cheek and calling to her. 'Rita. Wake up. Come on now, we got to go.'

I wandered over to the pool house, which had open, pavilion-style doors. There was something laying in the doorway. I bent down and picked it up with one finger. It was a soggy white terry cloth towel. Or rather, it had been white. Now it had big red splotches of red on it. The splotches were wet too, and slightly sticky to the touch. I dropped the towel quickly.

My heart was pounding as I moved slowly into the pool house. It was one large room, with a mirror-backed bar at one end, an elaborate teak billiard table at the other end. The music was coming from a CD player mounted in a media center to the right of the bar. The loud, grating scratches and heavy bass beat of the rap music was getting damned annoying. I walked over to the media center to switch the music off. Out of the corner of my eye, I saw something behind the bar. When I went behind it to look, I nearly stepped on the outstretched hand of Stu Hightower.

The body was on its side, the face turned away from me. But I recognized Stu Hightower by the deep tan and the silver ponytail. He was nude now, however, and despite the shock of finding him that way, my detail-oriented brain noted that there were no tan lines. He liked to sunbathe in the buff.

The other detail I noticed was a small neat hole in his back, just below his shoulder blade, and a puddle of blood on the white tile floor.

I knelt down and touched his neck. The body was still faintly warm. He hadn't been dead long. 'Oh shit,' I said. I almost backed into Vonette, who'd walked up without a sound and was now staring down at the nude body of her former benefactor.

'I know that's right,' she said.

'Mama,' Kenyatta called urgently from the door of the pool house. 'The cops are here. And I can't make Rita wake up. What are we gonna do?'

My heart sank. Vonette and I turned our attention from Stu Hightower, who was past helping, to see for ourselves. Sure enough, there were cops, and there were two of them scurrying down the pathway toward us. But they were dressed in yellow shirts and brown pants. 'Rent-a-cops,' I said, breathing a little easier.

'I'll bet those guns aren't rented,' Vonette said.

At the sight of the intruder, the men had unholstered their revolvers, and were now standing still, pointing them at Kenyatta.

'Don't move,' one of them yelled at her. The other got a walkie-talkie out of his belt pack and held it up to his face. 'Dispatch, this is Unit Seven. Requesting assistance from Fulton PD. We have apprehended a suspect and will wait for backup.'

The rent-a-cops apparently hadn't spotted us yet.

'What do we do?' Vonette whispered. 'You think those guns are loaded?'

'I'm hoping not to find out,' I told her. Then I hollered as loud as I could. 'There are two more of us in the pool house. We're walking out right now. We're not burglars and we're not armed.'

With Vonette close behind, I came slowly out of the pool house. Now both men had their pistols pointed at us. One of the men looked around fifty, with a ratty little blond mustache and blond slicked-back hair. His partner was all of nineteen, if that, with mirrored sunglasses and a smirk that said he'd apprehended his first big-time crooks.

The men moved slowly down the steps toward us. 'Hey, there's another one, on this chair,' the younger one said, edging over toward Rita, who still wasn't moving. 'What's she doing, taking a little nap?'

'She's unconscious,' I said. 'I'm a licensed private detective, and she's my client. I would suggest that you get back on that walkie-talkie and ask them to have Fulton County send a homicide detective and the crime scene unit. There's a man in that pool house, and he's been shot to death.'

The younger one's smirk dissolved. 'Stay here,' his partner ordered. With the pistol still drawn, the blond edged around the doorway of the pool house.

'Behind the bar,' I said helpfully.

When he came out of the pool house, blondie was much paler. 'He's dead all right,' he told his partner. 'You tell dispatch about the body?'

'I told 'em,' sunglasses said.

The two of them stood there then, weapons pointed at us. After five minutes of this, my back was starting to hurt. And Kenyatta and Vonette were so scared I thought they might pass out.

'Look,' I said. 'We came out here looking for my client. We're not criminals. So we're going to sit down at that table now, while we all wait for the real cops. That okay with you?'

The security guard didn't look happy, but he reluctantly put his weapon away. Vonette sat down on the chaise longue beside Rita, looking worried. 'I've never seen her this bad before,' she said. 'You think she's all right?'

There was an ice bucket on the table beside the chaise longue. 'Take some ice and rub it on her wrists,' I suggested. 'Maybe the cold will bring her around.'

Rita shivered and moaned when the ice was applied to her skin, but she still didn't come to. It was another long ten minutes before we heard sirens coming our way. 'It's gonna be a long night,' I told Vonette and her daughter.

The keening wail of the sirens grew louder, and all of a sudden, Rita sat up on the lounge chair. Her hair was wild, and her eyes puffy and swollen. She looked at us with bewilderment. 'What's goin' on?' she said, glancing from the rent-a-cops to us. 'What are y'all doin' here? Where's Stu? Why are the cops here?'

'We came lookin' for you,' Vonette said, her voice taut with anger and fear. 'We got here, and started looking around. Found you passed out right here. Stu's in the pool house. Dead. We must have set off some kind of an alarm when Kenyatta tried that back door. Rita Louise

Fontaine, tell me right now, tell me you didn't kill Stu Hightower.'

'Dead?' Rita said, blinking. She shook her head, as if to shake off the words. 'What are you talking about?'

The rent-a-cops moved closer now. We heard voices and footsteps coming from the front of the house. 'Save it for later,' I hissed. 'The real cops will be down here in about one minute. Tell them you'll be happy to give them a statement, after you've called your lawyer. Don't say a word, Rita, until your lawyer is there.'

'What do I need a lawyer for?' she asked, rubbing at her eyes with her fist.

'You just tell them you want to call David Korznick,' Vonette hissed. 'Do like Callahan says. We're all in a shitpot of trouble right now, thanks to you.'

10

The real cops swarmed all over the place, measuring, photographing, fingerprinting. They took my statement, which I gave in as cut and dried a fashion as I could muster. I made the whole thing sound absolutely boring and mundane. They tried to talk to Rita, but all she would tell them was her name. So far, so good.

About forty minutes later, two plainclothes detectives arrived. The taller of the two looked to be in his late fifties. He was tall and muscular, with frizzy, close-cropped gray hair and bifocals that rested at the end of a long, ethnic-looking nose. He paused on the top step down to the patio, surveying the scene, while his partner, a deeply tanned blond guy with a designer suit scurried over to a cluster of uniformed officers.

The tall guy was staring at me, frowning. 'Don't I know you?'

I was hoping he'd forgotten. It had been twelve years at least. But Artie DiPima had reason to remember. I'd been out of the academy only a couple of months. I was off duty, and a friend and I were sitting outside a convenience store on Roswell Road when we noticed two suspicious-looking characters sitting in a fancy sports car next to ours. A swarthy-looking Italian guy behind the wheel of an expensive DeLorean, handing an envelope to a black dude draped in gold jewelry. Anybody would have done what I did. Right?

Well, maybe they wouldn't have drawn their service revolver out of their jeans pocket, and maybe they wouldn't have demanded that the driver submit to a body search, and maybe they wouldn't have blown a two-hundred-thousand-dollar drug buy. But I did, so maybe Artie DiPima had a right.

'Callahan Garrity,' I said, standing up and holding out my hand for a civilized handshake. 'We met years ago when I was with the Atlanta PD.'

He kept his hand in his pants pocket and looked me up and down, hard black eyes transmitting nothing. 'Oh yeah,' he said softly. His voice sounded hoarse, with remnants of a Boston or New England accent, I didn't know which. 'So what, you got tired of fucking up stuff down at Atlanta, you decided to come up here and fuck up my homicide scene?'

'No,' I said evenly. 'I left the Atlanta PD five years ago. I'm a private investigator. My clients and I,' I said, turning and gesturing toward Vonette and Kenyatta, 'came out here looking for another client, and in the course of looking for her, I discovered the body.'

'Clients, huh?' His eyes swept dismissively over the women. 'What kind of work you doing for them?'

'It's a private matter.'

'Okay,' he said lightly. 'Be back in a minute.'

He walked over to his partner, and the two of them had a quick conference with the uniformed officers.

'Miss Fontaine?' DiPima's partner stood over Rita, unsmiling. 'My name is Detective Carter. I'd like you to go down to the precinct with me, tell us about what went on here tonight. All right?'

Rita's face crumpled. 'Do I have to?' She looked from me to Vonette, questioningly.

I nodded my head. Carter helped her up from the chair and took her arm as they walked away. 'Call David,' I told her. 'Right away.'

A moment later, DiPima was back. 'Okay, Garrity,' he said. 'Let's you and your other clients take a ride over to the station.'

'I've already given a statement,' I pointed out. 'To that officer right there.'

'Good,' DiPima said, unimpressed. 'That was a rehearsal. Now it's show time. Let's go.'

Carter and Rita were a dozen yards ahead of us, Rita stumbling slightly, holding onto the detective's arm for support. Kenyatta and Vonette walked side by side, the younger woman hanging onto her mother's arm. I heard Kenyatta crying softly.

The next time we saw Rita was hours later, in the early hours of Tuesday morning.

I told DiPima the same thing I'd told the uniformed officer. That we were concerned about Rita after she had received the legal papers telling her that Hightower owned the rights to the VelvetTeens identity. We knew she'd been drinking and were afraid she might confront Stuart Hightower, so we went to his home to try to stop her.

'And the security guards just waved you on through?'

101

DiPima had a very sarcastic way of treating people.
Yankee.

'I believe the security guards were under the impression that we were delivering a pizza,' I said quickly.

He didn't believe it any more than I would have, but he wrote it down anyway.

After an hour or more of the same thing, he told me I could go. But Vonette and Kenyatta sat in the hallway outside the homicide office, scared and exhausted. I couldn't leave them there like that. I sat down and waited for them to get through with questioning.

By now it was after two in the morning. I'd called Edna as soon as I got to the precinct to tell her what had happened.

'You want me to call Kate Reilly?'

'I don't think I'll need an attorney,' I said. 'Vonette and Kenyatta can back me up. I'm gonna hang around here to see what happens with Rita. Can you get the girls going in the morning? I don't know what time I'll get home.'

'I'll handle it,' she said sleepily. 'See you then.'

By three o'clock the floor around our chairs in the hallway outside the homicide office was littered with empty paper coffee cups, candy wrappers, and cracker packages. We'd dined from the station house vending machine.

At four o'clock, a tall, thin dark-haired man came striding down the hallway from the reception area. 'David,' Vonette said, jumping up. She hugged the younger man around the neck. 'Rita's in bad trouble,' she whispered. 'Stuart Hightower is dead, and the police think she did it.'

102

David Korznick looked calm and unruffled, as though he'd just stepped from the shower. 'I'm going in to see her now,' he said. 'I know it's late, but can you wait around until I'm done in there? I'll want to talk to all of you.'

An hour later, when Korznick came out, his face was etched with weariness, his suit unreasonably rumpled. He stood over the three of us, Vonette and Kenyatta asleep, leaning on each other, teepee style.

'You're Callahan, the private investigator, right? Think you can stand another cup of coffee?'

We walked slowly toward the vending area. The hall was empty, except for a white uniformed jail trustee who was mopping the floor in idle, inefficient circles.

'Did you get a chance to talk to her alone?' I asked.

He nodded. 'For just a few minutes.'

'Did she tell you what happened?'

He grimaced. 'What she can remember of it. The first part, you know. She got home from work, saw the injunction, and went ballistic. She drank some more at home, stopped at a bar for some more drinks, then headed out toward Hightower's house.'

'How the hell did she get past the security guards?'

'Who knows? Anyway, she said she drove around until she found the house. She parked in the driveway, knocked, and rang, but there was no answer. She heard music coming from the rear of the house, so she walked around, looking for Hightower.'

'And there was nobody else there when she got there?'

'Not outside,' Korznick said. 'She tried the doorknob to the French door, but she said it was locked.'

103

'Locked?' I said. 'Was she sure about that? That door was unlocked when we got there. Kenyatta opened it and that's when we must have set off the silent alarm.'

He took out a tiny black leather notebook from his suit pocket and jotted down a note. 'I'll ask her about the door again,' he said. 'If she was as drunk as she says, she might have gotten that wrong.'

'Or maybe there was somebody else there after all,' I pointed out.

'If we're lucky,' Korznick said. 'After she tried the door, Rita says she walked around the pool, calling Hightower's name. Then she walked into the pool house, saw the bar, and helped herself to a bottle of Hightower's Scotch. The music was loud, and it was rap music, which she hates, so she turned the volume way down. Then she took the Scotch and the ice bucket and a glass out to a chair by the pool, sat down and proceeded to drink herself into a coma.'

'And she didn't hear or see anything until the cops got there,' I repeated. 'Where did the gun come from? Does she remember firing it or even having it?'

'Rita claims she never saw the gun before,' Korznick said, grimacing.' And no, she certainly doesn't remember firing it, or so she tells me.' He looked at me closely. 'You know the lady. What do you think?'

I shrugged and sipped my coffee. I'd been at the copshop too long. It was starting to taste good to me.

'She told her son and Vonette and Kenyatta that she'd kill Hightower.'

'When was this?' he said. 'Were there any other witnesses?'

'Only a whole roomful,' I said. I told him about Rita's altercation with Hightower at the party for Junebug.

He listened carefully. A good sign in a lawyer. 'But that was the day before Hightower filed the injunction. You mean she was still angry with him after all those years? Was there anything else going on between them besides that?'

'I don't know,' I said slowly. 'It never occurred to me. She and Vonette both hated Hightower because he dropped them and essentially killed their singing careers. According to Vonette, Rita never got over it. She's working in a nursing home these days, you know, living with her son. She's had a drinking problem for years. This VelvetTeen comeback was her last big chance. Then Hightower finds out and steps in to screw it up. I know you don't want to hear this, but she definitely had a motive. And Hightower couldn't have been dead long. I touched the body when I got there at around nine thirty. It was still warm.'

Korznick crumpled the cardboard coffee cup and tossed it in the trash can in the vending area. 'Good or bad, I need to know it all.'

'Does that mean the cops are going to charge her?'

He nodded and looked at his watch. 'They've set a bond hearing for one o'clock before Judge Workman. Guess I'd better talk to Vonette about that. They're going to ask for a high figure, maybe as high as five hundred thousand.'

I was stunned. 'Can she come up with that kind of dough?'

Korznick smiled. 'Vonette is a very astute business-woman. A couple of apartment houses, a little strip of shopping center over on Cascade. If she's willing to do it, she could co-sign for her cousin's bond with no problem.'

'What are the chances the judge will go for it? I mean, it is a homicide.'

'Who knows?' he said. 'I can't figure out Annette Workman. One minute she's giving the death penalty to a battered woman who shoots her husband in self-defense, the next day she's busting the DA's chops for prosecuting too many prostitution cases. We'll line up some character witnesses, tell the judge she's no flight risk, see which way the wind blows.'

'Do you need me there?' I asked, trying to stifle a yawn.

'Not for that,' he said quickly. 'But you'll probably want to sit in. I know Vonette's hired you to find Rita's sister Delores. But if she okays it, would you be willing to assist me in an investigation? If we're going to get Rita off, it's going to take a lot of work, and fast.'

Personally, I thought Rita was something of a hopeless cause. If the autopsy found that the bullet in Hightower's body came from the gun Rita was holding, the Velvet-Teens would be making a comeback without their lead singer. And Rita would be singing gospel with the choir down at the state prison for women.

'What do you need?' I asked.

'Do you still have that pizza delivery sign?'

11

It took some convincing, but I finally persuaded Vonette and Kenyatta to go home and get some sleep before showing up at Rita's bond hearing.

'You've got to look like a successful businesswoman who can afford to make bond,' I told Vonette pointedly. She looked down at the rumpled and soiled pants suit and sighed. 'This thing's ready for the ragbag,' she said.

'And I need a shower, Mama,' Kenyatta said plaintively.

We agreed to meet up at Rita's bond hearing, which was set for 1:00 p.m.

Vonette wasn't the only one who looked the worse for wear. I was dog tired and filthy. A shower and a change of clothes would have to substitute for the eight hours of sleep my body clamored for.

Back at home, I filled Edna in while I jumped into a clean sleeveless cotton blouse and a pair of tailored white slacks. I'd have to look fairly respectable if I hoped to make it past those guards at Riverbend during the daytime.

'It's been all over the television news,' Edna said,

flicking her cigarette ashes into her coffee saucer. 'They broke into *The Price Is Right* for a news special on Channel Two. Showed aerial views of the house and all those cops waving people away from those big stone gates. I don't know why you didn't take me out there when you went.'

'Damn,' I muttered. A media circus wouldn't make my job any easier. And I still didn't have a plan for getting back to Hightower's house.

As I was heading out the door Edna handed me a warm biscuit slathered with butter and fig preserves and a cold can of diet Coke.

I shoved the biscuit into my mouth. Heaven. 'Thanks,' I said, through a mouthful of crumbs. 'Everybody get to their jobs okay this morning?'

'You think I can't run things without you?' she said sharply. 'Everything's fine. Now get out of my hair.'

I drove Edna's car as a cover, and parked on the shoulder of the road across from Riverbend. I hadn't noticed before, but the subdivision's golf course ran along both sides of Old Alabama. A line of tall magnolias kept the side of the street opposite the subdivision buffered from a putting green. Television satellite trucks, radio-equipped news cars and vans bristling with video equipment were parked along the road. I got out and sat on the bumper, searching for an idea.

'This sucks, don't it?' I looked around to see who had read my thoughts.

The speaker was a short red-faced man with a shock of sandy hair that fell across one eye. He was leaning out the open window of a white Escort with a Hertz sticker on the windshield.

He got out of the car and joined me on my bumper. He was no taller than Edna, maybe five two, and his face was covered with freckles. 'Mick Coyle,' he said, thrusting out a hand. '*Global Examiner.*' He had a pronounced accent, British, I thought, or maybe Australian.

'Callahan Garrity,' I said, 'uh, *Atlanta Beacon.*' There was no such animal, but then my new friend worked for one of those grocery store tabloids that insisted you could lose weight by rubbing hemorrhoid cream on your thighs.

He nodded to a throng of uniformed guards who stood in front of the gates to Riverbend, their arms folded defiantly across their chests. 'You'd think the bloody friggin' president was visitin',' he said bleakly.

'I know,' I said.

'And I know that if I don't get in there and get something by six this afternoon, I'm screwed. Totally and completely screwed.'

'Me too,' I said. 'My editor wants this story bad. Lots of press out here, huh?'

'It's June, innit?' he said. 'Slow week. I got pulled off a UFO sighting in Nebraska for this number.'

'Really?' I was fascinated. 'What happened?'

He shrugged. 'Same old thing. LGMs were hovering over a cornfield. Some old gal with bunions seen it, come out of the farmhouse, and the next thing you know, she's up on a table inside a stainless-steel bubble getting a free plumbing inspection.'

'LGMs?'

'Yeah. You know. Little Green Men.'

'And they raped this woman?'

'No, no,' he said impatiently. 'More like an exam, really. See, your extraterrestrials always want to know how humans procreate.'

While Coyle was talking, he was watching the scene across the street with a pair of high-powered binoculars. 'Bloody hell,' he said, dropping the glasses in disgust.

'What?'

'See that black van in the carpark there? That's Jimbo Walls. Fucker wants this story as bad as I do. And if he gets it, well, that's it for old Mick.'

'Who's he work for?' I asked.

'Everybody,' Coyle said. 'He's a stringer. Used to be with *The National Enquirer*, but he struck off on his own, and now he hires out to whoever pays the most. He's probably over there waving hundred-dollar bills in those coppers' faces.'

'May I?' I picked up the binoculars and took a look. Jimbo Walls was having an agitated conversation with one of the guards, who kept shouting and gesturing for Walls to move the van.

'He must have found an honest man,' I said. 'They're making him move on.'

We watched while the black van backed up and sped down the road.

'Good on him,' Coyle said. 'But look around you. See that red Accord and the woman with the long blond hair? That's *People* magazine. The white Geo and the tall drink of water? *Entertainment Weekly*.' He pointed a finger at the row of cars and vans and ticked off the list of occupants. '*Hard Copy. Entertainment Tonight. L.A. Times. A Current Affair*. And that's just the faces I recognize. No telling how many stringers are on this. Fuckin' bloodsuckers. I couldn't even charter a chopper today. Every single one in a hundred-mile radius was hired out before nine this morning.'

He sighed again. I didn't blame him. The media folks were milling about, with the print reporters interviewing each other and jotting notes in their notebooks, while the television types practiced their standups using the gates to the subdivision as a backdrop. There were four different crews across the street, each of them with a cameraman filming a report. As I watched, one of those cute electric golf carts bumped across the street, paused briefly at the gates and was quickly waved inside.

'Hey,' I said.

'What's that?' Coyle said. His chin was resting in his fists and he looked for all the world like a leprechaun who'd lost his pot of gold.

'See that golf cart?' His eyes followed where I pointed.

'Stu Hightower's house backs up to the golf course,' I said. Beyond the gates we could see the bright green swathe of grass dotted with golfers and their carts.

'Yeah?' He was sitting forward, eyes shining.

'Do you tabloid reporters really pay for stories?'

His eyes narrowed a little. 'Sometimes. What've you got in mind?'

The pro shop was humming with activity. We stood

outside and watched while the Cadillacs and Mercedes pulled up, parked, and their golf-minded occupants got out and strode inside, golf bags slung over their shoulders. A narrow concrete path led from the back of the building to the front, and out into the course.

'Back here,' I said. We sauntered around the back of the building. A deeply tanned college kid in khaki shorts and a white polo shirt was checking out the last cart in the shed to a pair of white-haired women in bright pink and blue golfing duds.

'Shit,' Coyle said, turning around. 'I knew this wouldn't work.'

'Not so fast,' I said.

The women drove the cart slowly toward the front of the building. I sprinted along behind them, then hesitated while they pulled the cart up to a new-looking Buick Electra. The driver got out, popped the trunk of the car and started transferring gear onto the cart.

I caught up just as she was locking the trunk.

'Excuse me ma'am,' I said, softening my voice and deepening my Atlanta accent.

The passenger, a tiny woman wearing a white billed cap that proclaimed her a 'Golfin' Granny' turned and gave me a smile.

'Yes?'

'I know this is goin' to sound strange,' I told her, 'but my friend here is in town from England just for today, and I promised him we'd play a round at the best club in Atlanta. Daddy is a charter member. Maybe ya'll know Daddy, Ashmead Peal?'

Ashmead Peal was actually one of the House Mouse's former cleaning clients before he'd moved to Riverbend and his wife had insisted on hiring a Jamaican couple as live-in help. Snob.

The driver, a tall thin woman who'd smeared sunscreen all over her cheeks nodded. 'We know Ashmead. And you're his daughter?'

'Yay-us,' I said, giggling. 'First marriage. Miss Caroline doesn't tell a lot of people she's got a step-daughter who's only two years younger than she is.'

The shorter woman tittered and looked at me expectantly.

'The thing is, all the carts are rented for the day, and I can't get a tee time,' I said, letting my lower lip stick out in a cute little pout. 'So I know it's askin' a lot, but I was just wonderin'...'

Mick stepped forward and elbowed me aside. His hand came forward and I saw a fan of hundred dollar bills. 'Me plane leaves in three hours,' he said. 'How about it then?'

Golfin' Granny plucked the bills out of his hand and tucked them into the pocket of her golfing skirt with a speed that belied her years.

'It's too hot to play today anyway, RuthAnne,' she said. 'We'll have a nice lunch at the club. Praline chicken salad and extra-dry martinis sounds a lot better than eighteen holes, don't you think?'

RuthAnne got out of the cart, handed me the keys and started to move her golf bag. But Mick stepped in front of her and another handful of hundred dollar bills materialized.

'Didn't bring me own clubs,' he said, chuckling. 'Silly twit. All right if we borrow yours then?'

RuthAnne thought about it for about a second. 'We'll meet you back here at one. I don't mean to be distrustful, but why don't you just let me keep your car keys as a little deposit? Just to make sure we get our things back? That's a new set of Pings the children gave me for Mother's Day.'

'May I?' I said, gently nodding toward her hat, a white billed affair with a Ping-Pong-ball-sized pompom on top. She nodded and put the cap on my head.

Mick dug in his pockets and handed her the keys to his rental van.

'I'll drive,' I said, hopping behind the wheel. He slung a large canvas duffel bag into the back with the golf bags, fiddled around with his gear for a moment, and we were off.

He gave me a critical look. 'That's the silliest hat I've ever seen on a grownup.'

'Worse than that crap the queen wears?' I asked, adjusting the cap so it didn't sit quite so high on my head.

'There is that,' he admitted, fastening the seat belt. 'You sure this'll work?'

I pointed to the Riverbend logo sticker on the windshield of the cart. 'Sit back and act like you're a member of the idle rich,' I instructed.

I held my breath for a moment when I pulled the cart up to the gates, but the guard smiled and waved me through. 'Have a good game,' was all he said.

'Okay,' I said, exhaling as we left the gates behind. I

drove the cart slowly on the cart path, trying to get my bearings. Things looked different in the bright mid-morning sunlight. 'I think we follow this path along to the right, and that should take us to the back edge of Hightower's property. It's a pale pink stucco number.'

'What's that, luv?' Coyle had turned around in his seat and was rummaging through the women's golf equipment.

'Oh lovely,' he said, opening a small ice chest and spying a dozen chilled cans of beer. He plunged his hand into the ice and retrieved a brew, but his face fell when he saw the label.

'Lite beer. Nasty shit this. How do you people drink the stuff?'

'Tastes great, less filling,' I said. The cart bumped along the path slowly. It was hard to tell what part of the subdivision we were in. I could see patios and pools off through a screen of trees that separated the homes from the golf course, but the houses all looked different from the back.

At the sixteenth hole, I spied the rear of what looked like the pool house where we'd found Hightower's body the night before. I pulled the cart off the path and drove through a small grove of pinetrees and oaks. 'I'm pretty sure this is the house.'

'Right then,' he said, grabbing a camera with a long lens out of his bag and hopping out before I'd stopped the cart.

For reasons I can't explain, I didn't want him getting ahead of me. I rolled to a stop, grabbed my notebook, and followed him through the trees.

'Get down,' he hissed suddenly.

I dropped to my knees and crawled forward to where he was crouching in the pine needles behind a water oak.

His camera was trained on a group of three people who were standing in front of the pool house. The two men looked like DiPima and the other detective who'd grilled us last night. All I could see of the woman was a fall of shimmering dark hair.

Coyle grinned widely and began shooting. The whir of the camera's motor drive was the only sound.

'That's it darling,' he crooned softly. 'Turn toward Mick and give a big tearful look of concern, would you?'

'Who is it?' I wanted to know.

'It's Serena, you twit,' he said. 'What the hell kind of paper did you say you worked for?'

'I couldn't see her from here,' I said quickly. 'Are you sure it's her?'

'As sure as the front-page bonus I'm gonna get for this caper,' he said, snapping away. 'Lovely darling, just lovely. You've never looked better.'

'Oops, time to reload.' He put the camera down for a moment and dug in his pants' pocket for another roll of film.

While he did, I snatched the camera up and looked through the lens. Serena, I was surprised to note, looked Oriental. Her skin was honey colored, and she dabbed at her eyes with a scrap of tissue, all the time gesturing with graceful hands that chopped the air as she talked animatedly to the cops.

'Is she Chinese?' I asked.

Coyle snatched the camera away from me, then busied himself loading it with a fresh roll of film.

'Korean,' he said. 'Or I should say Korean-American. She gets bent out of shape when people call her Korean.'

He lifted the camera up to shoot again, but dropped it with disgust.

'Bloody hell!' he said.

While we'd talked, Serena and the cops had moved into the house. We just saw the back of her bright pink shorts as she disappeared through the patio doors into the house.

I stood up and brushed the pine needles from the knees of my slacks.

Coyle scrambled to his feet and tucked the camera inside the neck of the windbreaker he was wearing.

'What's your plan?' I asked.

He winked. 'Never know until it happens. I'll meet you back here in an hour. That all right?'

I nodded. I didn't have a plan myself, other than to stay out of Artie DiPima's line of sight.

By sticking close to the tree line I managed to work my way along the east side of Hightower's house and out to the street.

A Fulton County patrol car and crime scene van were parked in Hightower's driveway, but other than that, the street was quiet.

At the house next to Hightower's, an older woman wearing a floppy straw hat, an oversized man's white shirt and white trousers was clipping away at a rosebush.

I wandered into her yard and tried to look casual. She saw me approach and put the clippers into a basket at her feet.

'Yes?' she said warily.

I held out my hand to shake hers. 'J. C. Garrity,' I said, trying to sound official. 'I'm working on the Hightower homicide. Could we step inside so I could ask some questions?'

She was in her late fifties or early sixties, with pale blond hair and a fine network of lines around her bright blue eyes. It was pushing things a bit to invite myself inside her home, but I didn't want DiPima glancing over to see me interrogating this woman right next door.

'All right,' she said, picking up the basket and clippers. 'But I'm telling you right now, I didn't see anything and I hardly knew the man.'

I followed her into the house, and she gestured for me to sit on a mahogany bench in the marble-floored entry hall. She obviously didn't relish the idea of having cops in her parlor.

'Mrs...?' I started.

'Powers,' she said quickly. 'Mary Louise Powers.'

'Mrs Powers, did you see or hear anything happening at the house next door last night?'

'Last night?' she said. 'Heavens no. I've told your people already. Gardner and I were at the Heart Fund Ball. Casino night, you know. We didn't get home until after midnight. That's when we saw all the police and the neighbors, standing around outside.'

'And you didn't know Mr Hightower?'

She looked down at her hands and frowned. 'Well no,

not really. He doesn't golf at all. And he's in show business you know.'

'I know,' I said.

'Rock and roll,' she sniffed. 'Gardner and I like Big Band music. Sinatra, Dorsey, that type of thing.'

'What about earlier?' I asked.

'Earlier?'

'Before the ball.'

She wrinkled her nose and thought. 'Let's see. I got home from the hairdressers around four. I remember seeing his car, the Jaguar, you know, parked in front of the garage. He has a Mercedes too, one of the big sedans, or he did until that woman took a sledge hammer to it.'

'Serena?' I said, trying not to show my excitement. 'She took a sledge hammer to Mr Hightower's car?'

She hesitated. 'Maybe it was a crowbar. I know it was a heavy iron tool, because Gardner said she did at least ten thousand dollars' worth of body damage to the car.'

'When was this? Do you have any idea why she did it?'

Mary Louise Powers sighed happily. I had the feeling she didn't have much color in her own life. Bridge club. Face-lifts. Manicures. Having a ringside seat to the domestic trials of Stuart Hightower was probably the brightest spot in her deprived WASP life.

'She moved out, oh, I guess it was back around Valentine's Day. No, Easter. One time, I remember, he locked her out of the house. So she stripped down to nothing, stood in the driveway of the house and shot out every window over there with a target pistol. Let me tell you, Gardner Powers memorized every detail of that girl's body, because he stood in that upstairs window so long I thought his eyeballs would fall out on the floor.'

'So they've been estranged since the car incident?'

She shrugged. 'As estranged as you can be when you move to a townhouse directly across the sixteenth hole from your ex-husband.'

'Really?' I said, letting one eyebrow rise.

'Um-hum. She drove past the house all the time. Not that I don't have anything better to do with my time, but you can't hardly miss that red Mercedes convertible, now can you?'

'No, you can't,' I agreed. 'You didn't see her car over at Mr Hightower's house yesterday, did you?'

She pursed her lips. 'No. The only other car I saw over there yesterday was an old green truck, which I believe belongs to Mr Hightower's pool man. And that was early in the morning, around eight, I think.'

'No other cars, other visitors?'

She shook her head regretfully. 'I was gone most of the day.'

'And you didn't notice a Nova over there, say sometime after eight p.m.?'

'No ma'am. Gardner got home late from the office and we were rushing to get to a pre-ball cocktail party. The only thing I noticed was that loud music of his. But there was always loud music over there. Our community association was going to draw up an anti-noise ordinance next month, just to deal with that. I guess we won't have to now.'

While she talked, I was watching the street through the sidelights of her front door. I saw DiPima and his partner walk across the street, and ring the doorbell of a house. After a moment, someone answered, and they stepped inside.

'Thanks,' I told Mrs Powers quickly. I shut my notebook and let myself out of the front door. Then I walked quickly across the street myself, to the house next to the one DiPima and his friend were visiting. It was a cream two-story stucco affair, with a wrought-iron gate set into a stucco wall that surrounded the house. Through the gate I could see a small lushly planted courtyard.

Suddenly I heard a door open next door. DiPima and Carter had struck out. I unlatched the iron gate and slipped inside quickly, pulling the door shut after me.

I stepped to the side of the gate, squarely on a bed of pink and red flowers, and peeked through the iron at the two men. They stood for a moment in the driveway, talking. Once, DiPima glanced over to where I was standing, and I jumped backward to avoid being seen.

After a moment, I ventured another look. They were heading over towards Mrs Powers' house.

'Damn,' I said out loud.

'May I help you?'

12

Startled, I dropped my pad to the ground. I stooped down to get it, then turned around to see where the voice was coming from.

I was in a courtyard garden, lushly planted, with vine-covered stucco walls. Huge terra-cotta pots held palm trees and fiddle-leaf figs drooping from the heat, and the brick floor was crowded with baskets and pots of ferns, hostas, begonias, and impatiens. It was still except for the droning of insects, and the hot damp air smelled of gardenias and something else, like coconut. In the corner, a black wrought-iron chaise longue blended into the greenery. A thin, deeply tanned man wearing a brief red bikini swimsuit regarded me with a look of amusement. His hair was graying, cut close to his scalp, and a pair of black bifocals perched on the end of a bony aristocratic nose.

'Hiding out from the men in blue are we?' He jiggled the ice cubes in a crystal highball glass. 'Naughty, naughty.'

'Oh, uh, well,' I stammered. I was caught off-guard, shocked into truthfulness.

'I'm a private detective,' I admitted. 'And I lied my

123

way past the security guards at your front gate. But if those cops catch me here, they'll throw me out. And I've got a job to do. Can I stay until they've gone? Then I'll leave, right away. Okay?'

'Good Lord,' he drawled. His voice was deep, theatrical sounding. 'Stay as long as you like. It's nothing to me. I'm just the little old housesitter.'

'In fact,' he said, sitting up and patting a matching chair next to his, 'come sit down by Uncle Eric and tell us what all the commotion is about next door. Has our Serena been trying to burn down the big bad wolf's house again?'

I sat down. 'You really don't know what happened?'

He shook his head. 'It's one of my little affectations. When I'm housesitting I try not to watch television or read the newspaper. It's strictly classical CDs, the latest best-seller, and lots of gin and tonics. That way I pretend I'm on vacation too. Now give.'

He got up and padded over to a table against the wall, dropping ice cubes into a glass, adding a jigger of gin, a splash of tonic water, and a final twist of lime. His bathing suit sagged in the seat. Chronic butt deficit. God, life is unfair. He brought the glass over and thrust it into my hand.

'Now don't try telling me you're on duty,' he said. 'It's ninety-eight degrees out here. A girl needs her fluids.'

I took a small seemly sip and looked at him over the rim of the glass.

'What'd you say your name was again?'

'Eric Glenn,' he said. 'You're stalling.'

I sucked on an ice cube. My throat was dry, and I suddenly realized how thirsty I was. If I wasn't careful, I'd knock back the cocktail in one gulp and be half-tanked before noon.

'Stu Hightower was murdered last night,' I said. 'Shot to death. They found the body in the pool house. The reason I'm here is that the police think my client did it. Unfortunately, I was the one who discovered the body, and when I got to the house, I found my client, passed out cold, with the gun that was probably the murder weapon, in her hand.'

'Tsk tsk,' he clucked. 'Bad break for your client. For Stu-Baby too, come to think of it. Your client isn't Serena, is it?'

'No,' I said slowly, trying to decide how much to tell him.

'Oh, come on,' he said impatiently. 'You can tell me. I don't live here. I don't even live in Georgia. I'm not a cop, I'm not a reporter, I'm not even a lawyer. Just your average nosy housesitter. Besides,' he added coyly, 'You show me yours and I'll show you mine. That's how it works, isn't it?'

I rubbed the cold sweaty glass across my sweat-dampened brow. I wanted to take the whole ice bucket and dump it down my shirt. 'Did you see or hear anything last night?'

'Ah, ah, ah,' he said, shaking his highball glass again. 'You first.'

'All right,' I said. 'Her name is Rita Fontaine. Do you remember a girl group from the early sixties, the VelvetTeens? Rita was the lead singer.'

'Maybe,' he said doubtfully. 'I was always more of a jazz buff. That and show tunes. But go on.'

'There's not a lot to tell,' I said. 'Rita and her cousin hired me to find the third member of their group. They haven't heard from her in about twenty years, and they need to find her so they can make a comeback. There's a Hollywood type who wants to use them in a movie, using their big hit single as the movie's theme song.'

'Who's the director?' he asked.

'Davis Zimmerman,' I said. 'Why, do you know him?'

'Of him,' Eric said. 'I'm in the business myself. A set designer, but I haven't worked with Davis. Right now I'm housesitting for old friends who own this house while they summer at their place in Maine. I'm having the kitchen of my house in Malibu ripped out, and it's just too traumatic to live with.'

He paused and frowned. 'But how do these Velvet-Teens or this Rita Fontaine person fit in with Stu-Baby? I thought he was the big rap master.'

'He is,' I said. 'But years ago when he was just starting out, he discovered the girls. Signed them to a long-term, multi-record exclusive contract. He managed them, produced them, the whole works. He made his stars, and then, when the British Invasion hit and their records stopped going gold, he dropped the VelvetTeens like a bad habit.'

'Careers go bust all the time,' Eric said. 'So all these years later your client decides to get her revenge and whack Stuart? Has she ever heard of the phrase "get a life"?'

'She's had a rough time,' I said. 'Raised a son by

herself, worked as an aide at some nursing home, and she's battled a booze problem. Did I mention that she and the others never saw any of the millions SkyHi made off the VelvetTeens? Now it looks like the girls have a shot at a comeback, and Hightower steps in and files an injunction to keep them from performing as the VelvetTeens. He claims he owns the name, not the girls.'

'Ooh,' Eric said. 'I'll bet Davis Zimmerman is not going to like this piece of news. Not one little bit. Producers hate controversy.'

'That's his problem,' I said. I got up to help myself to some more tonic water and ice. 'Your turn. Were you here last night?'

'I was and I wasn't,' he said. 'You see, I had some people in for drinks, and one of the gang brought these darling little amyl nitrate poppers, and one thing lead to another.'

'You had your own party,' I suggested.

'Exactamento,' Eric said. 'I do remember seeing an old car over there. A junker really. You don't see many rust buckets like that here at the dear old Riverbend. I just assumed it belonged to the cleaning lady or someone like that.'

I let the snide reference to cleaning ladies pass without comment. Maybe I'd leave one of my House Mouse business cards. I didn't think Eric Glenn was much of a tidy-upper.

'You didn't see any other cars?'

'I told you, I was entertaining,' he said. He picked up a small black plastic tube from the table next to his chaise, squeezed a dollop of lotion into the palm of his hand and started rubbing it vigorously into his thin tobacco-colored arms. That explained the Mai-Tai smell.

'Did you see Hightower's car there last night?'

'Cars. Plural,' he said. 'A silver Jaguar, one of the old ones from the sixties. A beautiful thing. And a navy Mercedes sedan for when Stu was feeling corporate. I think I saw both of them in the garage at some point during the late afternoon.'

'What about noises?' I persisted. 'Any loud voices arguing? What about gunshots? He was probably killed sometime after seven p.m.'

'Gunshots?' He waved a hand dismissively. 'You couldn't hear cannon-fire with that rap music of his. He played it nonstop, every night. I swear, he must have speakers the size of my car. The neighbors had all filed complaints with the Homeowner's Association, of course, and he was fined repeatedly, but he just kept up with it. Not a very nice asset to the community, I assure you. Richard and Jane, my friends who own this house, are going to be thrilled when I tell them the news. Jane gets migraines, you know.'

'What about Serena?' I asked. 'Did you see her car over there yesterday? The red Mercedes convertible?'

He considered. 'Maybe. But I'm thinking it was earlier in the day. Like around lunchtime, when I went out for refreshments for my little get-together. Seems to me I saw her car over there when I was leaving for the store, but I don't remember seeing it when I got back around one thirty or two.'

Something he'd said earlier struck a chord. 'Hey. You asked me if Serena had tried to burn down Hightower's house – again. What's that supposed to mean?'

He got up from his chaise and walked over to the wrought iron gate.

'Come here,' he said, crooking his index finger.

I stood still.

'Come on,' he said impatiently. 'The cops are gone. I want you to see something.'

I walked over and stood beside him. He pointed to the east corner of Hightower's house. 'See that upstairs window on the far right? See the black stains on the stucco? That's some of Miss Serena's handiwork.'

'She tried to set it on fire? When was this?'

'Late April,' he said promptly. 'I'd been here a week. It was around four in the morning, and I was dead to the world, I promise you. But I hear this banging at the door, and the doorbell's ringing, and somebody's yelling for help. So I go downstairs and there is Stuart Hightower himself, barefoot, wearing nothing but a pair of shorts, and he asks me to call the fire department and nine one. I took a look, and there were flames just shooting out of that window.'

'Did he tell you she'd set it on fire?'

'We stood out in the driveway together, waiting for the fire trucks. He just kept shaking his head. 'She's crazy man, fuckin' crazy. My suits, all my clothes, she fuckin' burned them up.'

'Meaning Serena?'

'Exactamento,' he said. 'He didn't tell me much, but I hung around when the arson investigators got there.

129

After all, it was my driveway. Or actually, it's Richard and Jane's driveway. But I heard him tell the investigator there had been a domestic dispute, that's what he called it, over some song Serena wanted to record that he'd given to another recording artist. She got mad, waited until he'd gone to bed, then she took a bottle of Smirnoff, sprinkled it all over the clothes in his closet, wadded up some papers and threw them around the closet and bedroom, and threw a match on it.'

'Whew,' I said.

'Well, she's not much better at arson than she is at singing,' Eric sniffed. 'She managed to trash the closet and the master bedroom, but the fire went out before the fireboys even got here.'

'What happened to Serena?' I asked. 'Did he have her arrested?'

'Nooo,' he drawled. 'Bad press and all that. I think they may have reconciled for a while there. Men,' he said, shrugging. 'Can't live with 'em, can't live without 'em.'

I thought of the man in my own life and had to agree.

13

Mick Coyle was exchanging putting tips with an elderly gentleman in lime green slacks and a lilac shirt when I motored up to him on the sixteenth hole.

'Keep your head down,' he called behind him as we scooted off on the cart.

'You get what you came for?' I asked when we were out of earshot.

His face was an alarming shade of crimson, and his shirt was plastered to his back and belly. But he smiled gleefully and rubbed the palms of his hands together. 'Did I?' he chortled. 'Front page stuff, that. Coppers swarming around the house, Serena being grilled by the coppers. Serena in tears. Lovely stuff. Absolutely lovely. Wait till Jimbo Walls sees it. He'll have a stroke at the very least. I'm in for a bonus on this one, and it's all thanks to you, luv.'

The way he said it, 'luv,' reminded me of my misspent adolescence, when my friend DebraLyn Justus and I used to swoon over the likes of the Monkees and Paul Revere and the Raiders. We wore Yardley of London makeup, because we thought it terribly hip, and knock-offs of Mary Quant miniskirts, because we thought it made us look fresh from Carnaby Street. In a way, we probably contributed indirectly to the woes of groups like the VelvetTeens.

'Get any good tips on the murder?' I said carelessly.

'Oh yeah,' he said, crossing his legs and reaching into the cooler for one of RuthAnne's beers. He popped the top, took a long swig and sighed. 'No wonder people are killing each other all the time down here. If I were this hot all the time I'd be up in a tower picking people off with an assault rifle for sport. How do you stand this heat, then?'

'You get used to it,' I told him. 'What'd you find out?'

'That reminds me,' he said, snapping his fingers. 'You think that paper of yours has any snaps of an old rock and roll group from the sixties? A girl group called the VelvetTeens?'

'The VelvetTeens?' I said, allowing a puzzled look to cross my face. 'Who are they? Why do you want it?'

He took a long gulp of beer, then another, belched loudly then tossed the empty can onto the manicured green. 'I owe you, don't I? All right then. It turns out the cops have arrested this woman, Rita Fontaine, who used to be the lead singer for this group. Stuart Hightower was their Svengali, in the same sort of way Berry Gordy was for the Supremes. He discovered 'em and managed 'em, and years later, lovely Rita punches his meter.' He looked pleased with himself. 'Hey, there's the headline. I can't wait to get back to my room. Ever have a story that practically wrote itself?'

I didn't answer, and he wasn't paying attention anyway, scribbling frantically in his notebook.

We crossed by the guard shack on the way back across the street, and Mick leaned way out of the cart, waving happily to all the reporters who were clustered around in sweaty little clots. 'Pathetic sods,' he called out, as they watched in amazement. 'See you in the funny papers!'

When we got back to the pro shop, RuthAnne and her friend were waiting patiently, leaning on each other in a loopy gin-induced embrace.

Mick loaded his canvas camera bag and hopped out. 'Thanks luv,' he said, pecking each woman on the cheek. 'It really is true what they say about Dixie.'

I was getting into the car when he came around to the window. 'You ever want some stringing work, ring me up,' he said, thrusting a business card in my face. 'I could use someone with your brains.'

I tucked the card in my purse and gunned the engine. I had thirty minutes to make it to Rita's bond hearing. I only hoped Mick hadn't found out about it, too. The last thing Rita needed was to have her face plastered across every supermarket tabloid in America.

Rita was already seated at the defense table next to David Korznick in the front of the courtroom when I slid onto the bench next to Vonette. The courtroom was half empty, an encouraging sign. I recognized reporters from the local television stations, and Jingle Hice, a reporter for the *Atlanta Constitution* whom I'd seen around town over the years, but thankfully, the rest of the media pack seemed to have missed out on the hearing.

My client didn't look good. She'd showered, and her hair was still damp, but her face was wan, with a greenish tint, and her almond-shaped eyes were rimmed with dark circles, the whites criss-crossed with a network of red veins. Hung over and in jail charged with murder was a combination guaranteed to keep a girl from looking her best. The orange jail scrubs didn't do much for her either.

Vonette sat erect on the bench. She looked like the successful realtor she was, dressed in a bronze-colored silk suit, with sedate gold jewelry and her hair smoothed back in a French twist. Kenyatta wore a dark flower-printed dress that floated around her ankles. Mother and daughter looked like they should have been in church instead of a supercooled courtroom, watching their cousin be arraigned for murder. A man I didn't recognize sat on the other side of Kenyatta. He looked to be in his late twenties or early thirties, and he wore an ill-fitting blue blazer over some kind of blue uniform shirt. I wondered if he was Andre, Rita's son.

When the bailiff called Rita's name, the assistant district attorney got up and stood before the bench. Christine Stroman was a small birdlike young woman a severe dark suit. She outlined the facts of the case in a clear slightly high-pitched voice and asked that Rita be kept in jail.

Korznick got up later and argued the reverse, reminding the judge that Rita had never been arrested, had a job and ties to the community, and a relative willing to post bond.

Annette Workman jotted notes as she listened. She

had graying blond curls and surprisingly beautiful hands, the nails long and polished, with diamonds glittering on both hands. She blinked her eyes rapidly as she worked, as though her contact lens were hurting.

When both sides were done she looked up and put her pen down.

'Ms Fontaine?' she said. 'I remember you well from your entertainment days. I'm disappointed to see you today in my courtroom. The police report, here,' she said, glancing down at the papers in front of her, 'says you had a blood alcohol level high enough to kill a bull moose. And you were in an alcoholic stupor when you were arrested, is that correct?'

Rita nodded, her lips pressed close together.

'Mr Korznick,' Judge Workman said, 'does your client acknowledge that she has a substance abuse problem?'

Korznick leaned over and whispered something to Rita. She shook her head violently, and Korznick whispered something else. Rita looked at the judge reluctantly. 'Yes ma'am,' she said.

The judge nodded agreement and wrote something on the paper in front of her.

'Mr Korznick,' she said, not looking up. 'I'm going to set bond at three hundred thousand. With an additional provision of bond being that your client admit herself immediately to an alcohol treatment program approved by this court.'

Rita's shoulders sagged, and she hung her head. Beside me, Vonette exhaled loudly. 'Thank you, Jesus,' she whispered. She grabbed Kenyatta's hand and mine and squeezed.

At the end of the hearing, the four of us, myself, Vonette, Kenyatta, and the man who was indeed Rita's son, gathered at the back of the courtroom.

'You're gonna be okay,' Vonette said. 'You're not going back to that jail cell, honey.'

'Mama?' Andre said, putting his arms around her awkwardly.

Rita collapsed in her son's arms. 'I'm sorry,' she sobbed. 'Baby, I'm sorry.'

Rita and her son walked away from us for a moment, toward the table Rita had just left.

'Excuse me,' Korznick told Vonette, with whom he'd been speaking. He pulled me away from the others. 'You have any luck?'

'Some,' I said. 'Hightower's ex-wife, Serena, the disco chick? She lives right across the green from Stu. And they had a fairly explosive relationship. She tried to burn the house down not long ago. And she definitely knows how to use a gun.'

'Good,' Korznick said, his narrow face breaking into a smile. 'I've got to go with Rita and do some paperwork. Can you call me at the office later and fill me in? Or better yet, give me a typed report?'

'Sure,' I said, my eyes wandering toward Andre. 'Meanwhile, I want to talk to Rita's son.'

After Korznick, Vonette, and Rita had gone back to arrange the bond, Andre sank down onto one of the scarred oak benches. He sat with his arms thrown over the back of the bench, his eyes fixed on some invisible spot on the ceiling.

'Andre?' I said, sliding in beside him.

He looked at me briefly, then away again. 'You're the detective,' he said.

'David has me doing some research, to help in your mother's defense,' I said. 'I understand you were working last night?'

'All day yesterday and this morning until around four,' he said. 'I work part-time as a security guard at the Towne Pointe office complex over in Sandy Springs. That's why Vonette couldn't reach me. I'm not in any one place, you see, it's an eight-story building.'

'Can you tell me what happened after you talked to your mother yesterday?'

'I called Mama while she was at work yesterday, and she sounded all right. Tired, and embarrassed because she knew I knew she'd been drinking. Then I called again, around four thirty, after she got off work, to see how things were going. I guess she'd just gotten the papers. She was like a crazy person, fussing and cussing about Stu Hightower, what all she was going to do to him. I couldn't get her to calm down. As soon as I got off my day job at the warehouse I ran home to change my uniform and check on her. That's when I saw she'd been drinking.'

'Do you happen to know anything about the gun Rita was holding when we found her? A little chrome-plated twenty-two?'

He shook his head. 'I've got a deer rifle, but I keep it at a buddy's house.' He looked a little embarrassed. 'With Mama drinking, I don't like to take chances. But I never had a twenty-two, and if she had one, I never knew about it.'

'Does your mother know how to use a gun?'

He scratched at the thin shadow of stubble on his chin. 'Not that I know of, but then, there's a lot I'm finding out I don't know about her.'

'Did your mother ever mention Stuart Hightower before all this VelvetTeen business came up?'

'No,' he said quickly. 'She never wanted to talk about the old days. Even when Vonette started in telling old stories, Mama just clammed up.'

'I wonder why?'

'I've wondered too,' Andre admitted. 'She's had it hard all those years since. I guess . . . I don't know, maybe she didn't want to be reminded of how she was once on top.'

'That makes sense,' I said. 'Listen. She had a lot of booze in her system. How long had she been drinking like that? Did she pass out often? Was she ever violent before?'

His eyes fell to his hands. He fidgeted with a loose gold button on the cuff of his jacket. Leaned over to retie one of his tennis shoes.

'When I was a kid, Mama was never like that. I mean, never. We were poor, sure, but she made sure I kept straight, and everything in our life was straight. Things were a lot better when my step-daddy was around. But after he left . . .' A look of pain crossed Andre's face. 'Mama kept on working, but she'd call home and my butt had better be in that chair doing my homework. She wouldn't let me stay in the streets. No sir. Not Andre Strong. She'd whup my butt if I brought home a C on a report card.'

'When did the drinking start?'

He looked intensely unhappy. 'Probably when I was in the army. I was stationed in Germany for four years. She married and divorced this no-account dude while I was away. The first time I came home, things were different. The place was a mess. She was a mess. Slept late, and instead of fixin' dinner, she'd send me out for fried chicken or Chinese. It took a while for me to figure out what was going on.'

'So that's what, six or seven years?'

'About that. I was married in Germany, but it didn't work out. I moved back here two years ago, after Vonette wrote and told me what was going on with Mama.'

'Has she ever gotten violent?'

'What do you want me to say? This is my mother we're talking about.'

'I know,' I said, trying to sound soothing and coming up short. 'I'm on her side – remember?'

'It's not so bad when she's drinking beer. Usually she just gets sleepy and passes out. I just have to worry about her falling asleep with a lit cigarette. But when she drinks hard liquor, vodka or Scotch, I don't know. It's like she's looking for a fight. She gets moody. Mean. That's not the real Rita Fontaine. Two or three times she's come home after drinking with cuts and bruises. I think she might get in fights with her drinking buddies.'

Great, I thought. A client who gets hostile and combative when she drinks liquor.

'Do you know where she might have done her drinking last night?'

'Some of it she did at the house,' he said. 'I found an empty bottle. I should have known better to have booze in the house. But she probably went out for more.'

He paused. 'There's a house. I guess it's somebody's house, over near that nursing home, Beverly Vue, where she works. They sell liquor by the drink, but it's not a real bar.'

'A shot house,' I said, interrupting. They're a common sight in poor neighborhoods, illegal, unlicensed joints that sell booze, cigarettes, and frequently dope to a clientele that can't afford to drink anyplace else. They're easy to find; just look for a house with a yard full of cars and a Coke machine on the front porch.

'Whatever,' he said, shrugging. 'She called the place B.J.'s. I only know about it because one time, she got so drunk she flushed her car keys down the toilet and she called me to come carry her home.'

'You think that's where she was before she went to Hightower's?'

'Payday's not till next week,' Andre said. 'They let her run a tab at B.J.'s.'

'Okay,' I said, flipping my notebook shut. 'Oh yeah, while we're at it, you got any idea where your Aunt Delores might be?'

'I haven't seen Delores since I was a little kid,' he said, smiling softly. He had a nice smile, with full lips that turned up at the corners. 'I remember her, though. She used to give me lipstick kisses. That's what she called them. If I was crying or something, she'd kiss me on the cheek, then blot it with a piece of Kleenex. She'd give it

140

to me to keep, for when she was gone. She'd say if I was sad, I'd have her kisses in my pocket.'

I had the feeling Andre Strong spent a lot of time being sad.

He gave me directions to the shot house, and I gave him my business card. Then I went home, and he went off to put his mother in a detox unit.

The house was quiet and cool. I turned on the ceiling fan in my bedroom, peeled off my sweaty clothes and lay down on my high wooden bed wearing nothing but my underwear. A stack of pink phone messages fluttered in the breeze from the fan. Mac had called twice, and the other messages were from a couple of particularly pesky House Mouse clients who like to take up my time trying to switch cleaning days. I tossed all the messages in the trash.

It had been a long time since my biscuit and Diet Coke breakfast. I went into the kitchen to forage for lunch.

There was a slab of cold meat loaf on the top shelf. Edna had cooked dinner for someone last night. Probably Mac. She adores the man and cossets him like some overgrown gray poodle.

I found a new loaf of Wonder bread, laid an inch-thick slab of meat loaf on it and dumped some Johnny Harris barbecue sauce on top. It's the mustardy kind, piquant, not too sweet. I poured myself a glass of iced tea and sat down at the kitchen table with a yellow legal pad at hand.

Between chews and swallows, I made notes to myself. David Korznick wanted me to find out about Stu

Hightower's financial well-being. That might take some doing. As far as I knew, BackTalk records was a privately held company. I don't own a CD player – the last tape I bought was Aretha Franklin's greatest hits. What I know about rap music and contemporary rock and roll in general you could put in your hat.

Matt Gordon, I thought. Call Matt. It's hard to believe he's not still the same runny-nosed kid knocking at my door, wanting to mow the grass for five bucks. A neighbor kid, Matt was always organizing garage bands, scrounging hundred-dollar gigs at flea-bitten clubs around town.

But I'd seen his father, Doug, at a cookout not long ago, and he'd said Matt was out of college, working for a local record distributor and managing a couple of rock bands.

I called Doug, and he gave me his son's number. 'He's not there, though,' Doug warned. 'Bat Guano makes its Atlanta debut tonight at The Point. The show starts at eleven if you want to track him down. I'd advise earplugs too.'

It looked like another late night. I went back to the refrigerator. Edna had stashed a casserole of peach cobbler at the back of the shelf. I ate it standing with the refrigerator door open, with a spoon, right out of the dish.

When the phone rang, I shoved the dish back in one quick guilt-ridden movement.

'You still mad at me?'

'I have a right.'

'She's my daughter,' Mac said. 'Maybe I shouldn't

have rushed over there. Maybe she is a spoiled little brat. She's the only kid I've got, you know.'

And she's still yanking your chain, playing the pitiful kid from a broken home routine, I thought.

'I know,' I said. I was tired of fighting. 'You miss me?'

'You miss me?' he countered.

'I asked first.'

'Yeah,' he said. 'As a matter of fact I do.'

'You planning on leaving the office anytime soon?'

'I might. If it were urgent.'

'I'm home alone, and I'm already stripped down to my underwear. I'd call that urgent.'

'I get your point,' he said. 'See you in fifteen.'

14

What is it with this man, I wondered? We were wrapped in a tangle of linens, and I marveled at the contrast between his deeply tanned arms and the white of the sheets. As often as he moved me to rage and tears I never failed to fall for his charm and humor.

I pinched his ankle with my toes, a trick I'd learned as a kid.

'You awake?'

He kissed my neck in answer and began running his hands along my belly. I slapped his hand away lightly. 'Don't start what you can't finish, MacAuliffe.'

'Have I got a surprise for you, Garrity,' he said, nibbling at my ear.

'Save it,' I said, turning to face him. 'Edna will be home soon, and I've got to work tonight.'

He groaned, but sat up and looked at the clock on my bedside table. 'It's nearly six,' he said, sounding surprised. 'Where did the time go?'

'Remember that song from the seventies, "Afternoon Delight"?'

He grinned and shook his head. 'Not my decade, the

seventies. Or the eighties for that matter. While you were listening to what passed for rock and roll, I was listening to Merle Haggard and George Jones.'

'I don't remember much of the eighties myself,' I told him. 'I think of it as the decade that gave us Nancy Reagan and Donald Trump, my two least favorite people in the world.'

I got out of bed and shrugged into my robe. 'Dibs on the first shower. How about turning on the news? I want to see if they've got anything about Stu Hightower's murder.'

When I got out of the shower he'd made up the bed and was stretched out on top of the quilt, watching the weather report. 'You just missed an update on your client,' he said. 'Somebody dug up some old black-and-white footage of the VelvetTeens singing at the Royal Peacock, over on Auburn Avenue. Now I bet that's someplace you've never been.'

He was right about that. By the time I was a teenager, the Peacock, in the heart of Sweet Auburn, which is Atlanta's black business district, had long since closed. Instead we'd flocked to hear a bunch of disreputable kids from Macon called the Allman Joys at concert halls like the Great Southeast Music Hall. I still maintain that the Allman Brothers version of 'One Way Out' should be our state song. Ray Charles doing 'Georgia on My Mind' is okay, but what's wrong with having a state song that rocks?

'Did they have anything really new?' I asked, sitting down on the bed beside him to towel dry my hair.

'The gun they found in her hand is the same caliber as

the bullet they removed from Hightower's body,' he said.

'Figures,' I said glumly. 'Poor Rita can't get a break.' 'Did she do it?'

'She honestly doesn't remember,' I said. 'The woman was blind drunk. She was still passed out when we got to the house and didn't come to until all there was all the commotion of the police getting there.'

'I don't suppose there were any witnesses?' Mac asked.

'None that I know of,' I said. 'I did talk to neighbors who saw Hightower's ex-wife's car there earlier in the day. But nobody heard any gunshots because he had the music in the guest house turned up so loud.'

'Could anybody else have been at the house that night?'

'That's on my list of things to do,' I said. 'I want to see if those security guards at the subdivision gate keep a logbook of visitors. And it's a big house. So I think Hightower must have had help, like a maid or a yardman at the very least. I'll get David, Rita's lawyer, to make some phone calls, see if he can get the cops to cooperate.'

'Why wouldn't they?'

I smiled grimly. 'The detective in charge of the investigation, a jerk named Artie DiPima, and I go back.'

'But not in a good way.'

'Unfortunately, no.'

He took the towel from me and began massaging my scalp with it. 'What about your original assignment? Do they still want you to find Delores Eisner?'

'This murder thing has kind of sidetracked me,' I admitted. 'I did make some calls before you got here. I found a booking agency in Nashville that used to book Delores into small clubs, and they got her some local radio and television commercial work.'

'That's great,' Mac said. 'So she's in Nashville.'

'Well, maybe not. The last job they booked her was fourteen months ago. And the phone number they had for her has been disconnected. They'd put her name in their inactive files.'

'Still, you're closing the gap. Fourteen months ago she was in Tennessee. Chances are she's still around.'

'Maybe.' I wasn't optimistic. 'I talked to an ad agency that used her with two other singers for an ice cream jingle. The director gave me the names of the two other singers. I did reach one of the women.'

'And?'

'She didn't remember much. Just that Delores was real professional. Arrived on time, knew the lyrics and the music. Mary Frances Hanemayer, that's the singer's name. A real mouthful, huh? Anyway, Mary Frances said Delores looks good, real trim and petite. The only other thing she remembered was that as she was leaving the studio, Delores handed her a tract.'

'A tract?' He was puzzled.

'Like a religious pamphlet. You know, 'Get right with God,' that kind of thing.'

'Does she still have it?'

'She remembered sticking it in her pocketbook. I gave her my address. She promised to mail it to me if she found it.'

As I was talking, my robe slipped down off my shoulder, leaving my left breast bare. He traced the small white arc of scar tissue with his finger. 'Have you talked to Dr Kappler lately?'

I pulled the robe up and knotted the belt tighter. 'I called him the last time Edna clipped out one of those newspaper stories about the tamoxifen trials. She's driving me crazy on this, Mac. Just because one of the doctors in the study might have falsified or distorted his findings, she's convinced the whole thing was a big boondoggle.'

My mother and I find lots of things to bicker about – show me two women who live together who don't – but the biggest thing we fight about is my health.

Three years ago I had a small lump removed from my breast. Noninvasive ductal carcinoma was the technical term; cancer was what Edna was screeching about. She has a right to scream: her own mother died of breast cancer when Edna was a teenager; Edna had a mastectomy years ago.

When I read in the newspapers about an experimental drug being used for premenopausal women who were at high risk for breast cancer, I insisted my doctor enroll me in the drug trial. And the whole time I was taking the little pink pills, my mother was terrified I was poisoning myself.

'You did have some nasty side effects,' Mac reminded me.

'And it could have been the flu. Or something else. Dr Kappler admitted as much to me. Anyway, I quit taking the pills. And we don't know for sure that I wasn't taking some placebo in the first place. My latest blood work was fine. Everything was perfectly normal. My bilirubin levels are absolutely prize winning. I'm coming up on the three-year mark now. Even Kappler, that old sourpuss, is pleased. So why can't Edna lay off?'

'She loves you,' he said. 'Me too.'

'Well, you're both pains in the ass sometimes,' I said.

We were watching *Jeopardy* on the television in the den when Edna came dragging home.

She was wearing a wrinkled and smudged pink House Mouse smock, carrying one of our caddies full of cleaning supplies. She put the caddie in the kitchen, stripped off the smock and sank down into one of the easy chairs.

'I'm whipped,' she said. 'Agnes's sister-in-law just had back surgery, and as a favor to Agnes, I said I'd touch the place up before Faye got home from the hospital. Agnes never mentioned the place is two stories, four bedrooms and two bathrooms. Plus it's packed to the rafters with stuff. I never saw so many gee-gaws and what-nots in my life.'

She slipped off her shoes and closed her eyes. 'Are you two up to fixing dinner for us? I can't move another step.'

After some rummaging around in the kitchen cabinets, we settled on a menu of spaghetti à la bottled Prego sauce, a tossed salad and garlic bread made on what was actually Wonder bread.

We ate dinner in front of the television, watching CNN's coverage of the Stu Hightower murder. They'd put together a hokey segment called 'The Day the Music

Stopped,' featuring the life and times of celebrated record industry giant Stu Hightower. There was more of the grainy black-and-white footage of the VelvetTeens that Mac had seen, paparazzi shots of Hightower's lavish show biz marriage to Serena, and then new film showing Rita and Vonette leaving the courthouse, with Rita trying to hide her face in David Korznick's sports coat.

The phone rang seconds after the segment ended. It was Korznick.

'You watching the news?'

'It doesn't look good, does it?' I asked. 'If you go to trial, will it hurt Rita's chances of getting a decent jury?'

'It's way too early to tell,' Korznick said. 'I'm monitoring the news, taping everything. But listen, I talked to Rita this afternoon. Her recollection of what happened at Hightower's house is shaky at best.'

'Did you ask her about that back door being open?'

'I did,' he said. 'And she insists it was locked. And you know, I tend to believe her. If it had been open, as drunk as she was, she probably would have gone in and trashed the place.'

'Did she see any cars there?'

'She says the garage doors were closed.'

'They were closed when we got there too,' I said. 'Although I wonder if Serena would have kept her automatic garage door opener.'

'That's something we'll want to find out,' Korznick said. 'And do we know where Serena was last night?'

'The cops were talking to her today when I was out there. They took her inside the house to look around.'

I heard scratching noises on the other side of the phone. 'I'm adding her to my list,' Korznick said. 'Call me tomorrow to tell me what you've learned. And I'll want you to get together with Rita, so we can brainstorm on some other possibilities.'

Edna had been eavesdropping on my end of the conversation. She had suddenly regained some energy.

'You got anything you need me to do?' she asked hopefully.

I thought about it. It was useless to try to keep her out of my cases. If I didn't give her a specific assignment, she'd come up with something on her own.

'Actually, you could do some courthouse research for me,' I said. 'I need you to go downtown to the Fulton County courthouse and look up the records of Serena and Hightower's divorce.'

Edna whipped a pad of paper off the table at her elbow and started writing. 'She got a last name, this Serena person?'

'She's a pop star, Ma,' I said. 'Like Madonna or Cher.'

'Or Elvis,' Mac put in.

'Make sure you get the name of Hightower's divorce lawyer too,' I said. 'I want to know what he thinks about Stu's relationship with his ex.'

'Anything else?'

'That should take care of it. I'll have to go poke around BackTalk myself. Which reminds me. I'd better get going if I'm going to check out Rita's favorite gin mill before I meet Matt Gordon.'

Mac got up to leave. 'Want to go with me?' I asked. It wasn't that I was afraid to go to the shot house by myself, it was just that I thought I might feel more comfortable if there was at least one other white face in the joint.

He got a funny look on his face. 'Can't,' he said. 'I've got to get up early in the morning to run over to Birmingham. I promised Stephanie I'd take a look at an apartment she's interested in.'

'For whom?'

'I knew you'd react like this,' Mac said. 'That's why I didn't mention it earlier. It's for Steph. I told her if she could find a safe, inexpensive apartment for the summer, I'd pay the rent. Just until she starts back to school in the fall. She and Barb really need a break from each other.'

'And you're going to pay the rent?'

He nodded.

'On top of the child support and alimony you already shell out to Barbara?'

He pursed his lips together and nodded.

I threw my hands up in defeat. 'You're right. It's none of my business. She's your daughter. It's your money. Do what you want.'

Edna glanced nervously at me and then at Mac. She started to say something, but I glared at her, so she thought better of it.

I turned on my heel, stalked back to my bedroom, got my nine-millimeter pistol, checked the chamber, checked the safety, and gingerly set it in the bottom of my purse. When I go out at night now, to a part of town I'm not familiar with, I take my gun. I don't like it, but Atlanta has changed. This ain't Mayberry no more.

When I got back to the kitchen, Mac was gone. I heard his car start up, then back out of the driveway.

We were right back where we'd started. 'Shit,' I muttered.

A light drizzle began to fall before I reached Rita's watering hole. I'd been driving fast, my speed fueled by anger and frustration, but it was approaching dark, and the asphalt was slick and treacherous looking, so I slowed down. At the same time I forced myself to examine my reaction to what had happened at home.

Why was I so irked about Mac's attention to Stephanie? She was his daughter after all. Something about the whole business bugged the hell out of me. Was it the fact that he'd gotten on civil terms with Barbara? Mac rarely talked about her, or their marriage. I knew they'd been high school sweethearts, married as soon as Mac got back from Vietnam. The marriage fizzled in the late seventies, he said, when Stephanie was just a toddler. Barbara had taken their daughter and moved back to Birmingham, where she had family.

I'd never met Mac's ex-wife, never even seen a picture of her. Suddenly, I was dying to know what Barbara McAuliffe was like. She was petite, I'd bet. Something I definitely am not. I'd met Stephanie, of course. She had strawberry blond hair that fell softly to her shoulders, big blue eyes, and a stubborn chin that reminded me of her father's. The smile was shy, tenuous. She rarely talked when she was around me. Did she get that from Barbara, along with the red hair?

'Damn.' I was doing a lot of swearing tonight. I'd missed the turn at the traffic light. The Beverly Vue nursing home where Rita worked was on the southside of Atlanta, not far from Southlake Mall. Her favorite drinking establishment was four or five miles away. At the next intersection I turned around and doubled back. I made a right, went a couple of miles and turned again. Whitehead Boulevard had been the main drag of a solid working neighborhood a long time ago. But the old storefronts had seen better days. Now the shopping centers were home to check-cashing operations, video arcades, coin laundries, and storefront churches.

I leaned forward to see the street signs better through the rain. I made a left at Landry Drive. For the first couple of blocks the houses looked tidy and cared for. Small, but decent, with postage-stamp-sized yards with flowers and cars lined up neatly in driveways, lights flickering behind curtained front windows.

Then the niceness ran out with a surprising abruptness. Now the houses looked tired, shrunk into mud-caked grassless yards littered with broken-down lawn furniture, beer bottles and fast-food wrappers. Doors with busted out screens hung half-open on their hinges and junk cars crowded each other at the curbs. I slowed down as I approached the house Andre had described.

Eight sixty-eight Landry stood out from its neighbors because it had a narrow wooden porch tacked onto its façade. The floor looked buckled and the roof sagged. There was a Coke machine on the porch and the front door stood slightly ajar, letting the sounds of loud music drift out to the street.

155

My stomach knotted as I parked the van and looked around. I felt like the stranger in one of those old Western movies we kids used to watch on Saturday morning. I could see those saloon doors parting, the stranger hesitantly stepping inside, where conversation abruptly halts, and all eyes are focused on the intruder.

I swallowed hard, took a deep breath and walked up the front steps. An old man leaned against the weathered boards of the house. He was bare chested, and his flesh fell in blue-black slabs and hung down over the waistband of time-worn tan work pants. He sipped from a long-neck beer bottle, looked at me with rheumy, red-rimmed eyes, then looked away again.

I pushed open the door of the house. The air was hot and thick: a mixture of stale beer; rancid grease; and the sweet, pungent tang of marijuana.

In the dim half-light, I saw that what had once been a living room had been transferred into a makeshift cocktail bar. Half a dozen people lounged on old sofas pushed against the walls. Beer bottles and cigarette butts littered the scattered tabletops, and the only real light in the room came from the glowing dials of an elaborate stereo CD player and from a wall-mounted color television set. A box fan whirred ineffectively in a window.

I felt the stares, but the loud conversation hushed for only a moment before an ongoing argument about the merits of the National League versus the American League was resumed.

A thin woman wearing hip-hugger shorts and a

halter top that showed a skeletal set of ribs sauntered up to me, her rubber thongs making soft slapping noises on the bare wooden floor. Her hair was reddish and piled on top of her head, and she wore eyeglasses with the thickest lenses I had ever seen.

'Get you something?' It was more of a challenge than a question.

'Uh, yeah,' I said. 'What kind of beer do you have?'

'You didn't come in here for no beer,' she said flatly.

'Are you the manager?' I asked.

'As far as you're concerned,' she said. A long thin scar ran down the right side of her face, puckering the skin of her upper lip, so that she wore a perpetual half-sneer.

'Then I'd like a beer. Lite if you've got it.'

She shrugged, walked into the other room and came back with a cold can of Bud Lite.

'In here,' she said, jerking her thumb toward a small room that opened off the lounge.

It was apparently a dining room, furnished with a cheap round oak table and some aluminum and plastic kitchen chairs. A small gray kitten had stretched itself out on the table, but she swept it off, and the cat disappeared into the smoke of the other room. 'You with the county?' she wanted to know.

'No,' I said quickly. 'And I'm not a cop either.'

'What you want in here then?' She tilted her chair on its back legs and gave me a critical stare.

'I'm a private detective,' I said. 'I'm trying to find out if one of your regular customers, Rita Fontaine, was in here Monday night.'

'Did she say she was in here?' She held onto the table

with her hands and rocked the chair back and forth. 'Is Rita in some kind of trouble?'

'So she is a regular?'

'She comes around.'

'Did she come around last night, like after she got off work?'

'What kind of trouble?' the woman persisted.

I knew I'd get no answers to my questions until I answered hers.

'She's been arrested. Charged with murdering a man. I've been hired by her attorney to find out where she went and what she did that night. Now can you help me or not?'

The woman set the chair down, raised herself off the chair and retrieved a pack of cigarettes from her hip pocket. She lit one, inhaled and then exhaled, letting the smoke out slowly.

'Who'd they say she killed?'

'A man she used to work for,' I said, struggling to stay patient. 'The name was Stuart Hightower. Was Rita here last night?'

'I heard about that on the news,' she said. 'Didn't say it was old Rita. Maybe I was falling asleep when it came on.'

Her eyes were expressionless behind the thick lenses. 'Yeah. Rita come in last night. Got here around six-thirty or seven. I didn't see what time she left.'

'Did you talk to her?'

'Rita wasn't in a talkin' mood. She was about half-lit when she got here. I brought her three or four beers myself. She was talking to herself mostly. Saying how she wouldn't put up with something, how this was her big chance, all that kind of mess. Liquor talk. The more she drank, the louder she got. She was talking about getting even. 'I'll get his ass,' she told me. 'I'll kill him.'

'Did she have a gun?' I asked anxiously. 'Have you ever seen her with a gun?'

The woman shook her head vigorously. 'House rules say no guns. Rita knew that. She don't have no gun. She spend all her spare money on drinking. I never seen her with a gun.'

Which didn't mean Rita wasn't smart enough to keep that cute little .22 tucked in her purse. It was small enough. 'Did Rita say who she was mad at?'

She raised her chin and let her eyes concentrate on the ceiling. 'Stu-Baby she called him. She said she's gonna go out to his house and take care of his ass.'

I opened my purse, fished out a five dollar bill and handed it to her to pay for the beer and the conversation. 'You sure you don't know what time Rita left? It's kind of important.'

She put her hand over the bill and smiled slyly, showing a gold-capped front tooth. 'What time you want me to say she left?'

I shook my head. 'I don't want you to lie. Just tell me the truth, what time did she leave, really?'

'Well.' She thought about it some more. '*Sanford and Son* was coming on the TV. I don't miss that. Not for nothing. We were laughing at something on that show. Rita, she slammed down some money and marched on out of here. Say eight. That'd be close.'

It was at least forty miles to Hightower's house from

this no-name bar. But Rita could have driven there, gotten in, killed Hightower, and drunk herself to sleep easily before we arrived on the scene.

'Okay,' I said. 'Thanks.'

I got out my notebook and pen and made some quick notes. 'What did you say your name was?'

'Does this mean the cops will be comin' around, messing with me?'

'I'm not gonna be the one to send them.'

'Shit.' She stubbed out her cigarette. 'Mattie. Mattie Green. I just run the place. I don't own it. The cops shut me down, that's Mr Joe's problem, not mine.'

'Hey Mattie?'

'What?'

'How often did Rita come in here?'

'Once a week, sometimes more. Usually around payday, when she had some cash money.'

'What was she like, when she was drinking here?'

'What do you mean? I ain't her best friend or nothing like that. She drank. She'd come in, have a few beers, kept to herself mostly. All she ever told me was that her son lived with her, and he didn't like her to be drinking. Sometimes she'd ask me for gum or mints, so he wouldn't smell it on her.'

'She ever get violent?'

'Rita? Well now, a couple times, she might have met a man here, drank some vodka or something. Come to think of it, she did act out a couple times. One time, we had to call her son, have him come get her. I forget why.'

I handed Mattie Green one of my business cards, and asked her to call if she remembered anything else.

160

I was almost out the door when I heard her call my name.

'Callahan?'

I turned around.

'Rita, she's all right. You ask me, if she did do it, the dude probably needed killing.'

15

It was my night for smoky bars. Matt's band, Bat
Guano, had attracted an overflow crowd to The Point.
At least I assumed Bat Guano was the draw, because I
couldn't actually see the stage. I pushed my way
through the teeming, throbbing crowd of twenty-some-
things. They were thrashing and gyrating to some
heavy-metal favorite, which meant I kept getting
elbowed and kneed. I finally made it to the bar.

Matt Gordon had his back to the bar, arms crossed, a
look of rapt concentration on his face. His dad was right,
the kid had grown up. His blond hair reached past his
shoulder, and he had a gold earring and a tattoo of a
possum on his forearm. The nineties version of the All-
American kid.

He didn't notice me until I touched his elbow. 'Matt?' I
had to shout to make myself heard.

The smile was the same as that lawn boy's of long ago.
'Hey, Miss Garrity,' he said, grinning wide.

I gave him a quick hug. 'None of that Miss Garrity
shit. It's Callahan. Are we gonna be able to talk in here?'

'Probably not,' he said. 'Wanna go someplace else?'

'Can you leave?'

'Yeah, they're smokin' tonight,' Matt said. 'I'll be back for the second set, and they won't even notice I'm gone.'

We fought our way back to the door. The drizzle had stopped and now the humidity outside was about 2000 percent. Still, the air here was cooler and fresher than it had been in The Point.

I pointed down the block to my own favorite hangout, The Euclid Avenue Yacht Club. 'How 'bout the yacht club?' I asked.

We caught up on each other's lives during the short walk.

Tinkles met us inside the door. 'Garrity,' he said, giving Matt an openly suspicious stare. 'Where'd you pick up the jail bait?'

'He's a family friend and he's twenty-two, all proper and legal,' I said. We headed for a table in the corner, and Tinkles was back a few moments later with a Jack Daniel's and water for me.

'We don't got no Happy Meals,' he said pointedly.

'Rolling Rock,' Matt said, ignoring the jibe.

When Tinkles was gone, I told Matt what I needed. He excused himself, went to the phone booth near the men's room at the back of the bar and stayed nearly fifteen minutes. While he was gone I watched the highlights of the night's Braves game.

'Okay,' he said, sliding into his chair. He took a long drink of the beer Tinkles had left. 'The buzz is that Stu Hightower might have had BackTalk on the block. A couple of big corporate labels were supposedly very interested, including AKA.'

'Really? I didn't know BackTalk was such a big deal.'

'Oh yeah,' Matt said. 'BackTalk's been a real hit maker. Supposedly it's one of the best indy labels around. It's small, well run, with a good stable of writers, producers and artists. And Stu really knew rock. He could smell a trend a mile away. Take Junebug, that new act of his. The kid's first single went gold before he could take his driver's test. And the new one, "Dis Diss," I hear is gonna be mega mega.'

'So if Hightower sold BackTalk he'd make millions,' I said. 'He could sit back and enjoy spending all that cash. I wonder who might have been pissed off about this merger deal.'

Matt's eyes widened a little. 'Well, Serena. That's a no-brainer. After they split up, she still had two albums left in a three-album deal. I heard she cut one, but Hightower just left it on the shelf. He told her it was a dog, and he wasn't contractually obligated to release it.'

'Was it?'

He shrugged. 'If you like dance-pop, I guess her stuff is okay. I do know that she had the same writers and the same producer as she had with her first album, the one that went platinum.'

'That's interesting, but I already have Serena down as a prime candidate. Can you think of anybody else who might have had it in for Stu-Baby?'

'I hear old Stu was quite the swordsman,' Matt said.

I guess I looked shocked.

'Come on, Callahan,' he said. 'I'm twenty-two. Remember? I lost my cherry a long time ago. I'm just saying Hightower had a rep, that's all.'

'Which was?'

He blushed a tiny bit. 'I heard he'd screw anything with two legs. There's a girl in a group I know, she cut a demo for Hightower. When the guys were packing up to leave, he asked her to stay behind, said he wanted her to play a chord again. So, of course, once he gets her alone, he tries to jump her bones.'

'And she went along with it?'

He gave me an indulgent look. 'We're talking about Stu Hightower here. Somebody like him makes or breaks your career. Yeah, she went along with it. Not too many chicks I know wouldn't. Hell, not too many guys would refuse him.'

So the casting couch was alive and well. Why wasn't I surprised?

'Who'd be affected if somebody like AKA took over BackTalk?' I asked.

He chewed on his thumbnail while he thought about it.

'Well, if a big label like them came in, they could decide to drop some of Stu's more marginal acts.'

'Like who?'

'You ever hear of the Joanses?'

'Should I?'

'Probably not,' he said. 'Unless you listen to the college stations, you know, WRAS and WREK.'

I shook my head no.

'They're two black chicks. Pretty decent talent, but they've had two CDs and I don't think they did too hot. Jonette, the girl who sings lead, is gay, but now, I heard a rumor that old Stu was doin' the wild thing with Rikki. And Rikki, man, that is one tough chick. If she found out that BackTalk was gonna dump the Joanses, she would cut his ass up.'

I was jotting notes down as fast as I could while he talked. 'Have you ever heard of any funny business at BackTalk?'

'Like what?'

'I don't know,' I admitted. 'Anything at all. Fraud. Cooking the books. Or don't you generation Xers know anything about white-collar crime?

He pushed his hair back from his eyebrows.

'Oh yeah,' he said. 'We got whole new ways to fuck the system. But it's people like Stu Hightower who invented the wheel.'

'Give me a for instance.'

A smile flitted about his face. 'You probably heard about payola? Wasn't there like some big deal about that back in the sixties?'

'Yeah,' I said. 'Back in the dark ages. You're telling me it still goes on?'

'Absolutely,' he said. 'Just about every label I know of has a stash of goodies to hand out to radio stations to make sure their new releases get heavy rotation.'

'Are we talking cash?'

'Cash, drugs, sex, concert tickets, athletic shoes, plane tickets. Every kind of freebie you can think of. There's supposedly a set price at some stations; you make a little present to the program director or the DJ on a hot drive-time show.'

'You're kidding.'

Matt looked immensely pleased that he knew something of value to me.

'Would BackTalk have paid off radio stations?'

'Why not? I told you. Everybody does it.'

He'd given me something new to think about. If Stu Hightower had access to a large stash of cash and drugs, maybe robbery could have been the motive for his murder.

'So how much does it cost to get a release on a radio playlist?'

'I'm not sure,' he admitted. 'The bands I represent are so small, it's a big deal if we take a program director out to dinner. I do know that it depends on the market. It'd cost more in LA or Miami or New York than it would in Atlanta.'

'Well what are we talking? Five thousand? Ten thousand?'

'Could be. Remember, for an important release, a label might need to get airplay in ten or twelve markets. If you buy off two stations in each market, that's twenty-four stations, and if it's only five thousand, well that's still one hundred and twenty thousand dollars. In cash, mind you.'

'Jesus,' I said.

'And you wonder why CDs cost sixteen ninety-nine. But hey, if a label budgets half a million in promo money for a new album, that's just a drop in the budget, and unlike with advertising, you get guaranteed play with cash under the table. It's a good deal for everybody.'

'But you don't know for a fact that Hightower was involved in payola – right?'

He glanced furtively around the room, to see if anyone

close was listening. 'Actually, I do. My friend that I just called? He had a grunt job at BackTalk last summer. You know, making coffee, typing, sending and delivering faxes around the office. One of his jobs was to pick up Stu's outgoing mail two or three times a day. He barged into Hightower's office without knocking one day, and caught Hightower handing a wad to Gary Armstrong, the program director at Monster 104.'

I'd seen the Monster 104 party wagon around town, with loudspeakers mounted on the roof, blaring raucous music into oncoming traffic.

'BackTalk needs Monster 104,' Matt explained. 'It's the number one urban contemporary station in Atlanta, in the South, for that matter. But you probably listen to Peach, right?'

'Gimme a break you little twerp,' I growled. 'I'm not all that old.'

'Right. But I'll bet you listen to oldies.'

He had me there. I listen to Fox 97 and sing really loud to Gary Puckett and the Union Gap.

'Your friend saw the money?'

'A big wad of hundreds,' Matt said smugly. 'After that, he made a point of watching Hightower's visitors. Apparently, Fridays were candy days. Lots of local radio types paraded through his office; and they always left with a big smile on their faces and a bulge in their pockets.'

I took a long sip of my drink. What Matt said was fascinating, but it didn't necessarily prove that Hightower was involved in payola. After all, this was really just secondhand gossip. Potent, but not toxic.

'You have any idea who'll take over the management of BackTalk now?' I asked.

'Lemme think,' he said. 'I can see the woman's face. She's black, from New Orleans, pretty, maybe older than you, but a really sharp dresser for someone her age. Danielle. Yeah. Danielle something. She's head of A and R. That's "artists and repertoire." Yeah. Danielle Manigault. She's been with Hightower for years, started with him when he had his first record company.'

'You mean SkyHi,' I said. 'She must be ancient. So, do you think this Danielle person will really be running the company?'

'That's the buzz,' he said. 'There's all kinds of vice presidents and shit like that, but my friend said Danielle Manigault was the power behind the power.'

'Okay,' I said wearily, closing my notepad. 'You've been great, Matt. I really appreciate all the help. Would you be insulted if I left money to buy you dinner? I'd stay and eat with you, but it's way past my bedtime, and I've got work to do tomorrow.'

'No way,' he said. 'You don't need to do that. I'm working, Callahan. I can buy my own dinner.'

I dropped a kiss on the top of his head and a twenty on the table. 'I know you can, Matt. Humor the old girl. Okay?'

16

'Y'all know what tomorrow is?'

It was Wednesday morning and Neva Jean was standing in front of the calendar, drawing pink hearts and flowers and arrows and exclamation marks on one particular day of the week.

'Sweet potato appreciation day?' I asked.

Jackie gave me an exaggerated wink. 'Pest control week?'

'You're both wrong,' said Ruby, trying to stifle a giggle. 'It's the twentieth anniversary of my varicose vein surgery.'

'Aw now, cut it out,' Neva Jean whined. 'It's my birthday and you know it.'

'Your birthday?' I said, trying to act shocked. 'Already?'

'And I know just what I want Swannelle to get me,' Neva Jean said excitedly.

She pulled a Polaroid photograph out of her smock pocket and laid it on the table in front of me.

The image was blurry, but it looked like somebody's television set.

'I thought Swannelle got that big-screen TV for

himself for your anniversary last year,' I said. 'What do you need another television set for?'

She leaned over my shoulder and thumped the photo with her fingernail.

'No, silly, it's not the television, it's what's on the television.'

I looked again, but for the life of me it looked like she'd taken a photo of a test pattern.

'What is it?'

She picked up the photo and passed it to Ruby and Jackie.

'Just the most beautiful two-carat cubic zirconia tennis bracelet you've ever seen, that's all. I know y'all don't watch Home Shopping Network, so I took this picture so you can get a look at it.'

I squinted, then tilted my head to get a better perspective on the thing. 'Is that somebody's hand or a map of Sardinia?'

She snatched the photo away from me and put it in her pocket.

'Quit teasing,' she said. 'I want that bracelet so bad I can taste it. Swannelle's bowling tournament banquet is next month. We're sitting at the head table because Swannelle's president pro-tem of the league. I've got me a red satin dress and matching red satin elbow-length gloves on layaway at Betty's Bridal Boutique. That bracelet was made for my ensemble.'

'How much?' Jackie asked.

She fluttered her eyelashes a little. 'Not that much. Not as much as the camouflage hunting outfit I got him for his birthday. And anyway, last year he didn't give me a birthday present at all cause I'd kicked him out of the house the week before. I think he deliberately provoked me into doing it so he'd get out of giving me a present and going to mama's for my birthday dinner.'

Ruby patted Neva Jean's hand gently. 'I think it's a beautiful bracelet. I'm gonna add you and your birthday wish to my prayer list.'

She looked suddenly concerned. 'I wonder if Pastor Carmichael would think a diamond bracelet is too worldly a concern for a prayer list?'

'It ain't real diamonds,' Neva Jean assured her.

'That's right,' Ruby said, shaking her head in agreement. 'I'll start prayin' over it tonight.'

'Have you told Swannelle what you want?' I asked. Neva Jean's husband has never been one to shower her with extravagant gifts. One year, for Christmas, he gave her a new set of mudflaps for his truck. 'So all your friends'll know what a good provider I am,' he'd explained.

'Oh, I got that all taken care of,' Neva Jean said. 'I went to the Radio Shack and got me a new remote control. Every time a commercial comes on ESPN or The Nashville Network, I switch real quick to Home Shopping Network, and then I make over how beautiful that bracelet is and how much I'd love to have one.'

'That does sound like a good plan,' I admitted. 'Especially that spare remote control. I need to get one of those to keep around here, for when Edna's watching those gawdawful unsolved crime shows of hers.'

The back door opened then, and Edna herself stepped inside.

'Did I hear my name being taken in vain?' she asked.

'No more than usual,' I said. 'Neva Jean's been dropping big hints to get Swannelle to buy her this cubic zirconia tennis bracelet for her birthday.'

'Good luck with that,' Edna said. 'Getting Swannelle McComb to take a hint is like getting a hog to use a fork. Don't go getting your hopes up, Neva Jean.'

Neva Jean's face clouded over.

'What did you find out at the courthouse?' I asked, changing the subject.

She pulled a small blue spiral-bound notebook from her purse, and sat down beside me at the kitchen table. 'Is there any coffee left?'

I got up and fixed her a cup. 'Give,' I said.

Edna looked meaningfully at the girls. 'Aren't y'all supposed to be at work?'

Neva Jean knew better than to argue with Edna. Even though I'm supposedly the boss, nobody fights with Edna Mae Garrity. She picked up her pocketbook and a cleaning caddy from the counter.

'Come on girls,' she said, 'I got my car this morning. I'll drop y'all off.'

Once the girls had departed, Edna lit a cigarette and took a deep drag, then another. 'They got no smoking signs all over that courthouse,' she said. 'They got some nerve telling taxpayers what they can and can't do. I'm calling my county commissioner and give him an earful. Just as soon as I smoke a couple packs and get my nerves calmed down.

'Come on, Edna,' I begged. 'Quit keeping me in suspense.'

'All right,' she said. She put her cigarette in the ashtray and put on her bifocals. Then she leafed through the notebook till she got to the right page.

'I hate to disappoint you,' she started, 'But Stu Hightower settled the divorce out of court and had the records sealed.'

'Damn,' I said. 'You were sure gone a long time to come back with so little.'

'Not so fast,' she said. 'The records for the divorce itself were sealed. But I did see Serena's original documents. She was asking for a bundle. Half the equity in the Riverbend house, the deed to the condo in LA which the court papers say was worth four hundred thousand, the red Mercedes, assorted pieces of jewelry which he'd given her as gifts, including a pair of four-carat diamond earrings with pear-shaped dangle – stones worth seventy-five thousand – a tennis bracelet with thirty-five stones totaling five carats worth ten thousand, and a flawless five-carat diamond engagement ring worth one hundred thousand.'

'Yow,' I said. 'Old Stu was right generous with the baubles.'

'There's more,' she said, looking up from her notes. 'She wanted furnishings and antiques from the big house: china, crystal, silver, stuff like that. Then she wanted stock in BackTalk Records, too. A quarter interest share, to be exact. The court papers claim she was instrumental in helping build the business and in getting influential writers and producers to sign with the label.'

'Damn,' I said. 'I'm surprised Stu didn't try to

knock off Serena, instead of the other way around.'

'Well, there's no way of knowing whether she got what she was asking for,' Edna pointed out.

'Anything juicy in those papers?' I asked.

'The usual charges of adultery,' Edna said. 'She named names too. Ever hear of someone named Rikki Banks?'

'Funny you should ask,' I said. 'Rikki is part of an act that records on BackTalk. And I hear she's a tough little cookie, too.'

'Serena also charged that Hightower had defrauded her of profits she should have made from her last album by not promoting and properly distributing it,' Edna said. 'And she claims that Hightower ripped her off again by persuading her to use an agent who actually worked for the label's interests and not hers. His divorce attorney was Scott Streethaus. Hers is Celestine Little.'

'Anything else?' I asked.

'Well, I did manage to strike up a conversation with one of those cute little clerks they have working down there,' she said. 'She's going to be calling about getting us to clean her condo. I quoted her sixty dollars, since she was so talkative and all.'

I sighed. Edna can't get over the habit of giving away our services at bargain prices to people she runs across.

'Anyway,' Edna continued, 'I told this girl, her name's Miranda, what I was looking for, and of course, she knew every record Serena had ever cut, and she knew all about BackTalk too. She suggested I check the defendant and plaintiff dockets for more dirt on Hightower.'

'Great idea,' I said. 'What'd you find?'

She took her bifocals off and wiped them on the hem of her blouse. 'Good stuff. Stu Hightower sued people right and left. There were four or five suits against contractors and suppliers who'd done work or sold him stuff for the house. Not an easy man to work for, the late Mr Hightower. He also filed a lawsuit against someone named Jack Rabin, charging him with assault and battery. But Rabin countersued and charged Hightower with defamation of character and conspiracy to harm.'

'Jacky Rabbit,' I said. 'That's his real name. He used to be a disc jockey here in town. I talked to him hoping he might have a lead on where to look for Delores. No wonder he had such nasty things to say about Hightower. He never mentioned a word about any of this when I talked to him. I wonder how Hightower was defaming him. Was the suit ever settled?'

'Not that I could find,' Edna said. 'And then there was one more lawsuit against Hightower too, filed by a plastic surgeon named Lyman Woodall.'

'What? Did Hightower stiff the guy for his face-lift fees?'

'I don't know how it started, but by the looks of the suit, Dr Woodall and Stu Hightower had a long-simmering feud. Woodall filed suit against Hightower claiming that his swimming pool was a criminal nuisance because Woodall's pedigree show Pekinese wandered over to Hightower's, somehow fell in the pool and drowned.'

'Just like that? How odd.'

'Dr Woodall apparently thought so too,' Edna said. 'The words *suspicious death* popped up in the lawsuit.'

I reached over and got her notebook, and tore out a blank page. I wrote Lyman Woodall's name on it. If the doctor was having a feud with Hightower, chances were good he might want to talk to me.

Then we both got busy working on the company books. Edna had gotten on an organizational kick and was insisting we get the account books unsnarled. For once, she was right. The books were a mess, with receipts stuck haphazardly in the back, and all kinds of unintelligible postings made my me. We finally stopped working on the files for a late lunch at three o'clock.

At three thirty, just as we were finishing our tuna salad on whole wheat with home-grown tomatoes, C. W. Hunsecker knocked on the back door.

The screen door was unlatched, so I waved him in. 'Want a sandwich?' I asked, offering him half of mine.

It must have been ninety degrees out, but C.W. had on a dark brown suit, starched dress shirt, and tightly knotted silk tie. The annoying thing was that he didn't seem miserable in that stifling getup.

'Nothing for me,' he said, sitting down at the table. 'But I will take a glass of that iced tea if there's any left.'

Edna poured the tea, and we chatted for a bit about sports and the weather and the charade we call city hall politics in Atlanta.

Finally, I could stand it no more. 'Come on, Hunsecker,' I said. 'You didn't come over here in the middle of a workday for a tea party with the Garrity girls. What's the deal?'

Now he started to look uncomfortable. 'You got to get out of this Hightower business, Callahan. Vonette hired you to find her cousin, not mess in a murder investigation.'

'What?' I asked, incredulous. 'Goddammnit, C.W., you're the one that dragged me into this thing in the first place. I never wanted anything to do with Vonette or Rita Fontaine. I only took the case as a favor to you. Now you tell me to back off? No effin' way, Hunsecker. I'm not some faucet you turn off and on.'

He rubbed his long elegant fingers over his dark face, which was now gleaming with perspiration. There were fatigue lines around his eyes, and a sag to his shoulders I hadn't noticed before.

'Artie DiPima got on you about me, didn't he?'

'Who's that?' Edna wanted to know.

'He's the detective in charge of the Stuart Hightower homicide investigation,' C.W. said. 'He's a solid investigator.'

'He's an arrogant asshole and he hates my guts,' I put in.

'Don't you see the position this puts me in?' C.W. said angrily. 'My ex-wife's cousin is found at the scene of a high-profile homicide, and the victim is someone she assaulted and threatened to kill only hours earlier. She's found holding the possible murder weapon. And my ex and my daughter are also found at the scene. How do you think that makes me look around the department?'

'Has anybody suggested Vonette or Kenyatta had any involvement in the murder?' I demanded. 'Has anybody suggested that you acted improperly? Or that I've acted improperly?'

He shook his head in exasperation. 'You all were trespassing on private property out there, Garrity. DiPima could have nailed all of you, if he'd wanted to. Man, I never should have told Vonette to call you.'

'Well you did,' I said calmly, folding my arms across my chest. 'Vonette hired me, she's paying me with her own money, and there's not a damn thing you can do about it. So you can tell Artie DiPima he can kiss my ass.'

He shoved back his chair, scraping wood against the linoleum. 'I knew you'd react like this. Thanks for the tea, Edna.'

Then he moved over to where I was still sitting. He stood in back of me and clamped his hands down on my shoulders. 'You keep Kenyatta out of this, Garrity. I got no control over what Vonette does, you're right about that. But Kenyatta is my baby. I don't want her riding around town with you, poking into stuff that don't concern her. I don't want to see her in any courtroom, or on the six o'clock news, and I don't want her messin' in any of this. You got that?'

His fingers dug into my shoulders. I shook out of his grip.

'She's a grown-up, C.W. She can do as she pleases, and there's nothing you can do to stop her. Besides, she's not involved. I'm investigating, not her.'

'Better not be,' he growled.

Unexpectedly, he patted the same shoulder he'd been gripping like a vise. 'She's my baby, Garrity. I don't want her hurt.'

I looked up and patted my friend's hand. Sometimes, when we butted heads like this, it was hard to remember that he is my friend.

'We'll leave Kenyatta at home, C.W. I swear. Anyway, I know it looks bad for Rita, but Stu Hightower had lots of enemies. Rita's a drunk, and a mean one at that, but I don't think she shot Hightower.'

'You never think your clients are guilty,' he said.

'Usually they're not,' I shot back.

'You gonna be able to persuade Artie DiPima of that?'

'Look,' I said. 'Hightower's ex-wife, the disco chick? She had several violent blowouts with Stu. I talked to a neighbor who said she tried to burn the house down with him in it. He apparently screwed her on her record deal, and now he's got some deal cooking to sell the label to a corporate biggie, which could end several careers. And he's feuding with other folks, too,' I said. 'Give me some credit, C.W., I know what I'm doing.'

'You're getting my ass in a crack, that's what you're doing,' he said. But I know C.W. well enough to know he'd given up on talking me out of the case.

'I got to go now,' he said, heading for the back door. 'This whole trip over here was a waste of time.'

I gathered up a paper sackful of tomatoes from the garden and pressed them into his hands. Then I walked him out to his car, a dark blue unmarked city car parked at the curb.

'So, how's Linda feeling? She worshiping at the porcelain altar?'

He opened the car door and slid onto the seat. 'She doesn't ever throw up. Just feels like she's going to. And now she can't stand the smell of food cooking. So we've been eating rice and tuna and angel food cake for a week. And orange juice. I'll bet she drinks a quart a day.' He grimaced at the thought of it.

'Relax,' I said. 'I hear that stuff's only during the first trimester. Have you guys told Kenyatta about the baby yet?'

'No,' he said. 'I keep meaning to, but this thing with Rita's got me nuts.'

'That's all that's keeping you from telling her? Just Rita? You're not worried about how Vonette will take the news?'

His car radio crackled then, and the dispatcher called his name. He picked up the microphone. 'Hunsecker here. I'm ten twenty-seven right now.'

He shrugged. 'Gotta roll. Then he turned the key in the ignition. 'You know something? All of a sudden, I got way too many women in my life, complicating things. You know what I mean?'

'So go back to the cop shop,' I suggested. 'There's plenty of good ol' boys there.'

He pulled his door closed and shot down the street.

17

I'd expected BackTalk studios, the biggest independent record label south of Nashville to be a glitzy, show-bizzy place. But after I called the studios, and got directions by telling them I was a courier with a package to deliver, I was a little disappointed.

Instead of a gleaming glass tower I found an anonymous brick box plopped in the middle of a weed-strewn asphalt parking lot. A small plaque beside the front door told me I'd found the home of BackTalk.

A receptionist sat behind a curved smoked Lucite desk in the middle of a small reception area. She was young, with marcelled blond hair that contrasted with the smooth cocoa-colored skin. She was turned around in her chair, intently watching a music video playing on one of three screens mounted in the wall behind her desk.

I glanced around the room. Black walls, industrial gray carpet, black leather sofas and chairs, and a smoked glass coffee table holding the latest issues of *Variety*, *Cashbox*, *Rolling Stone*, *Vibe*, and some other magazines I'd never seen before.

The video was of a rap group: three tough-looking

young chicks who had been transported to the moon via video magic. Very surreal, but the receptionist was obviously digging it, drumming her fingertips and bobbing her head to the staccato beat.

'Excuse me,' I said finally.

She whirled around in her chair.

'Yo,' she said. She pointed to the screen. 'That's Vaseline Dream. Stu, I mean Mr Hightower, produced that video himself. They finished postproduction work Friday. We were gonna screen it Monday.'

She blinked back tears. I was surprised at the sentiment. I'd pictured Hightower as an egotistical monster, not someone who inspired this kind of emotions from the help.

'I'm here to see Danielle Manigault,' I said coolly.

'Can I tell her your name?'

'Callahan Garrity,' I said, deliberately curt. 'I'm investigating the Hightower homicide.'

I didn't add that I was doing so on behalf of the woman charged with the murder.

The receptionist picked up the telephone on her desktop and pushed a button. 'Danielle? Oh, hi Jeannie. There's someone here to see Danielle. It's about Mr Hightower. You know...'

She held her hand over the receiver. 'They're looking for her. Things have been crazy around here. But I guess you're kind of used to that. Right?'

I nodded. 'I'll wait.' I sat down on one of the leather sofas, crossed my legs and tried to look businesslike.

A moment later, a young woman, this time a white girl with chopped-off poker-straight black hair and a clownlike powdered white face poked her head out of a door.

'Hi,' she said, looking at me questioningly. 'You're here to see Danielle? What's your name please?'

'Callahan Garrity,' I said, standing up and smoothing my skirt.

I followed the secretary down a wide hallway. This too was black, but someone had painted bright surrealistic murals the length of the hallway, cartoon scenes of ghetto life.

The girl stopped for a moment, touched a painted thug who had a chartreuse knife stuck in another thug's neck. 'Joe E did these paintings. He did Madonna's last album cover. You know Joe E?'

'No,' I said. She shrugged, clearly contemptuous of my lack of culture. 'It cost sixty thousand dollars. Sixty thousand. You fuckin' believe that?'

'Hmmm,' I said, trying for a neutral stance. I have a six-year-old niece who does much better dogs and humans than Joe E. I guess it's all in who you know.

The secretary lead me past a large office with glass block walls. She opened the door and stepped into the room. From the sound of the argument within, Danielle Manigault wasn't alone.

'Look, Arlene,' she said. 'The tour's set. We've booked the musicians, the crew, everything. The paper has the press release already. Junebug's contract specifically states that he will tour to support and promote the new album. You know that as well as I do. Stu's death doesn't change that.'

Another woman's voice was shrill, agitated. 'Crappy dates, crappy halls,' I heard her say.

'Face it, Arlene,' Danielle said, her voice sharp. 'Junebug is a tremendous talent. Tremendous. And BackTalk is going to make him a major star. But he's not there yet. He won't be for a while. First he has to pay his dues. And you know what that means. He plays Macon and Birmingham and Knoxville and Indianapolis. He's not ready for the bigger venues. Not yet.'

'Fuck that,' the other woman said. I heard something thrown hard, against a wall, and then the tinkling of shattered glass.

The door flew open and a woman stormed past me. Petite, and wearing very high heels. I'd seen her standing backstage chatting with Hightower just before Rita had charged him. Of course. She was Junebug's mother.

'Hi, Mrs Trotter,' the secretary chirped, but Arlene Trotter steamed down the hallway, oblivious in her anger.

The secretary pushed the door open, and I followed her inside, uninvited.

Danielle Manigault was bent over, picking up a framed gold album with shattered glass. She walked over to the secretary, handed her the album. 'Jeannie, have someone drop this by the framer's today please. Tell them to put Plexiglas over it this time. And send the bill to Arlene Trotter.'

She turned to face me. 'Sorry. This is a temperamental business, meaning we deal with temperamental people. Won't you sit down Ms . . .'

Danielle Manigault's office had three glass block walls, the one solid wall was painted a rosy pink. It was the first surface at BackTalk that wasn't painted black.

She'd probably had her personal color adviser pick the shade. Danielle had to be in her fifties if she'd been there at the start of SkyHi Records. But she looked much younger, late thirties tops, with long gleaming dark hair that brushed her collarbone, creamy coffee-colored skin, high cheekbones, and big dark eyes behind fashionable tortoiseshell framed glasses. She wore a simple taupe suit with a long tailored jacket and a skirt whose hem reached the upper regions of her thighs. She had the legs and the figure for the whole deal.

The office walls were lined with framed citations and framed gold and platinum record albums. I'd never heard of most of the groups represented on those walls, The Honeys, Attitude Adjustment, Dynamic Dissonance, BizzyB. But there was a single gold record, 'Happy Never After,' by the VelvetTeens, and 'Never Give Up,' by another sixties group I remembered, the SinSations.

Danielle sat down behind her desk and nodded at the secretary. 'Just hold the calls. I'm sure this won't take long. Will it?'

'Not long at all,' I agreed pleasantly.

Then I pulled a notebook out of my purse. 'Did you see Stuart Hightower at all on Monday?'

'No,' she said. 'But I've told the police that already. I was out in L.A. on business. Didn't someone already put this in a file somewhere?'

I didn't dare stop asking questions, for fear she'd kick me out. 'Sorry,' I said. 'What about anyone else from the company? Was anyone else from BackTalk supposed to be out at the house on Monday night? Mr Hightower's secretary for instance?'

'No one,' she said firmly. 'Everyone worked the listening party Sunday afternoon. Stu gave everybody Monday afternoon off. To make up for the overtime. I know I told Detective DiPima this already.'

'Was anyone at BackTalk angry with Mr Hightower?' I continued. 'An act who felt they weren't being promoted properly? Maybe an employee who was fired or demoted?'

A smile flitted about her lips. 'I see you overheard part of my conversation with Arlene Trotter. It probably sounded much worse than it actually was. Everyone in the business considers screaming matches to be part of the game. Arlene's a little upset because she thinks her son, Junebug, should be playing the Rose Bowl. She doesn't understand the mechanics of booking a tour. She'll calm down. As for anyone around here possibly being connected with Stu's murder. Well, I hardly think that's likely. Stu was a respected businessman. A pillar of this industry.'

Two small red spots appeared on her cheeks. 'You people arrested a woman out there at the house. She's been charged with murder, I was told. Why are you asking all these questions about our people?'

'We have to cover all the bases,' I said. Without looking up from my notebook, I continued. 'What about these rumors that BackTalk was to be sold to a much bigger company? Somebody like AKA. Can you give me any details about that?'

'That was Stu's department,' she said stiffly. 'I was not involved in those negotiations. And it was really only in a very preliminary stage. Nothing had been decided yet.'

'But it had been discussed. How would a sale have affected the company? Would you, for instance, have kept your position as executive vice president?'

'Of course,' she said quickly. 'But what the hell has this got to do with Stu's murder?'

'Hey,' she said, narrowing her eyes. 'You're not a police detective. Are you?'

'No,' I said pleasantly. 'I worked with the Atlanta P.D. for several years. I'm sorry if you got the impression I was still with them. Actually, I'm a private detective.'

'Working for Rita Fontaine,' she said slowly. 'I think you'd better leave.'

But I had to stay. Danielle Manigault knew a lot that I needed to know.

'I see you have a gold record for "Happy Never After,"' I said, pointing to the wall. 'So you knew Rita and Delores and Vonette.'

'I sang background on several of their singles,' Danielle said. Her expression seemed to soften, just a little. 'I was supposed to be Stu's secretary. But like everybody else hanging around in those days, I really wanted to sing. I bugged Stu till he gave in and let me sing background and do handclaps. For five dollars a session. Big money, I thought.'

'From what Vonette and Rita have told me, they didn't get paid much more than that,' I pointed out.

Her eyes narrowed. 'Oh yes. I see you've heard their

"poor pitiful me" routine. Listen. Those girls made good money, and at the time they were happy to get it. They were just a bunch of no-talents when Stu found them hanging around that candy store. He gave them the material. He wrote the songs, taught 'em how to sing, how to dress, act, move, talk. If it hadn't been for Stu Hightower, and SkyHi, each of those girls would have been like everybody else in their neighborhood, just another welfare mother living in the projects.'

'None of them was over eighteen when she signed those contracts,' I said. 'Stu acted as their manager. SkyHi hired their lawyers. It was a blatant conflict of interest. He'd never get away with that stuff now.'

Danielle laughed. 'And they'd never make it in the business now. That doesn't change the facts, Ms Garrity. Rita Fontaine was enraged when Stu got that order prohibiting them from using the VelvetTeens identity. She went out there, shot him to death in cold blood. She was too damn drunk to take off. Pathetic. Maybe her lawyer can get her a reduced sentence with one of those alcohol poisoning defenses you read about these days. It's not my problem. I've got a business to run. I'll let you find your own way out.'

She started to pick up the telephone again. 'What about Serena?' I asked. 'Stu dumped her, professionally and personally. She tried to burn his house down once, and he got the divorce settled out of court, probably for a lot less than she was asking. Are you telling me you don't think Serena is capable of this?'

Her glasses slipped to the end of her nose. She pushed them back up with one pale-painted nail. 'Serena wasn't found at the house, passed out with the murder weapon in her hand. Rita Fontaine was.'

I got up to leave. Danielle Manigault obviously wasn't going to cooperate with me.

'How can I get in touch with Arlene Trotter?' I asked.

She picked up the telephone on her desk. 'I'm calling security now.'

'No problem, I'm leaving,' I said, heading for the door. I went into the black night of Joe E's consciousness.

18

I woke up Matt Gordon to get Junebug's address.

'Late night,' he said sleepily. 'Wait a minute.'

The phone fell to the floor with a clatter, then I heard water running and a toilet flushing.

'Okay,' he said when he came back. 'That's better. What did you say you wanted?'

'Junebug's address,' I said patiently. 'Do you know how I can get it?'

'Everybody in Atlanta knows he lives at Peachtree Palisades,' Matt said. 'He's on the fourteenth floor. Just follow the music.'

The Palisades was one of those glossy new high-rise buildings that were sprouting along Peachtree Street in Buckhead like a particularly pernicious fungus. It makes me cranky to see these buildings where once had been some of Atlanta's most gracious homes. The Palisades made me especially cranky because to build it the developers had torn down Edith Wellman's house. Miss Edith, as generations of children called her, had been a drama teacher who gave acting lessons and put on children's plays in the big ballroom of the white columned Greek revival home she'd inherited from her parents.

She was a true Southern eccentric, Miss Edith was, dressing in flowing chiffon pants outfits with matching turbans and smoking skinny black cigarillos in a spangly cigarette holder. She'd come from a prominent Atlanta family, but Edna said Miss Edith taught drama because she was so poor she otherwise didn't have a pot to pee in.

One of Edna's socially connected friends had arranged for all the neighborhood kids to take acting lessons from Miss Edith, not because we had any aspirations for the stage but, Edna said, to give us poise. So I'd spent many a Saturday morning not watching cartoons, as I would have preferred, but reciting the likes of 'The Song of Hiawatha' dressed in a brown fringed crêpe paper Indian dress, with the other children ringed around beating on oatmeal box tomtoms.

I don't think I acquired much poise, but I can still remember the hand motions I learned to conjure up visions of the wigwam of Nokomis, Daughter of the Moon, Nokomis.

The Palisades had a uniformed doorman outside, and an imposing marble security desk just inside the big glass double doors leading into the lobby.

I changed into a clean House Mouse smock in the van, and pulled right up to the doorman. The van chugged to a stop, but then the engine knocked for a full minute before backfiring and cutting out.

'Can I help you?' He gave me the look doormen in that part of town are trained to give people like me.

'Is this valet parking?' I asked, trying to look humble.

He made a waving, dismissive motion with his hand. 'The entrance to the garage is in the back. Park in a visitor slot. And it's five dollars for non-residents.'

He obviously didn't think I had five bucks.

'Okay,' I said. I started the van and drove around to the basement entrance.

There was another security desk blocking the elevator. These people were serious about security.

I got a cleaning caddy out of the back of the van and approached the guard, whose eyes were glued to the bank of television monitors in front of him.

'I'm cleaning for the Duvalls,' I said.

'Go on up,' he said. His eyes didn't leave the screen. I craned my neck to see what he was watching. The fuzzy black-and-white image showed a slender young woman standing in the corner of what looked like an elevator car, with her skirt hiked around her waist, adjusting her pantyhose.

'Pervert,' I said under my breath.

The elevator I was in had a television camera too. I waited until I got off on the fourteenth floor to take off the smock and stuff it and the caddy behind a potted palm in the hallway.

As soon as the elevator doors opened I knew which way to turn for the House of Junebug. Not because of the music, but from the sound of colliding billiard balls. The door to the unit was ajar, and I could see Junebug, bare chested and dressed in baggy, billowing shorts, stretched across a pool table, pool cue poised

I waited quietly until the kid made his shot (common

barroom etiquette) and then knocked once. 'What it is?' he shouted, without turning to see who was at the door. His opponent was an elderly man, emaciated, except for a pair of ropey tattooed forearms. He had wispy white hair and wore a pair of zip front blue coveralls. The older man rubbed the tip of his cue with a chalk square and chortled happily while Junebug's solid balls bumped gently but ineffectively in all four corners of the table. 'You're dead meat, Bug,' he said. 'You set me up fine as froghair. Now watch the master.'

'Excuse me,' I said quickly, stepping inside the door. 'I'm Callahan Garrity.'

'Mama's in the office,' the kid said, pointing through a doorway in the room. He looked at me without curiosity. Junebug appeared younger offstage. He had a raging case of adolescent acne, and a flabby, hairless chest, but an angelic face, the kind grannies love to pinch.

I edged past the pool players quickly. The room was meant to be a living room, with a handsome black marble fireplace and black and white checked marble floors, but the only furniture was the pool table, a space-age television the size of a drive-in movie screen, and a white leather sectional that currently held a drowsing Doberman pinscher. As I walked past, the dog raised his head, pricked up its cropped ears, and showed me his teeth. They were big and fine and sharp.

'Hitler!' Junebug said sharply. The dog looked at its master, then at me, then back at Junebug. Then he put his muzzle on his paws, and laid his ears back flat.

'Thanks,' I said meaningfully.

Arlene Trotter's office looked like the real heart of the home. It had pale wood paneling, a wall of bookshelves that held mostly video and stereo equipment, and a large French provincial desk topped with a computer. On the wall behind her was a console holding a photocopy machine, a fax machine, and a printer. The fax was whining away, and the printer was printing. Arlene Trotter's one-woman empire was cooking on high.

The product was everywhere. Color photos of Junebug posing with music industry luminaries, politicians, and people I didn't recognize. There were more photos of Junebug as a baby, Junebug the tiny tot, already belting out a tune into a miniature microphone, Junebug at the Grammies, Junebug on Soul Train, and the cover art for his first album.

Arlene was on the phone when I walked in, but she gestured for me to sit down and wait. I could see where the kid got his looks. She had high cheekbones, a generous mouth and a dimple in her chin. The nose, I decided, had come courtesy of a plastic surgeon's wish book. She got off the phone in a hurry and glanced around the chair where I was sitting.

'Didn't you bring any sketches?' she asked, obviously annoyed at something. Her accent was deep South, but she'd been trying hard to tame it, making the speech oddly precise.

'Sketches?'

'Your ideas for Junebug's outfits. We wanted fabric samples too. I thought I made that clear on the phone.'

'Oh,' I said. 'I'm sorry. I'm not the costume designer. I'm Callahan Garrity. I'm a private detective.'

'BackTalk provides all our security,' she said quickly, looking down at a sheaf of phone messages in front of her. She still didn't get it.

'Actually, it's BackTalk I came to talk to you about,' I said, recognizing an opening. 'I've been hired to investigate Stu Hightower's murder.'

That got her attention. 'Hired by who?'

'Rita Fontaine's attorney,' I said.

'Oh,' she said. 'The woman who was screaming at Stu at Junebug's listening party. Wasn't she drunk or something?'

'Something,' I said. 'She was very upset with Mr Hightower.'

'I guess so, since she put a bullet in his chest,' Arlene said carelessly. 'Look, what do you need from me? I've got about a hundred phone calls I need to make here.'

'It won't take long,' I promised. 'Just a few questions.'

'Like what?'

'Well, I was wondering about your relationship with Mr Hightower.'

Instantly tears began to well up in her eyes. 'Stu was like a daddy to Junebug,' she said. 'Not like a lot of these other record executives. He really cared about us. He found Junebug himself, you know. Bug had come to Atlanta with his aunt, and he was in a mall, hanging around outside this record store. They were playing a CD on the sound system, and Bug was rapping along with it, just improvising new words. Stu saw him, took

198

my sister-in-law aside, and said he wanted to have Bug cut a demo. The rest is history.' She beamed at the memory of the meeting.

'I came to Atlanta, and we had a heart-to-heart. So many kids in this business go bad, you know? Drugs, booze, groupies. I told Stu the only way Bug could work was if I was his personal manager. And he understood. He agreed completely. My boy comes first. I help choose the material, manage his investments, co-write some of the songs. And I'm going to produce his next album at BackTalk.'

'That's great,' I said. 'But I understand there was talk that the label might be sold to a bigger company. If that happened, had Hightower discussed what would happen with Junebug's career?'

She smiled. 'Junebug is a star. It doesn't matter what happens to this label or that label. My boy is cream. And cream rises to the top.'

'Well, did Stu discuss the possibility of a sale with you?'

'No,' she said, the smile thinning a little. 'I don't believe there was going to be a sale. Why would he do that?'

I shrugged. 'To make several million dollars?'

'No,' she repeated. 'Stu was richer than God. BackTalk was his baby. He wouldn't sell.'

From what I'd heard, Stu Hightower was the kind of businessman who'd sell his left testicle if there was a viable donor market, but I decided not to pursue the matter with Arlene Trotter, who was obviously suffering from tunnel vision.

'What about you? How was your relationship with Stu?'

She cocked her head. 'What are you suggesting?'

'Nothing,' I assured her. 'It's just that Stu liked the ladies and the ladies liked him. I know you were friends, and business associates, but . . .'

'I am a married woman, Miss Garrity,' she said, her voice frosty.

'Oh,' I said. 'I didn't know.'

'Married with four precious children.'

I looked around. The place didn't look too family oriented. 'Really?'

'My husband and the girls are still in Easley. That's Easley, South Carolina. The girls are in school, but Junebug's career is here. Once things are settled, we'll sell the condo and build a house. Junebug has his heart set on his own recording studio, and the girls would like to have horses. Right now though, we have to concentrate on the Bug. I don't have time for anything else right now. My son comes first, second, and third.'

Certainly, I thought. The girls probably weren't pulling down the kind of bucks big brother was.

Something Arlene had said when we first started talking reminded me of something else. 'You were right there when Rita, my client, was yelling at Mr Hightower, at the club. Did you happen to hear what he said that got her so angry?'

'No,' she said quickly. 'I was concentrating on Bug's performance. I didn't even see her until she started screaming that she was going to kill him.' She stared at me then, as though she hadn't really seen me before.

Her eyes narrowed. 'You,' she said, her voice rising. 'You're the one who came charging backstage screaming something about being a fire marshal. People were stampeding for the doors. You ruined Bug's party. He never even got to do his second number because of you. I'm going to report you to the police for impersonating a fireman.'

She picked up the telephone, punched in a number and asked the operator for the number for the police. They must not have 911 in Easley, South Carolina.

While she was calling the fuzz, I was getting up and hurrying for the door. Clearly our little chat was at an end.

When I reached the sofa the dog lifted his head and growled at me menacingly. The teeth had gotten longer and sharper since I'd arrived.

'Hitler!' I said sharply. But nobody pays any attention to middle-aged white women any more. He gave one short warning bark before he was off the sofa and lunging for me. I was wearing rubber-soled tennis shoes that gave me the advantage of traction. Hitler was not. He slipped and skidded on the slippery marble floor, while Junebug and his friend watched. I dashed for the door and slammed it hard behind me.

From the other side of the door I heard a dull thud, and then a sharp yelp of fury as one hundred twenty pounds of teeth and fur met the steel fire door. I didn't wait for the elevator, and I didn't stop to get my cleaning caddy, taking the stairs, two at a time, the whole way down instead.

* * *

201

One of Matt's friends had arranged for me to meet the Joanses at a coffee house in Virginia Highlands, which is Atlanta headquarters for the young and the hip at heart. Espresso Express was right next door to a beauty salon called Key Lime Pie. When the place first opened my girlfriend Paula and I tried to go in there for a late dessert after we'd been to see a play at the experimental theater in the next block. We were keenly disappointed to find that the only mousse served at Key Lime Pie was the kind you put in your hair.

By the time I caught my breath from my emergency exit from the Palisades and drove across town to Virginia Highland, it was after 4:00 p.m. Even that early the coffee house was full of Generation Xers, sipping four-dollar thimbles of cappuccino and nibbling on three-dollar-a-whack biscotti. It made me wonder why all these wholesome, healthy types weren't doing what my contemporaries were doing at this time in the afternoon, namely pounding brews over at Manuels Tavern or the yacht club.

I spotted the Joanses right off. People were busy whispering loudly and pretending not to look at the celebrities in their midst. I was probably the only person in the place who'd never heard their music.

The Joanses would have made arresting characters even if they weren't famous. The taller of the two women had hair cut so short it was almost a buzz. But she had a beautiful swanlike neck and a high, regal forehead. For her, hair was just an accessory.

The shorter woman wore round tinted granny glasses, a discreet nose ring and hair that had been plaited and woven tightly with bright beads and metallic thread. Both her arms were covered in silver bangles from elbow to wrist.

'Rikki? Jonette? I'm Callahan.'

'How ya doin?' was the easy reply from the woman with the braids, who quickly introduced herself as Jonette.

She sat back in her chair, giving me an unabashed once-over. 'So you're the lady dick. That's cool, man. I like it. You ever, like, shoot anybody?'

'Jonette!' her partner said.

'It's okay,' I said, relieved to find myself liking them. 'Actually, my work is more investigative than preventative. I mostly just ask a lot of questions.'

'We heard,' Rikki said. 'Why did you want to talk to us? We were doing a gig down in Miami when the thing with Stu went down.'

I hadn't begun to ask questions, but Rikki was already making damn sure I knew she had an alibi. An alibi I intended to check.

'I'm trying to figure out what was happening at the label, at BackTalk,' I explained. 'Stu Hightower was powerful, successful, and rich. I think maybe that's what got him killed.'

'Yo,' Jonette said. 'Check it out. What probably got him killed was his puttin' his dick where it didn't belong. Word.'

'Shut up,' Rikki said.

'Hey,' Jonette countered. 'The whole world knows

what a stud Stu thought he was. And they know you and him were gettin' it on. So get over it, okay?'

Rikki sipped her cup of joe and sulked.

'I've been talking to people in the business,' I said. 'Somebody told me Stu was making noises about dumping the Joanses. I know there was talk too that the company might be bought out by a much bigger label.'

'We were doin' great,' Jonette said, leaning forward and keeping her voice low to avoid being overheard. 'All the urban contemporary stations were giving airplay to "Cured of Love," our first single. But those assholes over at BackTalk, they kept saying it wasn't sellin' like it should. That the returns were out of line. Our manager was freakin'. He wanted our accountant to look at the label's books, see what was what. When Stu heard, he went apeshit.'

'Totally,' Rikki agreed.

'After that, man, we weren't shit around there,' Jonette said. 'See, they're not used to ballsy black chicks. Danielle, man, she's not even really black, as far as I can tell. She's kinda tan, you know?'

'House nigger,' Rikki sneered. 'She did what Stu said. Vice president of nothing, that's Danielle.'

'What happened with your audit?' I asked. 'Did you find anything wrong?'

'Who knows?' Rikki said. 'The accountant said it looked like they had shipped a lot more CDs than we thought, but there were also a lot of returns in the warehouse. BackTalk gave us some jive about how it would turn up in the next royalty statement. I don't believe nothin' any of 'em say.'

'What happens to you guys now?'

The women both shrugged. 'BackTalk released *City of Pain* last month,' Jonette said glumly. 'No promotion, no tour. Nothing. We couldn't get airplay for nothing. It went in the toilet.'

'It bombed,' Rikki agreed. 'And that album was twice as good as *Cured of Love*. I think Stu stiffed us on purpose.'

'Did you talk to him about it?'

'Talk? We screamed, yelled, threatened to sue his ass, we did everything we could think of.'

I looked at Rikki. 'Weren't you two seeing each other? How did this thing with the new release affect the relationship?'

'Relationship?' Rikki said. 'Shit. I was a piece of tail to Stu. That's all. As soon as I figured it out, I quit going over there. He just pretended like it never happened. Last time I called, he told his secretary not to put me through. He was on the speaker phone. I heard him. He didn't care.'

'She's over it,' Jonette said.

'You went out to his house?'

'Sometimes,' Rikki said. 'When we knew Serena was out of town.'

'Did you ever see Stu with a gun? A twenty-two?'

Rikki made a face. 'I'm not into guns,' she said. 'But Stu had a whole cabinet full of them. Shotguns, rifles, that kind of stuff. I couldn't tell you what all they were. He kept that cabinet locked, and I stayed as far away from it as I could.'

'What happens now, to the Joanses, I mean?'

'We're writing material for our next album. Jonette's got some jammin' ideas. And Sugar Jackson promised us a couple numbers. We got labels looking at us. The Joanses ain't done. Not by a long shot.'

'Sugar Jackson?'

'The composer,' Rikki said. 'You know? The dude who wrote "Spirit Lover" for En Vogue?'

I'd never heard of Sugar Jackson or En Vogue, but I nodded my head to signify my hipness.

'You guys weren't the only ones Stu Hightower shafted, not by a long shot,' I said. 'Have you heard about anybody else at the company who had run-ins with him?'

The women exchanged a look. 'You heard anything about Junebug?'

'He's just a kid,' I said cautiously.

'Yeah, but his mama, she ain't playin',' Jonette said. 'What's her name, Arlene something? I heard her in Stu's office once, she didn't like something about the bass line on "Diss Dis," and she was screaming! I never heard anybody yell at Stu like that. He was taking it, too. What I heard is, she was really mad cause Stu gave Sugar's new song to another act, instead of to Junebug, like he promised. Once Stu starts that shit, it's over, man.'

'We ought to know,' Rikki said.

'Hey,' Jonette said. 'Maybe old Arlene offed Stu. How about that?'

'I like it,' Rikki said, nodding her head happily. 'If it turns out she did it, you be sure and tell her the Joanses said thanks.' Then she reached into the pocket of her

flowered baby doll minidress and brought out a wad of
dollar bills.

'Here,' she said, letting the dollars flutter down to the
tabletop. 'Give her this. Tell her it's our contribution to
her legal defense fund.'

19

Vonette insisted I come for dinner before our powwow with Rita and Korznick.

'Honey, I got all this food and all this nervous energy. Cooking and cleaning are the only things keeping me sane right now,' she said.

So I was 'honey' now. I guess she decided to forgive me my friendship with Linda Nickells and C.W.

She'd stuffed chicken breasts with goat cheese and herbs, topped with a mushroom and white wine sauce. There was a salad of baby greens, wild rice, and for dessert, a fresh peach sorbet.

Rita sat silently as usual, picking with her fork, pushing food around the plate, but eating little.

'I'll bet you were expecting soul food, right?' Vonette said, trying to break the awkward quiet.

'Uh, no, not necessarily.'

'Well, I used to cook that way,' Vonette said. 'Fatback in everything, fried this and that, cream gravy and biscuits, cakes or pie every night. Isn't that right, Baby,' she said, addressing Kenyatta.

Kenyatta took a sip of water. 'I miss that fried chicken, Mama.'

'Now that stuff is heart attack on a plate,' Vonette declared. 'After the divorce, I was bored, wanting to lose some weight. I started watching the cooking shows on public television. You know, Pierre Franey, the Frugal Gourmet, and that lady, what's her name? Lives right here in Atlanta, always got pie dough down in her diamond rings?'

'Nathalie Dupree?'

'Yeah, her. Well, I saw how they were doing, and I got some cookbooks, and here we are. I lost twenty pounds right off the bat.'

'I'd kill for fried chicken. Just one little old drumstick and a thigh,' Kenyatta said mournfully.

Maybe, I thought, I could get Edna to watch some of those cooking shows. Or maybe Kenyatta and I should just swap mothers for a few months.

Rita looked up at Kenyatta. 'You come on to my house, Baby,' she said. 'Me and Andre, we still like our greens cooked with streak-o'lean. How 'bout sweet potato pie? Yams came over here from Africa, did you know that? A little yam never hurt nobody.'

Vonette raised her eyebrows in surprise. This was the most words Rita had managed to string together all evening.

Rita saw Vonette's expression. 'What's wrong with you?' she demanded. 'I was a good cook before I got to drinking, and I ain't forgot none of it.'

'You ever have okra fritters?' Rita asked, directing her comments to me now.

'Don't think so,' I said.

'I could make my mama's okra fritters in my sleep,'

Rita affirmed. 'Just okra and onion and cornmeal, with some bacon grease in a black-iron skillet. When we're done with this business, if they don't put me in prison, I'll show you how it's done.'

'If she gives you Aunt Louise's fritter recipe, you'll have to give me back the money I'm paying you, Callahan,' Vonette said, getting up to start clearing the table. 'I've been begging her to show it to me for years, but she never would.'

'Thought you said all that grease was poison,' Rita sniped.

Her generous mood had ended as quickly as it had begun. Vonette just shrugged. She was used to it.

David Korznick showed up as we were having decaf in the living room.

'Good news,' he said, snapping open the briefcase he'd placed in the middle of the coffee table. 'The judge assigned to the case is Frank Bryson.'

'So?' Rita said, yawning.

'He's new to the bench. Just appointed to fill a vacancy. He was on the law review two years ahead of me at Emory. Decent guy. Did I mention he's black?'

'Yippee,' Rita said.

Vonette frowned. 'Tell David how it went at Peach-crest, why don't you?'

'Fine,' Rita said.

Korznick and Vonette exchanged a look.

'I met her counselor and the staff therapist,' Vonette said. 'Very nice. Very concerned.'

'Okay,' Korznick said. 'Callahan, what have you got for us?'

I briefed them on what I'd found out about Stu Hightower's business dealings, and the rumors that he planned to sell the company, and the implications it could have on its artists, including Serena.

I also told Korznick about my conversation with Danielle Manigault.

'Now there's a name I haven't thought about in nearly thirty years,' Vonette said. 'Remember her, Rita? I always thought she was jealous of us, didn't you?'

'Sneaky little bitch,' Rita said. 'Stu used to have her spy on us. She'd tell if she found a beer bottle or a cigarette in your dressing room.'

'We were supposed to be ladies at all times,' Vonette explained. 'We couldn't leave the house unless we had on girdles and stockings, heels, and gloves. The works.'

'I hated those garter belts,' Rita said. 'Felt like a mule in harness.'

'And to think Danielle is running the company now,' Vonette marveled.

'Slept her way to the top,' Rita said.

'Never mind,' Vonette said, glancing nervously at Kenyatta, who was laughing to herself.

'All right now,' Korznick said. 'Callahan needs for you to go over in some detail what happened Monday night, Rita.'

Rita rubbed at her eyes with her fist. 'We done that already.'

'We'll be going over and over and over it when we go to trial,' Korznick said.

I marveled at his patience with his recalcitrant client.

'You already know about those papers Stu put on us, right? Rita said. 'That son of a bitch...'

'Never mind that,' Korznick said sharply.

'I read about how he could keep us from being the VelvetTeens again. And I wanted to kill him. That's God's truth. You want me sayin' that in court?'

'Just say you were angry,' Korznick said.

'Angry.' She shook her head in disbelief. 'If you say so. I had a few pops at home. But I drank it all. And I needed more. So I went to B.J.'s.'

'The shot house,' I put in. 'I talked to the woman who runs the place. Mattie Green. She confirms that Rita was in there Monday night.'

'I had a few beers,' Rita continued. 'Made me a plan. About going to see Stu.'

David leaned forward, his face tense with concentration. 'What did you plan to do when you saw him?'

'Kill him,' she said calmly.

'With what?' I said. 'You told David you'd never seen that twenty-two before.'

'I hadn't,' Rita said. 'Had me a thirty-eight Smith and Wesson a long time ago, but it got stolen out of my car. I had me a plan, I guess. Had a knife in my purse. I was just going to go out there and scare him. You know, let him know he couldn't keep on messing with me. Not after all this time. I was done being messed with.'

'Did you see a gun at Stu's house? Maybe pick it up to look at it?'

'No sir,' she said, shaking her head emphatically. 'I don't remember seeing no gun. But then, I'd had a lot to drink.'

213

Vonette buried her face in her hands.

'Mattie Green says you told her you were going to kill Stu,' I said. 'Are you sure you didn't take that gun out there? This is important, Rita. We need to know where the murder weapon came from.'

'I told you I had a knife,' Rita insisted. 'Where would I get a gun?'

'You said you made a plan,' Korznick said. 'What was the plan?'

'Some of it I remember,' Rita said. 'I know I was thinking about where Stu lived. Out there with all those horse farms and the rich people. I didn't know they had those gates and guards all over the place. I just thought, now, I'll ring the doorbell, and when Stu comes out, I'll show him the knife. And tell him he better tear those papers up. He better tell those lawyers to leave us alone. Because we,' she said, looking from Vonette to Kenyatta, 'are the fabulous VelvetTeens. And nobody else. Not nobody else.'

'What did you plan to do if he wouldn't tear them up?' her lawyer asked.

'See now,' she laughed and the laugh turned into a long coughing spell. 'I didn't have a plan for that. That knife couldn't cut butter, you want the truth.'

'All right,' Korznick said, pleased with Rita's answers. 'We can say you never intended to harm Hightower. Where is the knife now, do you know? We can say that you don't remember having a gun. Maybe it was Hightower's gun. Maybe you picked it up and fired it at him in self-defense. But you didn't take a gun out there planning to kill him with it. The fact that you stayed on the scene and didn't attempt to flee should support that statement.'

'I don't know where the knife is,' she admitted. 'Could be in my car.'

'What you said just now,' she continued. 'Does that mean you're gonna say I did kill Stu?'

'Not necessarily,' Korznick said. 'But unless we can come up with someone else who would have motive and means to kill Hightower, we need to consider that an option. Yes. It may be necessary to plead guilty. We'll plea bargain it down to a minimal sentence.'

'No,' Vonette said angrily. 'Rita did not kill that man. I've known her all her life. And I'm not going to let you or anybody else say she did. They'll give her the death penalty. That's what happens when a black person kills a white person. This is Georgia. They'll give her the chair. I know it.'

'Now wait, Vonette,' I said. 'The D.A. hasn't said anything about asking for the death penalty. And he can't. You have to have extenuating circumstances for a capital case in this state. Like committing a murder during the commission of another felony, like armed robbery. Or murder and rape, or a murder where the victim is tortured, or murder for hire. None of that applies in this case. And even if she got convicted, in Georgia a life sentence can mean as little as seven years. Sooner maybe. And Rita's drinking problem, David can bring that up in court. He can show she wasn't responsible because she was drunk.'

'I said no,' Vonette said, raising her voice. 'Rita and I talked about this, didn't we Rita?'

'That's right,' Rita said. 'I messed up Andre's life enough already. If I go to prison, tell folks I'm a murderer, folks will put it on him. Anyway, I don't remember shooting Stu. Hell, I don't even remember seeing him that night.'

'Never mind,' David said hastily. 'Let's forget about the plea for the moment. Tell us about what happened when you got to the house.'

'How'd you get in there anyway?' Kenyatta asked. 'How'd you get past those redneck guards?'

That was what I'd been wondering.

'I didn't have any time to think about it,' Rita said, shrugging. 'I pulled in to those gates, and the guard came right up to the car window, actin' snotty, like I didn't have a right to be there. So I started crying. Big old crocodile tears. I told him my cat got out of my car and ran through the gate, and he had to let me find it, cause it was my son's pet. He started to tell me no, so I cried and hollered. Then a car came up behind me and started honking its horn. I had the driveway blocked. So the guard got disgusted and told me to go on and look.'

Kenyatta was giggling again. 'If you had thought of that Callahan, Mama wouldn't have ruined her outfit in that smelly old trunk.'

'How'd you find the house?' Vonette asked.

'Saw it in some magazine at work. It stuck in my mind, I guess.'

'Tell us what happened next,' David said.

'Again?' Rita frowned. 'I went to the front door like I told you. I rang for probably five, ten minutes. I could hear music coming from somewhere, so I knew the son of a bitch was home. I tried the garage door, but it was locked. Then I walked around to the back of the house, toward where the music was coming from.'

'Do you think anybody saw you?' David asked. 'This is important, Rita. Think. Did you hear or see anybody while you were there?'

'Well I know I must have made a racket,' Rita said with a look of grim satisfaction on her face. 'I was calling Stu's name, banging on that door. Tellin' him to quit hiding 'cause I knew he was home. I threw a rock at the side of the house. Broke the glass in a little-bitty window up on the second floor.'

David scribbled away on his notepad. 'Good. Broken window. Hardly the act of someone who hopes to commit a murder and then sneak away unnoticed. Go on.'

'I never saw anybody,' Rita said. 'I walked all around that house. Maybe that's when I lost that knife. The back door was locked too. I went to that little house, the one by the pool. That's where the music was coming from. He had more equipment in there than any recording studio I ever saw. Then I saw a bottle of Dewar's on the bar. There were glasses right there. I decided I'd have a drink while I waited for Stu to come back. Maybe he was in the house taking a leak. Or maybe he went out to buy more booze. I didn't know and I didn't care. I took the bottle, sat down in a chair by the pool. The music was so loud it gave me a headache. I fixed it. After that I guess I went to sleep. That's all I remember.'

Korznick looked excited again, like a kid who's just

spotted the ice cream truck. 'Did you actually touch the stereo? The dials, anything like that?'

'Yeah,' Rita said. 'Is that good?'

'If you left fingerprints we can show that you tried to shut the music off. The murderer would have wanted the music on to hide the sound of the gunshots.'

'Wait a minute,' I said. 'When we got there, the music was turned on full blast. Are you sure you turned it off, Rita?'

She shrugged. 'Thought so. I remember trying to.'

Korznick scribbled a note on his pad. 'We may want to see if you've suffered any organic brain damage from the years of alcohol abuse: memory loss, that kind of thing.'

'You don't remember anything after taking the bottle out to the patio?' Korznick pressed. 'No gunshots, doors opening or closing, that kind of thing?'

'I was asleep,' Rita protested.

'Passed out,' Vonette corrected her. 'You passed out in a drunken stupor.'

'Mama!' Kenyatta looked shocked.

'Her therapist says she has to admit she is a drunk before she can start to get better,' Vonette said. 'Her family has to admit it too. They want me and Andre to go to family counseling over there at Peachcrest. So we can figure out how to help Rita figure out why she does like she does.'

'"The Way You Do the Things You Do,"' Rita said. She hummed a little of the music. 'Wasn't that Smokey Robinson and the Miracles? That Smokey was one sexy dude, wasn't he?'

'Never mind,' Vonette said sharply.

'We're done anyway,' Korznick said, shutting his briefcase. 'Unless Callahan has something else she needs to tell us.'

I glanced down at my own notes. I wanted to go back and talk to Jack Rabin, and the neighbor, Lyman Woodall, before I raised anybody's hopes.

'Oh yeah,' I said. 'This may be a moot point now, but I think I've traced Delores to Nashville.'

'You did?' Rita sat upright in her chair and leaned forward, her voice urgent. 'Did you talk to her? Did you tell her about – what's happened?'

'No,' I said. 'I haven't really found her yet. I just know she was in Nashville fourteen months ago. I don't know if she's still there. I just know she was working there.'

'Was she singing?' Rita asked. 'That's good. She's still in the business. We won't have so much catching up to do.'

I was surprised at Rita's sudden interest in her long-lost sister and the project to revitalize their careers. Maybe she was capable of ditching the booze.

'She was singing for a radio commercial,' I said. 'I talked to a woman who had worked with her. I'm afraid she couldn't tell me much.'

I glanced at Vonette, who was busy stacking cups and saucers on a tray. 'I can keep looking, unless you think the movie deal will be called off because of all this.'

Vonette held the tray tightly with both hands. 'You keep looking. Zimmerman called this afternoon. He's seen the news reports, of course. He says he keeps CNN on in his office all day long. He thinks all this is great publicity for the movie. Providing,' she made a face, 'Rita isn't found guilty. He even says he's thinking of writing a murder scene into the movie. For creative suspense, he says.'

'Man is fuckin' nuts,' Rita muttered.

Korznick didn't look pleased. 'Look,' he said. 'You all have got to keep quiet about this movie thing. It could look bad to some people, the judge, a jury. It could look like we're trying to promote a movie and make money off Stu Hightower's death. It doesn't matter that you had the movie deal before the murder. It looks bad. Real bad. Vonette, I want you to call Zimmerman and tell him we have to put the movie on the back burner until we've figured this thing out. All right?'

Vonette's face fell. 'All right,' she said softly. 'I guess it can't be helped.'

'Ain't that the way,' Rita said, following her cousin into the kitchen. 'Stu's dead, and he's still finding ways to screw us.'

20

Thursday morning Edna baked one of her special red velvet cakes, the one with the cream cheese frosting. We decorated the kitchen with crêpe paper streamers and balloons. The coffee was brewing and Ruby and Jackie and Baby and Sister were already there. Neva Jean was due at nine. We'd made a special point of telling her she had a job with a new client and we needed to give her the key.

The balloon blowing up took a long time, mostly because Baby and Sister, who'd been assigned the job, would not quit bickering.

They'd come in the door at 8:00 a.m. fussing at each other. First Sister stomped in, letting the screened door slam in Baby's face. Before Edna could ask what the problem was, Baby let her know.

'She's wearing my teeth,' Baby said, her dentures clacking loudly.

'Am not,' Sister said loudly, sending a shower of spittle into the atmosphere. 'Guess I know my own teeth. Been wearing 'em twenty years.'

'If she's tellin' you I had twenty beers last night she's lying right through her stolen false teeth,' Baby retorted. 'It was only three beers, 'cause I been savin' my money for my bus trip to Myrtle Beach. Miss Sister has got her bowels in an uproar because certain people have been paying me more attention than Her Worshipful Highness. That's why she went and stole my dentures. Cause they're nicer than hers, is why.'

'I been puttin' my teeth in the same teacup with the same pink roses and gold rim since I got 'em,' Sister said. 'Now all of a sudden, Miss Hotpants thinks they're hers. But they're not. And I'm not a-giving mine up so that she can smooch some smelly old man in the back of an air-cooled motorcoach.'

'Now what's she saying?' Baby demanded. 'Did she tell you she like to bit my finger off when I tried to get my very own property back? Did she?'

'Now y'all hush,' Ruby said gently, moving between the two warring factions. 'I just heard Neva Jean pull up outside. She's gonna hear you two fighting and it'll ruin the surprise.'

We all hid behind the kitchen door and jumped out and yelled 'Surprise! Happy Birthday!' when Neva Jean pushed open the screened door.

But the surprise was on us. Instead of shrieking that we shouldn't have and that she'd never in a million years have guessed what we were up to, Neva Jean sniffed loudly and collapsed into one of the kitchen chairs.

Her eyes were red and swollen, and her face blotchy. A quick check of her hands revealed no tennis bracelet.

'Happy Birthday!' Baby hollered again, a couple minutes late.

Two big tears rolled down Neva Jeans pale round cheeks. 'How did y'all know it was my birthday?' she said, chins quivering.

'Just a wild guess,' Edna said.

Neva Jean stared at the small pile of wrapped packages on the table, all marked 'Happy Birthday Neva Jean.' 'Now y'all didn't have to do this.'

'Shut up and open mine first,' Jackie said. She and Neva Jean have a strange and wonderful relationship: strange because Jackie regards Neva Jean as an unreconstructed redneck and Neva Jean still refers to Jackie as colored, wonderful because they had somehow found a way to genuinely care for each other.

Neva Jean opened a bright red package with a big gold bow. She held up a screaming fuchsia pair of panties with black lace trim. Digging back into the box she brought out a matching fuchsia brassiere with cups so large they could have served as punch bowls for the party.

'Wow,' Edna said admiringly.

'My favorite,' Neva Jean said, choking back a sob. 'Jackie, how on earth did you find these? There's only a couple places left that sell these crotchless panties and the bras with the nipples cut out.'

'I know,' Jackie said, clearly pleased at the reaction her gift had brought. 'I found an ad for 'em in the back of one of Miss Baby's *True Confession* magazines. Had to send away clear to Passaic, New Jersey, to get 'em.'

The other gifts were met with equally passionate sorrow on the part of Neva Jean. She sobbed through the gift certificate for ten games of Putt-Putt (Ruby), the box of peanut brittle from Sister, the dusty blue bottle of *Evening in Paris* eau de cologne from Baby, and the boxed set of Elvis videos from Edna and myself.

'*Speedway* and *Roustabout* and *Blue Hawaii*.' Neva Jean wailed. 'Y'all must have spent a fortune.'

'Don't forget *Change of Habit* with Mary Tyler Moore,' Edna reminded her. 'I just loved her as a guitar-playing nun, didn't you?'

'Did you see we found *Kid Creole*?' I said anxiously. 'And *Viva Las Vegas*?'

At the mention of a movie featuring her idol, Ann Margret, Neva Jean dissolved into a torrent of tears. 'At least my friends care about my taste,' she said, choking.

Jackie came over and put her arms around Neva Jean. 'What happened, hon? Aren't you having a good birthday?'

Edna motioned with her head toward Neva Jean's naked hand. 'I guess Swannelle didn't come up with the bracelet, huh? Maybe it's on back order or something.'

'It ain't on back order,' Neva Jean said shrilly. 'The horse's ass never even tried to get it for me. You know what he did get? You'll never believe it in a million years. It's awful. When I opened the box, I threw it right back in his face and stormed out of the house. I hope I never see his miserable face again.'

'Not a set of metric wrenches?' I said. 'Tell me you didn't throw a set of metric wrenches in Swannelle's face. Those people at the emergency room are going to start getting nosy about all these strange injuries Swannelle keeps sustaining.'

It had only been a year since Neva Jean had atomized Swannelle with half a can of roach spray, so I was afraid they might have her name in some kind of computer databank of folks who assault people with insecticides.

'It didn't hurt him none,' she groused. 'Hurt the hell out of my hand though. This is much worse,' she said. 'A custom-drilled bowling ball.'

'He didn't,' Jackie said.

'You *were* high man on the House Mouse bowling team this past fall,' Edna said tactfully. 'Swannelle was awful proud of you about that.'

'He got me a damn bowling ball 'cause he thinks it might make me want to hang around the damn Bowl-A-Rama while he bowls every night of the week,' Neva Jean said. 'Bowling messes up my nails. Only reason I played on y'all's team was because Callahan said I could have a shirt with my name on it.'

'Never mind,' Edna said. 'You can make him take the ball back and spend the refund money on the bracelet.'

'They won't take it back,' Neva Jean said. 'It's custom made.'

'Oh,' Edna said.

'I'll tell you what you do,' Jackie offered. 'Take the credit card out of his pants pocket when he's asleep tonight, call up and charge the bracelet to Swannelle McComb. He won't find out for at least a month, and by then, you'll have found a way to get away with it.'

'You think so?' Neva Jean was dubious.

'I know so,' Jackie said.

After we'd had our cake and coffee and sent the girls out, Baby and Sister settled in at the table, refilling the cleaning supply caddies we sent out with all the girls. Then I went through the ritual of trying to reach Serena again. I'd been dialing her manager's number all week long, but I kept getting an answering machine.

Edna watched my calls with interest. 'You know, I think it's time you let us girls help out on this case.'

'Forget it, Ma,' I said.

'Who was it got you that information about Hightower's divorce? Who found about those other lawsuits? Me, that's who.'

I hate it when my mother is right. 'Rita's arraignment date is coming up,' I said. 'We need to make some headway if we're going to keep from having her plead guilty. What did you have in mind?'

'Baby and Sister here are right good at snooping, isn't that right, ladies?'

Sister smiled modestly, her eyes glinting behind the thick-lensed glasses. 'We like to help,' she said.

'Why not send them out to Serena's to take a look around?' Edna said.

'I can't even get her manager on the phone,' I said. 'How do you suggest we find Serena and talk her into letting us clean her house?'

Edna got up and got the thick Atlanta business telephone directory and sat back down at the table. 'I got that all figured out. Sit back and take notes now.' She shook her head. 'You know, I'm disappointed in you. For a former cop, you sure are dense about some things.'

She turned the pages of the phone book, found the listing she wanted and dialed.

'Hello,' she said. 'Is this the security gate?' A beat. 'It is? Thank heavens. I was getting some groceries out of my car in the parking lot of the condos this morning and I accidentally bumped a bright red sports car. Well, the car alarm is just screeching and screeching. I need to call the owner and tell her what happened, so she can disarm it.'

'Yes, I'll wait,' she said. Edna gave me a winning smile. 'Very helpful, these guards.'

'Oh, Serena Choi? And that's her full name? All right. Thanks so much.'

She wrote a number on the margin of the phone book, clicked the receiver then started dialing again.

'Good morning,' she said after a moment. 'Is this Ms Choi? It is? Ms Choi, I'm Edna Garrity of the House Mouse. We're a full-service residential cleaning business located here in Atlanta. Your neighbor, Mrs Jackson, referred me to you. Now, Ms Choi, I'm sure you already employ a cleaning service. Oh. Tidy-Brite? Yes. I'm sure they do an, um, adequate job.' She paused a moment here. 'I personally feel it's wonderful of Tidy-Brite to help those who've been incarcerated in the past by offering them gainful employment. However, my clients insist on having personnel of a slightly higher caliber. We feel that being fully bonded and insured and submitting our people to weekly lie detector tests ensures their honesty.'

She waited another moment. I was amazed at the ease

with which she lied. But my mother is a fluent, effortless liar.

'Ms Choi,' she continued, 'I feel so certain that you'll prefer the House Mouse that I'd like to offer you a free introductory residential servicing.'

The voice on the other end interrupted for a moment, but Edna was unphased.

'No ma'am. We're not selling timeshares. No, we're not offering Amway products. No, not the waterless cookwear either. No. I'm really only offering you the opportunity to experience the House Mouse difference.'

'Yes ma'am,' Edna said, smiling broadly. 'Actually, the first time we service a new client we prefer that the homeowner be present. To observe our honest, but relentless cleaning methods.'

'You can't? What a shame. No, I'm sorry. It's out of the question.'

There was a torrent of chatter on the other end of the line, audible even to me.

'Well,' Edna said, letting uncertainty creep into her voice. 'I suppose since your neighbor spoke so highly of you, perhaps I could make an exception. It happens that I have a cancellation this afternoon. Would that be convenient? Fine. Will there be a problem getting to your home?'

Edna's smile grew broader yet. She tapped her pencil merrily on the tabletop. 'Excellent. Yes. Two o'clock.'

She hung up the phone and held her hands over her head in a gesture of triumph. 'Serena's meeting with her attorneys this afternoon. Very busy. I thought she was going to hang up for a minute there.'

'You sure can tell a story Miss Edna,' Sister said admiringly. 'I bet you could charm the earrings off of a gypsy. Ain't that right Baby? Ain't Miss Edna a wonder?

Baby slapped the table for emphasis. 'She's the beatenist,' she said.

'I was sure she'd hang up too,' I admitted. 'Serena can obviously afford to pay for a full-time staff. Wonder why she'd take you up on a bogus offer like this?'

'That's the point,' Edna said. 'I learned a long time ago, when I worked full-time at the Salon de'Beaute. There's nothing a rich person enjoys more than gettin' something for nothing. A rich woman would go to the end of the earth for a free sample of perfume or a twenty-cent off coupon for a bottle of toilet-bowl disinfectant. That's why they're rich. Cause they're cheap.'

'Two o'clock today?' I said thoughtfully. 'I'd planned to try to talk to Jack Rabin and Lyman Woodall this afternoon.'

'You go right ahead on,' Edna said. 'Ruby and Jackie and Neva Jean are booked solid today, but me and Baby and Sister, we're gonna help Serena experience the House Mouse clean.'

Baby giggled happily. 'Hee hee. Miss Edna, I believe you like peeking in other folkses business.'

'Why Baby,' Edna said primly. 'All I'm going to do is help you and Sister make sure we get that deep-down clean we promised our client.'

'She likes to snoop,' Sister said. 'And that's a natural fact.'

Before Edna could protest her innocence anymore,

the doorbell rang, a sure sign that our caller was a stranger. Anybody who knows us comes around to the back door.

The caller was Mick Coyle, the tabloid reporter I'd met on my scouting expedition at the Country Club of the South. He was holding a folded newspaper under his arm.

I opened the door, not exactly happy to see him. 'How the hell did you find out where I live?' I demanded.

Coyle stepped into the living room, uninvited. 'I'm a reporter, remember? It's my job. Although I don't believe it's your job. In fact, my spies tell me you're a private detective working for Rita Fontaine. Can we talk?'

There wasn't much I could do to keep him from talking. Besides, I was curious about what he knew. He trailed me back toward the kitchen, where I introduced him to Edna and the Easterbrooks girls.

'The *Global Examiner*? I know you,' Baby said, peering at Coyle. 'You're the one wrote that story about how eatin' sauerkraut makes a person's IQ ten points higher. And you did that one about the lady in New Zealand giving birth to that lizardboy.'

While Baby was gushing on and on about Coyle, Edna was looking over his shoulder at the paper he held in his hand. 'Uh-oh,' she said, taking it away from him.

She showed me the headline.

'Rock 'n' Roll Renegade Slain by Singer with Sordid Secrets.' Somebody had pasted together two photographs, one of Hightower and one of Rita Fontaine, obviously taken decades apart. Under the photo there was another headline. 'Former VelvetTeen Had Love Child by High-Powered Hi-Fi Guy Stu Hightower.'

'What?' I screeched.

Coyle nodded. 'You didn't know? That son of hers, Andre? Hightower was the father.'

'Uh, uh,' I said slowly. 'I don't believe it. Rita hates the guy. She was married to the bus driver who drove the VelvetTeens last tour. Cleveland Strong. He's Andre's father.'

'Not bloody likely,' Coyle said smugly.

'Says who?'

'Says Cleveland Strong,' he said.

'You paid him off.'

Coyle shrugged. 'Mr Strong was paid fair compensation for consulting services. To show his regard for the *Global Examiner*, and also because he wishes to set the record straight, he confided in me that he was not, in fact, the father of Andre Strong. Although he admits he married Ms Fontaine in 1966, he says he later learned that she was two months pregnant at the time they first engaged in the old bumpty-bump. Ms Fontaine at first denied the pregnancy, and later she tried to make Mr Strong believe that her ten-pound, eight-ounce son was premature.'

'My cousin Maxine had one of them ten-pound preemies,' Edna said thoughtfully. 'Child was so big she practically walked back from the delivery room. Course my Aunt Ernestine swore big preemies ran in the family.'

'Maybe Strong wasn't the father,' I said. 'Big deal. That doesn't prove that Hightower was.'

'Rita Fontaine admitted it to Strong,' Coyle said. 'They'd both been drinking heavily, and there was a fight. She actually taunted him with it. The next day, she swore Strong made it up. He left shortly thereafter.'

I took the newspaper, balled it up into a wad and threw it at the trash can by the back door. 'You're full of shit, and so is that rag you work for,' I told Coyle. 'What the hell do you want here, anyway?'

He smiled, showing a set of bad teeth. 'I want an exclusive with Rita Fontaine. This is an advance copy of the paper. It was couriered to me from our printing plant in Florida this morning. Once it hits the news-stands, every television, newspaper, and magazine reporter in the country will be after Rita Fontaine's story. I just wanted to afford her advance warning, a chance to tell her story. You know, "He Sentenced Me to a Life of Shame", that kind of thing.'

'You're the last person she'd talk to,' I said.

'Probably,' he agreed. 'But the *Global Examiner* is willing to pay fifty thousand for an exclusive. That'll pay for a nice bit of legal fees, give her a chance to get sympathy. From what I hear, Hightower was a bloody beast.'

'You've already smeared her with that crap,' I said. 'You do realize her son thinks his father was Cleveland Strong? Andre is a a nice man. Very religious. He works two jobs. He wants to help his mother get her life back together. What do you think a story like this will do to him. Will do to her?'

'Not my problem,' Coyle said airily. 'My job is merely to present the truth. You Americans have a delightful institution called the Constitution. And the First Amendment clearly states...'

'Screw the First Amendment,' I said, shoving him toward the back door. 'Out of my house. Now.'

He let himself be pushed. 'I've had a copy of the story delivered to Ms Fontaine,' he said. 'And I've put our offer in writing. Believe me. It's the best one she'll get.'

21

Sister was quietly transferring all the leftover birthday cake to a piece of aluminum foil. She hadn't missed any of my conversation with Mick Coyle. 'My, my, my,' she muttered to herself as she deftly wrapped the cake and slipped the package into the pocket of her housedress. The cake was followed by the ribbon from Neva Jean's presents, a wad of Happy Birthday paper napkins, and two used envelopes, which she lovingly pressed into shape with her long wrinkled fingers.

'You believe any of what he said?' Edna asked, taking her good silver-plate cake knife and putting it into the sink before Sister could appropriate it, too.

'True or not, it'll come as a shock to poor Andre,' I said. I reached for the phone. 'Keep your fingers crossed that Rita hasn't already gotten that envelope. She's been staying over at Vonette's house. Maybe Coyle doesn't know that. If he sends it to Andre's house, we can intercept it in time.'

Vonette said Rita was at the outpatient center, having group therapy. 'She'll be back here around four thirty,' Vonette said.

'There wasn't a package delivered for her this morning, was there?'

'Yeah,' Vonette said. 'Wonder what that's about?'

I should have known. Coyle's spies were everywhere. 'Put it away,' I said quickly. 'I'll try to be at your house when Rita gets there. Just don't let her see it or open it until I get there.'

'You better tell me what this is about if you know,' Vonette said, clearly alarmed. 'You know I can open that envelope if I want to. I got a right. She's staying with me, and she's my responsibility.'

I swallowed hard. 'One of those supermarket tabloids has gotten hold of some pretty devastating stuff about Rita. It's going to be published tomorrow. There's a copy of the story in the envelope – and an offer of fifty thousand dollars if she'll give them an exclusive.'

'Fifty thousand!' she yelped. 'That's a big pile of money. Why would they give that to Rita?'

I paused. I didn't have the right to tell Vonette her cousin's secret. Even if the world would know tomorrow. 'I'm sorry,' I said. 'If she wants to tell you, that's up to her. I wish I didn't know.'

'That's a lot of money,' Vonette repeated. 'These lawyer's fees aren't cheap, you know. And neither are yours, while we're on the subject.'

Here it came again. 'I never wanted to take this case in the first place, Vonette,' I said hotly. 'I only did it as a favor to C.W.'

She was silent for a moment. 'What's the old fool up to, anyway?'

'Do you really want to know or are you just hoping I'll say something bad?'

'I resent that,' she said sharply. And then. 'Ah, well. Look. We were married for almost twenty years. We had a child together. Like it or not, we're connected. You know, going through these sessions with Rita got me thinking. Wondering, you know if C.W. and I had paid more attention to things. If we could have made it.'

'What did you decide?'

She laughed suddenly. 'That it was a miracle we made it as long as we did. We're different people, that's all.'

I wondered if Barbara, Mac's ex-wife, ever had any regrets about their splitup.

'When was the last time you and C.W. saw each other face to face?' I asked.

She laughed again. It made her seem young, girlish even. 'Not for a long time. For the past three years, it's been mostly on the phone. I think he's still afraid of me after what I did to his suits.'

It was my turn to laugh now. 'You made an impression on him, all right,' I said. 'But you never did anything physical, did you?'

'Tell you the truth, I read an article about how Al Green's girlfriend or ex-wife or whatever dumped a pot of scalding hot grits on him while he was in the bathtub. When C.W. first walked out, I used to fantasize all the time about doing the same thing to him.'

'You wouldn't have, would you?'

'And waste a good pot of hominy on his sorry black ass? Hell no,' she said spiritedly.

I glanced quickly at the kitchen clock. It was already after ten o'clock, and I had people I needed to talk to.

'Look, Vonette,' I said. 'The stuff in that envelope is just explosive. I'm wondering if maybe we should talk to her doctor about it. I'm worried she might go off on a bender again.'

'She'll be all right,' Vonette said. 'She doesn't like to talk about it, but I notice she's got a little Bible Andre gave her, open beside her bed. She's been marking verses, making notes in the margin. And Andre's been over a lot this week, in between work, talking and praying with her. She's getting strong. You'll see.'

I cringed a little at the mention of Andre's name. If Coyle was right, finding out who his father really was would be a test of Andre's own faith.

'I'll be over at four thirty,' I repeated. 'We'll talk about it then.'

Edna had cleared away the breakfast dishes, and Baby and Sister were in the other room watching *Regis and Kathy Lee* on television, waiting for their big assignment.

'You be careful,' I told her as my mother as I went out the door. 'Don't take anything. Just browse. Get in and get out. And don't forget to do a good job. If she's innocent, Serena might make a good client.'

I'd already decided to ambush Jack Rabin at work. Before I left the house I'd called WPCH and learned he'd be there until after one o'clock. I saw his car, the battered station wagon in the parking lot, and jotted the license tag down on a piece of paper. The sky above was bright blue and nearly cloudless, the heat in the parking lot searing, making the asphalt slightly gooey under my feet.

Inside the station, I told the receptionist who I wanted to see, but Rabin was on the phone, so I had to wait. The station piped in the music being played on the air. It had been years since I'd heard the Mitch Miller Orchestra. And I had no idea Mantovani had done a cover of 'Light My Fire.'

I was about to cover my ears with my hands when Rabin appeared in the waiting area. He obviously remembered my face but not my name. 'Oh hello,' he said, his voice registering mild surprise. 'How are you coming along with the search for the missing VelvetTeen?'

'Not too badly,' I said pleasantly. 'But I'm really here to talk about another matter. Could we go in your office and talk?'

He frowned, the fleshy dewlaps around his mouth dropping like a depressed basset hound's. 'I've got a marketing meeting this afternoon.'

'It's early,' I pointed out. 'And I really think you'd prefer to talk to me about Stu Hightower here than in court.'

He wheeled around to see if the receptionist had overheard me. But she was busy on the phone. 'Come on back,' he said.

His office was a tiny windowless square, just big enough to hold a desk, two green vinyl chairs and dozens of boxes of promotional bumper stickers, T-shirts, and china coffee mugs, all bearing the station's logo. He pushed a giant peach-shaped beachball out of his chair and sat down. I sat down in the opposite chair without being invited.

He popped up out of the chair, looked down the hallway, then shut the office door. When he turned around his face was suddenly white, pinched with fear.

'That thing in Houston was bullshit,' he said without preamble. 'I was told if I cooperated before the grand jury, it would be confidential. They gave me immunity. That rat fuck Hightower,' he said bitterly. 'He told you what went on, didn't he? He was spreading stuff all over town. That's why I sued.'

I had no idea what Rabin was talking about. And for once, I didn't have the time or the inclination to bluff.

'Hightower didn't tell me anything,' I said. 'I've been retained by Rita Fontaine's defense attorney. I'm sure you know she's been charged with Hightower's murder. I wanted to see you about the lawsuits. What was it all about?'

He leaned back in his chair, took a deep breath, then exhaled slowly, his hands folded on his high round belly. 'I don't have to tell you anything,' he said.

'True,' I agreed. 'I could just call every radio station in Houston until I find the one you worked for. I could search one of those computer databases for newspaper stories from Houston until I find what I want. Or I could call the personnel director of this station to find out where you worked in Texas. Or would you prefer I skipped that and called the station manager?'

The fear was back in his face. 'You mention anything about Houston and I'll be fired,' he said. 'I'd be through in the business. In this town. Every town. Hightower knew that.'

Rabin was dressed for business today. A dark blue suit coat hung on the back of his closed office door. He wore a light blue dress shirt, and there were dark patches of perspiration under the arms. He tugged at his collar, which was also damp.

'I'm not looking to get you fired,' I said. 'But my client didn't kill Stu Hightower. She was set up. I need to know what was going on with you and Hightower. Believe me, if I can find out about these lawsuits, so can the cops.'

'Jesus,' Rabin said. 'I wish to God I'd never met him. Dealing with him was the worst thing that's ever happened to me.'

'Did you kill him?'

'No,' Rabin said, looking horrified. 'Don't say that. The news said Rita Fontaine killed him. That she was found with the gun. At his house.'

'The news doesn't always get everything right,' I said. 'It seems to me that there are several people who might have had a motive to kill Hightower. Like you. You just told me he could have ruined your life.'

'He would have,' Rabin said, dabbing at the beads of perspiration on his forehead. 'As soon as I came back to Atlanta, he was on the phone, telling me he'd never forgotten what had gone down in Houston. He swore he'd tell everybody. I guess he was just too busy screwing other people to get around to me.'

I leaned forward, gave Rabin a conspiratorial smile. 'Why don't you tell me what happened? If you didn't kill anybody, how bad could it be?'

'The worst,' Rabin said. 'You just don't know.'

He breathed heavily for a while, dabbed at his gleaming wet face again. I wondered if he were going to have a heart attack right on the spot.

Finally he started to unravel the story.

'I left Atlanta in seventy-eight. Things were changing. I'd split with my first wife. Houston seemed like as good a place as any. I hated disco. And country was suddenly hot. I got a spot as a morning drivetime jock. They were between programming directors, so I did that too. Lonestar Jack, I called myself. And I was doin' good. The numbers were up, the sponsors were happy. There was a lot of money floating around, you know what I mean?'

'Payola?'

He shuddered. 'Christ. Don't even say that word in this office. In this building.'

'You got caught?'

He nodded, his dewlaps drooping again.

'You know the stupid thing? It wasn't even that much money. A couple hundred dollars a week and the occasional gram of coke. And I probably would have played most of the records anyway. It wasn't me they were after. The justice department wanted to prove this big conspiracy among all the big record labels.'

'How did Hightower get involved?'

'He'd switched over to country once it was clear Motown was dead. SkyHi was one of the labels doling out the goodies,' Rabin said.

Now I was really confused. 'If he provided the payola, wasn't he just as guilty as you?'

Rabin looked briefly amused at my expense. 'You don't know nothing about the music business, do you? It was Hightower's label. This was before he started up BackTalk. But he had an independent promoter, a guy named Johnny Balfa working with the radio stations. The promoter was the one who put the cash and coke in the cassette boxes and mailed 'em to the radio stations every week. That way, the record companies could say they didn't know anything about the payments. They just paid the promoters to get the songs on the radio; they didn't know nothing about how they accomplished it.'

'What happened?'

He sighed. 'There was a grand jury investigation. The dumb fuck Balfa kept records in his house of every payment, every date. I got called to testify. What the hell else could I do? Hightower got called too. He denied everything, naturally. But Balfa was smart about one thing. He taped a couple of his phone conversations with Hightower. I could have sworn we were all going to jail for a long, long time.'

Obviously though, they hadn't.

Rabin noticed my puzzled look. 'It's the one and only time I got lucky in that whole deal. Balfa got cancer right in the middle of everything. Testicular. He knew he was gonna die anyhow, so once he got sick, he told the feds to take a leap, he wasn't testifying about nothing. What could they do? Before they knew it, Balfa was dead. And their case was down the toilet.' He wore a look of grim satisfaction on his face. Another man's death sentence had been Rabin's reprieve. And Hightower's.

'That's some story,' I said. 'It still means the same thing. Hightower hated you. He would have ruined your career if he could have. So you've got a great motive for wanting him dead.'

Rabin was looking more and more uncomfortable.

I took a shot in the dark. 'You were out at his house Monday night, weren't you? Right around the time he was killed? Were you trying to talk him out of getting you fired? Is that what happened?'

'No way,' Rabin said, hopping out of his chair again.

'Way,' I said. I'd obviously touched a nerve here. 'I've seen your car, remember? I saw it out in the parking lot again today. The security guards out at Country Club of the South keep records of all the cars going in and out. The cops have the list, Jack. You know what? I'll bet you were out there that night.'

He sank back down into his chair. 'You can't prove anything,' he muttered. I could see that the whole back of his shirt was drenched in sweat. I'll bet he made a lousy poker player.

'You'll be surprised at what I can prove,' I told him, getting up to leave. 'My client didn't kill Hightower. If you did, your ass is grass, and I'm the lawn mower.'

22

I'd tried calling Lyman Woodall's office once before leaving home. The receptionist put me on hold for ten minutes, and I finally got tired of waiting and hung up. This time when I called back, I quickly told the receptionist I was calling long distance. From my car phone, everything sounds long distance.

'Oh, he's not here,' the receptionist said. 'He's at a medical conference in Aspen. He won't be back until the middle of next week. Dr Hansen is handling his caseload. Would you like to speak to his appointment clerk?'

No I wouldn't. Instead I asked how long Dr Woodall had been gone.

'Let's see,' she said. I could hear pages flipping. 'He always takes two weeks for his vacation, so it's been almost three weeks he's been gone now.'

'Has he been in town at all?' I asked. 'I thought I saw him at Lenox Square Mall last week.'

'Must have been his twin brother,' she said, chuckling. 'Dr Woodall does these bird-watching expeditions. I think he was in Guatemala this time. Or Ecuador. I can't keep those rain forest places straight. Are you sure you wouldn't like to speak to Dr Hansen's secretary?'

So much for Lyman Woodall. If I'd had a checklist of potential suspects, I would have crossed his name off the list there and then. He might have hated Hightower, but he probably hadn't sneaked back into town from the rain forest just to do away with a pesky neighbor.

I bit my lip and drummed my fingers on the steering wheel of the van. There was no getting around it. I was going to have to pay a call on Artie DiPima. Korznick had filed a motion to get all the cop's preliminary reports and lab results forwarded to us. It was early yet, but I needed some of that information.

On the way to the police precinct I went over my approach. I'd be pleasant. Cordial. Without any sucking up. We had a right to see any evidence the cops had against Rita. And they knew it.

DiPima was seated at a computer terminal, his back facing me, pecking with two fingers at the keyboard.

I slid into a chair beside his desk. 'Hi, Artie,' I said.

He looked up briefly, then went back to typing. 'Who let you in here, Garrity?'

'I'm fine, thanks. How are the wife and kids? Good, I hope.'

'I'm single,' he said. 'What is it you want?'

I took a deep breath. 'To start with, I'd like to see the results of the gun powder residue tests you ran on Rita Fontaine. And I'm interested in the forensics report also. We want to know whether the bullet that killed Hightower came from that twenty-two.'

'Bad news,' he drawled. 'Your client had gunpowder residue all over her hands.'

I took a deep breath. I didn't want DiPima to think he had me beaten. 'She was drunk,' I said. 'Maybe she found the gun on the ground and picked it up and fired it in the air. To get Hightower's attention. That doesn't mean she shot Hightower. What about the bullet that killed him?'

He shook his head. 'The forensics report's not back yet. Don't expect it for at least another week.' He gestured toward a stack of incident reports beside his computer. 'You might say this is our busy season, Garrity. We got six homicides for June already. Atlanta's got a dozen that I know of. The state lab is always backed up. Even you ought to know that.'

DiPima was right. Georgia's one crime lab serves all 159 counties. From my cop days I knew how busy the lab was. I knew it, but I had to try anyway.

'What about the twenty-two?' I asked. 'Whose was it?'

The smart-aleck grin on DiPima's face faded. 'Registered to Stuart Hightower,' he said. 'But that proves nothing.'

'Except that Rita Fontaine didn't go out there with a gun intending to kill Stu Hightower,' I said. 'This whole thing stinks of a setup, Artie, and you know it.'

'It stinks like a homicide, that's what I know,' DiPima said. 'What are you telling me, that there's a conspiracy against Rita Fontaine? What, you think there were two gunmen on that grassy knoll in Dallas too?'

I decided to ignore that last comment. 'What about the guards at the security gates out at Riverbend? Have you gotten a list from them of cars that went in and out that night?'

He had gone back to typing, but he stopped again. 'To a point.'

'What does that mean? What point?'

He reached over to the in basket on top of his desk and shuffled paper until he came to the one he wanted. He glanced at it and handed it over to me.

It was a photocopied page from the Riverbend security logbook. Monday's date was scribbled at the top of the page, along with a pair of nearly indecipherable sets of initials.

There were only four times listed on the sheet, and four hastily scrawled license plate numbers.

'Only four cars?' I said incredulously. 'In twenty-four hours? They didn't even list Rita Fontaine's car here. Vonette's isn't on here either. Where's the rest of the list?'

He shrugged. 'You think we're happy about this? We ran all those tags. The numbers are all screwed up. The dipshit rent-a-cops didn't even bother to write down real numbers. As soon as the security people saw the logbook they canned the two guys who were working that night. Of course, now I'm sure we'll be able to find these two clowns again when we go to trial.'

I looked down at the paper again, my hands twitching I was so angry. I was positive Rabin had been out to see Hightower on Monday. Now I'd have to find some other way to prove it.

'Can you give me the guards' names and phone numbers?'

He started to say no, but I cut him off at the pass. 'We'll get it one way or another. How about we cut the bullshit and you give it to me now?'

DiPima opened a file folder, leafed through the pages, found what he was looking for and copied down some names on a scrap of paper, which he then passed over to me. 'Knock yourself out,' he said. 'They did manage to positively ID your client.'

I decided to try a change in tack. 'How about the lab results from the pool house? Have the fingerprints come back yet? Was the stereo system fingerprinted?'

DiPima crossed his arms over his chest and gave me a long, slow stare.

'What?' He was making me uncomfortable, a sensation he undoubtedly enjoyed.

'Found a nice set of partials on that stereo belonging to your client,' DiPima said. 'What I can't figure out is why you stick with such a loser of a case. Rita Fontaine was found with the murder weapon, on the scene. She's a raving alcoholic, for Christ's sake. I find it hard to believe that anyone, even you, could believe that she's innocent. And by the way, I had a call from your buddy, C. W. Hunsecker.'

He saw the surprised look on my face.

'Nah. He knows better than to try to interfere in a case. Especially one where his family is involved up to their asses.'

'Vonette is his ex-wife,' I said, correcting him.

'Whatever. Hunsecker wanted me to know that you're on the up and up. Me and him go back a ways. He says you two go back a ways too. Says you're buddies with his new wife. I told him straight out. No favors. 'Fine' he says. 'But you don't have to go out of your way to give Garrity a hard time. Right?' So that's what I'm doing right now. Not giving you a hard time.'

You could have fooled me.

'So Artie,' I said. 'Now that we're friends and all, have you taken a good look at all the people who work for BackTalk?'

'We've talked to them,' he said cautiously.

'Have you talked to Danielle Manigault?'

'That's the woman who was second in command?'

'Yes.'

'She was one of the first ones we interviewed,' DiPima said. 'She said she was at some record distributor's convention in LA. Her plane didn't land at Hartsfield until nine forty-five p.m. Monday.'

'Are you sure she was in LA?' I asked. 'Sure she came back on the flight she booked? Danielle Manigault is in line to take over the business, you know.'

DiPima frowned. 'If you keep telling me how to do my job, we're not gonna stay friends for very long, Garrity. But for your information, Ms Manigault was one of only half a dozen first-class passengers on that Delta flight. She had a little hissy when they didn't have her favorite brand of bottled water on board, and then when they didn't have the vegetarian dinner she'd preordered, she really made a scene. The flight attendants all remembered her. One woman even described in detail what Ms Manigault was wearing that night. Everything was just like she'd told us.'

'Fine,' I said, trying to hide my disappointment.

'Are you aware that Hightower also had a feud with a disc jockey here in town? Jack Rabin, over at WPCH?'

'Rabin?' DiPima looked puzzled.

'Did you grow up around Atlanta, DiPima?'

'Nah,' he said. 'I'm from Savannah.'

'Never mind,' I said. 'He was Jacky Rabbit back in the sixties, when Hightower was starting SkyHi Records, the label the VelvetTeens recorded for.'

'So?' DiPima looked bored. Maybe he didn't like sixties music.

'So, Rabin was mixed up in a payola scandal when he worked in Houston. He got called before a federal grand jury and he testified about kickbacks he'd gotten: money and drugs funneled to him by a promoter hired by Hightower. Hightower very nearly went to prison for his role in the deal.'

DiPima suddenly looked interested. 'How do you happen to know so much about this?'

I told him what I'd learned from Rabin, and most of what I'd learned from Matt Gordon about BackTalk's recent history.

'If BackTalk is sold to a bigger, mainstream label, it's a whole new ball game over there,' I pointed out. 'Danielle Manigault stands to lose her big fancy job, and some of the other artists might get left out in the cold too.'

I thought back to the scene I'd witnessed between Danielle and Junebug's mother, Arlene Trotter. 'This was a multi-multimillion-dollar deal,' I said. 'Lots of people's futures were hanging by a thread.'

DiPima was still dubious. 'Yeah, this is all real fascinating, Garrity. But none of it puts anybody else out there at that house with a gun in their hand.'

'Somebody else was out there,' I said stubbornly.

'You want my advice?' DiPima said. 'You tell Rita Fontaine's lawyer to start planning a sentencing strategy. She did it, and we can prove it. We got so much other shit going on, it would save everybody a lot of grief if she'd just go ahead and plead out.'

I got up to leave. 'That's not going to happen,' I said.

The phone on DiPima's desk started to buzz before I was at the door. He listened for a moment, then held out a hand to tell me not to leave. He listened intently.

'That's good,' he told the caller. 'I got their boss right here. Yeah. I'll call you back.'

He hung up the phone. 'Say Garrity,' he said, allowing himself a brief smirk. 'That was one of our uniformed officers. A guy named Barnhart. He's got a complaint from a woman over at Riverbend. Stu Hightower's ex-wife hired a cleaning business to clean her house today. When she comes home unannounced to check up on them, she finds three old ladies ransacking the place. One of them claims to be your mother. You know anything about this?'

23

'This is all a misunderstanding,' I told DiPima as I followed him down the hall to the property crimes unit.

'I'll bet,' DiPima said, unsmiling.

Baby and Sister were huddled together on a small green leather sofa in the burglary unit office. Edna sat stiffly on a chair nearby, silently fuming. A petite Oriental woman with waist-length black hair was standing in front of a desk, berating a black plainclothes detective.

'Put these people in the hokey,' she said loudly. 'They are thieves. They steal from me.'

DiPima stood in the doorway, arms folded across his chest, enjoying the scene. The other man looked up at us, questioningly.

'Detective Steadman, this is Callahan Garrity. Ms Garrity owns the cleaning business that employs these people.'

Serena whirled around to face me. She was classically beautiful, with a pale round face and huge almond-shaped eyes. She wore a bright red linen city shorts suit and big gold hoop earrings. 'You're the one. You send thieves into my home. You're not a cleaning business. You're a detective. You're working for the woman who killed Stu. I saw you on the news on television. I'm going to have these thieves locked up. I'm going to sue you and put you out of business...' Then she lapsed into a language I assumed must be Korean.

While she was berating me, I stepped up to Steadman's desk. 'Look, Detective Steadman, this is all a mistake. My employees are not thieves. They were at Ms Choi's home to clean, with her approval. She even left word at the security gate that they were to be admitted. She hired us.'

'Is that true?' Steadman asked.

'I never hire them to rickrack my house,' Serena shrieked. She pointed to Baby, who was tightly clutching Sister's hand. The elderly women were clearly frightened. 'That one was in my bedroom, taking my dresser drawers apart.'

Baby blinked innocently. 'What's that lady saying? I can't hear too good.'

I walked over to Baby and bent down close to her ear, giving her a broad wink. 'She thinks you were going through her dresser drawers looking for something.'

'Sure was,' Baby said. 'I was looking for an old nylon stocking to scrub that nasty commode of hers. I seen cleaner gas station bathrooms than what she's got.' She looked up at Serena. 'I like nylon stockings better than them scrub brushes you buy. And try some of that new Clorox cleaner. It works real good on scum like you got.'

Serena's eyes bulged at the insult to her cleanliness. She whipped around and pointed at Edna. 'This one had all the papers pulled out of my desk, reading them. Why a cleaning lady need to read my papers? She was looking for money to steal. That's what.'

I gave my mother a very stern expression. 'Is what she says right, Edna?'

Edna laughed. 'Well, she might have thought I was going through her desk. It might have looked that way. What I was trying to do was find a pencil to leave her a message about that dining room rug of hers.'

She looked up at Serena, all helpfulness. 'You got some bad stains on that nice Oriental rug. Looks like somebody's dog needs housebreaking. We spot cleaned it, but I believe you need to send it out to Sharian's to be cleaned. He does a real good job.' Edna turned to Detective Steadman. 'Our customers get a ten percent discount with a House Mouse referral. You want one of our business cards?'

Steadman gamely accepted the card Edna held out to him, tucking it into the breast pocket of his starched white shirt.

I had to clamp my hand over my mouth to keep myself from breaking into a fit of giggles. Serena heard my suppressed laugh and was not amused.

'You think this is funny? I'm a widow. My husband was killed this week. You people invade my home. I'm not laughing.'

She shook a tiny scarlet painted fingernail under my nose. 'You think you can come in my house and steal my stuff. Hah! I know nobody cleans house for free. I leave the house, go out, drive around a while, then snick back and catch the three thieves. Trying to steal. I call the cops.'

Serena glared at me. 'Who you think you dealing with here? I'm not fresh off the boat.'

I gently pushed her finger away. Then I looked at Steadman, who was practicing his best poker face.

'These women are my employees. The House Mouse is a licensed, bonded, residential cleaning business. We offered Ms Choi a complimentary cleaning because we're trying to expand our client base in North Fulton County. I'm sorry she wasn't happy with our performance, but I think if she had let my girls finish she wouldn't have had any basis for complaint.'

Steadman looked from me to Serena, then to Baby, Sister and Edna.

'Aren't these women a little old to be cleaning houses, Ms Garrity?'

Edna gasped angrily. 'Who are you calling old?' She shot daggers at Steadman.

Now it was my turn for finger pointing. 'Detective Steadman,' I said. 'I'm surprised at you. Surely you aren't suggesting that I should engage in age discrimination?'

'Uh, no,' Steadman sputtered. 'I didn't mean they couldn't work, I was just surprised that they were so ...'

'Can we go now, Callahan?' Sister said plaintively. 'It's time for my medicine.'

The only medicine Sister takes with any regularity is a tablespoon full of Old Grand-Dad in the winter for colds. It was actually time for the Easterbrookses' favorite soap opera, which they never miss, but I didn't share that with the authorities.

'Has Ms Choi actually filed any charges?' I wanted to know. 'My girls entered the house with a key she left them, so it wasn't breaking and entering. And there wasn't anything taken – right?'

'Hah!' Serena said triumphantly. 'The blind one had this in her purse. It's mine, obviously.'

She held out her hand. Resting in the palm was a pale pink tissue holding a pair of long black fake eyelashes.

I took the tissue and walked over to Sister, who was peering around, trying to see what Serena was accusing her of stealing.

'Miss Sister,' I said gently. 'Did you mean to take this lady's eyelashes?'

'No ma'am,' Sister said firmly. 'I found them things on the bathroom floor. I started in stompin' on it cuz I thought it was a big old poison spider. I scooped it up with a tissue, and I put it in my pocketbook for safe-keeping, cuz I was gonna tell that lady she needs to call the bug man. I wouldn't steal nothing. The Lord knows that. You know it, don't you Callahan?'

Steadman's lips twitched in a suspicious manner.

'Detective Steadman,' I said. 'Miss Sister here is eighty-two years old. She's the president of the senior deaconesses at First Maranatha AME and a worthy matron in the Eastern Star. Why would she want to steal a pair of five-dollar phony eyelashes?'

'Those are custom made in Nepal from human hair,' Serena protested. 'They cost forty-five dollars wholesale.'

I handed the tissue back to Serena with deliberate dignity. 'Then you'd best not leave them on the bathroom floor. I'm terribly sorry for the misunderstanding.'

I addressed myself to Steadman then. 'If charges aren't going to be filed, I'll take the ladies home with me. Is that all right?'

Steadman looked at DiPima, who looked at me. 'That okay with you?' DiPima asked him.

Then Steadman turned to Serena. 'Ma'am, since you did give the ladies permission to enter your home and nothing was taken or vandalized, I don't really have a reason to detain these women. I'm sorry.'

'Sorry,' Serena said loudly. 'I want these spies put in jail. These are not maids. These are secret agents.'

'Nothing I can do, ma'am,' Steadman repeated.

The girls and I beat a hasty retreat to the parking lot, with Serena hot on our trail, cursing us the whole way in a mixture of English and Korean.

I helped Baby and Sister into the van, with Serena standing by, hands on hips. 'Spies,' she hissed.

Edna followed me home in the land yacht. When we got there, she walked straight to the refrigerator door and pulled out three long-necked bottles of beer. She handed one each to Baby and Sister, and kept the third for herself.

She didn't say a word until she'd taken a long slow gulp of the cold brew. Then she set the bottle on the scarred oak kitchen table with a bang.

'That,' she said loudly, 'was a damn close call. Wasn't it girls?'

'Ooh-whee,' Sister said, collapsing into a chair. 'I was

258

in the kitchen when that lady jumped out at me. I near about wet my knickers, she scared me so bad.'

'She screaming and hollering about us stealing from her,' Baby agreed. 'That was a bad scare, wasn't it, Miss Edna?'

'It's just a good thing I don't have heart problems,' Edna said. 'Or I would have been laid out right there on that nasty Oriental rug of hers, dead of a myocardial infarction.'

Edna reached into the pocket of her pink cleaning smock and pulled out a pack of cigarettes. She lit up and inhaled deeply. 'I can't talk any more for a while now,' she said. 'I need to smoke me about a pack of cigarettes to calm my nerves down.'

'I know that's right,' Baby said. 'You got any Brown Mule in that pocket of yours, Miss Edna?'

Baby settled for one of Edna's filter-tips. The two of them enveloped themselves in a cloud of smoke, until Sister started coughing and waving ineffectively at the fumes. She picked up her pocketbook and dug around until she found a handkerchief, which she promptly dropped on the floor.

When she bent over to get it, a small plastic object fell onto the floor beside the handkerchief.

Sister picked it up and put it on the table. 'I nearly forgot about this. I was just so mad she found them eyelashes. I was gonna wear those on my trip to Myrtle Beach, South Carolina. That hussy didn't need no more eyelashes. She got 'bout two dozen right there in that dressing table of hers.'

It was a microcassette tape.

'Where did this come from?' I asked.

Edna leaned her head back and blew a series of smoke rings toward the ceiling. 'Now where do you think? It's Serena's.'

'Oh no,' I said. 'She'll go home and find it missing and call the cops on us again. We've got to get rid of this thing.'

'Don't be so paranoid,' Edna said calmly. 'There was a whole drawerful of tapes by her answering machine. I stuck another one in the machine. She'll never know.'

'What about the announcement? You're not exactly fluent in Korean.'

'There was a little cassette tape player right by the phone. She apparently likes to listen to herself sing an awful lot. Sounds like shit, by the way. She sings through her nose just like that Diana Ross. I rerecorded her announcement onto another tape. Then I gave her tape to Sister to hide in the safe.'

'My bosom,' Sister said proudly. 'Any mans tries to touch that, he gonna draw back a bloody stump.'

'Let's play it,' Edna said. 'Then I'll tell you what little we found before the suspicious bitch hijacked us. I sure hope there's something good on there after we did all that hard work and nearly got thrown in jail.'

I looked over at the kitchen clock and jumped out of my chair. It was nearly four o'clock.

'We'll listen when I get back,' I promised. 'Pay Baby and Sister and take 'em home, will you? And give them each twenty-five extra for combat duty.'

24

Vonette and I waited together for Rita to get back from her therapy session. She'd sent Kenyatta to pick her up at the hospital. I was wishing I'd had a beer with Edna and the girls. I'm not good at scenes. And although I'm usually nosy to a fault, this was the one time I wished I didn't know somebody else's secrets.

Vonette was anxious too. She kept hopping up and down, running into the kitchen to check on the tuna steaks she was marinating for dinner. When she sat down opposite me on the sofa, I noticed she was twisting a large diamond solitaire ring on her right hand, turning the stone around and around. I hadn't noticed the ring before.

'That's a beautiful ring,' I said. 'Was it a gift from C.W.?'

'On a cop's paycheck?' The notion seemed to amuse her. 'Actually, Stu gave all of us these rings to wear the first time we went on *The Ed Sullivan Show*.'

A dreamy look came into her eyes. 'He had gowns made for us too, black strapless ones, with sequins all over. They fit like a mermaid's skin. I was worried to death my boobs would fall out right there in front of old Ed

Sullivan. We'd seen the gowns for the fittings, of course. But the night of the show, Stu picked us up at our hotel in a big old limo. He put us up in the Waldorf-Astoria. And then he gave each of us these rings. You could have knocked me down with a feather.'

I eyed the ring with newfound admiration. 'He was pretty generous, huh?'

She looked down at the ring. 'I'll say this for Stu. He wanted us to have everything first class. Nothing was too good for the VelvetTeens. We were treated like princesses. Can you imagine? Three little colored girls from the projects in Atlanta, Georgia. And Stu was color blind too. As much as anybody could be back then. It made him furious when he sent us out on tour the first time and we had to sleep on the bus because motels in the South wouldn't rent to black folks. After that he got us a bus with a real bathroom and even a little shower.'

She sighed heavily. 'That's why it was such a shock, when he dropped us.' She snapped her fingers. 'Just like that. We were done. As far as Stu was concerned, it was just business.'

We heard a car in the driveway then, and the sound of doors slamming. She hopped up from the sofa. 'What should I do? Can I be with her when you show her what's in that envelope? Rita needs me.'

I gripped the Federal Express envelope in my right hand, half-afraid of the contents. 'Why don't you leave us by ourselves while I tell her? I'll call you if it looks like things are going badly.'

Rita opened the front door and walked in smiling, trailed by Kenyatta. I'd never seen her looking so relaxed. She'd put on makeup that emphasized her amazing eyes and a touch of lipstick. Her hair had been trimmed, close to her head, in a sort of modified pixie cut. She'd taken pains with her clothes, too. She wore a slim pair of black jeans with a white-and-black striped T-shirt tucked at the waist, and a pair of black sandals. She was laughing at something Kenyatta had said. For the first time I could visualize the Rita Fontaine who'd made grown men howl like wild animals.

'Hey,' she said when she saw me. She stopped laughing, but for once she wasn't scowling, either.

'Hey, Baby,' Vonette said, giving her cousin a quick hug. 'How did it go today? Better?'

'Not bad,' Rita admitted. 'Group was all right. I think maybe I'll get there.'

Vonette patted her arm. 'I know you will.' She gave me a nervous glance. 'Callahan's got something she needs to talk to you about now. Kenyatta and I need to go out to the kitchen to check on dinner.'

Rita sat down on one of the champagne-colored armchairs. I sat on the sofa, unsure of how to proceed.

'How bad can it be?' Rita said, clasping her hands behind her head. 'I'm facing a murder trial, I'm a drunk in recovery. The way I figure it, ain't too much bad stuff hasn't already happened.'

She gazed at me steadily, expectantly.

I handed her the envelope. 'There's a newspaper story in there. And a check. A reporter for the *Global Examiner*, one of those trashy supermarket papers, dug up a lot of old stuff about you.' I took a deep breath. 'He tracked down Cleveland Strong, Rita. Strong told the paper he's not Andre's father. He told them Stu Hightower was the father. And the story runs tomorrow. It's too late to stop it. They're offering you fifty thousand dollars if you'll give them your exclusive story. They want to run it next week.'

She blinked a couple of times, but her face remained expressionless. She opened the envelope slowly, taking the paper pull tab and placing it in a clean ashtray on the table. She unfolded the photocopied article and studied it intently. She took out the check, looked at it, then put it back in the envelope, folded the story, and put it back in too.

'My mama would say the other shoe has dropped,' she said, when she finally spoke. 'I wondered how long it would be before somebody found out.'

'Are you worried about how Andre will take the news?' I asked. 'We could call him at work, have him paged . . .'

'I'll need to tell him it's going to be in the paper. But he knows who his father was. Been knowing a long time.'

'You told him?'

She put the envelope down on the sofa. 'Wait a minute.'

She got up and walked into the kitchen. She was in there for maybe ten minutes. When she came back, Vonette and Kenyatta came with her. All three of them were teary-eyed, with Vonette making a valiant attempt to smile.

'I told them,' Rita said, her voice a little shaky.

'We never knew,' Vonette said, dabbing at her eyes with a tissue. 'I mean, nobody ever suspected. I don't see how you kept it a secret all these years. Andre was light skinned, but you're light skinned, and so was Aunt Louise.'

'You didn't know there was a whitey in the woodpile, did you?'

Rita seemed pleased at her joke, but Vonette was still shocked, still shaking her head.

Rita was rubbing her fingertips together. 'Man, I would kill for a cigarette right now. I mean, I seriously need a smoke.'

Vonette hesitated, then pushed the ashtray toward her cousin. Rita pushed it away. 'Later. Anyway, I'm out of smokes right now.'

I hesitated a moment. The family bonding was touching and all, but it was time to talk facts. I needed to call Rita's lawyer and alert him to what was going on.

'Rita, you said Andre knew about Stu,' I said. 'How did he find out?'

'I had just broken up with Earl, my second husband. Actually, he walked out on me. Andre, he was about fourteen or fifteen. As soon as there wasn't a man around any more, he was uncontrollable. Staying out all night, running in the streets, cutting school. He wouldn't listen to nothing I said, smarted off at me all the time. One time, we had a big fight. He told me he was gonna go live with his father, with Cleveland.'

'But he was just a baby when you and Cleve broke up,' Vonette said. 'Andre never even knew Cleve.'

'Yeah, well, a daddy you ain't never met is still better than nothin',' Rita said dryly. 'He kept at me about finding Cleve. Wanting to know where he was, whether he had any other kids. That boy wore me down. One Saturday morning, he came out of his room with a little suitcase all packed. 'I'm leaving to go stay with my daddy,' he tells me.'

Her smile was grim. 'I was sober at the time too. Funny, huh? So I just sat him down and told him the truth. 'Your daddy is not Cleveland Strong,' I said. 'That's a lie I told you for a long, long time because I was young and scared when I found out I was going to have a baby.'

'Andre, he got real quiet,' Rita continued. 'He didn't want to believe me. He was mad as hell that I took away the make believe daddy he had all these years and then ran off Earl, who was no kind of daddy at all to him, but at least he was a man.'

She looked over at Vonette. 'Remember that time Andre ran away from home, and the police put him in that youth detention center?'

'I remember that,' Kenyatta said. 'Me and Mama went and visited him. It was awful.'

Vonette nodded. 'That's the only time that child ever acted out or got in trouble.'

'You're right,' Rita said. 'He was used to being the grownup in the house, because the Lord knows I never was one. After he came home from the YDC, one night he came to me. 'You need to tell me who my real daddy is,' he said. So serious. Andre was always so solemn. He was a serious baby even. So I told him. I gave him a picture of Stu, an old one, the only one I'd kept. And we never talked about it again after that night.'

'Did Stu know?' Vonette asked. 'Did you tell him you were pregnant?'

Rita's lips tightened. 'I never said a word. The only person in the world who knew the truth was Delores.'

Vonette was weeping softly. 'You told Delores, but you never breathed a word to me. Why? Baby, didn't you know I'd help you, take care of you? You didn't have to go and marry Cleve. Me and Delores, we were family. We would have taken care of you.'

Rita looked as if she might break down too. 'This was right at the same time Stu was getting ready to drop us. Y'all didn't know nothing about it, but what he really was planning was to break up the VelvetTeens. We'd been sleeping together for a couple months, but it was a big secret. All those rehearsals I told y'all I was doing? All of it was on a mattress in the company suite at the Ambassador Hotel downtown. Stu said the VelvetTeens were holding me back. He was gonna make me bigger than Mary Wells or Aretha Franklin or anybody.'

'That motherfucker,' Vonette said. 'Mo-therfuck!'

'Mama,' Kenyatta said, obviously shocked.

'She's got a right,' Rita said. 'Of course, what I didn't know was that he was singing the same tune to Delores.'

'He was cheating on you with your own sister?' Kenyatta gasped.

'Or cheating on Delores with her own sister,' Rita said, appreciating the irony. 'Once I found out, I didn't stick around to find out which was which.'

She looked at Vonette apologetically. 'I'm sorry, Vonne. I was drinking bad. And then it all blew up in my face. Stu had set up a recording session for me. I got so nervous about singing alone, I drank a whole bottle of Couvoisier and passed out cold in the bathroom of my apartment. I never made the session. The next day, Stu called me up. He said we were through. I'd violated my contract, and I was a disgusting drunk. That's what he said. Disgusting. And he said the VelvetTeens were through, too.'

'Motherfucker,' Vonette mumbled.

'So there I was,' Rita said. 'Twenty years old. Pregnant, hung over, washed up. Cleve had been giving me the eye on our last tour. The next time he put his hand on my leg, I let it stay there.'

'And before we knew it, Delores had run off and married David Eisner on the rebound,' Vonette said. 'What a mess.'

'Well, now,' Rita cautioned. 'From what little Delores told me before she left, she and Stu hadn't really gotten down to any serious business. She thought maybe he was just playing around, flirting for the sake of flirting. She went along because he was the boss. But I think she'd really fallen hard for David. She always did have a thing for little short white dudes.'

'Wow,' I said, getting up to use the phone. 'I'd better call Korznick. This is going to add a complication he hadn't planned on. Unfortunately,' I added, 'from the DA's point of view, this just means your motive to kill Hightower was that much stronger.'

I paused, wondering if I should let her know that the cops could prove she'd fired the gun that probably killed Hightower, then decided to let Korznick make that decision. I'd put enough stuff on Rita Fontaine today. The rest could wait until later.

Rita stroked the envelope in her lap. 'There's a check in

here too, Vonne,' she said softly. 'Fifty thousand dollars if I tell my story to that paper.' She stuck out her chin. 'I could pay the lawyer myself. Put some money aside for Andre. Start paying you back for all the times you bailed me out.'

In answer, Vonette snatched the envelope out of her cousin's hands. 'I put up with a lot from you over the years, Rita Fontaine. But I won't put up with your having anything to do with this mess. We'll take care of this like we have everything else. You've got to respect yourself, girl,' she scolded. 'You made your mistakes. But the person you hurt the most was you. Now it's time to go ahead on. Let the past take care of itself.'

I used the phone in the kitchen. Korznick wasn't exactly thrilled with the news that his client had a grown son by the man she was accused of murdering.

'Christ,' he grumbled, 'what else hasn't she told me?'

'I hope this is it,' I said. 'If it makes you feel any better, she's refused to give the *Global Examiner* the exclusive they wanted. Vonette talked her out of it.'

'At least one member of that family has some common sense,'

Korznick said. 'All right. I guess it's time for some damage control. I'm going to call the ABC news bureau here in town. There's a producer there whose kid is on my kid's Little League team. He's had a reporter leaving messages on my machine, looking for an interview with Rita. He's a decent guy. If we play it right, maybe we can manage to make Rita the victim here, play to the public's sympathy, that kind of thing.'

I didn't much like the idea. 'What if it backfires?' I asked. 'What if your buddy does a piece that leaves Rita looking guilty as hell? Then what?'

'It's a risk,' he agreed. 'But that *Global Examiner* rag will be in every store in America by tomorrow morning. We've got to get our version of the truth out now, and the best way to do that is through a reputable outfit like the networks.'

I begged off having dinner with the VelvetTeens. Vonette protested halfheartedly, but I could tell there were old issues that needed settling, preferably without any outsiders around.

At home, Edna was sitting in the den, watching the news and eating a bacon, lettuce, and tomato sandwich off a tray.

'You got any more of those?'

'The bread's by the toaster, the bacon's cooked, and the tomatoes are sliced,' she said. 'The Lord helps those who help themselves.'

I fixed myself a plate and joined her in the den. She motioned to the table beside her, where a tape player the size of a cigarette pack sat on top of a pad of paper.

'I borrowed that tape player from Kevin,' she said.

'And you've already listened to the tape from Serena's house, right?'

She pointed the remote control at the television and turned down the volume. 'Getting that tape almost landed me in jail today,' she said. 'I got a right.'

I took a bite of my sandwich. The bacon crunched under my teeth and a trail of tomato juice dribbled down my chin. Edna had left the den windows open, and outside crickets were chirping in the lengthening shadows around the house. The smell of night-blooming jasmine drifted in, along with the smell of charcoal from somebody's grill. From next door I heard Mr Byerly cursing at his dog, Homer, for digging in his garden.

I could listen to the tape as well as Edna could, and I would, eventually. But right now she was dying to tell me all about it. 'Was it worth the trouble?' I asked.

She picked up the writing pad and scanned her notes.

'There were lots of hangups, calls from girlfriends, crap like that. But then there were two calls from a man. One was made Saturday. He just says 'it's me.' No name. On the first call, he's wanting to know when she's going to sign some papers. He says she's had them for a month, and he's tired of her playing games.'

'Hightower,' I said. 'Probably something about the divorce settlement. Good. So they were still feuding. What else?'

'The second call, which was made on Monday, is the winner,' Edna said excitedly. She pushed her bifocals to the end of her nose and read from her notes.

'I need to see you,' he says. 'What's this shit your lawyer is trying to pull now? I thought we had everything worked out. Can you come over so we can talk about this like civilized adults? I'll be home after nine.'

Edna put the pad down in her lap. 'The next phone call on the tape is from Artie DiPima, saying he needs her to get in touch with him because something has happened at her ex-husband's house.'

I chewed on my sandwich and thought things over.

Hightower had asked Serena to come over, after nine. So he must have either been planning to go out, or he expected company. But by nine, he wasn't taking any more meetings. He was dead.

Had Serena come over earlier, quarreled and then shot him? Maybe he was dead by the time Rita arrived. Maybe Serena killed him after Rita got there and passed out.

'Good stuff, huh?' Edna asked.

'Not bad,' I admitted. 'The problem is, the caller doesn't identify himself. It could have been any of Serena's business associates. And of course, by removing the tape from her house, we've tampered with evidence.'

'I didn't tamper with anything,' Edna protested. 'I just copied the tape. Why couldn't the cops go in there and get the original? They've got labs and stuff. I bet they could prove that was Hightower's voice on there.'

I hated to dash her hopes. 'We'll turn your copy of the tape over to Korznick,' I promised. 'Let him decide what to do with it – Okay?'

'Okay,' she said reluctantly. 'But I hope the cops nail her.'

25

Surviving a bungled burglary and interrogation had apparently tuckered Edna clean out. By 7:00 p.m. she was asleep in her chair, snoring her way through *Jeopardy*'s 'Tournament of Champions.' With effort, I coaxed her off the chair and onto the sofa, where I draped my grandmother's tattered double wedding ring quilt over her. I turned off the television and the lights. Strange sensation, tucking your mother into bed.

I sat at the computer for a while, updating my notes on the case. I even called the background singer in Nashville to see whether she'd found the tract Delores had given her. She had. On the back someone had rubber stamped the name and address for a church: The Cathedral of the Word Incarnate. There was a phone number too, for a twenty-four-hour prayer hot line.

Instead of a prayerful voice I got a tape recording instructing me to leave a message about who I wanted prayed over. As an aside, the voice said I could make a donation to the cathedral by charging it to Visa, Discovery, or Master Card. I left my name and phone number, but left off the credit card information.

I almost called Mac. He'd slammed out of the house in a huff earlier in the week, and I hadn't heard from him since. It's not unusual for us to fight. But usually we cool down in less than twenty-four hours. It had been a lot more than that this time. Come to think of it, the spaces in between our fights seemed shorter lately, our relationship unusually rocky.

On a whim, I decided to patch things up. It was early yet. I'd ride out to his house and surprise him. I went into the kitchen and grabbed a fifteen-dollar bottle of wine I'd been saving for a special occasion. I took a quick shower and spritzed myself behind the ears with some cologne, then gathered a change of clothing and left Edna a note saying I'd be home in the morning.

But Mac's Jeep wasn't in his driveway. The back door, which he rarely even bothers to close, was locked. And there was no sign of Rufus.

I have a key to Mac's house. I could have waited. Instead I hopped back in the van and headed home. My scalp was prickling, my palms sweaty. I had a good idea where Mac was. When I got off Georgia 400 and onto Interstate 285, instead of heading east toward Atlanta, I turned the van west. A few miles down the road I turned west again, onto Interstate 20. Toward Birmingham.

There's an old, uneven rivalry between Atlanta and Birmingham. Back in the early sixties, when the towns were approximately equal in size and stature, Atlanta somehow surged ahead of Birmingham. Atlanta attracted Major League baseball, football, and basketball franchises, a slew of *Fortune* 500 companies, and an airport that became the major transportation hub for the Southeast. And Birmingham ... didn't.

Atlantans are unreasonably smug about their city's supposed superiority. From the time I was a child I can remember my folks commenting that the best thing ever to come out of Birmingham was I-20.

Anger and suspicion powered the two-hour trip. It wasn't until I saw the first exit ramp to Birmingham that it occurred to me that I didn't have the slightest idea where Mac's ex-wife lived.

I took the next exit off the interstate and pulled into one of those gas station-convenience store combinations. I used the bathroom, bought myself a diet Coke, and found a phone book where I looked up the address for Barbara J. McAuliffe.

The cashier's English extended only to the phrase 'cash or credit card?' and my command of Urdu is limited, so my efforts to get directions to her house were thwarted. Instead I followed the road to a strip shopping center that housed a large Piggly-Wiggly supermarket a mom-and-pop Italian restaurant, and a video rental store.

Twenty minutes and three stops later I had my directions.

I dialed the ex's number on the car phone. A woman answered on the fourth ring. I scowled in the dark and hung up. She was home. And I was certain she had company.

The house was in a nice middle-class neighborhood about thirty miles from the shopping center. It was cream-colored brick, prewar construction. It looked solid, respectable. A black-and-white striped awning over the front door gave the façade a certain jaunty air. I hated it.

There's a one-hour time difference between Atlanta and Birmingham, so it was only 8:30 by the time I parked the van across the street, out of sight of the bay window of the ex's house. That's how I'd been thinking of her the whole way from Atlanta. The ex. That's how Mac had referred to her too, until lately.

One of the girls had left a floppy straw hat in the back of the van. I jammed it on my head and pulled the brim down low over my face. Then I got out of the van and locked it. I forced myself to stroll, an unnatural gait for a woman like me who is always careening through life at full-throttle. But I did it. I stuck my hands in the pockets of my jeans and sauntered slowly past the house, a neighbor out for an early evening stroll. There were three cars in the ex's driveway: a blue Honda Prelude, a white Ford Escort, and Mac's Jeep, which was parked close to the sidewalk. The windows were rolled part way down, and a big black lab's head lolled mournfully out on the passenger side.

Rufus's ears pricked up when he saw me. He wasn't as stupid as I thought, or my disguise was a joke. Either way, he started barking happily at my appearance, and then whining when he saw that I wasn't going to come over and take him out for a run.

I tried to shush him, but he kept whimpering. If he didn't shut up, he'd blow my cover. Some stake-out. I jogged back to the van and rooted around on the floor until I found an old McDonald's bag with a handful of cold, calcified french fries. When I tossed them in the window to Rufus he got so busy scarfing them down he forgot to bark.

The house next door was dark. A 'For Sale' sign was planted in the overgrown front yard. I walked nonchalantly up the driveway of the vacant house, then cut across its weed-filled backyard. There was a rusty old swingset in the corner of the yard, facing the ex's house.

I sat down on the one remaining swing. The chain screeched and the metal seat sagged under my weight.

One wing of the ex's house jutted out at right angles to the rest of the house. It was the dining room, and the ideal American family was having a quiet Norman Rockwell-type dinner.

There were candles lit on the table, and soft music floated out from a set of open French doors. A petite, dark-haired woman sat at one side of the table. Her strawberry blond daughter sat beside her, and across the table sat a fiftyish white-haired traitor who should have been back in Atlanta sitting at my table, laughing at my jokes, sipping my wine.

They sat and ate and drank for a long time, it seemed to me. My butt began to ache. I had my gun in the van. The swingset would have been the perfect vantage point for a sniper. But I had neither the ability nor the will. I did go back to the van. I got the bottle of red wine. I hadn't thought to bring a corkscrew. Instead I wrapped the neck of the bottle in a clean House Mouse cleaning smock and rapped it smartly against the edge of the concrete curb. Some of the wine flowed out along with the top of the bottle, but since I was drinking solo tonight I'd still have plenty.

I took the bottle back to the swingset. It was full dark now, and fireflies flitted in the treetops and in the tall grass. I'd read somewhere that there are hundreds of different varieties of fireflies and that each had a different blinking pattern, a handy signaling device that allowed boy blue-bellied fireflies to flash their romantic intentions to blue-bellied girl fireflies.

The wine was drier than I usually like, but that was because I'd bought it for Mac. It was his favorite. I drank quite a lot of it, sitting in that swing, watching the fireflies and Mac and his ex. At some point Stephanie cleared the dishes from the table and left the room.

Mac and the ex stayed, drinking wine and talking. I didn't have anyone to talk to, but that was all right, because I kept busy swatting the mosquitoes who were swarming my lightly perfumed skin, and trying to distinguish all the different firefly blinking patterns.

After a while, Mac and the ex got up, and she blew out the candles in the dining room. The room went dark. A minute later, a light went on in another part of the house, and still a little later, that light went out too.

I tossed the empty wine bottle into the ex's backyard, and then lurched unsteadily back to the van.

Sunlight streaked in through the dust motes, burning my eyes. I closed them, then opened them again, with great effort. My head was pounding, and my mouth tasted like the inside of an old sneaker.

I sat up slowly. I was in the back of the van, lying in a

nest of wadded-up cleaning smocks. My hands and face and ankles were itching, stinging. They were bright red, covered with pale welts, dozens and dozens of mosquito bites.

'What the hell?' It was Mac's voice. He was standing beside the van, looking in through the open window. He was dressed for work; starched, striped dress shirt, dark suit, and the silk Jerry Garcia necktie I'd given him for his last birthday. It cost fifty-four dollars.

'Yes?' I lifted my head slowly. It hurt to move.

'What the hell are you doing here?' he demanded.

I managed to get on all fours and crawl toward the front of the van. I climbed into the driver's seat and leaned my head back on the headrest, exhausted from the effort. I shut my eyes and opened them again. He was still there, hands on his hips, his lips white with rage.

'What the hell are *you* doing here?' was the best retort I could come up with.

'You know why I'm here,' he said, spitting words like bullets. 'I've been helping Steph look for an apartment.'

'Oh,' I said weakly. 'Oh, that's all right. My mistake. From the looks of things last night, I thought you were here to fuck Barb.'

He stepped away from the van as though he'd been slapped. 'You've been here all night,' he said. 'You followed me over here like I was some kind of common crook, and then you staked-out the house. You're crazy, Callahan, fucking crazy.'

My temples were throbbing with twin tympanies of pain.

'You slept with her,' I screamed. 'You've been sleeping with her all along. You cheated on me with your ex-wife, you son of a bitch.'

I was yelling and crying so loudly that Rufus heard me and started to bark.

'Shut up,' Mac said quickly. 'You'll wake up the whole goddamned neighborhood.'

'You're a lying, cheating scumbag' I screamed. If it would embarrass Mac, I intended to wake up that neighborhood and several other Birmingham suburbs too. 'I never want to see you again.'

Now alarm replaced his anger.

'Wait,' he said quietly. 'Let's don't do this. Don't do this here. We need to talk.'

'Fuck you,' I said hotly. 'There's nothing left to say.' I turned the key in the ignition, but he reached in quickly and turned it off.

'Give me a chance,' he pleaded. 'There's a Dunkin Donuts two blocks over. You can follow me there. Please? We can talk. Just talk. I can explain everything. You owe me that much.'

'I don't owe you shit,' I said through clenched teeth. I wanted to put my hands on that fifty-four-dollar silk necktie and twist the ends until he choked and passed out. I wanted to run over him, right there on the street, and then back the van up and run over him again. Instead, I waited until he backed the Jeep out of her driveway, and I followed him to the Dunkin Donuts.

I had to pee like a racehorse, and I also thought I might need to puke before I freshened up for the morning. Afterward, I splashed cold water onto my face and looked in the mirror at my red, swollen, bug-bitten face. Not a pretty picture.

Mac was sitting in a booth in the corner. It was early yet, and the place was full of workers, stopping for a dunk and a cup of java before work. Two cups of coffee sat on the table. I slid onto the bench. He looked miserable, abject.

'You slept with her last night,' I said flatly.

'No, it's not like that,' he said quickly. 'Will you let me just explain before you start jumping all over me? I really did come over to help Steph find an apartment. Barb offered to fix me dinner because it was late by the time we got back.'

'You're denying you spent the night?' I couldn't believe his nerve. 'Mac, I was there all night. You never came out. I saw you having dinner. Laughing, guzzling wine. Dreamy music. Johnny Mathis. Christ! How corny can you get?'

'Stephanie was there all night,' he protested.

'Stephanie went to bed. Besides, she's a scheming kid. She's probably been plotting this the whole time, dropping out of school and then calling Daddy to come fix things and patch up her broken home. She's probably seen *The Parent Trap* a hundred times. I know I have.'

Mac was stony faced. He took a sip of his coffee and winced at the hotness of it. 'Why are you doing this? Sneaking around. Spying on me. You always said you hated that part of the business. That's why you wouldn't take divorce work. You know what I think? I think you got your rocks off watching us last night.'

His words stung. He'd never known how slimy, how

pathetic, how self-pitying I'd felt last night. 'You're wrong,' I said. 'I didn't get my rocks off. But I'm pretty sure you did.'

He pushed the cup away. It clattered against the china saucer. 'What if I told you you were right? Would that make you happy? Make you feel like a good detective?'

I felt my body go icy. I'd been waiting for him to deny everything, halfway ready to believe him. I wanted him to tell me he loved me, not her. I wanted him to say he'd never do me wrong, the way the boys did in those gooey old sixties songs. Instead he was sitting across the table from me in a Dunkin Donuts in Birmingham, Alabama, admitting he'd slept with his ex-wife.

My hands were cold. I gripped the coffee cup for warmth, but none came. I wanted to throw up. I felt frozen. I could feel my lips forming words, sentences, paragraphs even. I heard them, but they seemed to be coming from someplace else.

'You admit you slept with her.'

'Yes, goddamn it. I slept with her. Last night. For the first and only time. The last time. It was a mistake. I'm sorry.' He ran his fingers through his hair. An expression of frustration. 'God, I'm sorry. It's the last thing I wanted to have happen. We'd been drinking wine, and then we started talking, and she put on those old records we used to listen to back when we were dating. She played our song. Things ... got out of hand.'

'Okay, good-bye.' I felt myself put the coffee cup carefully down on the saucer. I got up and walked toward the door. I really did need some fresh air.

'Wait a minute,' he said. He was right beside me, blocking the door so that I couldn't walk out. 'Wait a minute, for God's sake. Come back and sit down. We need to talk.'

I don't think I knew I was crying again until I felt the sting of the salt on my mosquito bites. 'What's there to talk about? You slept with Barb. Was it as good as old times? I hear older women are great in the sack. Something about appreciating it more. I hope she appreciated you, Mac.'

He grabbed my arm angrily, put his face right up against mine. His voice was hoarse. 'Yes, she appreciated it. I wonder if you ever did. She didn't get up in the middle of the night to try to break into somebody else's house, and she didn't take a phone call from a client while I was making love to her. It was a one-time thing, Callahan, but by God, she put more into it than you have in a long time.'

He let go of my arm then, and walked back to the table. I got in my van and drove a couple of miles. I pulled into a gas station, opened the door wide and puked on the asphalt. Then I put my head on the steering wheel and cried like a baby.

26

Edna was in the kitchen working on the payroll when I got home. I said hello and rushed past her to the bathroom. I needed aspirin and a long shower.

When I finally emerged from the bathroom, the outside of me looked nearly normal. Inside I felt dead. I dried my hair, put on some clean clothes, and went out to the kitchen to see if I could manage my business life any better than I'd run my personal life.

I ignored Edna's curious stares and got out the telephone book. I flipped through the pages until I came to the listings for security companies and Acme Ace, the company in charge of security at Riverbend. I'd noticed their company logo on the guards' uniform shirts.

I needed to interview the guards who'd been on duty the night of Hightower's murder. They'd screwed up by not logging cars that passed through the gates, but maybe they could remember something. It was worth a try.

I told the woman who answered the phone at Acme Ace Security what I needed. 'I'm sorry,' she said curtly. 'We don't give out the names or phone numbers of current or former employees. Company policy.'

285

Maybe, I thought, the guards on duty out at Riverbend now could tell me how to find their former colleagues. My head was throbbing from the wine, and I dreaded seeing the inside of that van again, but duty called.

It was another hot, airless summer day. Traffic was sluggish on the interstate because an eighteen-wheeler had overturned across two northbound lanes, meaning the distance got measured in inches instead of miles. Traffic helicopters droned overhead, and the cops working the accident leaned lazily against their cruisers, instead of stepping forward to try to direct the mess.

By the time I got to Riverbend I was a sweaty, swearing mess. I pulled the van squarely in front of the guard shack, got out and walked up. The shack was small, the size of a closet, and its wraparound windows were streaked with condensed moisture from the over-worked air-conditioner.

One of the guards stepped outside the door. He was young, and Hispanic, about twenty-three, with biceps that bulged out of the sleeves of his dark blue uniform shirt. 'Help you?'

'I'm a reporter for the *Global Examiner*,' I said, glancing about furtively. 'Could we step inside and talk?'

He shrugged and opened the door. The guard inside had red hair and a military-style crewcut. He was reading the *TV Guide*. 'Lady says she's a reporter,' the first guard said. 'Wants to talk us about something.'

'Stu Hightower,' the second guard said. 'Am I

right?' He must have been workout partners with his colleague, because he had equally magnificent musculature.

'Bingo,' I said, pointing a finger at him proudly, as though he'd just recited the periodic table from memory.

'Fellas,' I said, drawing them into my confidence. 'I need your help. I've got to file a story for the *Global Examiner* this afternoon, and it looks like I'm suckin' wind. I was hoping you could help me out with some details.'

The Hispanic guard looked a little confused. 'Didn't that little guy with the rotten teeth who was out here yesterday say he was with the Global Examiner?' he asked his partner.

Mick Coyle, damn his soul, had beat me to the punch.

'Oh, you mean my partner, Mick. That's the way we do things at the *Examiner*. See, every detail of our story has to be independently corroborated. So they send two reporters out, and the second one checks up on the first one. Mick wasn't drinking yesterday, was he? These Brits are bad to get in the sauce.'

Crewcut looked dubious. 'We ran him off after he offered us a case of beer for confidential information. We're not allowed to talk to the media.'

So Mick had tried to buy information on the cheap. I was surprised and disappointed in his lack of finesse. I'd stopped at the instant bank teller on the way to Riverbend, and I had eight twenties burning a hole in the pocket of my skirt.

I took four twenties out and placed them conspicuously

atop the *TV Guide* the redhead had set down. 'I would never insult you boys by offering you alcoholic beverages,' I said. 'And what I need is not necessarily confidential information. All I'd like for you to share with me is some observations, that's all.'

'I don't know,' the Hispanic one said, shaking his head back and forth like one of those stuffed dogs people put in the back of their cars. 'Ralph and Allen screwed things up royally the other night. Now we got supervisors on our ass all the time. Can't even take a whiz without filling out a form in triplicate.'

'Ralph and Allen,' I said eagerly. 'Where do they live? Phone numbers?'

The redhead was getting nervous. He stood with his back to me, looking anxiously out the window, as though he expected to be caught with his pants down at any moment.

'Tell you what,' I said, placing two more twenties on the magazine. 'Let's start chatting. If a supervisor shows up, I just stepped inside to ask for directions. How's that?'

The redhead turned away from the window and put his hand on the magazine and palmed the bills. I hoped he was good at sharing.

'Can you tell me how to find Ralph and Allen – the guys who were working here the night of the murder?'

'Got no idea,' the Hispanic one said. 'The bossman took their badges and guns and holsters, and that's the last we seen of 'em. Ralph's got family in Baton Rouge,

though, so he may have gone back there. Last I seen of
Allen, he was living in a mobile home out in Smyrna. He
didn't have no phone, so we used to beep him when we
needed him.'

'What's the beeper number?' I asked, ready to write it
down.

'The beeper belonged to Ace Acme,' the redhead said.
'He had to give it back.'

I needed to talk to those guards to see who else might
have come though the Riverbend gates that night. Now
I'd have to piece it together without their help. I
massaged my aching temples with my fingertips and
thought it over.

'That logbook Ralph and Allen were supposed to be
keeping didn't have but four cars logged on it,' I said
casually. 'But I'd think a whole lot more people would be
coming through here.'

'Yeah, those two dipshits screwed it up for everybody,'
the redhead said. 'We got maybe a hundred cars a night
coming through here, more weekends.'

'Did Mr Hightower have a lot of visitors?' I asked. 'A
lot of women coming to see him?'

The guards looked at each other and grinned. Stu
Hightower apparently had a fan club.

'Yeah, old Stu liked to party,' the Hispanic one said.
'Lots of ladies come through here going to his house.
Good-looking ones too.'

'Then they'd probably show up on the logbook for
other nights, right?' I said. 'Where are those pages?'

'Right here,' the redhead said, thumping a black
looseleaf notebook that sat on his desktop.

'Could I take a peek?' I asked, putting two more twenties on the book. The Hispanic guard snatched them up and stuffed them in his pocket, then walked over and handed me the book.

'You gotta hurry though,' he added. 'The supervisor, he's been popping up here in the middle of the afternoon this week, checking up on us.'

I took the book and sat down in the only other chair in the room. Pages fell out of the book and onto the floor. The rest of the logbook wasn't much better kept than the pages the cops had seized. Pages were filed out of order, handwriting was nearly illegible and some pages weren't even dated.

'How is the system supposed to work?' I asked, looking up from the meaningless lines of tag numbers and names.

'If a homeowner is expecting company, he can call down here and tells us the person's name, and what the car looks like,' the Hispanic guard explained. 'When they show up, we just wave 'em through. That's what we usually did with Mr Hightower's guests. Some guys stop the cars and write down tag numbers, but if there's more than one car in line, it backs up traffic, and people get pissed.'

'So you just get a phone call, and then let people in? Do you have any way of verifying that the caller is really who he says he is? Like calling back to check?'

The redhead looked puzzled. 'Why would we do that?'

Never mind. I looked back at the logbook. No two

guards kept it the same way two days running. Some days were dated, with the guard's initials noted beside it, others weren't. Some days the guards had written down the names of the guests as well as their tag numbers, other days they hadn't bothered. Because of the inconsistencies, the logbook would probably be useless in court, both for the DA and for the defense.

I scanned the pages hastily. Danielle Manigault had been to see Hightower at least three times in the past month. I recognized the name of Sugar Jackson, the songwriter; Rikki Banks of the Joanses; and some other names I had seen on nameplates at BackTalk.

'If somebody wanted to get in here, somebody who was unauthorized, could they do it?' I asked. I didn't bother to tell them I'd already been to Riverbend twice by devious means.

'Hell no,' the redhead said, puffing out his chest. 'Not with us here.'

'Really?' I said, raising one eyebrow.

'Well, maybe,' the Hispanic one said. 'Like, if you came in the back way, walking through the woods. I've been back there. It's over a mile, and there's creeks and stuff so it's all marshy. No way you could get a car back there.'

'Or if it's a car with one of our Riverbend stickers, we wouldn't stop the car,' the other one said.

'But don't you only give those out to residents?' I asked.

'Yeah. But say somebody sells a car. They might not

go to the trouble of peeling the sticker off, even though they're supposed to.'

The Hispanic guard nudged the redhead. 'And what about all those stickers that turned up missing?'

'Shut up, man,' his friend said quickly. 'You wanna get us in the same boat as Allen and Ralph?'

'Hey, I'm not the cops,' I said. 'What about those stickers?'

The redhead looked unhappy. 'We keep a list of stickers by their serial numbers, and the stickers are kept with the book in the desk here in the shack. A couple weeks ago, we were logging in some new stickers, and Dwayne here notices the sticker he's issuing is out of sequence.'

'The last number logged was three oh eight. I was about to issue three fifteen,' Dwayne explained.

'Turns out seven stickers are unaccounted for,' his buddy said.

'What do you think happened?' I asked.

'Who knows?' Dwayne said. 'Nothing happened, as far as we're concerned. You think we're gonna tell Acme Ace or the homeowner's association about this? Like, excuse me, but seven stickers are missing, and they could have been stolen by an ax murderer? No way, man.'

While we were talking a white Mercedes-Benz had glided silently up beside the shack. The driver tooted his horn impatiently, and both men jumped as though they'd been goosed.

'Sorry ma'am,' Dwayne said. 'You gotta go. If we get caught talking to the press, it's adios amigo, right Jaime?'

His partner patted his now enriched pockets. 'Si. Enjoyed talking to you, though. Sure did.'

27

After I left Riverbend, I drove aimlessly around some backroads in the area. It was brutally hot, but the clouds had a dark rim around them, and there was the faint smell of rain in the air. I was dog tired. Sick of this case, sick of my life. Maybe Rita really had shot Stu Hightower. And maybe she should think twice about allowing Korznick to cop a plea for her. I didn't know. Didn't care at this point. All I wanted was some peace and some sleep.

Mac's angry voice kept coming back to me. 'She put more into it than you ever did,' he'd said. Implying what? That I hadn't really cared? Hadn't ever really committed myself to the relationship? His accusations stung. Maybe I was trying to stretch myself too thin, running both the House Mouse and the investigation business. Was I succeeding at either one?

I'd gotten into law enforcement because of some stupid conviction that I could fix things, that I could stop the bad guys from picking on the good guys. And when it turned out that my career was probably never going to take me anyplace besides the burglary squad room, I'd taken my toys and gone home. In a weird way, the cleaning business satisfied my need to create order out of chaos, and taking on an occasional criminal investigation gave me a chance to even the score with the bad guys. Somehow, I'd talked myself into believing Mac understood all that about me.

Wrong, wrong, wrong. Now here I was again, up another dead end. But I couldn't quit this case. Not until I'd proven some things to myself. I called Edna on the car phone to see what was shaking.

'Mac called while you were out,' she said.

'Oh yeah?'

'He sounded kinda funny. He wants you to call him.'

When hell freezes over, I thought. 'Okay,' I said. 'Anything else going on?'

'Neva Jean's tennis bracelet came FedEx,' Edna said. 'She just ran over here to show it to us. You ought to see that thing. Them fake diamonds are the size of bottlecaps.'

I listened politely to her chatter for as long as I could take it. 'I'm on the car phone,' I said finally. 'You can tell me the rest when I get home.'

Artie DiPima was thrilled to hear from me again.

'You're skating on thin ice, Garrity,' he said. 'Sending old ladies to do your surveillance work for you. Is that what they teach at that Mickey Mouse school you go to for your PI license?'

'I went to the same police academy you went to Artie – remember?'

'Next time, we'll charge 'em with burglary,' DiPima said. 'Keep it in mind.'

'I definitely will,' I pledged. 'In the meantime, have you got any idea where Hightower spent the earlier part of his evening the night he died?'

'Yeah,' he said. 'I got an idea. But if you want to know, get that Korznick guy to put it in writing. The DA says I don't gotta give you squat unless it's in writing.'

I was really enjoying our new, close working relationship.

The BackTalk parking lot was nearly empty. It was Friday, but it wasn't even four o'clock yet. Record companies must keep banker's hours, I thought.

When I walked inside, I could tell things were different. The woman working the front desk was not the one who'd been there earlier in the week. She was older, in her mid-fifties, with a bad perm and a prim cotton print dress. She didn't look like BackTalk material. What she looked like, I thought hopefully, was a temp.

'I'm here to see Danielle,' I said, moving confidently toward the door to the inner sanctum.

She grabbed a clipboard from the desktop and scanned it quickly. 'Is that Danielle Manigault?' I could see the clipboard had a typed list of names on it.

'I'll just go on back, because she's expecting me,' I said, keeping moving.

'She's not here,' the woman said, obviously flustered. 'They're all at a sales meeting. If you'll just leave your name and number . . .'

'I'll leave a note on her desk,' I said, and before she

could object, I was hurrying down the hallway. It's the first thing I learned when I started in this business; if people ask too many questions talk fast and keep moving.

I glanced backward over my shoulder to see if she was following me. Danielle Manigault's office door was closed. I tried the handle. Locked. She was a suspicious type.

Hightower's office was at the end of the hallway. The door was closed and the coast was clear. But the door was locked.

'Well, hell,' I said aloud.

'Excuse me?'

The voice was coming from the next door down from Hightower's. It was slightly ajar. I looked in. It was a small office, with a door that connected to Hightower's office. A young woman was standing in the middle of the room, surrounded by cardboard cartons.

She was dressed in cut-off jeans, and a faded Hard Rock Cafe T-shirt. Very casual, even for a place like BackTalk.

'I thought everybody was at a sales meeting,' I said.

'Everybody else is,' she said pointedly. 'I'm just packing up some stuff. Today was my last day.'

'I'm sorry,' I said, sniffing an opportunity. 'Is there anything I can do?'

'Who are you?' she said, but not in a threatening way.

'I'm a private detective. I'm looking into Stu Hightower's murder. Were you his secretary?'

Her eyes widened and she nodded yes. She wasn't

very pretty, really. Her straight brown hair was too fine and too straight, and her nose had a funny bump and it was too big for her narrow, pointed face. Her figure wasn't that great, either. Maybe Hightower really had hired her for her typing skills.

'I miss Stu,' she said quietly. She opened a desk drawer and started dumping its contents into one of the boxes. The box closest to her was already full of potted house plants, some framed photographs and a couple of those corny little Precious Moments porcelain figurines.

'They fired you? Why?'

Her voice quavered a little. 'Danielle has her own secretary. It's okay, though. The company gave me a decent separation package, and my dad has a friend at Equifax, so I've got an interview there Monday.'

I looked around at the mountain of boxes. 'You must have worked here a really long time.'

'Just four years,' she said. 'Stu hired me right out of junior college.' She saw me looking at the boxes. 'Oh, those aren't mine,' she said. 'They're Stu's. Danielle is moving into his old office, so I had to clean it out. He was a real packrat; never threw anything away.'

I was itching to get into those boxes. I stepped over and looked at one. It was full of manila file folders. 'What'll happen to all of this stuff?'

'Somebody from maintenance is supposed to take them and put them in storage,' she said. 'Hey, uh, what exactly are you trying to find out about Stu's murder? Are you working for Rita Fontaine, the lady they arrested?'

'Yeah,' I said, trying to read the writing on the file folders. 'Rita's my client. I'm trying to find out where Stu was and what he was doing the night he was killed. Do you think his calendar or appointment book might be in one of these boxes?'

'You know, I never heard of Rita Fontaine or the VelvetTeens until I saw something about it on the news,' the girl admitted. 'Stu wasn't one to sit around and talk about the old days, you know?'

'What about that calendar?' I repeated.

'Sorry,' she said. 'The police took all that kind of stuff. They've been all through the office. It was the biggest mess you ever saw.'

'I can imagine,' I said. 'Do you happen to know what Stu was doing on Monday?'

She started to say something and then stopped and frowned. 'Am I allowed to be talking to you? Because of the murder and all that?'

'What's your name?' I asked.

'Traci.'

'Traci,' I said, 'your boss is dead. Danielle Manigault fired you. You're not under arrest. As far as I can tell, you can say and do whatever you please. It's a free world, right?'

Her face flushed a little. 'Damned right.'

There was a computer terminal on her desk. She pulled a chair up to it and punched a few keys. The machine hummed to life. 'Good. They haven't killed my access code yet.'

A few keystrokes later she looked up at me. 'I always kept Stu's schedule in the computer too. So we'd both have a record. He was pretty meticulous about that kind of thing.'

'Traci,' I said, trying not to sound like a suck-up, 'I'll bet you were a hell of a secretary.'

'Damned right,' she said.

I moved over to the desk and peered over her shoulder at the computer screen. The screen held a date book of some sort, but the entries were all in something like hieroglyphics.

'Stu had his own kind of shorthand,' Traci said. 'I was the only one who could read it.'

She pointed a finger at the listing. 'His first appointment was at noon, with Scott Streethaus, his lawyer.'

Her finger moved down the screen. 'At two he met with Larry Bushman, our art director. At four thirty he saw Kim Prewatt, he's a producer who does a lot of work at BackTalk. Stu wanted to talk to him about some project he was interested in. That's the last business appointment.'

She tapped the screen lightly. 'Oh yeah, how could I forget? Monday night was the cocktail fund-raiser for the Children's Hospital. Stu is honorary chairman for the hospital guild. The cocktail party was at six, at the Ritz-Carlton in Buckhead.'

'Stu was interested in charity?' This was the first I'd heard that Stu Hightower had a social conscience.

'Oh yeah,' Traci said. 'Every year Stu picked one charity that the company would support. This year was the Children's Hospital. All our artists, everybody, were supposed to get involved in volunteering or fund-raising. Stu said it was good for business.'

'Do you have any idea who else was going to be at the cocktail party?' I asked. 'Like, were people from the company supposed to go?'

She'd gotten up from the computer and she was packing faster now, tossing letters and files into the trash can with gleeful abandon. 'I don't know who went,' she said. 'You'd have to ask Diana Faircloth about that.'

'Who's she?'

Traci picked a Rolodex out of one of the boxes and flipped the wheel around until she came to the spot she was looking for. She took a card out of the index and handed it to me.

'Stu was the chairman for fund-raising, but Diana Faircloth is head of the women's auxiliary,' she explained. 'She was the one who did most of the real work.'

I looked hopefully at the phone. 'Go ahead and use it,' Traci said boldly. 'I'm sure not going to stop you.'

'Thanks,' I said. The liberation of Traci was heart-warming indeed.

Diana Faircloth was on another line when I called, but after I told her who I was and what I wanted she got back to me in a real hurry.

'Oh my God,' she said breathlessly. 'I can't believe any of this is happening. I mean, I saw Stu Monday night. At the party. He kissed me and brought me a glass of chardonnay. We talked about the table decorations for the dinner dance. The next thing I know, my sister-in-law is on the phone telling me to turn on Channel Eleven, Stu Hightower has been shot to death. I cannot believe it.'

'It's tragic,' I said. 'I was wondering if you have a copy of the guest list for the party.'

'I had one,' she said. 'The police took it. But nobody at that party would have, I mean, I knew most of those people. Nobody there would have . . .'

'I'm sure,' I said soothingly, cutting her off again. 'How about the people from BackTalk? Were there many people there from the company?'

'Let me think,' she said. 'Stu gave me a list of about twenty people he wanted invited. Most of them I didn't really know.'

'How about that list?' I asked, crossing my fingers. 'Did the police take that?'

'No,' she said thoughtfully, 'because I folded his list into the master. Here it is.' She read the names. Some of them, like Danielle Manigault, Sugar Jackson, Rikki and Jonette from the Joanses, Arlene Trotter, and Larry Bushman, I recognized.

'Do you know which of those names actually showed up?' I asked.

'Are you kidding?' she said. 'We sent out over three hundred and fifty invitations. Unfortunately, people these days don't bother to RSVP. It's poor manners, but there you are. I blame it on all these people transferring in here from up north. I do know that Danielle Manigault did not come. Her secretary called very promptly and said Danielle would be out of town.

'Of course,' she continued, 'we'd planned on heavy appetizers and open bar for two hundred seventy-five. By seven thirty, we were out of everything except for the anchovy balls and the domestic beer.'

303

'Did you happen to notice what time Stu left the party?'

'The police asked me the same thing,' she said, sighing heavily. 'I was in the kitchen having words with the caterer about the smoked salmon, which we paid for but did not receive. When I came back to the party, he was gone. Or at least, I assume he was gone.'

'And you didn't see him talking with anyone in particular?'

She laughed. 'You didn't know Stu, did you? He talked to everyone. He was totally charming and utterly without morals. But he raised nearly a hundred thousand for the hospital this year.'

'I see,' I said, disappointed. I started to give her my name and phone number, in case she did remember seeing Hightower talking with someone or leaving with them.

'Oh,' she said suddenly, 'did I mention that Stu's ex-wife showed up?'

'What?' I said, nearly shouting. 'What was she doing there?'

'That was Stu's reaction when he saw her come in the door. She wasn't on the patron list, but the society section of the newspaper ran a little piece about the party, and of course, anyone with twenty-five dollars was welcome. I think Serena came just to embarrass Stu. From what he told me, the divorce was not going well.'

'Wait a minute,' I said. 'Does that mean any number of people who weren't invited could have been at that party?'

'Well, I suppose,' she said. 'I wasn't working the door, so I don't know. But yes, usually a dozen or so people will just show up and pay to come in. I think it makes them feel socially connected.'

'What about Serena?' I said. 'Did Stu talk to her? Did she make a scene?'

'I certainly didn't see them together,' Diana said. 'And as for making a scene, well, she was wearing this peek-a-boo black thing with her titties just flapping in the breeze for the whole world to see. Old Dr Ferguson, who is the hospital's chief of staff nearly had a coronary when he saw her. Is that the kind of scene you're talking about?'

It wasn't. As far as Diana Faircloth was concerned, Serena's excessive décolletage was nearly as shocking as her ex-husband's murder. I thanked her and hung up.

Traci was taping the boxes closed. There was a brief knock on the door, and a young guy in a gray work shirt stepped in, pulling a hand-truck behind him.

'Take 'em away,' Traci said, gesturing toward her former bosses' belongings. She picked up two boxes of her own. I picked up the third and followed her to her car.

She loaded the stuff in the trunk and looked around the deserted parking lot. 'I guess this is it,' she said. 'I never thought I'd be leaving like this. Working for Stu was so much fun, I just assumed I'd always be here. His being dead didn't hit me, not until just now, when they came to get his boxes.' She looked at me and forced a smile. 'Hey. It's Friday. Happy hour, right? You want to go get a glass of wine or something?'

The last thing in the world I wanted was a glass of wine. 'Yeah,' I said. 'Or something.'

28

'Let's go to Hooligan's,' Traci said. 'They have a free buffet and dollar mixed drinks during happy hour.'

There was a time when I thought a mixed drink for a buck was a good deal. That was before I could taste the difference between rotgut brands and the good stuff, before a bottle of red wine put me out of commission for twenty-four hours.

Happy hour was in full swing at Hooligan's, a fern bar over near Lenox Square Mall. It was crammed with the after-work office crowd: women in their cotton summer dresses, men with neckties loosened, suit coats slung over their shoulders. We found a small table in a corner, and Traci ordered herself a margarita while I opted for club soda with a twist of lime. She went to the 'free buffet' and brought back a plate of tepid Buffalo chicken wings and some soggy-looking cheese nachos.

When the waitress brought the drinks Traci emptied hers in one long slurp. 'I'll have another,' she told the waitress, who promptly brought it, and another club soda for me.

'None of my friends could understand why I was so loyal to Stu,' she said, picking at the nachos. 'But he was really good to me. He was intense, that's all. When he was working on something, he gave it one hundred percent. He didn't have time to notice who got short-changed or felt left out.'

I squeezed the lime into my club soda and took a sip. 'From what I've heard, a lot of people who'd worked for Stu felt they'd been treated unfairly, had their careers dropped or ignored. Do you have any idea who hated him enough to kill him?'

She shook her head. 'I've been thinking about it all week. Could it have something to do with this AKA deal Stu was working on?'

'The merger deal? You knew about that?'

'Not a lot,' she admitted. 'I booked Stu a flight to LA a month ago, and he said he wouldn't need a car because AKA was providing him with a car and a driver. And they also put him up at the Chateau Marmont, the place where John Belushi overdosed? Stu loved that. And for six months before that I made a lot of calls for him to LA. He got FedEx letters from them all the time. He wouldn't let me open any of them though. Stu could be very secretive at times.'

'The way I heard it, if the deal went through, a lot of careers would have been harmed. AKA probably wouldn't pick up Junebug or the Joanses, for instance. Definitely not Serena. A lot of people were starting to feel they'd been screwed.'

She put down the Buffalo wing she'd been nibbling on. 'I get so tired of hearing that kind of talk,' she said indignantly. 'Stu did everything for these people. He discovered them, he made their careers. And he was unbelievably generous. He gave people cars, jewelry, boats, motorcycles, clothes, even money to buy houses. Look at Rikki Banks. She's going around now saying how Stu dropped the Joanses. Does she mention that Stu gave her the down payment for that condo of hers in Midtown? And Arlene Trotter – Stu let her and Junebug stay in his guest house when they first moved to Atlanta. He gave Junebug a car, bought that pool table and color television for them. And he didn't expect anything in return. Just a thank you.'

Traci tilted the margarita goblet and drained the last drop out of it, then motioned to a passing waitress to bring her another.

While Traci was tossing back her third margarita I excused myself to go to the ladies room. What I really wanted to do was use the pay phone.

I caught Korznick just as he was trying to leave for the day.

'Do you know a guy named Scott Streethaus?' I asked.

'Stu Hightower's lawyer,' he said promptly. 'I know him. Why?'

'He was working on this merger deal with AKA Records,' I said, 'and he was also finalizing the divorce. Could you call him and see if he'll tell you anything about either one? I'm really interested in knowing whether or not the divorce was final, and if Serena will inherit anything.'

'I'll call,' he said, 'but Scott's not likely to tell me much, unless I file a motion to that effect.'

'How about calling him on an informal basis?' I said. 'Are you on that kind of terms with him?'

'We're on a bar association committee together,' Korznick muttered. 'It's worth a try.'

'Have you talked to DiPima lately?' I asked.

'Unfortunately, yes,' Korznick said.

'He told you about the gunshot residue on Rita's hands?'

'With gleeful abandon,' Korznick said. 'We could have gotten around that, maybe, but the ballistics thing, I tell you, I don't know how we get a jury to ignore that kind of evidence.'

'What?' I said. 'DiPima told me the tests weren't due back from the state crime lab until next week.'

'They weren't,' Korznick said. 'Until the DA started feeling the heat from all the media. It's a high-profile case, Callahan. I've got reporters calling me nonstop, wanting access to Rita.'

'What about the tests?' I said impatiently.

'Hightower was killed by a bullet fired from the gun Rita was holding,' he said glumly. 'It's not looking good. Not looking good at all.'

It hadn't been looking good for a while. But I was too damn stubborn to call it a night and go home. Go home to what? I didn't even have a cat. 'What if it's a setup?' I asked.

'You're joking, right?' He sounded as depressed as I was. But he gave me his home phone number and told me to call later in the evening.

Traci was working on what looked like her fourth margarita when I got back to the table. Her eyes were looking a little glazed, and she had a slight salt mustache on her upper lip.

'I'm curious about Stu's relationship with Danielle Manigault,' I told her. 'It seems like she's the only woman at the company he didn't sleep with.'

'Who says he didn't?' she shot back. 'I think she and Stu were lovers once. And maybe they got together for old time's sake every now and again.'

'Was he as generous to her as he was with the others?'

'Sure,' Traci said. 'That red Mercedes of hers, Stu gave her that when she turned forty – for the fifth time.' She giggled at her own joke.

'Was Danielle going to be part of the company if the AKA deal went through?'

The waitress arrived with another drink, and Traci took a long sip. 'I don't know,' she said. 'But I do know that Stu didn't take her with him to LA for those meetings, and he never had me make copies of the AKA correspondence for her. This was a really big deal, and when it came down to the big stuff, the only person Stu really trusted was Stu. And me, sometimes.'

She set her drink down hard, slopping some of it on the tabletop, and slumped down in her chair a little, her eyelids fluttering furiously. I think the tequila had finally taken hold.

'Traci,' I said loudly. She struggled to sit up straight. 'Did Stu have any dealings with a guy named Jack Rabin?'

'Jacky the wacky rabbit,' she said, giggling. 'That's

what Stu used to call him. He came to the office and had a big fight with Stu. I could hear them arguing pretty loudly. At one point it sounded like this Jack guy was threatening Stu. Hey! Maybe he did it – maybe he killed Stu.'

Her voice had gotten a little louder and a little shriller with the last drink. I saw a woman at the next table stare and then look away quickly when she saw me watching.

'What could Rabin use to threaten Stu?'

She swung her head wildly around, looking to see if anyone could overhear.

'Shh!' she said in a stage whisper. 'Nobody was supposed to know about the money. Only me.'

'What money?' I whispered back. 'How did Jack Rabin know about it?'

'That wacky wabbit,' she giggled again. 'It was the money for the radio stations. For the program directors and disc jockeys. Every Friday, I had to go to the bank and get cash. One thousand, sometimes two thousand, in twenties. Then I had to bring it back and divide it up and put it in little envelopes that went into the CD cases. Jewel boxes, they're called. Funny, huh?'

So Matt's gossip about BackTalk making payola was accurate. And Rabin had somehow found out about it. 'How did Rabin find out about the money?' I asked.

She shrugged. 'Somebody told him. Probably a disc jockey. These guys all know each other. Stu said Jacky Rabbit had been in radio a long time. He videotaped me, that sneaky little bunny.' She snickered.

'He followed me to the bank. He had a video camera. He taped me going in and getting the cash, and getting in my car, and dividing the money up and putting it in the cases.'

'You divided the money up in your car?' Not what you could call a clandestine operation.

Traci looked embarrassed. 'Just that one time. Stu was in a big hurry because he was going out of town on business, and he wanted to take some of the cases with him. I had to meet him at a restaurant where he was meeting one of the program directors. Jacky Rabbit got it all on tape, including the part where Stu handed the jewel box to the guy he was having lunch with that day.'

So Rabin could prove that Hightower was involved in payola again. Only this time he wasn't using an independent promoter. Maybe Rabin planned to blackmail Hightower into keeping quiet about Rabin's involvement in the Texas payola scandal.

'What did Stu do when he found out about the tape?' I asked.

'Nothing,' she said. 'I thought he'd be furious. It was all my fault. I was so stupid to do all that in my car where someone could see me. I offered to quit. But Stu wouldn't let me. He was mad, but he got over it.'

'And he just let Rabin get away with blackmailing him?'

'I think he was planning something,' Traci said, whispering again. 'He told me "I'm not through with that bastard, Traci. He'll learn to fuck with Stu Hightower." But then, he was killed.' A tear rolled down her cheek, and she slid down in her chair until her forehead was resting on the tabletop.

I looked at the lineup of empty glasses on our table. There were three the waitress hadn't had time to clear. Traci had drunk enough tequila to stupefy a horse. And I'd been so busy encouraging her to spill her guts I'd barely noticed. Now she was my responsibility.

I picked up her purse from the empty chair and managed to hoist her out of her chair. 'Are you okay?' I asked. 'Can you walk?'

'So sleepy,' she said woozily, her body going limp against mine. I left the money for the tab on the table. It was the least I could do for somebody who'd just lost a boss and a job all in the same week.

I half-walked, half-dragged Traci out to the parking lot. People looked on with interest, but no great shock. Hey, it was happy hour. Shit happens.

Our cars were parked side by side. I unlocked the van and hoisted her up into the seat and then fastened her seat belt. 'I'll take you home,' I said loudly, 'and then I'll get somebody to help me bring your car back later. Okay?'

Her head lolled back against the headrest. She was floating above the fray in a tequila-scented cloud of oblivion. Touchdown was going to be painful, I knew from experience. What I didn't know was where Traci lived.

I got in the van, opened her purse and found her driver's license in her billfold. It listed a street address on Roswell Road. Probably an apartment, but which one?'

'Traci,' I said loudly, pulling at her arm. 'Which apartment complex to you live in? What's the apartment number?'

She opened her eyes briefly. 'Post,' she mumbled.

Great. There are probably two dozen Post apartment complexes in and around Atlanta, all of them with names preceded by Post. There were Post Glenns and Post Brooks and Post Horizons, all of them anonymous banks of luxury apartments plunked down in the Post trademark of lush green and flowering landscapes.

'Which one?' I said, shaking her again. 'Which complex?'

'Post Hole,' she smirked. 'Thas wha my roomy calls it.'

I had to smile. Like nearly everybody in Atlanta under the age of forty, I'd lived in a Post apartment complex myself, when I was right out of college and newly emancipated from my parents. My three roommates and I considered ourselves the swingingest of singles. We'd referred to our own complex, on Powers Ferry Road, as Postcoital.

'What's it really called?' I said, renewing the shaking. 'Traci?'

The eyelids fluttered one more time. She must have sensed the urgency in my voice. 'Post Chase. Building four, Apartment two.' Then she was out again.

We'd stayed in Hooligan's long enough to let the last of the Friday rush hour traffic die down. I was optimistic enough about the traffic to chance heading south on Peachtree Road. I was pretty sure Post Chase was inside the Perimeter, which is what Atlantans call Interstate 285.

In ten minutes, I was turning into the flower-bedecked entrance to Post Chase. I parked in front of Traci's building and looked in her purse for her house key.

Her key chain jingled from the bottom of her pocketbook. It had a gold plastic CD hanging on a chain, with a label that said 'Diss Dis' – Junebug. Obviously a promotional giveaway from BackTalk.

Honestly, up until I saw that key chain gadget and all those keys, my only intentions were strictly of the Good Samaritan type. I'd planned to off load Traci, then get Edna or maybe Linda Nickells to follow me back to her complex with Traci's car. But once those keys were in my hand my fingers got that familiar tingly sensation.

I got out of the van and unloaded the nearly comatose Traci. I shook her awake enough to get her to move her feet in a poor imitation of walking, then half-walked, half-dragged her to her front door.

Once inside the apartment, her sense of steering seemed to take over. She stumbled into a bedroom and collapsed atop a bed. There was a quilt folded at the foot of the bed. I took off her shoes and put the quilt over her.

'Traci,' I said, leaning down and putting my face near hers, treating myself to a blast of sour-smelling tequila. 'I have to go back to BackTalk. My wallet must have fallen out when I was helping you move the boxes. Traci? Can you hear me? I need to get my wallet.'

'Too bad,' she said drowsily. 'Get it tomorrow.'

'I can't drive around Atlanta without my driver's license and credit cards,' I said. 'I've got your keys anyway. So I'll just go back to the office and get it. Will that be okay?'

'Okay,' she agreed.

Easy enough. And then I remembered. A place like BackTalk would have security. If I wasn't careful I'd end up in Artie DiPima's office myself, and this time he would not be amused.

'Will there be security guards there tonight?' I asked, shaking her awake again.

She pulled the quilt over her head. Her voice was muffled. 'No guards. Unlock back door. Wall panel to right. Punch in Star-eight-two-three, then push enter. Only got two minutes to do it. If alarm goes off, security company calls first. Tell 'em code word is *Rock*.'

'Okay,' I said, straightening up. 'I'll bring your car back tomorrow. Will you be okay?'

'Okay,' she repeated. 'Lemme sleep.'

29

After I'd tucked Traci in for the night, I called Korznick from the car phone. 'Did you call Scott Streethaus?' I asked.

'Caught him as he was leaving to go to dinner,' he said. 'It's Friday, you know.'

'I know what night it is,' I said. 'And I'm working.'

'Streethaus knows next to nothing about the AKA deal. A guy named Wegner, in his firm's LA office was handling that. I called him and left a message.'

'What about the divorce?' I asked. 'Was it final or not? What does Serena get?'

He chuckled. 'Maybe things aren't so bad after all, Garrity. I don't know about Serena, but I do know the lawyers on both sides are going to get rich on this one. The divorce was final three weeks ago. The settlement was too, or so Streethaus thought. Then Serena caught wind of this AKA deal and went ballistic. She's claiming he lied during deposition in order to conceal the pending sale of the company. Her lawyers are screaming fraud. They've filed a motion asking that the settlement be set aside.'

'Can she do that?'

'She can try,' Korznick said. 'And if she can prove Hightower tried to hide those assets, then, yeah, a judge might set the original settlement aside.'

'I don't get it,' I said. 'If it looked like she was going to get a bigger piece of the pie anyway, why kill him?'

'Maybe she didn't kill him,' Korznick said. 'But remember, this stuff isn't written in stone. A judge could throw out Serena's motion. Besides, how's this for a motive – what if Hightower didn't get around to changing his will after the divorce?'

'I don't know,' I said. 'You're the lawyer. You tell me what happens.'

'Most divorce agreements include a clause prohibiting former spouses from inheriting upon the death of the other,' he explained. 'But if there's an existing will specifically naming the surviving spouse as an heir, then the will prevails.'

'And Serena hits the jackpot,' I said. 'Do we know whether he changed the will?'

'Streethaus won't discuss it with me,' Korznick said regretfully. 'All he would tell me is that he met with Hightower on Monday so they could discuss strategy to keep the original settlement intact. He said Stu was adamant about not giving Serena another penny. If you ask me, Serena's who we need to concentrate on.'

'Yeah, but there are a couple of other people with really strong motives too,' I said. 'I want to do a little more digging before we put the full court press on Serena.'

'What have you got in mind?'

What I had in mind was finding the AKA file among Hightower's papers and checking them out. To do that, I planned what we security specialists sometimes call a covert action.

'You don't want to know,' I assured him. Then I hung up.

I cruised slowly past the BackTalk offices. It was only eight o'clock, not dark yet. The parking lot was empty; my pink House Mouse van would stick out like a nun in a nudist colony. Then I remembered Traci's sedate gray compact parked back at Hooligan's. If somebody happened to drive past and see her car, they'd just assume she had stayed late to finish packing.

I hated to go all the way back to the bar, but on the other hand, I had at least an hour to kill before it got dark. In the meantime, I had to arrange to get Traci's car back to her.

Linda Nickells sounded bored. 'C.W.'s over at Manuel's with the guys from the office and I'm home watching summer reruns,' she said. 'Girl, I'm up for anything tonight.'

'How come you didn't go with him?' I asked.

'That cigarette smoke and stale beer smell over there makes me nauseous,' she said. 'Hell, everything makes me nauseous. This pregnancy thing is already getting to be a drag. What are you up to?'

'It's too complicated to go into right now,' I said. 'I'll tell you when I see you. There's some other stuff I want to talk to you about too.'

Suddenly I needed to talk to somebody about Mac.

'Uh oh,' she said. 'Sounds like some heavy shit.'

'It is,' I blurted. 'I broke up with Mac last night. He was sleeping with Barb.'

'Say what?' Linda said. 'Who's Barb?'

'His ex-wife,' I said. 'Look, I can't talk about this right now. Just meet me at Hooligan's at eleven. Or is that going to make you nauseous too?'

'They've got a patio, don't they?' she said. 'I'm so bored I might just get really crazy and have me a diet Coke tonight.'

'That's your idea of getting crazy?'

'It's Hunsecker,' she said. 'He's like an old lady. Won't let me have any caffeine or any artificial sweeteners. No booze, not even wine or beer. Hell, he's nagged at me so much I've cut my running back to a mile a day. If he had his way I'd spend the next six months in a foam rubber room.'

'He's worried about you,' I said. 'I think it's sweet.'

'You're not the one giving up diet Coke for nine months,' she said sourly. 'I'll see you at eleven.'

Next I called Edna. She answered on the first ring. 'Making a long day of it, aren't you? You've had some calls. Mac called three times. And a reverend somebody called from some church in Nashville.'

'The Cathedral of the Word Incarnate?' I asked, my spirits lifting.

'Something like that,' she said. 'Neva Jean took the message. She wrote it down somewhere.'

'This could be a lead on Delores Eisner,' I said. 'Try to find that message, will you? I need a phone number. It's important. Any other messages?'

'Oh yeah,' Edna said. 'This is good, Jules. A man named Eric Glenn called about an hour ago.'

'Glenn,' I said. 'How do I know that name?'

'He said he's been house-sitting at the house across the street from Stu Hightower's,' she said. 'He claims he met you when you were out there snooping around the day after the murder.'

'I remember,' I said. 'The set designer. What did he have to say?'

'He wants you to call him. Said he'd be in tonight, but he's flying to California in the morning.'

She gave me his phone number. 'Where are you?' she wanted to know. 'Why haven't you called Mac?'

I looked at my watch. Nine o'clock. The last remnants of daylight were gone, and the parking lot at Hooligan's was overflowing with the Thank God It's Friday crowd.

'I've got a key to BackTalk,' I said. 'I'm going to take a ride over there and see if I can figure out who had the most to gain by getting rid of Hightower.'

'Jesus, Jules,' she said. 'If that DiPima character finds out you've been breaking and entering over there he'll put you where the sun doesn't shine.'

'It's not breaking and entering,' I said. 'One of the secretaries loaned me a key. I'm going to go in, look at the file on that merger deal and come right back out. I'm meeting Linda Nickells at Hooligan's at eleven, and I'll be home tucked in bed by midnight. Okay?'

'You still haven't told me why you haven't called Mac,' she said. 'He sounded frantic.'

'MYOB, Edna,' I said.

'What's that supposed to mean?'

'Mind your own business.'

Eric Glenn was terribly proud of himself.

'Well, I've solved your little murder,' he said.

'How nice. Have you told the police?'

'I haven't had drinks with the police,' he said pointedly. 'Now do you want to hear it, or not?'

'Please,' I said.

'All right,' he said eagerly. 'Remember, I told you I had a little get together Monday night? One of the gang, Eddie, left early because he had to be in Miami the next day for business. He called me today when he got back, and I told him about all the excitement he'd missed. That's when he mentioned seeing the car.'

'What car?'

'A white Range Rover,' Eric said triumphantly. 'Parked in Stuart Hightower's garage. He saw the doors open, and this Range Rover backed out and sped away.'

'What time was this?' I asked.

'Around eight thirty, quarter to nine. Eddie said he'd noticed the garage doors were closed earlier when he went out to get something from his car. He noticed, because he's a car buff, and he was just dying to know what kind of car someone like Stu Hightower drove. Star-fucker! Then when he left an hour later, Eddie said the Range Rover absolutely zoomed out of that driveway. Practically peeled rubber. The car must have belonged to the murderer,' he said ominously.

'Or it could have belonged to a friend who just stopped by,' I said.

'It was the murderer, I tell you,' Eric said. 'Isn't this

exciting? Just like one of those old Alfred Hitchcock movies.'

'It's a good lead,' I admitted. 'Those Range Rovers are pretty expensive, aren't they?'

'Forty thousand big ones,' he said. 'The ultimate playtoy. You'll call me as soon as there's an arrest, won't you?'

'You'll be one of the first to know,' I promised.

And then I thought of something, something that had been nagging at the back of my mind.

'Eric,' I shouted. 'Don't hang up.'

'Never,' he said. 'What's on your mind?'

'The music at Hightower's house,' I said. 'My client thinks she remembers turning that stereo off. But when I got there, it was blaring away.'

'My darling, the noise was unbearable.'

'And it was on all night? Nonstop?'

He was quiet. 'Let me think.'

'Well. What do you know? This is so exciting. Is it another clue? Because, now that you mention it, it does seem that the music let up for a short time.'

'What time?' I said anxiously.

'Oh heavens,' he said. 'Who knows the time? I do remember we'd all been shouting to make ourselves heard over the racket, and then somebody was telling a naughty joke in a very loud voice, and the music cut off and everybody but everybody in the room heard the punch-line, which was extremely risqué. Shall I tell you the joke?'

'No thanks,' I said. 'You're sure the music cut off?'

'Fairly sure,' he said. 'I mean, yes. Definitely. You'll call, won't you?'

I parked Traci's car around back, near the rear entrance. Like a good organized secretary, Traci had color-coded the keys on her ring. The one for her apartment had a red plastic dohickey on it, four or five others had blue ones, and her car key was yellow. The blue ones, I decided, were for the office.

The second key worked just fine. I opened the door, snapped on the flashlight I'd brought along and listened to the quiet beeping of the burglar alarm. Now I had two minutes to find the control panel. It was supposed to be to the right of the door, but all I could find was the fuse box.

I flashed the light around the area near the back door. There was a soft drink machine, a fire extinguisher and a large metal trash can full of aluminum cans for recycling. But no alarm panel.

Sweat beaded on my upper lip and trickled down my back. How many seconds since I'd tripped the alarm?

Calm, I told myself. Stay calm. It's here. By the door. But which door. The front one? Holding the flashlight in front of me, I yanked open the only door leading out of the room I was in. It lead into a long hallway. I'd been here before. I raced down the hall toward the lighted exit sign at the other end, opened that door and found myself in the reception area.

I played the light to the right of the door. There, half hidden by a drapery panel, I saw the tiny red glowing lights of the panel.

My hands were shaking as I went to punch in the code.

The code. My mind went blank. I'd chanted it in the car over and over after Traci gave it to me. Now it was gone. My stomach churned. Rivulets of sweat poured down my face. What was the number? I looked at my watch and saw the second hand sweeping around. What the hell was the code?

WHUP-WHUP-WHUP. the walls seemed to reverberate with the sound. I thought my heart would leap out of my chest. I wanted to run – to the car, to the parking lot, anywhere away from here.

The phone on the receptionist's desk rang. Steady, Garrity, I told myself. Answer the phone. Tell them the code word.

It rang again. I took a deep breath and picked it up.

'Is this the alarm company? Thank heavens. This is Traci, Mr Hightower's secretary,' I said breathlessly. 'I came back to get some files and the other line rang and I answered it, and then I remembered the alarm. It's okay,' I said. 'The code word is *Rock*.'

'Say again?' the woman on the other end said.

'Rock,' I said loudly. 'R-O-C-K. And the numerical code is Star-eight-two-three. Sorry for the bother.' The code number came back as soon as I'd quit trying to remember it.

'No problem,' the woman said. 'Do you know how to reset the alarm?'

'No,' I said, starting to panic. 'I never had to do that before. Nobody ever showed me.'

'Figures,' the woman muttered. 'Punch the code in

again, hit enter, and then reset,' she said. 'I'm at eight two two-oh oh oh oh one, operator thirty-two, if you have any more problems.'

I stretched the phone over to the panel and did as she instructed. The whooping faded away into the night.

'Thank you so much,' I said fervently. She had no idea how much I meant that.

After I hung up I peeked out the front door to see if any cop cars had responded to the alarm. Except for the pervasive chirping of the crickets, everything was quiet. No cops in sight.

Relieved, I left the reception area and walked briskly down the hallway. The black paint and lack of windows made the area as dark and noiseless as a tomb, except for the weird glow-in-the-dark paint from Joe E's sixty-thousand-dollar mural. Traci had said Hightower's files would be put in the storage room. Now all I had to do was find it, and hope I could get in.

I tried every door down the hallway. Most were offices. One appeared to be a break room, with tables and chairs and a kitchen area.

When the hallway was bisected by another hall I turned right. A nameplate on a set of double doors at the end of that hall said Studio A. The doors were locked tight. None of my keys fit. They weren't taking chances with any of that expensive equipment.

I went back to the other end of the hallway, where another set of double doors said I'd found Studio B. I didn't bother to try the keys.

A room next door to the studio was marked Tape

Vault. If I didn't find those file boxes someplace else, I'd come back here.

Retracing my steps back to the main hallway, I moved past Hightower's office. The door was locked. Traci's was locked also. There were three more rooms to try before the hallway ended in the rear entry. The first room was a copy and supply room. Three large photocopy machines, two fax machines and banks of cabinets lined the walls. I opened them all, but found no cardboard file boxes.

The next room was locked. I held the flashlight between my knees while I fumbled with the key chain. The first key fit.

I stepped inside. The room, like the others, was windowless and pitch dark. I decided to risk turning on the lights. This had been someone's office once. The desk was still there, complete with a telephone. But the rest of the room was full of cardboard storage boxes. The ones nearest the door looked like the ones I'd seen being removed from Traci's office earlier in the day.

I closed the door, leaving it open only a fraction of an inch. The boxes were stacked three high, with no identifying marks about the contents. I opened the top box and dug in.

It looked like Traci had opened her former boss's top desk drawer and dumped in the contents. There were airline flight schedules, matchbooks from various fancy restaurants, boxes of Stu Hightower's business cards, rubber bands, a leather-bound business card index, and a dozen or so pens and pencils. Then there was a half-roll of Certs and an envelope containing two tickets to a sold

329

out Rolling Stones concert scheduled for two weeks from now at the Georgia Dome. Stu Hightower wouldn't be needing those tickets now, but I couldn't quite bring myself to pocket them. I guess Traci couldn't either.

I set the box aside and opened the one underneath. This one looked more promising. File folders, alphabetically filed of course, A through H. I took the box and set it on the desk. There was no chair in the room, so I sat cross-legged on top of the desk.

The AKA file was right where it should be. Nice and thick too. I took it out of the box and started leafing through it. The first part of the file was correspondence from Hightower's LA attorney, Peter Wegner. Holding the flashlight on the paper, I practiced the speed-reading techniques I'd learned in college. There was a lot of discussion about a deal memo, and whether or not AKA would put Hightower on its board of directors, something Hightower was adamant about but that AKA's chairman, Leonard Fischer, was resisting.

There was a lot of legal mumbo-jumbo, but after pages and pages of boilerplate, it looked like AKA was prepared to offer Hightower twelve million in cash and AKA stock for BackTalk records, its publishing library, unreleased product, and other physical assets. Also included in the sale would be the publishing catalog of SkyHi records. The VelvetTeens had been passed along in the sale too.

Attached to the deal memo was the list of assets to be conveyed. Pages and pages of stuff; from the building I was sitting in, to every woofer and tweeter, every chair and desk, even the two company tickets to the Masters golf tournament in Augusta. I set that aside. If there was time, I'd photocopy the deal memo to take to Korznick.

The next document was an eye-opener. A confidential memo from Hightower to Fischer, containing his vision of the 'new' BackTalk Records: a division of AKA International.

As Matt Gordon had guessed, Hightower was resigned to taking BackTalk to a more conservative, mainstream audience. He'd already terminated Serena Choi's contract, Hightower wrote, and the Joanses second album, *City of Pain*, would be their last for BackTalk. As for The Honeys, Attitude Adjustment, and BizzyB, Hightower thought they would be a perfect fit for the new company.

As for Junebug, Hightower said he was willing to concede with Fischer that although talented, Junebug probably was indeed a 'novelty act' whose appeal as a young white rapper was extremely limited. 'He is fourteen now, and his voice is starting to change,' Hightower wrote. 'I've reluctantly concluded that your comments about his postpubescent lack of appeal are right on the money. He has a strong contract, however, and we may not be able to break it through the usual means. I am open to suggestions.'

From what I'd overheard in Danielle Manigault's office, BackTalk had decided to get rid of Junebug by treating him shabbily.

I glanced at my watch again. It was already 10:45. I gathered up the deal memo and a stack of other papers. There wouldn't be time to read everything now. I'd photocopy what I could and leave before my luck ran out.

I snapped the light out in the storage room and made my way down the hallway to the copy room. When I switched it on, the copier made a racket that seemed to echo in the big tile-floored room. I took the staples out of the papers and started feeding them into the machine, a page at a time. I started collating the pages as the machine spit them out.

Something on a page of the deal memo caught my eye. It was actually on the list of company assets that would be transferred to AKA at the completion of the sale. A list of company vehicles. I stopped copying and read closer.

Vehicles belonging to BackTalk included two 1989 Chevrolet panel trucks, a 1968 Jaguar, a 1993 Mercedes SEL, a 1993 Mercedes convertible, and a 1994 Range Rover.

The Range Rover. Was it the same one Eric Glenn's friend spotted in Hightower's driveway the night of the murder? And if it belonged to the company, who was driving it? Danielle Manigault? Serena, or perhaps someone else with the company? According to Glenn, Hightower drove the Jag and the blue Mercedes, and Serena drove the convertible.

I leafed through the stack of memos in my hand to see if there was a list detailing who drove which vehicles. But there were too many pages and I had too little time left. I switched the copier back on. When Linda and I took Traci's car back, I thought, I'd wake her up and ask her about the Range Rover.

I was almost done with the copying when I smelled something. I wrinkled my nose at the odor. Then the hair on the back of my neck started to prickle. Over the din of the copier I heard a loud, menacing growl.

I whirled around and the dog, all teeth and glowing eyes, lunged at me.

'Hitler!' Arlene Trotter shouted. She yanked on the chain-link leash and the dog jerked backward, still straining against her pull.

'Turn off that machine,' Arlene ordered. 'It makes the dog nervous.

I did as she said. I almost never argue with a lady who packs a Doberman and a thirty-eight.

30

'Stay,' Arlene snapped. The Doberman sat down on its haunches but kept its teeth bared and its ears pricked. I didn't move either.

She unclipped the chain from the dog's collar and tucked the pistol in the waistband of her jeans. 'If you move suddenly, Hitler will forget to stay,' she said evenly. 'If I were you, I'd just keep real still.'

My mouth was dry and I could feel the adrenaline pumping. I licked my lips and forced myself to speak. 'The car Stu gave Junebug. It was his white Range Rover, wasn't it? And it still had the Riverbend security sticker on it, I'll bet.'

She ignored my question and took the sheaf of papers out of my hand, leafing through it until she came to something of interest. It was Stu's memo to Leonard Fischer. As she skimmed, a muscle in her jaw twitched and her eyes hardened. She crumpled the paper into a ball with one hand and threw it against the wall.

'A novelty,' she said slowly. 'That's all my boy was to BackTalk. A novelty.' She looked up at me as though I were an afterthought.

'Put that stuff back in the folder,' she said.

I did as she told me.

'Now drop the folder on the floor.'

I did that too.

'That's Traci's car out there,' she said. 'Have you got her keys, too?'

'Yes,' I said. 'How did you get in here?'

She smiled. 'Stu left a spare set of keys in the pool house. I borrowed them. Give me yours now.'

I hesitated, watching the dog, who was growling down deep in the back of his throat.

'Hitler, stay!' she said. 'Get the keys out slowly. Put them on top of the copier. You don't have a gun, do you? Because if you make a move toward me this dog is going to be on you like white on rice. He'll rip your throat out before you can blink.'

'I don't have a gun,' I said, truthfully. I'd left it in the van. Silently I vowed to buy myself an ankle holster before I went on another covert action. If I ever went on another covert action.

I put the keys on top of the copier. Arlene took them, then waved the gun at me. 'We're going to the tape vault now. You know where that is?'

I nodded. 'It's locked.'

'That's all right. Traci had keys to everything over here. She was the only one Stu trusted.' She clipped the chain onto Hitler's collar again. 'Stay,' she warned.

To me, she said, 'walk on ahead of us. Unlock the door and go in. We'll be right behind you.'

The clicking of the Doberman's nails on the tile floor told me just how close he was.

My hands were shaking as I tried all the blue keys. Hitler stood by Arlene's side, growling as I fumbled with the keys. 'Hurry up,' she said tersely. Funny thing. Under pressure, Arlene's precise Eastern accent had vanished.

When the lock tumblers clicked into place I could have cried with relief. I opened the door and she reached around past me and turned on the light.

'Go on in,' she said, gesturing with the gun.

I stood in the doorway, terrified. I was positive she intended to shoot me, then lock my body in this tape vault. 'Why are you doing all this?' I asked. 'Because Stu was going to drop your son's contract? He's young, Arlene, just a kid. He has his whole life in front of him.'

'You don't know a damn thing about this business,' she said savagely. 'Junebug's the biggest talent this industry has ever seen. He could be another Elvis Presley, another Michael Jackson. He sings, he writes, he can act. And that bastard Hightower, he calls my boy a novelty.'

'This,' she said, motioning with the gun to the tapes in the vault, her mouth twisted in disgust, 'this garbage is the novelty. BizzyB, Dynamic Dissonance. Garbage. They're all no-talent amateurs. Where will they be in a year? Five years? Nowhere, that's where. You're right about one thing, though, my boy has his whole life ahead of him. That's what I'm going to make sure of. Nobody messes with him. Nobody.'

I was watching how she handled the gun. She gripped it loosely, gesturing wildly as she talked. She was definitely not a pro. On the other hand, she'd been proficient enough with a gun to kill Hightower. And she had Hitler on her side too.

'Walk down that aisle right there,' she said, pointing to the left side of the room. 'I want our masters.'

'Your what?' I was stalling. Things were going too fast and I needed to slow them down.

'The master tracks from Bug's next album, *Strictly Personal*. It'll say Junebug on the side. Get it and bring it here.'

I moved slowly down the row, reading the labels on the sides of the tape cases. 'Why do you need the master track?' I asked. 'None of this makes any sense, Arlene. The police are going to find out you killed Stu. One of the neighbors saw you leaving in the Range Rover that night. They'll figure out you set up Rita for the murder.'

She smiled, showing a set of perfect white teeth. 'Too bad about Rita Fontaine. I used to like the VelvetTeens in the sixties. I figured the cops would blame it on Serena or that bitch Danielle. But she walked in and set herself up. And anyway, she deserved it, ruining Bug's listening party like she did. Now I need Bug's master because I'm going to take it out to LA. A producer at RCA is interested in signing us. Stu had no intention of ever releasing *Strictly Personal*. He told me that, you know.'

'And that's why you killed him?'

She frowned. 'Quit talking and find that tape. Hurry, damn it, we don't have all night.'

The dog responded to the agitation in her voice, pricking its ears forward, whining, and straining against the leash.

She jerked viciously on the chain. 'Shut up, Hitler.'

I found the tape cartridge and took it off the shelf. I held it out to her. The case was bulky, two inches wide by about fourteen inches across. If she took it, she'd have to juggle the tape, the gun and the Doberman's leash. Maybe I could get the gun away from her.

She shook her head. 'You carry it. Come on.' With one hand she knocked a row of tapes onto the floor. The dog whimpered at the clatter, but she kept a tight grip on the chain. She turned off the light and left the door ajar. 'Looks like some snoopy private detective ransacked the place,' she said with satisfaction.

'Now down here.' She was pointing toward the end of the long hallway.

'Where are you taking me?' I asked. Oddly enough, I was starting to feel a little calmer. If she hadn't used the gun on me in the tape vault, she must have other plans. I sneaked a look at my watch. It was 11:15. The longer we were here, the better my chances. Edna knew where I was. Linda didn't, but she was notoriously impatient. If I was too late, she might call the house looking for me and raise the alarm. Or she might get disgusted and go home and go to bed.

'You're not goin' far,' Arlene said. She paused in front of the last door on the right side of the hall. 'Gimme them keys,' she said. I handed them over.

This door was unlocked. I opened the door and stepped inside. She shoved me forward into the darkness, then turned on the light.

It was a cleaning closet. The floor was cement, the walls were water-stained wallboard. One wall held a deep sink, with a shelf of cleaning supplies above it. In the corner stood a heavy galvanized tin mop bucket with a wringer attachment on the top. There were mops and brooms and a long-handled window squeegee in the corner. The room was tiny, no larger than six by nine.

Hitler's ears stood up, the fur on his neck was erect, his nose quivered at the stale, slightly pine-scented air.

'I hadn't really counted on running into you tonight,' Arlene said, frowning. 'I just wanted our master, that's all. Still, I think it'll work out. Folks'll just figure you came over here snoopin' around, busted your head by accident, passed out and maybe spilled some stuff in the process.' Her eyes wandered about the room until they lit on the shelf of supplies above the sink.

I needed to stall for time. 'How'd you know how to disarm the security system?' I asked.

'You mean the eight-two-three code?' she asked. 'Bug was part of a late session one night. We all went out to get pizza around four a.m. I watched while Stu set the alarm. It's the same kind we have at our condo. Nothing too tricky.'

It had been damn tricky for me, but I didn't feel like sharing that with Arlene Trotter. I did consider grabbing for the gun, but the dog inched forward, baring his teeth at me. I think he remembered the incident with the slamming door at the condo.

'Sit down there,' she said.

The concrete floor was cold and damp against the thin fabric of my cotton slacks. I decided to keep stalling for time. 'Why kill Stu?' I asked. 'You said your son is talented. Why not just switch record labels?'

'He lied to us,' she cried. 'I believed everything he said. Bug loved him like a daddy. And he betrayed our trust. I couldn't let him get away with that. I just couldn't. He deserved to die. He was scum.'

'The whole thing was pretty clever,' I said. 'Did you plan it that way?'

She flashed those beautiful teeth again. 'I never planned none of it. Carpe diem. That means seize the day. That's what I did. And it all worked out real nice.'

'You met up with Hightower at the cocktail party Monday night,' I suggested. 'Whose idea was it for you to go back to his house?'

She actually blushed. 'I had a lot of champagne at that party. It was my first big society party, and I was nervous. Stu kept bringing me champagne. He was flirting with me. I flirted back. He made me feel sexy, you know?'

'Stu Hightower was expert at making women feel sexy from what I've heard,' I said.

'We snorted some coke,' she said, sounding surprised at herself. 'In the stairwell of the hotel, at the party. Well, I snorted it. Stu said it gave him a headache. Now that was fine. Afterward, I couldn't wait to be alone with him. I'll tell you the truth. I had an itch that needed scratching after all these months up here without a man.'

'You followed him out to his house in the Range Rover.'

'He gave it to Junebug when we first come to town,' she said. 'A fourteen-year-old with a car like that. They tell me those things cost something like forty thousand.

It still had Stu's Riverbend sticker on the windshield. The guards waved me right on through. I parked in the garage and we closed the doors, in case Serena happened to cruise by. She did that all the time.'

'What happened at the house?' I asked.

'He gave me some more coke,' she said dreamily. 'I'll tell you, I could get used to that stuff if somebody else was doin' the buyin'. Then we had sex right there in the backyard on one of those lounge chairs. Then we went skinny dippin' and did it again. Afterward, I wanted to take a shower and wash my hair. There's a bedroom and bathroom right there in that pool house. Did you know that?'

I didn't. My exploration of the premises had stopped with the discovery of Stu Hightower's body.

'I was combing my hair in the bathroom, and I heard Stu talking on that cordless phone of his. He takes it everywhere. And he was talking about BackTalk. 'I don't care who you decide to dump,' I heard him say. 'That's not a deal breaker. He's a kid, he'll get over it.' And I knew right away. He'd sold us out. He'd already started hedging about the release date for *Strictly Personal*. I got dressed, got my gun out of my purse.'

'Stu's gun?' I asked, looking at the one in her hand.

'It was a present,' she said, laughing girlishly. 'Stu was big on presents. He said I'd need it for protection, living in the big city of Atlanta, a country girl like me. He didn't know how right he was. I didn't tell him I already had a gun of my own. This gun. Didn't seem polite to turn down a nice present like that.'

'So you shot him. With a gun he bought you.'

'Without a second thought,' she said. 'I stepped out of that bedroom and he was standing there, still naked, fixing himself a drink. I told him he was a lying son-of-a-bitch. I told him I knew what he was up to. He saw the gun and he laughed. 'What are you gonna do, Arlene,' he said, 'you gonna shoot me 'cause your son is gonna be on the streets?' Then he laughed again, and he turned to finish making his drink.'

'And you shot him.'

'Without another word,' she agreed. 'I was just getting ready to tear the place up. There was some coke left. I was gonna sprinkle it around, make it look like what the newspapers are all the time calling a drug-related slaying. And then your friend Rita showed up.'

'And walked into a murder rap.'

'I hid in the bathroom while she helped herself to a drink,' Arlene said. 'I was afraid she'd see Stu's body, but she was too busy guzzling that free booze. She never even knew I was there. She turned the music off, went out, and fell asleep.'

'You weren't afraid she'd wake up?'

'With the buzz she had on?' Arlene laughed harshly. 'She fell down twice while she was trying to get onto that lounge chair. After a little while, I turned the music way up, and I took the gun and put it in her hand, aimed it up in the air and fired. She didn't move a muscle.'

I looked up from where I was huddled on the floor. 'And now you're going to shoot me? Arlene, you'll never get away with it. Not twice. I told you, a witness saw your car that night. Traci knows I'm here, too.'

'You're lying,' she said. 'You'd say anything to save your own hide. I'd do the same thing. Carpe diem, right?' Then she reached over and brought the butt of the gun crashing down on my forehead.

31

When I came to, I was lying on my side, my knees curled close to my chest, coughing. My head throbbed and my nose and mouth and eyes were burning. I tried to breathe, but my lungs felt seared. I coughed uncontrollably, retching and gasping for air.

With my fists, I rubbed at my eyes, tears running down my face. The room was full of something, an acrid gas I'd smelled before. Yes, once, years ago, when I'd poured ammonia into a bathtub I'd already tried cleaning with bleach. Chlorine gas.

I struggled to my knees and peered into the inky dark. Nothing. I could see nothing. Blindly, I searched the wall for a switch, until I remembered Arlene turning the switch on the outside of the closet. I pawed wildly at the doorknob, but it turned only a fraction of an inch. Locked.

Coughing and choking, I got back down on the floor and crawled around the tiny space, looking for the source of the fumes. My head hit something hard and I cried out in pain. It was the edge of the mop sink. I pulled myself up by the edge and felt inside. It was dry.

I crawled to the other corner, and found a metal

345

container. The mop bucket. The chlorine smell was overpowering. My body was seized with racking spasms of coughs. I thought my lungs would tear in half from the effort.

Beside the bucket I felt a plastic jug with a handle. It was empty. I held it to my nose. It had held bleach. With my feet I managed to move the bucket. I could hear liquid slopping around inside. Arlene had mixed what felt like a gallon of bleach with something, an ammonia-based window cleaner, probably, intending to poison me with the fumes. It was working. The windowless room seemed airtight. No light entered from around the door.

I had to get air, had to get rid of the bleach solution. I pulled myself to my feet, gasping for air, my body doubled over from the effort of trying to breathe. The bucket was heavy, full of ammonia and bleach, and the wringer attachment at the top made it even bulkier.

I stripped my shirt off and tied the sleeves around the lower part of my face, covering my nose and mouth, Using my feet like a soccer player, I slowly scooted the bucket across the floor toward the sink. Liquid slopped over the sides, onto my calves and feet. Finally I picked the bucket up and dumped it awkwardly into the sink. More liquid spilled onto my bare chest and arms. I screeched at the shocking cold, and the burning sensation when the chemicals hit my skin.

I felt for the faucets, turning them on full blast, splashing water on my chest, arms and face. I splashed more on my ankles and feet, where the bleach had slopped. The water was ice cold, but that bleach was blistering my skin.

I was weak from coughing and my lungs felt scorched and blistered. Shaking uncontrollably, I managed to peel off my bleach and water-logged pants. I had to get the caustic chemicals away from my skin. I sank back against a wall, untied the shirt and tried to dry myself off. I felt cold metal against my back and reached around to see what I'd found.

My fingertips told me it was the window squeegee. It was maybe eight feet long, long enough to reach the farthest corner of those picture windows in the reception area. I couldn't see how high the ceiling was, but it was worth trying. Anything was worth trying.

I kicked the mop bucket over with my feet. But the wringer made it top heavy and it wouldn't stand upside down. I groped my way back to the sink. It was deep, and maybe four feet off the ground. Holding the squeegee in one hand, I threw a leg over into the sink, and holding onto the spigot, hauled myself into the sink.

I crouched there, my legs and thighs quivering from the effort, my ribs aching. Finally, I found the strength to stand erect. My equilibrium was thrown off by the dark, and I felt myself swaying, my body threatening to tip over and throw me ass over teakettle out of the sink. It would have been laughable if it hadn't been so awful. But I grasped the squeegee and held it with both hands, trying to steady myself. Then I thrust it upward as hard as I could, jabbing at the ceiling with the metal and rubber end of the tool.

Shards of acoustical tile rained down on my head and

shoulders. I ducked my head to keep the dust out of my eyes. I jabbed that pole upward, again and again. I didn't know if the ceiling was fake, but I hoped there might be an air shaft up there, something that would let oxygen flood into the poisoned air in my closet.

After whacking at the ceiling for five minutes, I was exhausted. I wanted to curl up in the corner and rest. But my eyes and nose stung, and my skin still burned from the bleach.

Reluctantly, I climbed down out of the sink and groped my way back to the door. I banged on it with my fists. It was solid and metal. I wanted to cry. Instead I bent down and picked up the mop bucket. Holding it by the wheeled bottom, I stepped away and swung the wringer end against the wall with all my might.

I was rewarded with a crunching and splintering sound. I groped the wall with both hands. The bucket had gouged a small depression in the wallboard.

I picked the bucket up again, moved away from the wall, then bashed it with every ounce of strength I possessed. My lungs felt like they would surely explode. But this time I heard the splinter of wood, and felt chunks of wallboard flying from the wall.

I put the bucket down and felt the wall. I could see a pinhole of light. There was a hole, a small one. No bigger than my thumbnail, but I'd broken a hole in the wall. I bashed again and again, maybe a dozen more times, grunting with the strain. The hole grew until it was fist-sized, and a weak beam of light from the outside hallway let me see my surroundings.

But now my legs would no longer support me. I sank

to the floor, my face turned to the hole. If I'd had the strength, I would have put my lips to it, to suck in a whole roomful of oxygen.

After a moment or two, I crawled over to the sink and pulled myself up again. Now I could see the shelf above the sink. I'd forgotten it was there, or hadn't noticed before I was plunged into darkness. On the shelf I found what had been hidden from me in the dark, a wooden handled toilet plunger. I felt giddy with relief.

Still gasping for air, I took the wooden end of the plunger and commenced to gouging at the wall. It was slow work. I was weak, wheezing and coughing, and my hands quickly blistered from the wood handle. After an eternity, the hole was as big as a small dinner plate, but with a wall stud running through it.

Again I wanted to cry. I could see the outside hallway, but the hole was too far from the door for me to be able to grasp the doorknob. Anyway, I had no more strength to hammer.

Anger and terror, terror at suffocating, closed in a locked, darkened closet full of poison had given me the will to survive, but now I could go no further. I put my head on my knees and cried. My sobs ended in coughing fits. Between the coughs I heard sounds coming from somewhere inside the building.

If it was Arlene, and she'd come back to check on me, she'd see the hole, hear my racking coughs and finish me off with the gun. I was past caring.

'Callahan?' A man's voice. Familiar.

'Jesus Christ, Callahan, are you in there?' It was C.W. Hunsecker.

'It's me,' I croaked. 'Get me out.'

I heard the doorknob turn, but not open. 'It's been locked with a key,' he called. 'Get away from the wall.'

The sounds of the bullets hitting metal seemed to explode in my ears. The door was thrown open, and then C.W. was grabbing me, grasping me by the arms and dragging me out, with me coughing and wheezing and sobbing all at the same time.

'Jesus,' he said, clearly stunned at my appearance. 'What happened?'

'Arlene,' I croaked. 'It was Arlene Trotter.'

32

While we waited for the ambulance, C.W. went into one of the offices to look for some dry clothes for me. He returned with an oversized black T-shirt with gold lettering on the front. It said 'Junebug' in big letters. And 'Diss Dis.' I put it on, then pointed at my bare legs. 'Pants?'

He grumbled, but went away again. When he came back, he had somebody's gym bag. He pulled out a smelly pair of gray gym shorts.

They were tight, but I put them on gratefully, pulling the shirt down over them. There were socks and shoes too, a pair of men's size twelve black baseball spikes. I put them on anyway. I didn't care. At some point, he called Edna and told her I was okay. He didn't share any details.

C.W. tried to get me to sip from a cup of water. But between the racking spasms of coughs I could get down only a tiny bit. He sat me up on the sofa in the reception area, his arms tight around my shoulders while I coughed and wheezed and gasped.

'I called home at ten thirty to check on Linda. She told me she wanted to go meet you at Hooligan's, to help you run an errand. "No way," I said. "No three-month-pregnant wife of mine is going running in the streets at midnight." We had a fight. She was pissed. But I told her I'd meet you over there instead. When you didn't show, I called her and woke her up, to make sure she had the right place. She got mad at me all over again. I think her hormones are all messed up. So she tried calling you at home, and that's when Edna admitted what you were up to over here. Somebody left the back door open a little, or you'd probably be dead.'

He shook me gently by the shoulders. 'Garrity, you dumb fuck, don't you ever learn?'

Slowly, with excruciating effort, I managed to whisper what had happened, how Arlene Trotter had killed Hightower, admitted it to me, then left me locked in that closet to die. My fury mounted with each detail.

When the Grady Hospital ambulance got there, the emergency medical technicians turned out to be old friends of C.W.'s, a couple of large, bossy black women named Flo and Janet.

'She's been exposed to chlorine gas,' C.W. told Flo, while she took my pulse. Janet was slipping an oxygen mask over my nose and mouth. 'Relax now, honey, and breathe,' she said. 'We gonna fix you right up good as new.'

'You didn't pass out from that gas?' Flo asked.

I shook my head no, tried to close my swollen and inflamed eyelids. My lips felt swollen too. I flashed them both hands twice, to let them know I'd only been in the closet for around twenty minutes.

'Only twenty minutes? Well, that's not too bad,' Flo

said. 'You can spend the night at Grady, let the doctors check you again in the morning and go on home by afternoon, if they like what they see.'

'Yeah, you were lucky, honey,' Janet said. 'Must have been some cracks in the wall somewhere, cause with chlorine gas, they usually pass right on out.'

I shook my head vehemently, and moved the mask away from my face for a moment. The coughing had subsided for the moment. 'I'm fine,' I whispered. 'I don't need to go to the hospital.'

C.W. grasped my wrist and squeezed. 'Cut out that shit, Garrity,' he said gruffly. 'You're going to the hospital. End of discussion.'

I had the oxygen mask back over my face now, and I was concentrating on trying to breathe deeply. My head throbbed where Arlene Trotter had bashed me. I raised my fingers and felt a knot and a cut with dried blood. But I was alive.

And goddamn it, I wasn't going to let her get away with it. But first I needed to breathe. I watched the minutes tick away on my watch while C.W. mounted futile arguments about why I should let myself be admitted to the hospital. When I'd been on the oxygen for twenty minutes, I unhooked the mask and handed it back to Flo. 'Thanks,' I whispered. 'I'm all right now.'

Hunsecker started to fuss again, this time at the EMTs.

'We can't make her go if she don't want to, Captain,' Janet reminded him.

They made me sign a consent form saying I wouldn't hold the city liable if I dropped dead or sustained a permanent injury, then they packed up their stuff and left.

'Where do you think you're going?' C.W. said, when I got up stiffly from the sofa.

'I'm going to that condo. Peachtree Palisades. I'm going after Arlene Trotter,' I said hoarsely. 'With you or without you.'

He cussed and fussed for a while, but in the end, C.W. knew it was useless to argue with me. We went out to his car and he used his car phone to wake up Artie DiPima, who was sound asleep in suburban Forsyth county, forty miles north of where we were. DiPima said he'd send a crime scene unit and be right over to BackTalk.

'Arlene Trotter's a flight risk,' Hunsecker told DiPima. She's armed and it sounds to me like she's mentally unbalanced.'

'Junebug will be with her,' I whispered. 'He's only fourteen.'

'Okay,' Hunsecker told me. 'She's got her kid with her too, Artie. We're ten minutes from there in my unit. We'll swing by the condo and see if she's still there. Have somebody call the airlines and see if she booked a flight.'

DiPima argued with him briefly, but Hunsecker held his ground. 'No time, damn it,' he said. 'We'll see you there.'

C.W. hung up the phone, reached for the floor, and got his emergency flasher. He clamped it to the dashboard. Then we took off.

As we sped north on Peachtree, Hunsecker glanced

over at me. 'You ought to be locked up, you know that?' Then, his voice softening, 'You okay, Garrity?'

I swallowed, licked my parched, swollen lips. 'Just get her, C.W. Promise me you won't let her get away.'

'Calm down, Garrity,' he said. 'She ain't goin' nowhere.'

When we were within a mile of the condominium, Hunsecker's phone buzzed. It was DiPima. C.W. listened and hung up. 'She and the kid have the two a.m. flight to LA.'

I looked at my watch. It was nearly one now, and it was a twenty minute trip to Hartsfield Airport.

'DiPima's got a couple units on the way there now. I got a backup on the way to Peachtree Palisades too. When we get there, you're going to stay in the unit. Understand?'

I started to object, but he cut me short. 'You're a civilian now, Garrity, not a cop. You know the rules. You want to get me fired?'

He didn't wait for my answer.

'How are you going to get Junebug away from his mother?' I asked. 'She's obsessed with him, C.W.'

He nodded gravely. 'There's an underground parking garage at those condos, right? Do the tenants have assigned spaces?'

'I don't know,' I admitted. 'I just parked in a visitor's slot. I wasn't paying attention to that kind of stuff.'

'You think she's still driving the Range Rover?'

I shrugged. 'I didn't see her tonight until it was too late. She knows that the car was spotted at Hightower's the night of the murder, so if she's smart, she will have dumped it by now.'

He nodded, dialed information and asked for Arlene Trotter's phone number. 'Unlisted,' he said, pounding the steering wheel in frustration. 'We'll cruise the garage, see if we spot her or the car, and try to intercept her before she leaves.'

We were in front of the condo tower now. The marble lobby was brightly lit, and through the floor-to-ceiling plate glass walls I saw a uniformed guard sitting at a desk, watching a closed circuit television monitor.

'I could go in, identify myself as a cop and get the phone number, then call up to see if she's left yet.'

He shook his head stubbornly. 'You're not a cop. You don't leave the unit. What if she comes out of the elevator and sees you? She'll know what's up.'

'The garage entrance is in the basement,' I said. 'That's where she'll be headed.'

'Unless she's decided to take a cab or a limo to the airport,' Hunsecker said. 'Then we're really screwed.'

'Let me go in to the lobby,' I pleaded. 'Swear to God, all I'll do is call up there. If she answers, I'll hang up and call you right back on the car phone. You can catch her as she leaves the elevator. If there's no answer, I'll boogie on out of there, take the service stairs and meet you in the basement.'

I could see he was softening. 'Listen, C.W.,' I said. 'The lobby is empty. The basement will be too, this time of night. Right here, right now is going to be the safest place to take her into custody. If we have to wait until she gets to Hartsfield, anything could happen.'

He knew I was right.

'Gimme your hand,' he said.

Puzzled, I held it out to him. He took a pen and scrawled some numbers on the back of it. 'That's the car phone number. Call me right away, then get the hell out of that lobby. I'll see you in the basement.'

I paused before opening the door. 'My weapon's in the van,' I said pointedly.

'Shit.' He reached across me and opened the glove box, digging among the maps and papers until he brought out a nine millimeter Colt semi-automatic. 'That's Linda's,' he said. 'You lose it, you'll have to deal with her. You fire it, you'll be dealing with me.'

'See you in the basement,' I said, tucking the gun into the waistband of my shorts and pulling the T-shirt down over it. Hunsecker's car glided noiselessly into the night.

The plate-glass lobby doors were locked, and the security guard's eyes were shut tight too. I rapped on the door hard. Tried to scream, 'Open up, Police,' but my throat was too raw. So I pounded on the glass until he woke up, saw me and wandered over to the door.

He was young, no more than twenty, and he wore an ill-fitting vaguely military blue jacket with gold braid and a pair of rumpled khaki pants.

'Atlanta Police,' I croaked. 'Open up. I need to use your phone.'

He looked startled, but let me in.

'Give me Arlene Trotter's phone number,' I said, wasting no time. 'Now. This is official police business.'

His sleepy nonchalance faded. 'Yes ma'am,' he said.

He opened a drawer, pulled out a looseleaf notebook and turned the pages rapidly. 'Here it is,' he said, pointing to the typewritten listing.

'Have you seen her or Junebug tonight? Has she called down and told you to expect a cab or limo?' I asked.

'No-o-b-body's called,' he stammered. 'I saw Junebug earlier. We shoot pool together sometimes. One of his friends dropped him off around nine.'

I dialed Arlene's number. The phone rang once, then four more times. I pressed down the receiver and called C.W. 'Nobody home,' I said when he picked up.

'Everything's quiet down here,' he said. 'Get your butt down here.'

'Gimme your hand,' I said to the kid. He held it out, and I picked up a pen and wrote the car phone number on it. 'If Mrs Trotter or Junebug comes into the lobby, call this number,' I said. 'You don't have to say anything. Just dial it, then hang up. Don't say anything to her. Just act normal. Got it?'

'Got it,' he said.

I ran for the stairs, but I was gasping for breath before I'd gone only a few feet. My chest ached and my lungs were screaming for mercy. I forced myself to keep going. When I opened the door into the basement, C.W.'s blue sedan was parked in front of the door. But the car was empty and the security desk was unmanned.

'Get in the front seat and lay down,' a low, disembodied voice called out. I looked around. The basement was in half-darkness. The light in front of the elevator doors was out. C.W. had planted himself flat against the elevator wall. His service pistol was drawn and in his right hand. 'Now,' he barked.

We both heard the elevator gears start grinding. I dove for the car, shut the door and pressed my face against the cool leather of the seats. Then I rolled to my side and edged Linda's Colt out of my waistband. I checked the safety and tried to catch my breath.

The elevator dinged softly. I heard the doors slide open. Heard Arlene Trotter's voice urging 'Get those bags now. We've got to hurry...'

And then C.W.'s voice. 'Arlene Trotter, Atlanta Police...' A woman screamed, high and long. And then there was a single gunshot that roared and echoed and reverberated in the cavernous garage.

I jumped out of the car. Everything happened so strangely. I had the impression of being in the middle of one of those flickering early silent motion pictures.

C.W. was slumped over, half-sitting, half-lying, clutching both hands to his belly where a deep crimson stain was spreading over his pale yellow golf shirt. Junebug knelt beside him. 'You shot him, Mama,' he screamed. 'What'd you do that for?'

Arlene was tugging at her son's arm then. 'Come on, Bug, leave him. We gotta go. Come on now.'

I ran toward my friend. 'Don't move,' I called, training the gun on her.

She hadn't seen me until now. She turned and raised the gun.

I fired first.

All my years with the department, I'd been only a middling marksman. I'd never fired my service revolver

359

anyplace except the practice range. That night, in the half-light of a garage, I held a gun I'd never handled before, pointed it at another human being, and did what I had been trained to do a long, long time ago. I took a life, and I saved a life. The life I saved has never been the same since.

Epilogue

September 15

It was Kenyatta's idea to have a party at my house to view the videotape of the grand reunion performance of the fabulous VelvetTeens. I wasn't all that keen on the notion. Lately, I haven't felt like much of a party animal.

'You've got a big living room,' she pointed out.

'Yours is bigger.'

'Your mama is a great cook, everybody loves her pound cake.'

'Vonette's a fabulous cook.'

'Okay, I'll bring all the food and the beer. All you have to do is open the front door.'

'Hah!' I said. If Kenyatta thought Edna would let somebody else fix all the food for a gathering at her own home, she didn't know my mother.

'What's this really about?' I demanded. 'Give.'

'Okay,' she relented. 'I want Daddy and Linda to come. Daddy's never seen me perform as a VelvetTeen. You know they'd never come to Mama's house. No way, no how. Your place is like, neutral territory.'

That's how Edna and I came to be spending a sunny

Sunday afternoon cleaning house and fixing party snacks.

Edna curled her upper lip in disgust when I told her I wanted her to open a can of chilli (no beans) and drop it into a saucepan full of melting Cheese Whiz to make my friend Paula's nacho dip. 'You planning to serve this glop to company?' she asked.

'You serve it with taco chips,' I explained. 'Paula says it's a real crowd pleaser.'

'Paula's idea of haute cuisine is Spam sandwiches washed down with Yoo-Hoo,' Edna retorted. 'Let me see that recipe.'

'It's on my dresser,' I said, not looking up from the platter of grapes and Brie and crackers I was arranging.

When she came back from my bedroom she had the recipe in one hand, a small gray business card in the other, and a funny expression on her face.

'You're seeing a shrink?'

It was as much a statement as a question. I snatched the card away from her. 'Drop it, Ma,' I warned.

It had been three long months since that night in the parking garage. And every night, in what little sleep I got, I relived the moment over and over again, until I awoke, inevitably, drenched in my own sweat, unable to scream, gasping for breath, my lungs still burning from the chlorine gas I'd been exposed to, even though my doctor swore there had been no residual damage.

In the dream, I was still holding a wadded-up towel over the spreading stain on C.W.'s belly, telling him over and over that he'd be all right. I saw the boy, Junebug, sobbing softly while the ambulance attendants zipped a burgundy-colored bag over his mother's body. The bag had the funeral home's name embroidered on the sides, in curving script letters.

C.W. Hunsecker was too tough to die, but he wouldn't really be all right. Arlene's bullet ripped through his intestines and nicked his spinal cord before exiting his body. There had been two surgeries – stabilization they called it – and two months of rehabilitation and therapy in Shepherd Spinal Center. He was in a wheelchair now, the doctors told Linda it was questionable whether he'd ever walk again.

She was glad just to have him alive. Always the pragmatist, Linda. Since he'd gotten home from the hospital, I'd seen C.W. exactly once. I didn't know where to look when I talked to him, didn't want to stare at the wheelchair, or at his now-lifeless legs.

'You're avoiding C.W. You blame yourself for everything, for Arlene's death, your friend's injury, the boy's trauma,' my shrink told me. 'That's a hell of a lot of guilt to be carrying around.'

'I'm Catholic,' I'd explained. 'We're the people who invented original sin, remember?'

I met Nancy Cook when she was treating my cousin's son Dylan. We'd kept in touch, and after two weeks of sleeplessness, I'd called her, in desperation, to ask for help. She was really a child psychologist, but for me, she said laughingly, she'd make an exception.

We were meeting a couple times a week. I felt funny the first few times, self-conscious and full of dread that she'd make me dig up all kinds of nasty long-forgotten dreck about my childhood and my parents.

I guess she's good at what she does. The dreams had started to fade a little bit, and there were nights now when I slept undisturbed until morning. But I hadn't discussed my visits with my mother.

Now she turned back to the cheese dip, stirring it slowly and tilting the saucepan to keep the bottom from burning.

'I'm glad you're seeing a doctor,' she said finally. 'I've been worried about you.'

'I'm fine,' I said, wiping my hands on a dishtowel. I took the fruit platter into the living room, set it on the coffee table, and moved the chairs around so that everyone would have a good view of the television, which I'd wheeled in from the den. I'd left a space clear for C.W.'s wheelchair, and moved a small table nearby so that he'd have a place to set his drink.

Edna bustled in with a bowl of pretzels and another of mixed nuts. She moved the fruit platter I'd just placed, and fussed around, readjusting the chairs.

'What does Dr Cook say about Mac?' she said, frowning at the extension cord I'd used to plug in the television. She wouldn't look me in the eye.

I sighed. Edna has never believed that my personal life was personal. She'd always had a soft spot for Mac, and she'd been bugging me for weeks, in a not-so-subtle way, wanting to know what had happened between us. I knew she'd been talking to him, but I hadn't let her tell me anything about their discussions. Linda and C.W.

had seen Mac too; I gathered he'd been a frequent visitor while C.W. was in the hospital.

'We haven't talked about Mac,' I said wearily. 'Could we please drop this now?'

That was a lie, of course. I'd told Dr Cook about the relationship with Mac, and how and why it ended. She'd said nothing specific, no advice really. But lately, she'd been talking a lot about forgiveness. 'It's time to forgive yourself,' she told me. 'Time to think about forgiveness in general.'

But I wasn't ready yet.

The doorbell rang just as Edna opened her mouth to ask me another question. 'I'll get it,' I said quickly.

Vonette and Kenyatta stood on the doorstep, their arms loaded down with foil-wrapped platters, a cooler at their feet. For the next few minutes, we busied ourself setting out the Buffalo chicken wings, vegetable platter, and trays of cookies Vonette had fixed. 'I told Mama, forget about that healthy mess,' Kenyatta said, gnawing happily on a chicken drummette. 'This is a party, not a health spa.'

A few moments later, Rita and Andre and a cute young thing with a familiar face came in. 'This is Jeannie,' Andre said, slipping his arm around her shoulder and beaming down at her. 'She works at BackTalk.' Ah yes, the blond receptionist.

I almost didn't recognize Rita. She was spaghetti thin, wearing a black knit one-piece catsuit and some vampy high heels. She'd put a red rinse in her hair and added false eyelashes to emphasize her almond-shaped eyes.

'Rita,' I said, 'Girlfriend, you are looking fine. Edna, did you see this goddess?'

While the others were exclaiming over how good she looked, Rita gave me a quick hug. 'I've been sober three months today,' she said proudly. 'That's the real good news.'

'Did you bring the tape?' Edna demanded.

Rita dug down in her shoulder bag and waved the videotape in the air. 'It just came yesterday. Delores called last night. She's got some scheme to sell the tapes through the mail. Some outfit in Nashville says we can make a fortune off the oldies market with it. Especially after the movie comes out.'

David Korznick arrived next and while Vonette was fixing him a drink, Kenyatta pulled me aside. 'Where are they? Are they coming?'

'They'll be here,' I promised. 'Linda's still getting used to driving the new van with the chairlift, we went to the mall last week and I swear, she drove only twenty miles an hour.'

The van had been a gift from C.W.'s homicide buddies. They'd held a barbecue fund-raiser to help pay for the expensive customized vehicle C.W. was going to need to get around in. Linda was steadfastly refusing to let me do anything to help out. 'It's not your fault,' she kept saying. 'C.W.'s a cop. It's his job. Quit blaming yourself.'

I couldn't, of course. When Vonette mailed me a check for five thousand dollars for finding Delores and getting the murder charges dropped against Rita, I cashed it, bought a money order and mailed it anonymously to the post office box designated for the wheelchair fund.

'Daddy swears he's gonna be driving that van himself in a few months,' Kenyatta said.

'Believe it,' I told her. 'Your father's a fighter. He's too damn stubborn to spend the rest of his life in a wheelchair.'

No sooner were the words out of my mouth than we heard a banging at the back door. Kenyatta peeked out the front door and spotted the van in the driveway. 'They're here,' she said, 'Linda must be bringing Daddy in through the kitchen.'

'I'll see if she needs any help,' I volunteered, heading that way.

When I got to the kitchen, Linda was holding the screened door open, while C.W. bumped his way over the door stop, his face twisted in concentration. He didn't see me watching him until they were both in the house.

'Nice going,' I said casually. He looked up. His face was much thinner, and he'd grown a beard since I'd seen him in the hospital. It had come in totally gray.

'Nickells,' I said, 'who's this old dude in the wheel-chair? Is that your grandpa?' I deliberately looked him over and kissed him on the cheek. Part of my therapy, making myself take an unflinching look at reality.

C.W. scowled at me, the scowl that told me he loved me anyway, and Linda laughed. She was six months pregnant, but you'd have to look hard to tell it. 'I love the beard,' she protested. 'It makes him look sexy, don't you think? Kind of a cross between Quincy Jones and that dude on the cop show on TV. I can't think of his name.'

'I was thinking more like a cross between Burl Ives and Santa Claus,' I said, 'but maybe you're right.'

We were teasing and laughing like that as we moved into the living room, but when C.W. saw Vonette standing there, chatting with David Korznick, I heard him draw his breath in. 'What the hell is this?'

Vonette was obviously just as shocked to see C.W. and Linda as he was to see her. Her face went pale, and the drink in her hand shook and spilled a little.

'Well Carver Washington Hunsecker,' she said finally, after a long painful silence fell over the room. 'You're looking good for yourself.'

C.W. twisted in his chair until he found Kenyatta, who was standing by the window, nervously biting her lip. I glanced over at Linda, who was standing stock-still behind C.W., taking it all in with those big dark eyes of hers. I could have sworn I saw a glimmer of amusement there.

'Young lady?' he said, his voice loud. 'Is this your idea of a joke?'

She hung her head for a moment, and I could see tears welling up in her eyes.

C.W. wheeled around to face me. 'No,' he said. 'Never mind. This looks like something you'd do, Garrity. You never could stay out of my business.'

'Hey,' I protested. 'I had no idea she had something like this planned. I figured both of you knew.'

'Kenyatta,' I said, grabbing her by the arm. 'Do you mean to tell me you didn't tell either one of your parents that the other would be here? What kind of a cruel stunt is that?'

Rita moved quickly to her cousin's side, throwing an arm around Kenyatta's shoulder and favoring both C.W. and me with a glare. 'Now y'all quit hollering at this girl. She didn't mean no harm. This here is a party. I thought we were gonna celebrate, not keep on fussin' at each other about all this old business.'

A minute later, Kenyatta was kneeling beside C.W.'s wheelchair, tugging at his hand, which he kept jerking away from her.

'Listen to me, Daddy,' she said, her voice breaking.

C.W. turned his head away, muttering under his breath.

'Listen, dammit,' Kenyatta said, grabbing both his arms with hers, forcing him to look at her.

'I didn't tell you Mama was coming, and I didn't tell Mama you and Linda were coming, because I'm sick of all this feuding. Rita's right. Everything that happened before is old business. So you got divorced. Big deal. Lots of people get divorced. You're happy now, aren't you?'

She raised her head and looked meaningfully at Linda's swollen belly, then over to Vonette, who stood with hands on her hips, ready for a confrontation.

'Did you know Mama got down on her knees and prayed for you, prayed every single night you were in the hospital?' Kenyatta demanded. C.W. looked sharply at his ex-wife, then back again at Linda.

Vonette looked surprised, and her face flushed.

'I heard you, Mama,' Kenyatta said. 'I was prayin' too. Can't you just tell him you're glad he lived? Tell him to his face?'

Slowly, her high heels clicking deliberately on the

wooden floor, Vonette approached C.W. She held her head high, but the fixed lines around her eyes and her mouth seemed to soften a little. When she was directly in front of him, she held out a long slim hand.

'She's right,' Vonette said simply. 'I am glad you're alive. And I'm sorry I've been acting like you were dead all this time. I wish you and Linda all the best. I hope you'd do the same for me.'

Grudgingly, C.W. took his hand in hers and squeezed it momentarily. But Vonette wouldn't let go. She kept holding on.

'Your turn,' she said, cracking a smile.

'Yeah,' Linda prompted. 'Your turn.'

'Thank you,' C.W. said. 'I do wish you the best.'

'And?' Linda coached.

He scowled again. 'You're not gonna make this easy for me, are you?'

'No,' Linda and Vonette answered in unison, breaking the awkward tension in the room and inducing a round of laughter from the others.

'And I'm proud of the comeback you and Kenyatta and Rita have made with the VelvetTeens,' he said quickly. 'I've always been proud of you. I mean it.'

They talked quietly for a while then, while the rest of us milled around, chatting, laughing, eating and drinking. Somebody put on one of my Motown's greatest hits tapes, and while we watched, Kenyatta, Jeannie, and Andre started singing along with the Temptations' 'Just My Imagination' adding an impromptu choreography of exaggerated sways spins and strolls, with a fillip of doo-wop choruses.

'Look at that,' Vonette said, gazing at her daughter. 'Watch how Kenyatta moves, how she holds herself. She's ten times better than we were in the old days.'

'Andre's not bad either,' I said, humming along with the tune.

'Maybe he should quit his day job and get into the business too.'

'He did quit the night job,' Rita said. 'It's the first time since he got out of the service that he hasn't worked two jobs.'

'That's right,' Vonette put in. 'Did you tell Callahan that David thinks Andre should have a claim to part of Stu's estate?'

Edna had walked over and as usual wasn't too proud to elbow her way into the conversation. 'What's that Serena woman going to have to say about Andre getting a piece of her action?'

'What can she say?' Vonette said. 'It's obvious that Andre is Stu's only living blood relative. Stu was an only child, his parents died years ago, and David found out Stu had a vasectomy in the mid-eighties. He never had any other children that anybody knows about.'

'Still, I'll bet Serena's fit to be tied,' Edna said, cackling. She had never forgiven Serena for nearly having her arrested for burglary.

'What happened with the record company?' Edna demanded.

'Serena's running it,' Rita said. 'That merger deal with the other record company fell through, did you hear?'

'So Serena inherited after all,' Edna said, making a face. 'Too bad.'

'Yeah, well, it's a mixed blessing,' Vonette replied. 'Since Jeannie started going out with Andre, she's been giving Rita and me the inside scoop. Serena's got a board of directors to deal with, and of course, she doesn't know anything about running a record label. So she's had to make Danielle Manigault president. According to Jeannie, Danielle is obviously a thorn in Serena's side, but there's nothing she can do about it, not if she wants the company to keep turning a profit.'

Vonette glanced at me, her face somber. 'Have you heard anything about Junebug?'

I swallowed hard. Reality time again. 'Yes,' I said, choosing my words carefully. 'He's gone back home to his father and sisters, back to South Carolina. Buddy Trotter is a genuinely decent man, it turns out. He'd been worried about Arlene for months, had been trying to talk her into coming home, or letting the rest of the family move up to Atlanta, but Arlene wouldn't hear of it. She wanted Junebug all to herself. It was a really unhealthy relationship, I think. She'd gotten delusional, talked herself into believing that Junebug was going to be the next Elvis Presley. The sad thing is, the kid didn't even like show business that much. He just wanted to go home and try out for the junior varsity wrestling team.'

'So you saved a life,' Vonette pointed out. 'Junebug's. Take it easy on yourself, Callahan. It wasn't your fault.'

'Right,' I said bitterly. 'Not my fault.'

'You're a blame placer,' Rita said, pointing her finger

at me and wagging it for emphasis. 'Just like I was. My fault, my fault. All my fault. We talk about that all the time at my AA meeting.'

'She broke up with Mac,' Edna piped up. 'Won't talk to him. Won't talk about it. Clams up when I try to get her to say why.'

'I don't want to talk about it,' I said, clenching my teeth. If I wasn't careful, I might be forced to throttle my darling blue-haired mother in front of a roomful of friends.

'Leave her alone,' Rita advised Edna. 'She needs time.'

Edna stomped off without saying another word, and we stood there for a while, trying to come up with conversation that wouldn't touch on the state of my mental health.

The kids took the Motown tape off, and somebody popped in one I hadn't heard before, the VelvetTeens doing a new, updated version of 'Happy Never After.' The booming cacophony of horns and drums from the old arrangement was gone now, replaced by swells of strings and piano, and a closer harmony on the chorus. These VelvetTeens had a sweeter, more mature sound. This time around, you believed there'd be no happy endings. 'I like that arrangement,' I told Rita. 'Whose idea was that?'

She grinned proudly. 'You really like it? Most of it was mine.'

'Yeah?'

'Yeah,' she said simply. 'I wrote four other new songs for the album too. I been writin' songs in my head for years. The whole time I was working in that nursing home, when I'd get a little time, I'd work on my songs. When I was drinkin' though, I never believed in myself enough to put 'em down on paper. I didn't think I was good enough.'

'This arrangement is terrific,' I said earnestly. 'Better than the original even.'

'That movie producer, Davis Zimmerman, he thinks so too,' Rita said. 'He wants to use 'em all for the movie soundtrack. Says they're killer. I told him, don't use that word *killer* around me. Not after what I been through.'

We shared a laugh together about that. 'You know, I can't believe Delores isn't sorry she's missing out on all this excitement,' I said. 'The movie, the tour, singing backup for Billy Joel's new video. That's some heavy stuff.'

Rita shrugged. 'Her choice. But to tell you the truth, I think that's her husband's influence. If it were up to Delores, I believe she'd be up there on stage with us right now.'

Linda had wandered over to join our discussion. Rita stiffened a little at her approach, but seemed to relax after Linda introduced herself as a fan. 'At least the VelvetTeens found each other and they're back in touch,' Linda said. 'That's one good thing that came out of all this. They can thank you for that, Callahan.'

I didn't know what to say. Some of what she said was true. I had tracked Delores Eisner through the Cathedral of the Word Incarnate. She'd beaten the odds and stayed married to Eisner all these years. They had led the gypsy life of professional musicians for a lot of that time, but eight years ago, at a Jews for Jesus rally in Portland, Oregon, Eisner had experienced a religious conversion. With Delores's support, he'd attended a charismatic Bible college in South Carolina and gotten himself ordained a minister. After his conversion to Christianity, Eisner had his name changed to Edwards. That's why I hit a dead end when I looked for Delores Eisner in Nashville. She'd used the name Eisner professionally, but personally, she was now Delores Edwards.

In Nashville, they started a little church together, with Eisner as pastor and Delores as minister of music. Their flock had grown, exploded really, gaining an impressive number of members who were apparently attracted by Eisner's feel-good brand of Christianity and Delores's Motown-inspired rafter-rocking church choirs.

'Catch me up,' Linda begged. 'What did Delores say when you told her the VelvetTeens wanted her to come back and perform with them?'

'She said no, right off the bat,' Rita said. 'I called her but she wouldn't hardly talk to me. So Callahan called her back and got her talking.'

'She was afraid you were still holding a grudge against her,' I explained. 'But after a while, she softened up. 'All these years,' she told me, 'every night, I've thought about Rita and Vonette. But it's been so long. I've changed so much. I can't be what they want me to be. I'm not a girl singer any more. I have a ministry, a calling. Rita could never understand that, I'm afraid.'

'She didn't know what kind of changes I'd been through myself,' Rita said, smiling ruefully. 'After Callahan told me what Delores said, I called her back. I told her, all that stuff with Stu Hightower was history almost as soon as it happened. I never blamed Delores for nothing. Stu used her. And he used me. He used everybody he ever knew.'

'After all the girls talked on the phone, they got Delores to agree to do at least one reunion concert. For old time's sake,' I told Linda.

'At her church up in Nashville,' Rita put in, laughing at the memory. 'The Cathedral of the Word Incarnate. You know how long it had been since I sang in church?'

'They all went up to Nashville for the weekend,' I said. 'Even Kenyatta and Andre and their Aunt Lillian. I can't wait to see that videotape.'

Neither, apparently, could some other people.

'Enough of this chitchat,' I heard C.W. say. He put the bottle of Heinekin he'd been drinking on a tabletop, wheeled over to Rita, snatched the videotape out of her hand, and wheeled back over to the VCR, popping it into the slot.

'Where's the remote control?' he demanded. 'And what about some real beer, Garrity? I've had enough of this fancy imported, light, ice-brewed mess. There's a ball game I want to see in an hour,' he said loudly. 'Let's rock and roll.'